# Addicted to You

## BOX SET

# K.M. SCOTT

## Books by K.M. Scott

Crash Into Me (Heart of Stone #1)

Fall Into Me (Heart of Stone #2)

Give In To Me (Heart of Stone #3)

Heart of Stone Volume One

Ever After (Heart of Stone #4)

A Heart of Stone Christmas (Heart of Stone #5)

Return To Me (Heart of Stone #6)

Forever With Me (Heart of Stone #7)

Heart of Stone Volume Two

Hard As Stone (Heart of Stone #8)

Set In Stone (Heart of Stone #9)

Silent As A Stone (Heart of Stone #10)

All of Me (Heart of Stone #11)

Temptation (Club X #1)

Surrender (Club X #2)

Possession (Club X #3)

Satisfaction (Club X #4)

Acceptance (Club X #5)

The Complete Club X Series Paperback

If I Dream (Corrupted Love #1)

If You Fight (Corrupted Love #2)

If We Fall (Corrupted Love #3)

Crave (Addicted To You #1)

Adore (Addicted To You #2)

Shatter (Addicted To You #3)

Claim (Addicted To You #4)
The Addicted To You Box Set

In The Darkness (Project Artemis #1)
After The Storm (Project Artemis #2)
Behind The Scenes (Project Artemis #3)

Hard Work (Standalone)

## Books by K.M. Scott writing as Gabrielle Bisset

Blood Avenged (Sons of Navarus #1)
Blood Betrayed (Sons of Navarus #2)
Blood Spirit (Sons of Navarus #3)
Blood Prophecy (Sons of Navarus #4)
Blood Craving (Sons of Navarus #5)
Blood Eclipse (Sons of Navarus #6)
Blood Ascendant (Sons of Navarus #7)

Stolen Destiny (Destined Ones Duology #1)
Destiny Redeemed (Destined Ones Duology #2)

Love's Master
Masquerade
The Victorian Erotic Romance Trilogy

# Contents

I want her. I crave her. She's my addiction.
The world knows me as Ian Anwell, New York Times bestselling author, but Kristina makes me want more.
Much more.

I need him. I love him. He's my obsession.
Everyone thinks they know Kristina Richards, but I'm more than what they see on the screen.
So much more.

I'm his muse, and this is our story.

For the first time ever, the entire FOUR books of the sensual ADDICTED TO YOU series in one paperback!

# Crave

## K.M. SCOTT

# CHAPTER ONE

## *Ian*

A WARM PUFF of air against my cheek rouses me from my sleep, reminding me that no matter how sunny it seemed as I looked out my window a few hours ago, fall has arrived with a vengeance. I roll over onto my back and stare up at the ceiling as the forced heat now blows over my head. The floor in my living room pushes hard against my back tonight. I should be used to the feeling, but I'm not and I wince from the pain shooting up from the base of my spine.

To my left on the floor next to me stands a half-empty bottle of twelve-year-old scotch, my companion tonight. Standing guard even as I dropped off, it waits for me to remember how much I love its contents.

Grabbing the neck, I cradle the bottle to my chest as I contemplate getting up and away from the air heating my head. I own a five million dollar apartment in New York City, and I spend my nights getting blasted and ending up on the floor. My neighbors would never imagine that's who I am. New York Times bestselling author Ian Anwell, author of historical fiction bestsellers Caligula's Dream and Nero's Nightmare and favorite of readers worldwide, a fall down drunk and forever recovering heroin addict.

My publisher keeps the whole addict thing carefully under wraps. Completely hush-hush. All I have to do is keep clean and continue writing one book a year for them, and they'll keep paying me the ridiculously large advances I've grown accustomed to. The problem is that keeping clean means something must replace the smack, so that's where alcohol comes in and why it's my nearly constant companion.

But I've grown tired of waking up on the floor in a drunken haze lately and the itch to go back to my old ways gets stronger and stronger every day. I'm an addict before I'm anything else, and I need a new fix.

My phone rings, so I make my way to the couch to answer it. Swiping the screen, I see it's my agent, Sheila Rogers. A likable woman, if not appealing, she seems to have been able to overcome what nature or God, depending on your beliefs, forced on her looks-wise to become a successful literary agent. Absurdly tall for a female, she reaches nearly my six foot two inch height, and on some days when she does her hair in this upswept thing she likes for formal affairs, she towers over me like some Amazon woman.

I've known tall women, but they've all been models. Poor Sheila could never be mistaken for a model, though.

Not that I give a fuck about what she looks like. I don't want to fuck her. I just need her to keep doing the bang up job selling my books she's always done for me. But I do wonder sometimes how a woman who looks like she does got past her appearance to get where she is today. An almost grotesquely tall woman with gangly limbs and a plain face isn't exactly what anyone imagines when they think of a successful woman, but she's achieved what others haven't and I'd be lost without her, at least professionally.

I answer the call and her one true blessing comes through loud and clear. Sheila's voice is what I imagine an angel's voice would sound like. Not too soft, not too rough, and smooth as silk, it's what's usually called a radio voice.

"Hi, Sheila," I croak out before I clear my throat.

"Ian, please tell me I didn't wake you up. It's not even eight o'clock on a Tuesday night. Are you okay?"

I want to say something about okay being relative, but that will only make her nervous and she'll call again every night until she's convinced I'm not filling my body full of shit again.

So I lie.

"I'm fine, Sheila. What are you doing working so late?"

"I have good news. I think we're close to selling the film rights to Caligula's Dream. I've gotten the deal to be as sweet as I think it can be, but you're going to like it. They have big plans for the film, and as you demanded, they're willing to let you be an executive producer and the main writer on the project."

"This is good news. I knew you'd get them to come around. You always do. You're my secret weapon, Sheila," I say, my words slurring slightly.

In all honesty, she's my only weapon since the agent I used to have for film deals dumped me after my last stint in rehab. Sheila stepped in to help without one complaint, like the savior she is.

"Ian, you sound wrong. Are you really okay?" she asks in her angelic voice I hate lying to.

"I'm fine. Well, maybe I'm coming down with something.

You know how it is when the seasons change. I think I'm going to hang out on the couch and nurse myself through whatever this is."

"Please promise me you're not planning on doing anything to derail your career, which I've so assiduously worked to make the stunning success that it is."

"I promise. Don't worry, Sheila."

She remains silent for a long moment, as if she's assessing the truthfulness of my words, and then finally changing the subject, she asks, "Have you gotten any ideas for your next book? They've already asked a few times."

They is my publisher, and I knew they would be. Nero's Nightmare soared up the charts, hitting the number one spot on the Times list the first week it was out. They'd be fools not to want to continue our relationship. But I don't have any ideas for the next book, even though they think asking me repeatedly will make the ideas come faster.

"I know, but you can't rush this kind of thing."

The truth is I haven't even tried to work in weeks. I simply have no ideas for what to do next.

"I understand, and you know how I appreciate the artistic temperament. I'll tell them you're working on ideas and put them off for a few weeks more. Just tell me you're going to work on it, Ian."

"I'm going to work on it," I lie.

Other than drinking, I have no plans to do anything except watch movies alone in my apartment, unless I can count craving the worst thing in the world as work.

"Okay. I'll check on you next week. You know you can call me whenever you need to, right?" she asks, omitting the other words she wants to say. I hear in her voice her fear that I'm about to turn back to the life she's had to rescue me from far too many times before.

"I know, and thank you, Sheila. Have a good night."

"You too, Ian. And congratulations again on Nero's Nightmare. You deserve it. That book's the best one yet."

"Thanks, Sheila. Goodbye."

I toss the phone on the couch next to me and lean back to close my eyes. She's right. Nero's Nightmare is my best work yet, but I want something different. My brain craves something new, something challenging. I'm sure I could find that if my brain could just let go and allow the ideas to come, but the scotch isn't doing the job.

A sharp craving stabs at me, and for a moment all my brain can think of is how to score. I have to fight the desire, but it's like second nature and my body wants it. My limbs ache as the phantom feeling of getting high flows through my mind. Just a little is all it would take.

Grabbing the remote, I turn on the TV and hope I can find something to take my mind off what I want more than anything at the moment. Clicking through channels, I see nothing to distract me. A thousand channels and nothing but shit.

Then I see her.

Long brown hair the color of cocoa, the truest brown I've ever seen. That's the first thing I notice about her. The camera moves in and I see her eyes, blue like the flowers on my mother's Corningware casserole dishes she had handed down to her from my grandmother. My eyes travel down to the woman's mouth with its full, deep pink lips, and I watch them as she speaks, not giving a damn about the words leaving her mouth but intensely focused on how it moves so seductively, like every word she utters is sexual and alluring.

Who is she?

I press the Info button on the remote and quickly scan the details about the film, my gaze coming to rest on her name.

Kristina Richards.

Kristina. I say her name, loving the feel of my tongue as it caresses the back of my teeth to form the second and third syllables. Kristina. I repeat it over and over until she's all I can think of.

The camera pans back and for the first time I can see her completely. She's thin but not sickly looking like so many skinny Hollywood actresses whose faces look beautiful but when you look below their necks their bodies are all sharp edges and boniness. She's standing next to some man who at the moment I want to kill I'm so jealous.

I watch the rest of the movie, unable to focus on anything but Kristina. When it's finished, I go back to where I began and watch it all over again. And again. And again five more times. Yet I have no idea what the film is about and I don't care.

All I care about is her.

At two a.m., I realize that I haven't touched a drop of scotch in hours. I pour myself a glass and set it on the coffee table in front of me as I return to studying Kristina Richards. I feel the obsession beginning and let it take me over, feeling it course through me. I've always loved the moment when what I'm addicted to begins to become part of me. The moment it becomes necessary to who I am. History. Writing. Heroin. Alcohol. The rare girlfriend or two I can truly say I cared for.

And now Kristina.

I wonder how it's possible I've never seen her before. As someone who spends the majority of his days in his home, I watch more television and movies than anyone else I've ever heard of, and yet she's eluded me until now.

The film I've found her in—a remake of The Misfits, I think—might be good. Not that I care. She's all I'm interested in. After I've watched it eight times, I need more, and with just a few clicks of my remote, I can watch every film she's ever made.

Netflix is like an addict's worst nightmare or best friend. I guess it depends on how you see people like me. I scroll through the choices and decide to start at the top. By the time the city below begins to come alive for another workday, I realize that I've seen some of these films but never saw her.

That's how it is with addictions and obsessions. One day something means nothing to you, and then the next day it's all you can think about.

By the third day, I need more. I've watched all her movies, but that's not enough. I want to see her in person. Thankfully, my success comes with certain perks that have nothing to do with being able to afford expensive things.

I can get things other people can't.

A quick call to my publicist will do the trick. Albert is night to Sheila's day. Where she's sweet and I think genuinely worries about me, he seems to be rushed and disinterested nearly all the time. His lack of appreciation for what I do irritates me too, but in this case, I'll tolerate him if he can help me get what I want.

"Ian Anwell, how the hell are you?" Albert asks in his

hurried way that tells me this is a rhetorical question. All the better. I'm not interested in talking about how I feel.

"Albert, I want you to set up a meeting with Kristina Richards."

"Who?"

"Kristina Richards, the actress. I want to meet her, so do your magic and make it happen."

He's silent for a minute and then says, "Okay. What should I tell her manager you want?"

The thought of what I want from her races through my mind, making my cock stiffen, and I lick my lips in anticipation. "Tell her I'm a fan. Tell her I'm interested in speaking to her to research my next book. For fuck's sake, Albert. I'm a New York Times bestselling author of four books."

"Actresses don't usually read much historical fiction, Ian."

Albert's place in my world seems to be to keep me humble. He's doing a hell of a job too. "Fine. Tell her I'm a huge fan."

"Okay, I'll see what I can do. I'll let you know what I find out."

I throw the phone away from me, disgusted by my publicist's humility refresher. I would have asked Sheila to do it, but that caring for me thing she does is a double-edged sword. She can't seem to keep good news to herself. At least Albert can, which is why I always ask him to do things like this.

Like when I needed to speak to a world-renowned expert on Roman sex practices and couldn't get past the man's officious secretary. I never did figure out why she took such a disliking to me from just one phone call, but she wasn't going to let me get to speak to him come hell or high water. Just one call from Albert, however, coupled with a bouquet of flowers and suddenly she couldn't have been more accommodating.

Things like that are the reason I don't fire Albert and look past how little I like him. But if he doesn't succeed with Kristina's manager, I might have to consider finding a new publicist.

I return to watching her movies, preferring not to research anything about her online. That might seem somewhat ironic considering what I do for a living, but as much as I love the idea of stalking someone on the Internet, I find it unfulfilling in practice. So what if I can learn every little thing about a person courtesy of nosy websites and hacks masquerading as journalists? That kind of research lacks vigor, lacks flesh and blood.

If I could learn about ancient cultures by living among them, I would. Instead, I'm forced to research in books and secondhand sources. Finding out about someone living now shouldn't be relegated to stalking from afar, hidden behind the anonymity of the Internet. That's the coward's way.

No, I want to meet Kristina in person. I want to look into those blue eyes. I want to listen to her soft voice as she sits just inches away from me. I want to smell her perfume and the scent her shampoo leaves in her hair. I want to feel the softness of her skin on mine. I want to taste her and savor the delicate flavor of her body on the tip of my tongue as I tease her just before I bury my face in her pussy.

I fantasize about how incredible it will be when I slide my cock into her until my phone ringing disturbs me from my daydreaming. Looking down at the screen, I see it's Albert.

"Ian, I was wrong about actresses not reading your stuff.

Seems you have a fan. She'll be at Jax's at seven tonight. I figured somewhere hidden away would be best. Her manager said she knew exactly what you look like. Thank God I convinced you to change that terrible light grey suit to the black one for your book jacket picture."

"Yeah, thanks Albert. Good call."

"Good luck, Ian."

Albert's good news spurs my creative juices, and I hurry over to my laptop to seize the moment before it leaves me. Sitting down, I begin to tap out whatever pops into my head, and in just minutes I sit amazed at the words on the screen in front of me. Instead of brainstorming for my next historical novel, I've written out the bones of the first scene of something far more erotic.

I let the words flow from my fingers, not caring that I don't usually write in this genre or that I can't imagine how Sheila would react if she found this in her inbox. I lose myself in the story of a woman who uses sex to keep her from her heroin addiction. It's smut, pure and simple, and I can't believe how much I like it.

By six, I've written four pages of my fantasy but it's time to get ready to meet Kristina. After a quick shower, I stand in front of the bathroom mirror checking out my look and questioning whether this meeting was a bad idea. My dark hair hangs in my eyes, and even when I push it back off my face, it still doesn't look right. I give myself a good, close shave, but the face that stares back at me still isn't convinced.

*She's a movie star, Ian. If this is all you're bringing, it's not much.*

Pointing at the mirror, I push back against that little voice inside my head. "Shut the fuck up. Don't start that shit."

So it whispers back a dark secret that never leaves me. *You'd be much better if you had just a little before you went.*

I will myself to forget that evil voice. I promised Sheila. I promised myself. I don't want to get back into that again. I'm clean and I want to stay that way.

My eyes tell the truth I don't want to admit. In their darkness, I see the voice is right. I would be much better if I could get my hands on some to take the edge off. Kristina won't like this Ian—this person who drinks too much to stop himself from doing something much worse and can't even look at himself in the mirror without hating what he sees.

I turn away from that truth, no matter how seductive it is to believe it. It's almost time to go meet Kristina. I can do this without help.

# CHAPTER TWO

## *Ian*

JAX'S IS AN out-of-the-way bar on the West side and a favorite of mine because there's not a booth in the place that isn't dark and secluded. That's how a bar should be. Unless you're some frat boy, getting blasted in public should be private affair. I walk in and nod at the bartender, a tall, thin man who looks to be in his late forties, if his slightly greying hair is any indication. The lighter color peppers near his temples and the top of his head giving him a look that reminds me of the serious cop on every TV police drama, and as I pass, he gives me the guy chin lift acknowledgement.

I scan the bar for any sign of Kristina and see her sitting with her head down at a booth all the way in the back. As I slowly make my way there, I notice how small she seems there surrounded by the high-backed wooden booth. Her brown hair is lighter than in her movies, but I like it this honeyed caramel color.

"Hi, Kristina," I say in a low voice.

She looks up and I see those gorgeous cornflower blue eyes. Even better in person, they sparkle with interest as she studies me for a quick moment before she says quietly, "It's nice to meet you, Ian. You look just like your picture on your books."

Her smile is far shyer than I expect from a Hollywood starlet, charming me more than I thought she could just seconds into our meeting. I sit down and stare across the table at this beautiful woman who I'm surprised even knows who I am. A thousand things come to me, but I say none of them, sure they're all wrong for this moment.

Instead, I smile and extend my hand to shake hers. "Hi, Kristina. Thanks for agreeing to meet me. It's an honor."

Her hand gently grips mine as she blushes from my compliment, but all I can think of is how excited my body immediately becomes from her touch. She says something about it being a bigger honor to meet a New York Times bestselling author, but I'm focused on the fantasy that's forming in my mind about her hand and how it would feel wrapped around my cock as she slides all of me into her mouth.

She takes her hand away and smiles shyly again, layering charm on top of my desire for her. "I was so excited to hear from my manager that you wanted to meet me. I've read all your books. I love history and your books make it even more interesting. You have a way of making your characters come alive right on the pages."

"Thank you. I guess we're both fans because I've seen every one of your films and love them. Every one of them."

Kristina blushes again. "That's so nice of you to say. I try to improve with each project. I've been very fortunate to be offered roles that allow me to stretch my abilities."

She continues to talk about her career, and to be honest, I find myself becoming more enchanted by the moment. Behind the beautiful exterior exists a serious actor. I hadn't expected that, and as she explains how she's hoping to snag a role in some film that begins to shoot in Canada in a few weeks, I'm genuinely interested in what she has to say.

It doesn't take long for our meeting to go a way I hadn't planned. I'd wanted to meet her and hopefully get her back to my place to fuck her, but as I listen to her speak about her films and my books, that idea is eclipsed by another.

I want her to be my muse. With every word that comes out of that gorgeous mouth, I'm more convinced that she's my muse for Silk, the erotica book I'm writing. I can't tell her that now, though, since I just met her. I don't want to scare her off.

"Listen to me rambling on about myself and my movies all this time. I'm sorry."

Her beautiful eyes fill with regret, but I shake my head, hoping to dispel any shame she feels. "It's wonderful to listen to someone so dedicated to their craft. Please don't feel like you should stop. I'm all ears."

"Tell me about you. I know what the blurb at the end of your books says, but I bet you're even more interesting than that. How do you come up with ideas for your books? It must be so difficult."

I admit something I never tell anyone, oddly comfortable enough already with her to share my secret. "It is. The pressure to create a story that not only stands up to the last one but surpasses it can make finding ideas very difficult."

Her eyes light up with a look of recognition. "You're like that too? I always try to do better than I did before, but it does put a lot of pressure on me. We're probably our own worst critics, you know that?"

A pretty waitress with her blond hair pulled tightly up into a bun interrupts us for our drink order and since the place is practically empty, she returns quickly with Kristina's white wine and my scotch. I know I shouldn't get drunk and even though this is going pretty well, I sense the demons inside whispering that I'm boring her and I could have been so much more interesting if I just snorted a little before I came here.

Kristina slips off her white sweater to reveal a pale pink long sleeve shirt that hugs her body in all the right places. The camera may add ten pounds, but she appears slightly heavier in person. Not heavy like fat but healthy looking, like a woman should be.

"Do you get to read a lot?" I ask, wondering if she might be willing to become my muse.

She shakes her head and frowns, like she's disappointed at the answer she's about to give. "No. My work schedule makes it difficult, but I always fit your books in."

"You don't have to say that. I know your life is probably far more exciting than reading my historical fiction."

I'm not usually so humble and self-effacing, but Kristina has charmed me into being something nicer than my usual self.

"Oh no. I always read your books as soon as they come out. I've been a fan since I read Caligula's Dream."

The idea that the gorgeous woman in front of me read my book on corruption in the reign of Caligula thrills me, oddly enough. I've been at signings where hundreds of people have waited in line for hours to talk to me as I scribble my name on the title page of their books and never felt as incredible as I do at the moment when she says that.

Raising my glass, I offer a toast to the two of us. "To fulfilling careers and meeting others who appreciate our work."

Kristina gently clinks her glass against mine. "And to finding new people who understand you."

I hear a sense of loneliness in her voice despite the smile she wears. A mouthful of scotch slides down my throat, warming my insides as it makes me feel braver by the second. I want to touch her left hand as it rests on the table. To reach over and run my fingertip over the knuckles and feel her soft skin against mine again.

"If only I'd thought to bring my book with me, then I could ask you to sign it," she says with sadness, her frown deeper now. "I can't believe I ran out of my apartment without remembering it."

"I can walk you back to your place and sign it there, if you like," I offer, hoping she'll take me up on it.

Her eyes light up again. "That would be great! You wouldn't mind?"

"It would be my pleasure."

"I don't have scotch at my place, though. All I have is wine. Is that okay?"

"I'm fine," I lie, as if drinking isn't an integral part of what keeps me together and off something much worse.

Kristina slips back into her sweater, ready to go. "Okay, then let's head there now! My place isn't too far."

I mentally file away the information that we both live in the same neighborhood and follow her out toward the street. As I walk behind her through the bar, my gaze fixes on her ass in a black skirt that falls to just above her knees and shows off her shapely lower body. Not generally a man who finds asses much to care about, I can't take my eyes off hers. Not too big and not too small, it fills out the skirt like the fabric knows exactly where to cling to make anyone behind her want to cup their hand over that ass.

We hit the bracing October air and it's like a hard slap to the face. Kristina seems unmoved by the chilliness, though, and takes my hand in hers. "It's just a few blocks so we can walk. Unless you want to take a cab? You look a little cold."

"I'm good. What kind of New Yorker would I be if I couldn't handle the little chill in the fall air that accompanies the turning of the leaves and that earthy autumn smell?"

She beams at me and tugs me toward her place. "I love the way you say things, Ian. Every word sounds so perfect."

If only she knew how imperfect and downright damaged the man she clung to at that moment was she might not be so enthralled by my choice of words.

We walk together as we talk about the weather, living in the city, and how she's going to hate being away if she has to leave to film in Vancouver, and all the while I feel my demons one by one retreat to their hiding places deep inside me until all that's left of me wants what she offers.

Sweetness.

Lightness.

Happiness.

But I don't know those anymore, so they're strangers to me. What I know is that the obsession that began as I watched her on my TV screen is morphing into something far more serious that I won't be able to fight.

Or won't want to fight.

I feel a tug on my arm and Kristina says, "Here we are! Up two flights and there I am."

Her building is a brownstone typical of many New York

neighborhoods. I let her lead me up the front stairs and then up two flights of stairs, listening to her talk about how she found this place before she hit it big and still loves it, even though everyone says she should move to a more upscale apartment. I sense she's nervous all of a sudden, if the speed of the words tumbling out of her mouth now is any indication.

Her apartment certainly isn't what a Hollywood star would usually have, but it's cozy. One bedroom, a kitchen, and a living room that looks out onto the street, it's got a charm that most small apartments in New York City don't possess. Decorated in no particular style, the walls have pictures of Kristina and her co-stars from some of her films hung beside inexpensive artwork of vases with flowers.

She offers me a seat on her couch, a leather piece that looks odd among much cheaper furnishings around it, and I sit down while she finds her copy of my book on her bookshelf. She hasn't lied. A floor to ceiling bookshelf covers one wall with all her books, and as I scan the titles, I'm impressed. Kristina reads many of my contemporaries in the historical fiction genre, a fact that surprises me, but I'm particularly impressed by three Colleen McCullough Masters of Rome books near mine.

"I'm situated amongst some greats there," I say as she pulls Caligula's Dream off a middle shelf.

"A few of these were my mother's. She always loved history, and I guess I take after her."

"Did you enjoy McCullough's Antony and Cleopatra?"

She sits next to me and holds my book out for me to take along with a pen. "I did. She has a wonderful way of making that time period come to life like you do. Thank you so much for this."

I sign my name and a few words about her being my biggest fan, but all I can think of is how her knee feels nudging against my thigh as she sits next to me with her legs folded underneath her. When I hand her the book, she smiles so sweetly at my inscription.

"Thank you. It's perfect."

More perfection from the world's most imperfect soul. If she only knew.

Kristina shifts her weight and begins to fidget with her hands. "I guess you know all about that whole thing with John Stinson and think I'm just the biggest fool, don't you?"

I truly have no idea what she's referring to, but I can see by the pain in her gorgeous eyes that it's something she's embarrassed by. With a smile, I say, "I don't know what you mean."

"You don't?"

Shaking my head, I explain I rarely watch anything that would tell me about Hollywood gossip. "So you see, I really don't know what you mean."

"Oh. I thought maybe that was why you didn't make a move when we got back here."

She presses her lips together as she waits for my answer, but I'm not in the mood to explain why I haven't tried to kiss her yet. Better to just do it. Sometimes words get in the way.

The fantasy that's been playing on a constant loop in my brain is about to come true. Taking her chin between my thumb and forefinger, I gently pull her face toward me to kiss that delicious mouth I first noticed days ago, dying to know what her perfectly formed lips will feel like as I press mine to them.

My cock is rock hard already, and I haven't even touched her yet. Normally, it takes at least some decent foreplay to get me going, but that's probably because of the poison flowing through me. Now my bulge is practically busting out of my pants before we even kiss.

Just before her mouth meets mine, she moans ever so slightly a tiny whimper, and then we kiss. Her lips are soft and full, and all I can think of as her tongue slides tentatively into my mouth is how much I want to feel those lips and tongue on my cock.

Her hands caress my cheeks as our kiss intensifies, and then she's on my lap straddling my hips, her black skirt up around her waist. My hands instinctively move to cup that beautiful ass I'd admired as we left the bar, and a jolt of excitement courses through me when I feel skin instead of the cotton or silk of panties. Fuck, she's wearing only a garter belt under her skirt!

That gorgeous, full ass feels incredible in my hands. My fingers knead her silky skin as she grinds against the front of my pants, and I lift my hips off the couch to push my cock against her.

Our kiss deepens and our tongues dance together. Kristina moans into my mouth, and I squeeze her cheeks hard, loving how eager she is. She tugs on my hair, her desire ratcheting up against mine and I slip a finger down toward her drenched pussy.

I want her. I want to live the fantasy that's played repeatedly in my mind since that first moment her beautiful face filled my eyes.

Kristina's fingers slide down over my neck to my shirt, and she begins to unbutton it, whispering against my lips, "I want you, Ian. That's why when my manager told me you wanted to meet me, I made the meeting for as soon as possible. Tell me you want me. Tell me what you want me to do."

I push her hands away and groan, "Take your sweater off."

She obeys my command and slips it off, revealing a pink lace bra. I want to see the gorgeous tits under it, so I quickly unhook it and throw it off to the side as I fill my eyes with the sight of her breasts. Full and firm, they look real, which thrills me even more than I imagined. I cup them in my hands and take one full, deep pink nipple in my mouth, sucking gently at first.

Looking up, I see her watching me, biting her lower lip and whimpering, "Yes...harder..."

Her wish is my command, and I suck her pebbled skin harder into my mouth. I close my eyes and listen to her moans as I bite down gently on her excited nipple. Fuck, she's responsive! I hadn't expected that.

Kristina rolls her hips and begins to rub up against me in earnest. I love the idea that my mouth on her is going to get her off even before I whip my cock out. I feel her juices dampen the front of my pants and look up to see her face show the ecstasy building inside her. Releasing her nipple, I move my head to the other one and take it into my mouth, sucking hard as she pulls my hair.

Her hand slides between us and she fingers her wet pussy, but it gets in my way, so I pull her hand away. Disappointed, she frowns and admits quietly, "That's the only way I can get off."

I say nothing but shake my head, determined now to make her come from anything but her fingers touching her clit.

Holding her hands behind her back, I slide my cock out of my pants and stroke it from base to head. I position it at her entrance and look up at her. "Not with me."

She smiles and rolls her hips, taking just the tip of my cock inside her. She's wet but tight. Lowering her mouth to mine, she kisses me long and deep and then slides onto me until I'm balls deep into her hot cunt. Releasing her hands, I grip her hips and won't let her move, loving the feel of being inside her. A rush unlike anything I've ever experienced before courses through me just as she breaks our kiss and whispers in my ear, "Fuck me. Make me come, Ian."

My brain shifts to pure pleasure, and every part of my body has a single goal. Make her come from me fucking her. I release my iron grip on her sides and begin guiding her up and down on my cock, loving the sight of her riding me. She's wild and uninhibited in her pursuit of the orgasm she craves. I want to give that to her as much as I want to come too.

Kristina rocks her hips back and forth, urging my cock to rub up against her G-spot. So open, so responsive, she seduces me and for one of the few times in life, I want another to feel pleasure as much as I feel. Her teeth sink into my shoulder as the first moments of her orgasm overtake her. The gentle squeeze of her cunt around my cock tells me I've given her what no one else has ever been able to give her.

I pull her hair roughly to force her to face me. "Don't look away. I want to see your face when you come."

Those blue eyes soften as her body gives in to mine, and then they close as she comes hard on my cock. I'm so close and the tender squeeze of her inner walls milking me sends me over the edge. I flood her cunt sending jets of cum inside her. The feeling is better than anything else I've ever experienced, even my other addictions.

And she is already an addiction. I know that.

"Oh my God," she moans softly as she collapses against my chest. "I've never been able to get off like that."

There's nothing a man loves to hear more than a woman tell him his cock was able to give her something no other man's cock ever could. It's something primal and animalistic, but it makes him feel like that woman is his.

I know no matter what twists and turns our time together might take, Kristina is mine now. But that has to remain our secret.

Smoothing her damp hair from her forehead, I look deep into her eyes and say, "I need you to promise me whatever we are together is kept private. Will you promise me that, Kristina?"

Her mouth turns down and a pained look crosses her face. "Why?"

I place a tiny kiss on the tip of her nose and shake my head. "Because of who we are. The rest of the world knowing would ruin this. Tabloids, paparazzi, gossip columns in the papers, all that would taint what we are. So I want to keep this like a delicious secret just between the two of us. Will you?"

"Are you ashamed of what we did?"

"No. I just don't want the rest of the world ruining this."

She wants to feel what I gave her again, and I want her more than anything else. She's already my muse, even though I haven't told her. I will when the time is right, which makes keeping us a secret all the more important.

Nodding her head, she whispers against my lips, "I

promise."

I kiss her and there as we sit with my cock still deep inside her, I think about how I want to taste that beautiful pussy on the tip of my tongue. Addiction is like that. Once is never enough.

# CHAPTER THREE

## Kristina

THE AUTUMN SUN streaming in through my bedroom window wakes me, and I stretch my limbs that still ache from the night before. Everything I did with Ian comes flooding back into my mind, and I'm ashamed that I've made the same mistake with another man. I always promise myself that I won't fall so quickly for them, but then I always do.

And then it always ends the same. They leave when I'm already too far gone in love with them and I'm devastated.

I cover my eyes with my arm and wish the regret away as the tears begin to fill my eyes. I can't handle my heart breaking again, but I already know even after just one night together that I'm lost.

If only he hadn't been able to get me off like he did.

No, that's not it. I was lost the moment he walked into that bar. So different from any of the usual men I date, he had a look that screamed sensuality as he approached me. Like he enjoyed life more than anyone I'd ever met before. His dark hair that refused to obey his command to stay off his forehead made him look tousled and casual, but his nearly black eyes made him look intense. The combination intrigued me.

Then he spoke and I knew he wasn't like anyone else I'd ever met. Every word that came out of his mouth seemed perfect, like he had a command of language I've never been able to call my own. When I speak, words seem to have a mind of their own and run out of my mouth before I can stop them, but his are so measured and carefully chosen, as if every one of them means the world to him.

I know this is infatuation. I realize that. But it doesn't change that I want to see him again, wishing even as I lie here that he could be next to me right now.

I fall hard and fast for every man, but for the first time, I feel like falling might not be a mistake with Ian. Usually, my boyfriends use me to help their careers by announcing our relationship to the media the day after our first date. Not that I'm not already into them, but it doesn't take long to find out that while I was falling, they were figuring out how being with me would catapult them to the next level and the next movie deal.

But Ian wants to keep what we are a secret. At first I thought he was ashamed of what we'd done, but I don't think so now.

I stretch again, this time feeling an ache in my lower abdomen I've never experienced before. It's a mixture of pain and need, like my body misses him. I look on my phone to check the time and see he's sent me a text. Suddenly I worry he's reconsidered and doesn't want to see me again, preferring to tell me this way instead of having to deal with me in person.

Fear fills me, but I click on the text and read the message he's sent, relief washing over me as I see his perfect words.

I want to be inside you right now, my cock stretching
your tight cunt. Until next time, I'll just have to be happy
with my memories. Ian

I read his words again and again as my pussy gets wet. I
know I shouldn't reply, that I should wait and not seem so
eager, but I can't. I type I wish you were here right now. Kristina
and click SEND, loving the achy need his message has created
inside me.

Closing my eyes, I let my hand wander to between my legs
to finger myself. Ian's message has made me want to feel like he
made me feel again, but then I remember his admonition to
me. I want—no, need—to get off again so much, though all I
can think of is him saying, "Not with me."

My phone buzzes with a message from him.

Remember, you must not touch yourself, Kristina, even
if you want to. Promise?

I stop my finger's movement over my tender clit and stare
at my phone in amazement. How could he know? With my
hand still between my legs, I use my other hand to type out a
text in return.

I promise but don't make me wait long.

My phone rings almost immediately. I know it's him, so I
answer it quickly. "You're torturing me."

"I want to break you of that habit."

"There's nothing wrong with masturbation," I say with a
giggle. "Cosmo says it's a healthy thing every woman should
do."

"Not my woman," he answers with a smile in his voice.

"So I'm your woman? You move fast."

"Do you want me to slow down?" he asks, his voice far more serious now.

A spike of fear tears through me at the thought of not seeing him again. That's what he means by slowing down. I know it.

I say, "No," hating that I've caused the conversation to turn like this.

He's quiet for a long time and then finally when he speaks again, the smile is back in his tone. "Good. I don't want to slow down either, Kristina. Meet me at the 79th Street entrance to Riverside Park at six tonight."

"Where are we going?"

"Somewhere you'll like."

"What should I wear?" I love the idea of surprises but figure I should be prepared.

In a voice that sends a pang of need straight to my core, he says, "Something you think I'll like."

I silently admit I barely know him, but I already know exactly what I want to wear. Something sexy yet sweet. Something that shows off my assets and hides the faults.

"Okay."

"I can't wait to see you again, Kristina."

"I can't wait either. I'll see you then."

He doesn't say goodbye. It's just that he's suddenly not there anymore and I'm alone again. I'm left wanting more of him, so I scroll back through our messages to read them over, loving how uninhibited he is and how just a few words from him can affect me so much.

The need for release returns with a vengeance, and I can't stop myself from letting my fingers get me off. I want to wait since I promised him, but it's too hard and he's gotten me too excited. There's no way I'll be able to wait another eight hours until I see him and then God knows how many hours more before I get the chance to come.

So I slide my middle finger through my slick folds and dip my fingertip inside me, dragging it up to my clit. Then with tiny circles I focus on that oh so sensitive bundle of nerves while I close my eyes and think of Ian fucking me just hours earlier. Every muscle in my body relaxes as I replay sitting on his lap riding his cock. How full I felt with him inside me. His nearly jet black eyes staring up full of lust. The taste of his tongue lashing against mine in the seconds just before he came, flooding me with his hot cum.

In just minutes, I'm dangling on the edge and know only one more gentle press of my finger will take me crashing over into the most sensual feeling there is. I think about my promise and wish I could stop, but I don't, instead sliding my fingertip over my clit one last time.

Everything around me ceases to exist. All my attention centers on my pussy and the delicious sensations my finger has created. My legs stiffen and then go weak, and I feel nothing but ecstasy as my orgasm overwhelms me.

I lie in bed unable to move, savoring the tiny aftershocks still pulsing through me. I've started every day like this since I was fifteen. At first I felt ashamed by my desires, like I shouldn't have needs like these, but over time I've accepted them. If men can jerk off every day, multiple times a day, and still be considered normal because they have urges, why can't women?

Ian simply doesn't know this is who I am. I know if he knew, he'd accept me too.

As I say that to myself, I sense my insecurities begin to file in, one by one until all I can think about is how he won't like me anymore if he finds out who I really am.

How he will leave like everyone else always has.

It happens the same way every time. They say they love me, that they can't live without me. And then slowly but surely, they do just that. By the time the press reports that another one of my relationships has ended, it's been over for a long time.

And every time I ask myself if I'm the problem. I must be, right? If every man leaves me, it must be me that's the problem. Not that I know what I'm doing wrong. I've tried to play hard to get, and I've tried giving them whatever they want. I've tried being bitchy, and I've tried being sweet. Every time it ends the same.

I just for once wish I could find someone who likes me for me. Slightly insecure, unsure of herself sometimes, but would never hurt anyone on purpose me.

*Don't ruin this like always. Just let it happen. Do what that doctor told you to do. Just be yourself and let your emotions flow naturally.*

But what if I do that and still another man leaves?

✧   ✧   ✧

I EXAMINE MY look in the mirror, nervously tugging and smoothing my black jersey dress over my thighs. If only they weren't so big. And my hips. Ugh! If only they weren't so wide.

Why did I have to get my mother's Scandinavian child-bearing hips? Why couldn't I have gotten my hips from my father's side of the family?

The fabric clings to every part of me I hate, but with my black knee-high boots, the dress looks terrific, so I'll stick with it. Running my hands through my hair, I let it fall in soft waves around my face and check my makeup. Thanks to my friend Marie and her makeup designer tricks, all my imperfections on my face are covered, highlighted, or diminished as perfectly as possible. If only everything in life could be this easy.

I look at my phone and see it's almost six o'clock. Afraid I'm going to be late, I hurry toward the door, grabbing my bag and keys. Riverside Park is only a few blocks away, so I should be on time.

Ian is already there when I arrive. Dressed in dark blue jeans and a deep green sweater, he's standing next to a tree that's nearly bare of its leaves. Just a few golden ones remain. I study his body language as I approach him, hoping he isn't angry I'm late.

When he turns to face me, I see my concern was for nothing. With a smile, he smooths his dark hair off his face and says, "You look beautiful, Kristina."

All my worries melt away as his gaze slides over me and I see how much he appreciates my look. He doesn't see my big hips or thick thighs like I do. "Thank you. I love your sweater. It looks great on you."

Ian slips his hand around my waist and leans in next to my ear to whisper, "Did you leave the underwear at home like last time?"

His warm breath on my neck thrills me. Leaning back, I

lower my head and feel the blush cover my cheeks. In a low voice, I answer, "Yes."

He runs his tongue over the seam of his full lips and smiles. "Good. Let's go. I have a surprise waiting for you."

Taking my hand, he leads me away from the park and up three blocks to his apartment in a large brick building much nicer than mine. We ride up in the elevator and I fill the empty space left by his silence with talk of the weather and other meaningless topics simply because if I don't, I might burst from nerves.

Finally, I ask, "Is something wrong? You're not saying much."

He levels his dark gaze on me and stares into my eyes. "I like listening to you talk."

"I just worried there might be something wrong."

Pulling me to him, he kisses me softly and my legs get weak from how tender he is when he whispers against my lips, "How could anything be wrong?"

I taste the scotch on his tongue like the night before and wish I'd had a drink before leaving my place. At least it might have calmed my nerves a little.

His question isn't meant to be answered, and as the elevator doors open, he takes my hand to lead me down the hall to his apartment. His long fingers press against the back of my hand, and even though the hallway is beautifully decorated, all I focus on is how strong his hand feels holding mine.

"Your building is very nice," I say when we stop at his door.

He turns to look at me and nods. "I hope you like my home."

I can't imagine why I wouldn't like it since it's obviously far nicer than mine, but as we step into his apartment, I'm stunned at just how much nicer it is. At least three times the size of my tiny rooms, his seem to go on forever because of the floor to ceiling windows that line the far wall. I feel him let go of my hand, but the view out those windows mesmerizes me, and I walk toward them, eager to see what he sees every day.

"I fell in love with that view the minute I stepped into this place. The realtor couldn't stop talking about stainless steel appliances and the number of bedrooms, but I was sold the minute I looked out those windows."

I can understand why. From his living room there on the top floor, he could see practically all of the West Side, and with the night sky as a backdrop, it looked like a painting deserving of being hung in a gallery.

"This must be stunning in the morning," I say as I stand as close as I can to those windows without touching them.

"I usually draw the blinds so the sun doesn't flood in, but on the rare occasion that I leave some open, it's gorgeous."

Ian wraps his arms around me, and a surge of need pushes through me straight to my core. Just his touch sends my body into overdrive so I want him even though I should be content with just standing there making small talk.

"I'm going to fuck you in front of these windows tonight. First, though, I want you to eat some of my world famous risotto."

His promise of what he plans to do to me makes a tiny whimper escape from my throat, but I try to hide my arousal with some comment about the meal he's made me. It doesn't work, though, and he says low in my ear, "I can't wait to be back inside you either, Kristina."

How would I make it through dinner when he already has me sopping wet just from a few words?

Ian guides me to a table set with fancy china dishes and crystal stemware. Two long taper candles placed in the middle of the table flicker their light over the cherry wood tabletop, the light for our meal since he dimmed the lights. He pulls my chair out and seats me like a gentleman before sitting down across from me and pouring me a glass of wine and serving me a plate of his famous risotto.

"You're going to love this," he says with pride as he hands me my dinner.

"I love that you made dinner for us. That's so sweet."

As he scoops out a spoonful of risotto onto his plate, he explains, "I didn't know if we'd be mobbed by photographers if we went out to a restaurant, so I thought I'd surprise you with my favorite dish."

Raising his wine glass, he says with a devilish smile, "To having all my favorites tonight."

I smile and raise my glass, admiring how handsome he looks in the candlelight. "To favorites."

The risotto tastes as good as he'd promised, and I eat every last bite of it on my plate. In contrast to his earlier promise of having me against those huge windows that look out over the city, he talks about where he learned to cook and how much he enjoys making his favorite foods when he has the chance. I make a few comments, but I can't help feel confused. We switched so quickly from talking about fucking so all the world could see to how risotto takes so long to make because of how the stock has to be added slowly that I don't know how to react.

"Is everything okay?" he asks as he clears the plates from the table.

I want to say that this all seems so domestic compared to our time together the night before. Not that I don't like a man cooking for me, but I guess I just expected something different. Instead I just smile and shake my head.

"No. Dinner was lovely."

"You seem quiet since we got here."

He's so observant compared to other men I've been with that I forget he notices things. Since all I'd done was pretty much chatter on about everything under the sun yesterday and this evening as we were coming up in the elevator, I must seem very different now.

I take a drink of my wine. "Your apartment is very nice."

Ian smiles and stands up from the table. He walks around behind me and leans over to kiss me on the neck. "You said that before, Kristina. Why don't you tell me what's wrong?"

God, his deep voice feels like it's traveling right to the center of my being. I close my eyes and say quietly, "I guess I'm just a little nervous."

As he gently fastens his hand on the front of my neck, he says in a voice so low I can barely hear him, "You look beautiful tonight. This dress accentuates all my favorite parts of your body. Did you know that?"

"No. I was afraid it make me look too hippy and showed off my worst part," I reluctantly admit as my hands move to cover my legs, afraid he'll agree with me or worse, say nothing.

He remains silent but takes my hand to lead me over to the windows. Standing behind me again, he places his hand back on my throat and nuzzles just under my ear, saying in a deep voice, "When I eat your pussy in a few minutes, anyone in that building there will be able to see your entire body because you'll be naked in front of all these windows. Do you know what they'll see?"

I lean back to melt into his body and answer, "No."

"They'll see a gorgeous woman being worshipped by a man who can't help but adore her. They won't see a body part. You're beautiful because of the sum of your parts, not for one part alone."

Closing my eyes, I let his wonderful words sink into my brain. All those times that I'd been so self-conscious about some part of my body, all I'd wanted to hear was something like that and no one has ever said it to me.

Until now.

# CHAPTER FOUR

## Kristina

HE COULD COMMAND me to do anything in the world, and after hearing those words I wouldn't refuse him. As I stand there looking out at the city in front of me, I don't want to refuse him. I don't know if it's the way he phrases things or the sound of his voice when he says them, but his words enchant me like no one's ever have before.

Ian wraps his arms around me, holding me tightly to him, and says low in my ear, "There's nothing sexier than a woman who knows how to give herself to a man, Kristina."

I want to say yes, that I wish I could be that kind of woman, but I push my insecurities down and remain silent. Maybe if I don't say anything, he won't see that I'm really not that woman he finds so desirable.

Not yet, anyway.

But I want to be that. I want to be the kind of woman who turns him on like no other.

His mouth presses against the tender skin just below my right ear and lingers there, sending ribbons of desire winding through my body. My gaze focuses on a light in an apartment in the building across the way as Ian's hands slowly slide my dress up to the top of my thighs, revealing my garter belt and bare pussy.

"Do you think he can see us?" he asks with a devilish lilt to his voice, as if having someone watch us is exactly what he hopes for.

"I don't know," I say quietly while his fingers tease the skin where my body meets my legs. Then a thought occurs to me. Has Ian put on this show with other women before? I don't want to think he has, but the idea quickly begins to grow in my mind, making me tense up when he slides his finger through my wet folds.

"Something wrong, Kristina?"

I hear in his voice a displeasure that upsets me even more than the thought of him with other women. Shaking my head, I whisper, "No."

His hand leaves my body, a sign he doesn't believe my lie. Walking around to face me, he stands in front of me, shielding me from the potential prying eyes of the person across the street. He stares with those dark eyes studying my expression and smiles. "Better?"

Smiling, I nod my head as he cradles my face in his hands, making me feel cherished and important. "Thank you."

"Tell me, did you obey my command not to touch yourself this morning?"

My heart pounds against my chest as my brain plays tug of war with itself. Do I lie again, only to be caught, or do I tell him the truth, surely upsetting our time together? His gaze zeroes in on my eyes, and I'm sure he sees right through me. I have no choice. I have to tell the truth.

Fearing I'm about to ruin our night, I take a deep breath

and bite my lip nervously. His eyes never veer from mine, silently commanding me once again to obey him. I can't stand up to his scrutiny and look away as I give my answer.

"No."

I feel entirely alone as I stare out the window, wishing the possible person across the street was there so I could pretend to speak to him to ease my tension as I wait for Ian to say something. One syllable and I fear it's revealed who I am and made him dislike me. I can't help but anticipate his next words, praying they aren't him telling me to leave.

He remains silent, but I can sense his stare on my cheek. The room feels like all the air has been sucked out, and I can't help but close my eyes to avoid the truth.

This is why everyone leaves. Who would want to be with someone who can't even do the simplest thing to show she can be trusted?

"Look at me, Kristina."

His words sound clipped, like he's working to keep his temper even. I don't immediately obey this command either, too scared to turn my head and face what will happen.

"Look at me now."

There's no mistaking his tone. He's angry. Quietly, I say, "I'm sorry," and hang my head.

His hand gently grips my jaw and turns my head so I have no choice but to face him. Opening my eyes, I see his dark eyes gleaming and his mouth hitched up into a smile.

"I knew you wouldn't do as I asked. Maybe it was unfair to make that demand," he says as he pushes my hair behind my left ear.

"You aren't angry with me?"

Ian shakes his head. "No. It's more important that you told me the truth. I need to know I can trust you. Making you ignore your natural urge to feel good wasn't the right way to find that out. I'm sorry."

"You can trust me, Ian. I promise. I'm sorry I couldn't stop myself, but your texts got me so excited…" I let my sentence trail off as I watch the smile slide from his face. Have I said something wrong?

"I want to ask you something, Kristina."

"Anything. You can ask me whatever you want."

"Will you be my muse?"

His question registers in my brain, but I can't understand how I could be his muse. "What do you mean? How could someone like me be a muse for an historical fiction writer?"

Ian traces his fingertip along the swell of my lower lip and leans in to kiss me softly. "I've begun to write something new, different from the books I usually write."

"What would I do as your muse?"

His eyes sparkle as he speaks. "You'd inspire me. That's what a muse does."

"How could I inspire you? What kind of book is this?"

"It's an erotic story. It came to me one night after watching a movie." His voice drops and he adds, "One of your movies."

I can't help but feel enchanted as I stand there listening to him confess he began writing something sensual after watching me. I kiss him softly on the lips and whisper, "I'd be honored to be your muse, Ian."

His smile thrills me, but then his expression changes to one far more serious. "I need you to promise me to keep this our secret, Kristina. No one else can know."

"Okay. Why?"

"Think of it like nude photos of yourself. While in context they might be tasteful and beautiful, if they got into the wrong hands, your career might suffer because of it."

"Are you worried your fans wouldn't like this new book?"

"Yes, so I'm going to be writing under a pseudonym. I don't want you hurt by this either, though, so unless you can promise this will remain a secret between us and only us, we can't go any further."

I sense him backing away even as he stands in front of me. I don't want to stop what we're doing. Never before have I felt so sexy and desirable with a man.

"No. I promise not to tell a soul. Just between you and me."

He strokes my cheek with the back of his hand and kisses me on the tip of my nose. "Good. Now about our friend across the way..."

Before I can ask what he means, Ian lowers himself to his knees and slides his palms over my thighs to the top of my garter belt. His soft touch thrills me. I close my eyes as he leans forward to press his mouth to my sex and his tongue flattens against my sensitive skin, sending a jolt of need to my core.

Leaning back, he looks up at me. "I'll let you stay dressed while I eat your pussy for him, but after you come the first time, I want him to see all of you as I take you right here."

Nothing in what he says asks permission or allows for any doubt on my part. I know this. If his words didn't make it clear, the look in his eyes does. He's hungry for me—as hungry for me as I am for him. It makes me want to please him even more.

"What if I want him to see you going down on me too?" I ask, almost daring him to deny me.

The sparkle in his eyes that's been there since he asked me to be his muse flashes the purest look of need I've ever seen and he says in a voice low and deep, "Take the dress off, Kristina."

I slide my dress over my head and then I'm standing in full view of anyone nearby in just my bra, garter belt, and stockings. Ian licks his lips and grins, but says nothing, instead grabbing the backs of my thighs and pulling me roughly to him. Without pause, he returns to devour my wet pussy, his tongue sending strings of delight through me as he flicks my needy clit.

The urge to close my eyes is strong, but I don't want to hide behind them and pretend. I want to be the sexual creature Ian sees me as—his beautiful and erotic muse. When he lifts my leg and slings it over his shoulder to bury his tongue deep inside my cunt, I dig my fingers into his collarbone to hang on, loving how I feel there on display.

His fingers spread me wide, and Ian sucks my clit between his lips. Just as I think I can't handle any more, I feel his teeth bite down gently and I'm lost. My leg buckles as my orgasm rushes over me, and every inch of my body feels like it's flying. I sense Ian's hands holding me up, but I can't feel anything but the complete and utter ecstasy of coming from the incredible sensations his mouth created in me.

"I bet he loved seeing that," Ian whispers as he plants tiny kisses along my inner thigh.

Looking down, I smile at how sexy he looks kneeling in front of me. Tousling his hair with my fingers, I want more. I want to feel him inside me, stretching me to take all of him.

"Come here."

Instead of standing, he pulls me down onto the floor and kisses me, his lips still wet from going down on me. I taste myself on his tongue as it teases mine. Moaning his name, I fumble with his zipper as I try to free his cock.

"Not yet," he warns as he moves my hand away.

"Why?" I don't mean to whine, but it comes out like that because I want more.

"Sit on my lap and straddle my legs."

I do as he tells me to and quickly realize what he has in mind when he removes my bra. Tugging his hair harder than I should, I pull him toward one nipple, and he roughly takes it into his mouth. He sucks hard, making my tender skin pebble instantly and my pussy run wet with the need to come again. I instinctively rock against him and feel his hard cock beneath his pants as I grind against the full length of him.

"You like it rough?" he asks as he leans back away from me.

"No, not usually," I answer as he pinches my excited nipple, sending a jolt of pleasure straight to my clit.

"You do with me."

Needy for more, I pull his hair hard to direct his mouth to my other breast, eager for his lips to repeat their delicious torture. He sucks it hard, his teeth sinking into the base of my nipple harder than before. His hands squeeze my tender flesh, one surrounding where his mouth is and the other pinching my other nipple so both get to enjoy his attention.

His touch borders on pain I'm not sure I can withstand, but I stop myself from crying out, wanting it more than I want him to stop. Just as I'm sure I can't take anymore, he slides his right hand down to my pussy and thrusts two fingers inside me. They graze a spot only he seems to find, and I whimper his name softly.

My nipple pops out of his mouth as he turns his focus to his fingers' movement, and instantly I miss the feel of his lips and teeth on me. He sees the loss on my face, and smiling a devilish grin, says, "My girl definitely likes it rough. We'll get back to that later, though."

"Later?" I ask, disappointment covering me as he slides his fingers out of me. "Why?"

"We have a show to put on for that man over there. We wouldn't want to let him down, would we?"

His mouth slants over mine in a kiss so passionate and deep that he nearly takes my breath away. This show excites him.

"You really like this thing with others seeing us, don't you?"

Ian draws his finger from my lips down between my breasts and nods. "I do. You do too."

I can't deny that something about a stranger in the dark watching us excites me. I've never been an exhibitionist, but with Ian I want to do things I've never considered. What does that man look like, though? Is he old? Young? Short? Who is he?

Standing, Ian pulls me to my feet and kisses me long and hard, his tongue forcing its way into my mouth play with mine. He turns me around to face the window so he's standing behind me and drags his fingertip up my wet slit.

"I want him to see all of you when I fuck your tight cunt."

"Yes," I whisper as I hear his pants drop to the floor and feel his hard cock nudge my ass. "Don't wait, Ian."

He rears back away from me and for a moment I'm alone waiting to feel him again. Then his hand is on my throat as he rams his cock into me and says in my ear, "Tell me how you feel, Kristina. Tell me everything."

"Full...hot...don't stop."

"Never. I need to feel you around me."

Ian thrusts his hips forward, stretching me for a long moment before he slowly slides out of me, leaving my body needy for more.

"Faster...please..."

My pleas are met with him slamming into me over and over, the swollen head of his cock rubbing that spot that feels like heaven. I come as his hand tightens around my throat and he says, "That's one. You want more?"

"Yes," I say breathlessly. My body aches for more.

Ian fucks me until I come twice more, but still he doesn't come. I wonder what's wrong, but he seems happy and content, whispering in my ear, "Ready to change the show for our friend?"

I turn to see him smiling and nod my agreement. "I want him to see you come."

"Then down on your knees."

Lowering myself to the wood floor, I feel the hardness press against my knees and instantly wish Ian had wanted something else. Never as big a fan of going down on men as other women are, it simply isn't what I consider my best position, and all I can think of as I stare up at him is that he'll be as disappointed with my performance as I usually am.

"Is something wrong, Kristina?"

I shake my head and press a smile onto my lips. "No."

Ian crouches down in front of me and takes my face in his hands. "Don't be scared. It's no different than what we were just doing. I want you to enjoy yourself."

My brows knit, and I know my face shows the concern filling me with dread. "I just—"

"Don't worry. There's no way a beautiful mouth like yours won't make me feel more incredible than I've ever felt before."

"Okay."

He stands and as he winks at me like a sign that we're in this together, he wraps his hand around his cock and feeds it to me, slowly sliding it into my waiting mouth. His skin tastes musky and has a hint of saltiness to it, and suddenly I realize I'm tasting me on him. My eyes open wide and for a moment I think about telling him I can't do this.

I've never done this before after a man's been inside me. A mixture of emotions fill my mind, but then I look up and see him staring down at me and I want to make him happy. To make him feel as good as he's made me feel tonight. So I push my fear and nerves aside and do just that.

Make him happy.

His cock is long and thicker than anyone I've been with, so it doesn't take long for my jaw to ache. I can only take about half his length into my mouth, but I work the bottom half with my hand, pumping his soft skin as I suck the top and head. His moans tell me I'm doing it right, but I can't help but wish I was better at this.

His hands slide through my hair and roughly tighten into fists. Pain skitters across my scalp as he tugs my head down onto his cock. My eyes closed now, I hear him say, "Let me see what that pretty mouth can really do."

He directs me to go as fast as he wants, easing my head down slowly until nearly all of his cock disappears into my mouth, and then he pulls my head up quickly so he nearly pops out from between my lips. Over and over, he does this as he groans how good it feels and how much he loves the feel of my mouth on him.

I feel his balls tighten near my hand and he tugs my hair so hard tears come to my eyes. About to come, he slides nearly all of his cock out of my mouth until just a few inches are left inside me and groans, "Take it all, baby."

His cock throbbing, he floods my mouth, and the hot liquid rolls down the back of my throat. I've never finished going down on a man, always choosing to stop before they came, so this is the first time I'm tasting anyone. The experience is strangely empowering as I look up and see Ian with his eyes closed and a look of complete ecstasy covering his face.

In that moment, I forget about the possible audience across the street and focus entirely on the man there with me. For the first time, it's just Ian and me, and I want more than anything to know I've made him happy.

# CHAPTER FIVE

## *Ian*

KRISTINA GENTLY SNORES next to me, easing me out of a sound sleep as my brain tries to figure out why there'd be a noise in my room. I'm not used to having someone in my bed, but as I open my eyes all the way to watch her, I like the feeling of having her there.

I push her brown hair off her face and see her mouth turns down into a tiny pout as she sleeps. It reminds me of every picture I've ever seen of babies sleeping. I reach out and softly touch her bottom lip, tracing the softness of her skin as I remember the pleasure her mouth gave me hours earlier.

Her confession afterward that she'd never finished a man surprised me, but that soon changed to a sense of pride that she'd been willing to do that for me. She's surprised me with her ability to be so forthcoming. Few women are that way, in my experience, and the ones who are quickly show themselves to be truthful more to gain something than to simply share a part of themselves.

But not Kristina.

Her candor charms me more than I thought I could be. I can't help but want her because of her openness. What began as a fascination—an obsession borne of infatuation—has grown to more far quicker than any of my other addictions, but unlike with them, I haven't thought even once to stop myself from falling.

She has no idea of the depth of my desire for her. No doubt to her I'm just a typical male who's wasted no time getting in her pants. I don't deny that part of my attraction to her, but there's more. The need to hear her soft voice, to see her blue eyes as she looks at me like she cares—the need to have these things around me begins the moment I wake up.

This is the life of an addict. I know this. I also know if I told her what I really am she'd likely run away and never want to come back. For now, all I want is her, but the time may come that I want alcohol or junk more than her.

Who am I kidding? It's not a matter of if but when. I know this, but as I look over at her sleeping so sweetly next to me, her mouth in a tiny pout that makes me want to take her in my arms and never let her go, I want to believe that this time will be different.

"Did I wake you?" she asks as she rubs the sleep from her eyes.

"No," I say, shaking my head, happy to lie to save her any amount of embarrassment.

"Is it late?"

"I don't know. I didn't check the time. I was just watching you sleep."

Kristina buries her head in the pillow and mumbles, "I snored, didn't I?"

"Not too bad. I had to get up anyway."

Giggling, she picks her head up and I see she's blushing.

"I'm so sorry. I snore like a lumberjack, or at least that's what my sister always says. She refused to sleep in a room with me when we were teenagers."

"No, not a lumberjack. More like an adorable little saw cutting through wood. Like something in a cartoon."

"That's still awful!" she says with a smile. "Sorry about that. If I do it again, just roll me over. That usually works."

"I'll keep that in mind."

"So not sexy, right? Actress Kristina Richards snores like an old man. I can see the cover of The Enquirer now."

"I promise it's our secret. I won't tell another living soul."

She touches my shoulder and traces her finger down over my collarbone. "That's two secrets now. I had no idea you were so cloak and dagger."

"I'm like the CIA—full of secrets," I say with a smile, my answer far more truthful than she can know.

"I think I like that. A man of mystery. Sounds sexy."

Her sweetness continues to charm me, even first thing in the morning before I've had my coffee. Is she always this cute when she wakes up?

I want to tell her nothing would make me happier than just lying there in bed with her all day, but that would probably come across as too much so early in the relationship. That's the kind of thing people say after they've moved in together, not on the second date.

Is it really just the second time we've been together? It feels like I've known her for ages.

"You're pretty quiet. Are you one of those people who hate mornings?"

"Not really. I'm just too dependent on coffee at this time of day. You're not like that?"

Kristina shakes her head and smiles. "No. I don't drink coffee. I'm a tea person. They say tea has more caffeine than coffee, though, so it's the same addiction. I'm guessing you don't have any tea here, though."

I stretch the sleep from my limbs and think if I have any tea in my kitchen. As someone who doesn't drink it, there wouldn't be much reason to have any, but I think my mother might have left some one time when she came to visit me. All of this runs through my head surprisingly fast for this time of day, and I nod. "Maybe. We can check when we finally get up."

A shy smile spreads across her beautiful mouth. "Oh. We're not getting up now?"

"No. I'm not ready to leave this bed just yet."

"Got anything in mind?"

"Yeah."

As I roll her over on her stomach, I can only think of one thing I want to do.

AFTER KRISTINA LEAVES, I get ready for a full day of planning this new project that more than ever has my attention. Silk, as I'm calling it, is the story of a woman who fights her addiction to heroin through her other addiction, sex. The main character, Kate Silk, is a famous actress who wants to be known as more than just some Hollywood starlet gone wrong. Her story is much like every famous star who's fallen on hard times, but she's determined to be the exception to the rule.

I sit down in front of my laptop and let the ideas flow from my fingers. Far quicker than when I brainstorm for my historical fiction, the story begins to take shape right there in front of me on the screen. Kate's appearance, her backstory, the conflict all come so easily, but then I see why.

They're Kristina.

Even though I know little about her life before we met, except for her work in films, because I still refuse to cyberstalk her instead of gleaning the information the old fashioned way—through conversation and serious moments together—I imagine the details so the story comes alive. Eventually, I'll find out about Kristina's past, but for now, what I create for Kate's past will work just fine.

Six hours later, I sit back proud of my work and satisfied with how Silk is shaping up. I've spent all day in Kate Silk's world, one I know all too well. I didn't plot out the parts about her addictions. I don't need to. I've lived it for so long that story is part of me, part of every day of my life.

For now, Kristina is my addiction, and after so many hours without her, I need to see her. I call her and just the sound of her voice eases the edginess I began to feel hours ago.

"Hi Ian! Did you miss me?" she asks playfully.

"I did. Am I seeing you tonight?"

"Another dinner planned or something different?"

"I'd like to tell you about the book you've inspired. I can order Chinese, if you like, and we can talk about it."

"I'd love that! Say eight?"

I quickly calculate how long until I can see her. Four hours. I can make it that long.

"Eight's good. Do you want me to get some wine for you? All I have here is scotch."

"I'll tell you what. I'll bring the wine, and you get the Chinese. I love General Tso's chicken. Not very Chinese, but the place a few blocks from you tastes great."

"Then it'll be you, me, and the General for dinner."

There's a pause in our conversation and then she asks, "Should I dress any particular way? I don't want to be underdressed if we're going somewhere."

"Wear whatever you love. I want you to be comfortable here."

"Okay. Eight o'clock with you and the General. It's a date. I'll see you then, Ian."

I PACE THE room back and forth, each time checking to see if the hand on the clock has moved any closer to eight. I've been doing this for thirty minutes, unable to keep my mind from thinking about her. This is obsession. This is addiction.

This is me.

The knock on my door makes my heart leap in my chest, but I stop myself from racing to the door and flinging it open to see if it's Kristina or the delivery man with our Chinese food. Neither one of them would understand my behavior.

Slowly, with measured steps, I make it to the door and open it to find her standing there smiling up at me. I want to take her in my arms and hold her to me. I don't only because I know she wouldn't understand.

*Don't want to come on too strong. Go easy at first or you'll scare her away.*

The words repeat in my mind as I welcome her in and escort her to the kitchen to open the wine. She's talking about something going on down on the street, but I'm focused on her white sweater that appears to have been made especially for her. It clings to her body perfectly, hugging her breasts as if to showcase them.

She's dressed this way for me. The fact makes keeping my hands off her next to impossible, but as she continues to explain something about a group of people in front of my building, I work to not touch her so soon, stuffing my hands into my pockets to hold myself back.

"I think they recognized me, but thankfully, something happened in the street and I was able to slip inside without having to wait for you to let me up. Thank God for your doorman."

I absentmindedly answer and smile even though I have no idea what she's talking about. Taking the wine bottle from her hands, I find the corkscrew and open it for her. Pouring her a glass, I hand it to her and receive one of her beautiful smiles in return.

"No drink for you?" she asks as she looks around for my glass.

"Not yet. I'm content as I am for now."

Kristina takes a sip of her wine and places the glass on the counter as she licks her lips. I watch her tongue moisten them like it's the most interesting act I've ever seen.

"Ian, is something wrong? You're staring at me and not saying much."

"No," I answer and shake my head.

"Okay." She steps toward me and kisses me, whispering against my mouth, "I thought about you today."

I taste the sweetness of the wine on her lips as my tongue slides into her mouth. It's fresh and natural, not syrupy, and it dances across my taste buds. This is what I'll think of when I want to remember how her kiss tastes.

Her fingers caress the tips of my ears, tickling me, and I pull her mouth to mine in a deeper kiss that makes my cock stiffen. I want her right there against the counter in my kitchen. I push my hand under her sweater and cup her breast through her bra. Under my touch, her nipple tightens into an excited peak, and I squeeze it hard between my thumb and forefinger, loving the sound of her whimpering into my mouth.

Reaching down, I slide my hand under her purple skirt to find the black tights she's wearing only go to the tops of her thighs. Above them, all I feel is soft skin because she's doesn't have panties or even a garter belt on. The need to be inside her makes my chest tighten with need, and I break our kiss to take a breath.

"I almost gave the whole world a show on my way here when a gust of wind blew my skirt up," she tells me with a cute smile, not knowing how jealous the idea of other people seeing her like that makes me.

She presses her body to mine and tilts her hips to feel the hardness of my cock. I know I should wait—that I shouldn't want to fuck her every time I see her—but just her being near me makes my body crave her. Inching my fingers up over her hip, I feel the smooth skin of her bare pussy and want to bury my face in her.

One finger slides over her clit, and I lick my lips at how incredible she feels. "I love how wet you are for me already."

Kristina moans and whispers hoarsely, "When I thought about you today, it was of how good it feels when you're inside me."

An ache comes over me when I hear those words, like the only way to make it go away is to bury myself balls deep in her and fuck the pain away. I unzip my pants and my cock practically springs out, ready and willing like the rest of me.

Lifting her, I thrust once and I'm inside her, loving the feel of her wet cunt around my cock. Her hands cling to my neck, and I grip her hips to absorb my stabs into her body. The need to come, to make her come, overtakes me so I can think of nothing else. I press her against the wall and fuck her hard, every plunge into her body another attempt to sate my need for her.

She meets my thrusts with her own, rocking her hips against me as she moans for me to fuck her harder. My hips hurt and my back aches, but I don't stop. I can't stop. I need the release she can give me. I need to make her come.

We hear the knock at the door and we look into each other's eyes, the two of us silently questioning whether the other one will stop. I shake my head and continue pounding into her, and she closes her eyes. I feel her body just seconds away from surrender.

She feels it too. In my ear, she sobs, "Don't stop. Please don't stop, Ian. I'm almost there."

I couldn't stop even if I wanted to. My body demands a reprieve from the cravings I've had all day, and Kristina is the only one who can give it to me. Another knock at the door drowns out our moans for a moment, and I say in her ear just as I feel her body begin to tighten around me, "Come for me. Give me all you have."

Her teeth clamp down on my shoulder as her orgasm explodes through her, sending streaks of pain across my back and neck, but I don't care. She could bite me to the bone. My body is too busy rejoicing in the feeling of her cunt milking my cock for me to give a fuck about anything but the perfect pleasure she brings out in me. I come hard into her, flooding her body until it streams down between us.

Panting, she says sweetly, "The Chinese delivery guy probably left."

"Unless I can go to the door just like this, I don't care."

Kristina kisses me tenderly and hugs me. Pressing her lips to my ear, she says quietly, "I want to say I didn't mean for this to happen again, but since I didn't wear anything under my skirt, I guess that would be a lie."

I lean back and look up at her. "Are we going too fast?"

For a moment, she's silent, but then she says, "I should say yes. I know that. I know we should know all sorts of things before we get to this point. My friends say I jump into relationships too fast. But I don't care. I like the way I feel when I'm with you."

I lie and say what I know I should say. "Just tell me if you want to slow down. We can take this slower."

She shakes her head and a tiny frown mars her beautiful face still covered in an after sex glow. "No. I didn't mean it that way. I love the way you can't seem to keep your hands off me. It makes me feel beautiful."

"You are beautiful."

Her smile in response to my compliment thrills me. I kiss her and slowly lower her to the floor. She looks down at my still hard cock and winks at me. "I'll check to see if the Chinese is still nearby. You get yourself straightened up."

I hand her the money and zip my cock back into my cum-soaked pants as I watch her walk toward the door and love the view of her from behind. Shaking my head, I try to focus on something else. I've just finished fucking her not five minutes before and all I can think of is doing it again.

Kristina somehow finds the delivery guy and closes the door, a bag containing our dinner in her arms. "He looked at me like he knew exactly what we were doing while he was out in the hallway. I gave him a big tip."

Taking the food from her hands, I kiss her and run my tongue over her lips. "As long as that's all you gave him."

"He's not my type. I prefer my men tall, lean, with dark hair and eyes darker than I've ever seen in another person."

I smile at her description of me as I unload the General Tso's Chicken and Moo Shu Pork from the bag. "Anything else you like in your men?"

She wraps her arms around my waist and presses her cheek to my back. "I like it when they know just the right words to say."

"I guess it's a good thing I'm an author then."

Pressing a light kiss onto my cheek, she snatches her food out from in front of me and walks toward the table. "I guess so. Are we eating in here?"

I think about how she likes what I do, even though what I write isn't usually sexy. "No, let's sit on the couch and eat. Then I can tell you about the story."

Peeking her head back into the kitchen, she says, "I can't wait. I'm dying to hear what a story inspired by me sounds like."

"Patience, grasshopper. All in good time," I joke as I follow her into the living room and sit down next to her, happier than I've been in too long.

# CHAPTER SIX

## *Ian*

K RISTINA SNUGGLES UP against my side and coos, "I can't eat another bite. I'm all General Tso'd out."

"I was Moo Shu'd about ten minutes ago. I should have stopped eating, but it's so good. Sure you don't want a taste? I've got a forkful or so left."

Shaking her head, she says, "No. I'm stuffed. I'm going to struggle to keep my eyes open after eating so much."

I put the fork down and lean back on the couch, holding her as my back settles in against the leather. "If the story was one of my usual ones, I could understand that."

She looks up at me with worry in her eyes. "No, that's not what I meant at all. I love all your work. I mean that." I hear in her voice the fear that she's offended me.

"It's okay. Except for other writers, this part isn't the exciting stuff anyway. I could understand if you didn't find it very interesting."

Kissing me on the side of my face, she repeats that she doesn't find my work boring. Even if she doesn't mean what she says, it's still nice to hear it.

"I want to know about all your writing, Ian. That you can

string words together like you do to make such fantastic books amazes me. People always think actors are the great ones, but they only deliver the lines. It's the people who write them who are truly the great ones."

I turn and kiss her on the top of the head. "We'll see if you still think that after I tell you about this new story."

She brings her legs up underneath her and sits up straight beside me. "I'm all ears."

"I guess I have a confession to make. I began to write this before we met."

"I thought I was your muse for this, though?"

"You are. I got the idea for this book after watching your movies," I say quietly and then wait for her response.

"You did? Something from one of my movies made you want to write this book?"

I look into her eyes and tell her the truth. "Not something. You. You made me want to write this book."

"Me?"

"Yeah. You."

I see in her expression what I've said confuses her, so I try to explain my creative process without putting her to sleep for real. "You see, for a writer, ideas can come from just about anything. A song. A scene I see outside the cab as I head to a friend's house. A movie. That's what happened. I was watching one of yours the other night and the story just came to me."

This isn't exactly the truth. I know this. But telling someone I became obsessed with her after watching every single movie she's ever made isn't as romantic as they make it sound in romance books.

"So my acting inspired you?"

I nod, choosing not to explain anymore since I'd probably say too much and ruin the moment.

"That's so wonderful. I always wonder how my work affects others. Usually I think it doesn't much at all. People watch the films and want to meet me, but it's mainly because they like how I look. But this shows me that there are people out there who see more than just the outside of me. That the way I play a part can show more of the inside of me. Which movie was it?"

Her question makes my heart skip a beat. I can't remember what movie it was. I watched every single one back to back for hours on end, but even at this moment I can't say what any one of them was about and certainly don't know their names.

"I'm terrible with remembering names and titles," I lie. An author who can't remember details. Not very believable. "I think it was the one that was the remake of The Misfits."

"Oh, I loved that part! Do you know Marilyn Monroe played it first, alongside Clark Gable?" she asks, her eyes wide with enthusiasm.

"I do. That's probably why I remembered."

I don't want to dampen her passion for talking about her job, but a few more questions about why I enjoy her acting and it will become clear I'm not a fan of the acting so much of her. I wait until she says a few more things about the film, and then I gently try to move her back toward talking about the book.

"You're a lot like the main character in Silk. I think being with you has influenced me a lot already." It's a tepid lie, but there's some truth in it.

"What's the story about?"

I choose my words carefully because I've just said she's like a heroin addict who uses sex to suppress her urges to get high.

"Kate Silk is sensitive and gentle, but she finds it difficult to deal with a lot of daily life because of that. She's beautiful and giving."

"You see me as sensitive and giving?" Kristina asks with tears in her eyes.

Kissing the tip of her nose, I smile. "Of course. Why wouldn't I?"

"Because I'm a Hollywood actress. All people generally see of me is the outside."

"Well, as an author, I see things other people might not."

"So what is her story, this sensitive and giving woman?" she asks and I can't avoid telling her the real plot.

"She's a recovering addict," I say quietly. "Every day she deals with the cravings her want for heroin force on her. The only way she finds she can master them is with sex."

Kristina's quiet for a long moment and finally says, "I bet it's way deeper than that, but you don't want to tell me because you think it would bore me. I bet she fights against those cravings every minute of the day and sex isn't just a physical act to her but a way to push down the need for something that hurts her."

Her blue eyes are filled with emotion as she speaks. I can't help but be impressed with how much she seems to understand addiction. "Have you ever been addicted to anything?"

Shaking her head, she smiles meekly. "No, but my old therapist used to tell me all the time that I'm addicted to people. I don't think she's right, but she says that's why all my relationships fail. Because I get addicted to the other person and he doesn't get addicted to me back."

Sounds like typical psychobabble bullshit therapists like to spew. Perhaps a person can be addicted to the feelings someone creates in them or the way they treat them, but addicted to a person? Bullshit.

"I wouldn't listen to her," I say with a smile. "She doesn't sound like she knows much about addiction, to be honest."

"Do you?"

Nodding, I wonder how much I should tell Kristina about who I really am. If she spends enough time with me, she's going to find out. It always returns like some ugly demon I push to the background but never really goes away. I could just lie and tell her about the drinking, but that's only something I use to calm the pangs of need for the real thing I'm addicted to that wash over me most days and threaten to drown me on the worst of them.

"Yeah."

Touching my arm in a gesture of sympathy, she says, "If you don't want to talk about it, Ian, you don't have to. Don't feel like you have to talk about anything you don't want to with me."

This is one of the problems with a relationship moving at warp speed. The sex twenty-four-seven is great, but along with that real life intrudes with all its ugliness and reality.

"It's not exactly what someone wants to hear the third time they're with someone, right?"

"Are you worried if you tell me something bad about yourself that I won't want to see you anymore?" she asks in a voice so sweet I can't help but want to confess everything about myself to her.

"It's not just bad. That's the problem."

Kristina turns my face toward her and kisses me softly.

"There's nothing you can tell me that would make me not want to see you, Ian. Do your worst."

As much as I want to believe her, I know the truth. It never leaves me. No matter how much I may look like the successful author my agent promotes me as or the man Kristina thinks I am, the truth is I'm an addict, pure and simple. An addict who when he isn't snorting junk up his nose searches for something else to become addicted to so he doesn't fuck up his life again.

"I never did any drugs in high school, strangely enough since that's when so many people are introduced to them. Even in college, all I did was smoke some pot. Nothing big. It wasn't until much later that I had my first taste of heroin."

She says nothing and I know I should stop. If I go much further, she'll know what I am and will probably want to leave and never see me again. I know this and still I keep going.

"It was my first editor who introduced me to heroin. I was so naïve back then. I thought the only way you could do heroin was shooting up, so when he first asked me if I'd ever done it, I was horrified. I hate needles, so there was no way I would've ever used any drug that required sticking myself with something."

Kristina says nothing, but her hold on my arm steadily grows stronger as I continue confessing who I am.

"The first time I did it all I felt was relaxed for around a half hour. I didn't think much of it and couldn't imagine what he was talking about when he said it would make me feel better than I'd ever felt before. Then everything changed. One minute all I felt was relaxed and almost sleepy and then the next minute I was flying. The rush was incredible. It was at that point that I knew just what he meant."

"Why did he give you drugs?"

"I was a mess with my first book. I knew how to write, but I didn't know how to handle everything that happens after you get the book written. People think authors get the words down on the page in some kind of magical way and then the book shows up in stores ready for them to read. It doesn't happen like that. What really happens is an author writes the book and then it goes into edits where it gets torn apart and put back together again."

"That sounds painful."

"It can be. We writers get very attached to our work. Our words are our creations, our babies. But then editors come in and carve into those babies. Their job is to make our work better, but it can hurt if you're not used to it. I wasn't with my first book. I'd gotten an agent with what I'd written and she'd gotten me a publishing deal, so I couldn't imagine what the editor would want to change. I was in for a rude awakening."

Kristina leans her head against my shoulder. "I like thinking of that guy who was so naïve. He sounds cute."

I look down at her and chuckle at her description of me back then. "I was such a newbie. I got my edits back and fell apart. The editor had to actually sit with me and calm me down, and that's when he gave me my first taste of heroin. It did what it was supposed to. I calmed down and then I felt better than I'd ever felt before in my life."

My story makes my addiction far more romantic than it actually is. Beginnings always are. It's that time after the initial wonder and excitement that shows what something really is.

"Were you immediately addicted to it?"

I think back to the days following that night I snorted

heroin with Robert and remember liking how I felt but not feeling some overwhelming need to feel like that again. "No. I liked feeling that way, but I think if I never had it again I wouldn't have missed it."

"But you did do it again. Why?"

"I had more edits to do. That's another misconception about books. Edits aren't something that just happen in a day or so and then the book's done. There are rounds of edits and sometimes they feel like they go on forever. So every time I got overwhelmed, my editor made sure I had something to calm me down and get me to a place where I wasn't overwhelmed."

"Why would he do that?"

"He's an addict and knew it would help me, so I guess he figured misery loves company. I got the book's edits completed and it went on to be a huge seller. But I was addicted by the time the book hit the bestseller lists."

"Do you still do heroin?" she asks and I hear what she can't mask. The judgment. The fear.

She has every right to be afraid. Anyone who lets a junkie into their life should be afraid. We wreck things.

I answer truthfully. "No. Do I want to? All the time. More than you can know. But I don't. I've been through rehab three times. After the second time, things got better for a while. For a long time, I didn't touch it. But then something triggered whatever it is inside me that wants that feeling and I went hard into it. That's when I went to rehab the third time and got clean. I've been off it for eight months now, and I just finished a book without it for the first time ever."

She kisses my cheek, but I know what I just told her is probably making her wonder if she should run away as fast as she can. She should, but I hope she won't.

"And that book just hit the New York Times bestsellers list, didn't it?"

I smile. I'm proud of that book for more than just the writing. "It did. That book showed me I can do it without turning to putting that shit up my nose."

"Ian, I don't understand why you'd want to write about a character who struggles with heroin addiction. Won't it make you think about how much you want it again?"

"It isn't really like that. I think about it all the time whether or not I want to, and writing a character that deals with what I go through every day of my life has been cathartic, to be honest."

Then she asks me a question I haven't thought of. "If the character uses sex to control her urges to do heroin, are you writing about yourself? Do you do that?"

"Yes and no. I have an addictive personality, so I can get addicted to anything. What I usually turn to when I want heroin is alcohol, but I'm not going to lie. I'm already addicted in some way to how it feels when you and I are together. I tell myself that I should keep my hands off you, like when you got here tonight, but then you kissed me and all I could think about was how much I wanted to be inside you."

All this confessing makes me feel exposed and more vulnerable than I like, so I get up to find myself some scotch to make the uneasiness go away. Kristina follows me and as I pour myself a drink, she wraps her arms around me like she did earlier in the kitchen and whispers against my back, "I know what you mean. I have a hard time being around you without touching you. I've never felt like this. I thought it was just me who had this weakness."

I swallow a gulp of the scotch, enjoying the warmth it spreads as it goes down my throat, and turn to face her. "I'm not sure what it is, but I don't want you to think I'm using you for sex because I'd rather be high. That's not it at all."

She gives me one of her sweet smiles and looks up at me with such caring in her eyes I want to believe she won't run.

"Your weaknesses don't frighten me off, Ian. I see in your face you're worried they do. They don't, though. As long as mine don't frighten you off."

I tuck her hair behind her left ear and trace my finger along her jaw. "That addiction to people your therapist claims you have? I can think of much worse things than having you addicted to me."

"I want you to know how much I think of you telling me all this tonight. I know you didn't have to confide in me like this. It means a lot to me."

There's no way I can avoid telling her the absolute truth now, so I kiss her and take her hand as we walk back to the couch. I don't let go of her hand as I say the words I know might make what she just said a lie. "I don't ever want to go back to where I was, but that doesn't mean it won't happen. I've never gone this long without it, but as much as I want to promise you I won't let it back into my life, it's something that haunts me every day and night."

"Will you promise me something?"

"Yes," I answer, happy to see the kindness in her eyes hasn't left yet.

"Promise me if you ever do want to go back that you'll tell me because I can't stand by and watch someone I care about ruin his life. I know what I'm supposed to say is that I'd be by your side and help you through it, but I can't promise that like you can't promise it won't ever happen again. I'm not strong enough."

"You'd leave if I went back to it?"

"I'm sorry, but yes, I would. That's not what people want to hear, but it's the truth, and I promise I will always tell you the truth. I can't watch you kill yourself. I care too much about you already to do that, and there's no way you'll want me more than some drug. I wish that wasn't the case, but I've been around enough people who do drugs in my business to know I'm no comparison. You'll choose the drug over me, if you have to make the choice."

I'm struck by her words. "I've never had anyone tell me they'd leave if I went back to using heroin. All they ever say is that they'll help me through it. Then I go back to it and they try to help, but you're right. I always choose the drugs over them. I don't want to do that this time, though."

Kristina rests her head on my chest and squeezes me to her. "I know, but if you do, you deserve to know what I'll do."

I stroke her soft hair and press a small kiss to the top of her head. "Thank you for being honest. Nobody's ever been honest like that with me before."

We talk for hours about the book and how I hope the story will turn out, but Kristina's promise to me that if I choose the drugs over her that I'll lose her never leaves my mind. That woman I saw on my television is far stronger than I ever could be. As we lay naked in each other's arms later, I already know there's no way I could give her up, no matter what.

Unlike my character, the sex isn't what I'm addicted to. I'm addicted to her, and she's as much a drug as anything I've ever snorted up my nose.

# CHAPTER SEVEN

## *Kristina*

I SIT IN Ian's living room as I have every night for the past week listening to him read me what he's written in our story that day. That's how I think of Silk. Our story. I know he's the one writing it and it's his talent that will make it a success, but when I hear his words on the page that are there because I'm his muse, I can believe it's our story.

He takes on a whole new look when he's writing, a look that enchants me even more than the one he had when we met. His features intensify, as if telling our story brings out all the emotion in him. I watch his face as he reads me the day's words and see the fire in his eyes when he reaches a part he's written from a memory of our being together. Those dark eyes become pools reflecting his desire just like when he makes love to me.

"I wrote a scene today I'm not sure I'll keep in the final draft."

"Is that how this works? I guess I just always thought you wrote the book from start to finish," I say as I take a drink of wine.

"I do write that way, essentially, but my muse is inspiring me to write things that I usually wouldn't."

Smiling, I lean in and kiss him on the cheek. "Your muse?"

He winks and gives me a crooked smile. "Yes, my muse. Would you like to hear more?"

"Always. I want to hear everything, and then when the book comes out, I'll buy dozens of copies and tell everyone I was the inspiration for it."

Ian's face suddenly morphs to a far more serious look. "No, Kristina. You can't tell anyone. Remember, you promised?"

The gorgeous desire in his eyes vanishes, leaving only the darkness that makes me feel like he's disappointed in me. Quickly, I take his hand in mine. "I know. I was just saying I'd be proud. Don't worry. I won't do anything."

"As long as you understand that telling anyone would mean ruin for me. I can't let the world know about this."

I cling to him, afraid he's angry with me. "I won't. I promise. I would never do anything to hurt you or your career, Ian. I know how important the public's perception is. As much as I want to tell everyone about you and me and this book, I won't. You can trust me."

I wait for him to answer, my heart pounding in my chest as I silently chastise myself for being so stupid. The man tells me I can't tell the world about us or his new book, and what do I say? That the first thing I'll do when it's released is tell everyone about us.

A slow smile spreads across his lips, and he kisses me on the forehead. "It's okay. I'm excited too. And I know you understand why we have to keep this quiet. I'm happy you want to share this with the world. I wish we could."

"We get to share it with each other. That's even better."

An awkward silence settles in between us as he goes back to

silently reading over what he wrote. After a few minutes, he looks up and says, "Ready for more?"

Nodding, I snuggle up next to him and listen as he tells me more of Kate Silk's story.

"I reach the top of the stairs and feel him behind me. His warm breath skims my shoulder as he leans in to put his key in the lock, and the hardness of his cock grazes my ass just light enough to make me want more. I look around to see the hallway empty and turn to face him. 'Feeling brave, Jake?' He says nothing, but I see in his eyes he knows what I want and wants it too."

Ian looks up from the paper and smiles. "What do you think?"

"That's not from anything you and I have done before. Fantasy? Or is this something you've done with someone else?"

A rush of jealousy takes me over at the thought of Ian with another woman. It's irrational, I know, but I don't want to think of him with anyone else. Just me.

"No one else. I just took what we did in the kitchen the other night and moved it to the hallway," he explains, much to my relief.

"Oh. I thought maybe..." I don't finish my sentence because it will just sound insecure and stupid.

Putting the paper down on the coffee table, he stares at me as if he knows what I was going to say. "Come here," he says as he pulls me onto his lap. "You don't think I could be with someone else other than you, do you?"

I'm not sure how to answer his question. Of course I think that. I've never been with a man who didn't cheat on me. "I don't know. This has all happened so fast."

He slides his hands down my back to cup my ass and pulls me into him. Pressing his lips to my ear, he says in a voice that makes me pool with wetness, "There is no one but you. Whether in real life or in the book, it's all you, Kristina."

Closing my eyes, I relish his words. *It's all you, Kristina.* I love the sound of his voice as he says them. It makes each syllable all the more special. It makes me feel special.

I lean back and smile at him staring up at me like he means what he says. "Will you read me anymore before I have to go?"

He shakes his head. "No, I'll save it for next time. Why do you have to leave so soon?"

My mouth opens to speak, but I'm distracted by his finger slowly sliding down over my damp panties. "I have to…I mean I have an appointment…Ian, I can't think when you touch me like that."

His gaze is fixed on my panties as he says, "I love it when your voice whines like that. It's cute."

My eyes roll back into my head when he slips the tip of his finger under the cotton and touches my clit, sending zings of need straight to my core. "And when you touch me like this, I can't think of anything but fucking. I can't do that, though, because I have to go to my meeting and I can't go smelling like sex."

"It's not sex," he whispers as he softly rubs the pad of his thumb in circles over my needy clit.

"If I come, it's sex."

His dark eyes flash up at me. "Then I won't let you come."

I knit my brows at the thought of him touching me like this and not letting me come. "Why would you want to torture me?"

Moving his hand lower, he slides his middle finger inside me. "You were the one who said you can't go to your meeting smelling like sex."

I begin to rock against his palm, but he stops me. Confused, I lean down to kiss him and whisper against his lips, "Please, Ian. Don't tease me."

"I'm not teasing," he says while he slides a second finger into my wet pussy. "No coming for you, Kristina."

"Then I'll just have to do it myself when I get home," I say with a pout.

"I thought I told you not to do that," he scolds, roughly pulling his fingers out of me.

I don't know what to say. He seems like he's being playful, but something in his expression—an edge that isn't normally there—makes me think he's angry with me. I still want to get off and feel a little angry that he's playing with me.

"Fine. I'll just go to my meeting now and go home to do nothing. Let me up."

Half-expecting him to refuse to release me, I'm surprised when he swings his hands out to the side giving me free passage to get off his lap. Straightening my skirt, I grab my purse and head for the door, hurt and confused by his behavior, but if I stay I'm liable to say something hurtful that I don't mean and ruin everything.

As my hand touches the doorknob, I feel him come up behind me. I don't turn around, part afraid of what I'll say and part hurt that he'd play with me like this. His arm slips around my waist, instantly making my resolve weaken.

In my ear, he says low and deep, "Don't leave."

Staring forward at the door, I close my eyes and steel

myself. I don't want to give in. I don't. But he has this effect on me. "I have to go."

"I know. Don't."

Slowly, I turn around to see him looking at me with such need in his eyes. I don't understand his behavior. "Ian, I don't like to be toyed with."

He leans down and kisses me like he's never kissed me before—deeper, longer, and more intense than anyone has ever kissed me. When I think I can't go on for another second longer, he pulls away and cradles my face. Looking deep into my eyes, he says in a voice that nearly breaks my heart, "Forgive me. That wasn't fair of me to test you like that."

"Test me? Why would you feel like you need to test me?" I ask as he presses his forehead to mine.

"I don't know. It's stupid and I'm sorry, Kristina. I just felt like you didn't care."

I look into those dark eyes and see he's truly worried I don't care about him. But how could he think that? Every night I come here to be with him. To listen to his deep voice speak those beautiful words he's written because of me. How could I not care?

"I care more than I should after just a few days of knowing you, Ian. We've been like a flood of emotions that's carried me away since the moment we met. I can't think of anything else but you when we're not together, and when we are, all I can think about is how much I want to feel your hands on my body. If I made you think I don't care, I'm sorry."

He shakes his head and frowns, making me feel worse. "No, you did nothing wrong. This is all my fault. Forgive me."

"How about I come back after my meeting and show you

how much I care? I shouldn't be too long."

Another kiss that makes my legs feel like they're jelly and he leans back away from me with a smile. "I'll be here."

"Okay. I'll be back."

✦   ✦   ✦

CAFÉ EUROPA IS crowded, like usual. Every table is full, and people even stand along the walls, obscuring the beautiful blue and grey mosaic design of what I imagine is supposed to be the Mediterranean. My friend Priscilla sits at a table in the back of our favorite café looking as gorgeous as ever. Her newest style includes a short cut for her blond hair and lots of brown for her smoky eye look. I don't know how she does it, but she pulls off wearing all that makeup in the middle of the day. I'd look like a hooker if I did it.

"Kristina! I was early, so I ordered us those delicious croissant sandwiches we love. Sit down and tell me what you've been up to lately. You look practically glowing. You're not pregnant, are you?"

The patrons at the tables around us turn to look at me after Priscilla's announcement, and I smile meekly hoping they will just return to their conversations and ignore me.

"Can you keep your voice down?" I whisper as I sit down. "Everyone doesn't need to know my business."

She rolls her eyes like I've said something ridiculous. "You know, for a celebrity, you're pretty shy about things. This is the age of TMZ, baby. Everybody wants to know everything."

"There's nothing to know. Everything there is to know is up on the screen, like it should be. What I do in my private time is just that. Private."

"Well, share what skincare regimen you're using because you look fantastic. Your skin has a glow to it that I've only seen in pregnant women."

"Well, I'm not pregnant, so you can stop saying that."

"Then I have to know what you're using because I want a case of it. My skin is starting to look like crepe paper."

I stare at her in disbelief. Priscilla is one of the most beautiful women in the world, and she has the men lining up around the block to prove it. Her skin looks as stunning and dew-kissed as it always has. Ten thousand dollar spa treatments do that for a woman.

"Can we talk about something that has some basis in reality?"

Arching one perfectly manicured eyebrow, she sneers at me. "You make fun, but this face is on its last leg. I'm going to need a full facelift before I'm thirty at this rate."

Thankfully, the waiter interrupts our ridiculous conversation with our tuna croissant sandwiches. Priscilla hadn't been wrong about them. They're delicious and the only reason I agreed to come here to spend time with her in such a public place.

Even their scrumptiousness doesn't stop Priscilla's need to talk, though, and it doesn't take long for her to get back to pumping me for information on why I look so happy. I want to tell her all about Ian. Smarter than most of my boyfriends, he's someone I'm proud to be with. The problem is that she has a big mouth, and she'll tell the entire world about us before the afternoon is up.

So I lie. Sort of.

"I've begun a cleanse I heard about from one of the makeup artists on my last film, so maybe that's why my skin is doing the glowing thing. I've also been seeing someone, but I think my giving up drinking hard liquor might also be helping me look better. You know what they say. Alcohol saps the youth right out of your face. Or is that smoking? I'm not sure."

Priscilla narrows her eyes to suspicious slits and leans forward, pointing her index finger toward me. "What was that middle part? Did you say you're seeing someone new?"

"Yes, but my guess is the lack of booze is what's making my skin glow. You should try it."

She raises her eyebrows as if I've just said something utterly ridiculous. "I'm never giving up alcohol, thank you, but stop trying to get off the topic. Who is he? I want all the deets!"

Taking the last bite of my sandwich, I make sure to chew far slower than I usually would to stem the tide of madness I know will come as soon as I begin speaking again. When I'm finally finished, I take a drink of my iced tea and smile, knowing Priscilla is about to go out of her mind with curiosity. I can't tell her much, but I will take a few moments to brag about Ian, albeit anonymously.

"He's just someone I met because of one of my movies."

"What the hell does that mean? Met because of one of my movies could mean some guy who asked you for your autograph on the street. I want real info, Kristina."

I see I'm not going to get out of this without some details, so I go with the obvious. She'll draw her own wrong conclusions, if I'm lucky. "He's a writer, okay? There. That's all I'm going to say about him other than he's a great guy and I'm having a great time with him."

"Oooooh, I love it! You haven't had a real romance since John, so it's about time."

Priscilla's mention of John makes my heart contract for a moment, but I make sure to smile so she doesn't see the effect on me from hearing his name. I don't love him anymore, but his leaving me for some waitress at a hotel bar in San Francisco still stings.

"It's not a big deal," I lie, hoping she'll drop this topic of conversation and return to her concern for her impending facelift.

"If you say so, but your face says something else. Whatever he's doing for you, keep it up. And when you're done with him, send that man my way so I can get whatever he's got for my face."

Quickly, I seize the opportunity to bring up the facelift again. "Are you really thinking of getting some work done, Cilla? I don't think you need it at twenty-six."

With her fingertips, she pushes the skin up from her jawline until she looks like she's shoving her head through a hole too small for it. "Gravity is such a bitch, Kristina. She's a bitch, I tell you. How will I ever get a man with these jowls?"

"You don't have jowls. You have a jaw that wishes you'd stop abusing it like that. As for getting a man, you never have a problem in that department. Just because you haven't dated anyone you like in months isn't a reason to go searching for a bridge to jump from, or in your case, a plastic surgeon to carve into you."

Cilla lifts her right hand up and pledges, "I'm deciding here and now to wait for you to be done with your mystery man writer so then I can look fantastic. Until then, it's the spa for me. I'm going after this. Want to come? Alexander's would be happy to have a star with them, even though you don't have an appointment. They're such celebrity whores."

"I can't. I have to meet with my agent. You know how Jennie gets. If I miss a meeting, she's sure I've run away to another agent behind her back."

I don't entirely lie, but my meeting with my agent isn't until the next day. I just don't want to get trapped in a seaweed wrap with Priscilla pumping me for information about Ian. I might not be able to stop myself from telling her something, and then I know it will only be a matter of hours before the paparazzi hunt us down like rabid dogs and ruin everything between Ian and me.

"Time for me to head out. When are you leaving for LA?" I ask as I stand to leave.

Priscilla looks up at me and smiles at my mention of LA. She hates New York as much as I love it, so I know she's eager to return to the sun of southern California. "Saturday. Marlie is having her annual Octoberfest party. I'm hoping it's not half-naked men in lederhosen again. I mean, they were hot, but lederhosen? What the fuck?"

"I'm glad I missed it. Men in lederhosen, no matter how hot, is not what I want to see," I say with a chuckle.

"I'll be back in town by Christmas, I think. Promise me we'll get together then, and I'm going to expect more details about this mystery man."

Leaning down, I hug her goodbye and promise I'll meet up with her for the holidays. Maybe by then I can tell her more about Ian too.

As I leave the café, a man standing on the sidewalk just

outside the door asks for my autograph and I politely sign a sheet of paper for him, hoping to avoid any photographers wanting to snap pictures of me this afternoon. Cilla may think I'm glowing, but that doesn't mean I want to be anything but a normal person just out for a bite to eat with a friend.

The fan smiles and thanks me, but from behind him a man lurches toward me and grabs my arm. Slightly taller than the first man, he's about my height and has a mousey look to him with a pointy nose and chin that reminds me of a rat. I recoil from his touch, but his fingers close in around my sweater.

"Kristina, I've waited so long to meet you!" he exclaims as he pushes closer to me. "You're the most beautiful woman I've ever seen."

Terrified, I merely nod and turn to get away, but his hold on me keeps me planted in place. I don't know what to do and as my emotions quickly spin out of control, I remember the last time a fan did this and I fell apart for weeks afterward. I open my mouth to cry for help, but thankfully the first fan helps me and tugs the man off me, giving me the chance to run away as a crowd of people begin to form a tight circle around us.

I quickly force my way through them and hurry to Ian's apartment instead of going home, checking over my shoulder for any cameras as I get out of the cab, but thankfully, I seem to have eluded them today. My legs haven't stopped shaking since that fan grabbed me, and I feel weak. In truth, with all the celebrity scandals from secret babies to repeated stints in drug rehabs, I'm relatively boring and not really fodder for the front pages of gossip magazines anymore.

Not that I miss that. But fans are a different story. They don't need drama to want to be next to me.

Ian answers his door wearing that smile I already love. Taking me in his arms, he nuzzles my neck. "How was your meeting?"

"Unproductive," I say, still shaking. "How was your afternoon?"

"Why are you shaking? What happened, Kristina?"

Closing the door, he escorts me to the living room, his hand on my lower back as always to guide me. I sit down and try to take in a full breath. "It wasn't a big deal. A fan just grabbed me and I got scared."

Ian holds my face in his hands and looks at me like all he sees is a broken bird. "Are you okay?"

"I am now. Tell me about your afternoon so I can forget that awful, rat-faced man who grabbed me.

"I wrote a little more and had lunch. Such is the exciting life of an author," he says as he holds me so my head rests on his chest.

I look up at him and ask, "Can I have a glass of that wine I brought over? It's one of those chilly October days and it would hit the spot right now."

He kisses me and stands up from the couch. "Sit down and relax. I'll get it."

I love how he dotes on me like this. Most men I've known would have sat down on the couch and pointed toward the kitchen, saying, "Sure. Grab me a glass too while you're at it."

But not Ian.

"Here you go," he says as he hands me the wine glass. "You're going to need more of that, so I'll pick it up when I go out later."

Most men wouldn't do that either.

"You're so sweet," I coo and he beams his happiness at my compliment.

"Not all sweet."

He turns to face me and kisses me hard, like he's missed me for the few hours I've been gone. Need coils in my abdomen as he snakes his tongue into my mouth and his hands close into fists in my hair, tugging it not so gently.

"I missed you," he says and then teases my lips with his tongue. "You taste good."

"I had tuna fish for lunch," I admit, my cheeks warming from a blush of embarrassment. "I wanted the wine because I was worried I had bad breath."

Ian shakes his head and kisses me again hard and full on the lips. "Nope. But it wouldn't matter if you did. I'd still want you more than my next breath at this moment."

His hand leaves my hair and travels down to slide up underneath my skirt. Grazing my panties, he slides his finger along the edge, sending chills up my spine. I can't help but want him as much as I did a few hours before when things went wrong.

His words…his touch…I'm his for the taking.

I clumsily try to unzip his pants, wishing for once he sat around his house naked so I could just sit on his lap and feel him slide inside me. Pushing my hand away, he finishes the job and pulls his boxer briefs down to reveal his cock hard and ready for me. I hike my skirt up around my waist, forgetting I wore underwear because I was meeting Cilla.

Looking down, I smile. "I usually don't wear those when I know I'm coming here."

Ian's gaze travels to my panties. I move to stand so I can

take them off, but in a flash he rips them off me and tosses them to the side. "Problem solved. Now get back here so I can bury my cock in your tight cunt."

He pulls me down hard onto him, filling me quickly until he's fully nested and stretching me to take all of him. His cock touches a spot inside me that sends strings of pleasure through my body, but when he lifts me off him to plunge back into me, I want to cry out in ecstasy.

"You like that?" he asks in a sexy voice.

"Yes," I say more as a moan than anything else as I begin to ride him.

"That's it, baby. Ride my cock. Let me see you come apart on top of me."

His fingers dig into my hips as he decides how fast I should go. I roll my hips so his cock slides over my G-spot and watch the look on his face as he sees how much I love the feel of him. He's power and desire, and I can't get enough of him.

I want to feel his touch on the rest of my body, so as I ride him, I strip off my sweater and bra. He senses what I need without a word spoken between us and cups my breasts in his hands, squeezing my nipples hard between his thumbs and fingers just the way he already knows I like it.

"Ohhhh....Ian," I moan. I'm close already. I just need him to stay right where he is and I'll come.

Then he touches my clit and as I close my eyes, everything looks like colors exploding in the darkness. My body surrenders to his, and I come harder than I thought I could, bucking wildly on him as he holds me down on his cock. The feeling is more incredible than anything I've ever felt in my life. Clinging to him as wave after wave of sensation fills me, I finally collapse against him, unsure even if I can hold myself up anymore.

"Oh, my God. That was mind blowing," I whisper in his ear. "But you didn't come yet."

"Not yet. I was thinking your mouth could do the job."

Leaning back, I feel his cock twitch inside me. "You do like that, don't you?"

He gives me a devilish smile. "You sucking my cock after I've made you come? Yeah. I think it's sexy that you can taste yourself on me as you suck me off."

"Then your wish is my command," I say as I ease myself off his lap to kneel in front of him. Taking his cock into my mouth, I taste myself on his skin. "Anything else you find sexy while I'm down here?" I joke.

"Yeah, but all in due time. For now, just watching you suck me off will be all I need."

I slowly take all of him into my mouth, tasting myself on his silky skin as each delicious inch of his cock slides over my lips. Staring up at him as ecstasy fills his expression, I push the uneasiness I still feel about my abilities out of my mind and enjoy the feeling of pure sensuality giving him pleasure gives me.

Never before have I felt so sexy, and I love it. And even though I know it might not be the best way to handle things, having sex with Ian helps take my mind off that awful fan and how frightened he made me.

# CHAPTER EIGHT

*Ian*

I WAKE UP alone and instantly miss Kristina's gentle touch against me first thing in the morning. The bed feels too big for one person now since she's been in it. Stretching my arm out to the side, I run my hand over the cool sheets where she would be. I bury my face in the pillow next to me and smell the faint scent of her perfume, soft and flowery.

Two weeks. That's all it's been and already I can't stand to be away from her for more than a few hours. My limbs ache from want as my mind replays our time together last night. The feel of her tight cunt gripping me like a glove as she rode me so wildly. The taste of wine on her lips when she kissed me just as she came so hard I thought she'd strangle my cock. The sound of her voice when she told me how much she'd miss me when she was leaving.

I know I should slow things down between us. The warning signs are all there. She's tender and sweet, and when she finds out the monster addiction makes me, she'll run away. I won't be able to let her, but she'll want to. She'll say it's too much—too fast—too overwhelming. I'll tell her I can't live without her and mean every syllable.

What I don't know is how she'll react after that. The problem is that I do know how I will react. As much as heroin or alcohol, I'm addicted to her, and just like with them, she controls every moment of my day.

And I can't imagine a day without her.

I take a deep breath and hold the air in my lungs until I can't hold it anymore, letting it out slowly until there's nothing left to release. I feel the tiny bit of control I still possess begin to slip away.

SHEILA'S OFFICE REMINDS me of what I imagine a study in a college professor's house would look like. The predominant color is brown. Dark walnut wood bookcases line the walls to each side of her desk, which is also dark walnut. The three leather chairs, including the one she sits in, are a caramel brown with black metal studs that look brown.

The room has a warm feel I've never found anywhere else in the world, no matter how many beautiful homes I've been in. That's pure Sheila, though. Warm. Comforting. Nurturing.

She's summoned me to her office to talk about my next book, which in fact doesn't even exist as the kernel of an idea yet. I haven't decided what I'm going to tell her when she gets around to asking about it. Right now, she's going on about the dozens of calls she's been fielding for another of her authors who committed the cardinal sin of sounding off on social media about some reviewer or something. This is why I pay people to be me online. I don't have the time for that bullshit.

"So I've been putting out fires for the last twenty-four

hours, and Ian, you have no idea how big this might have gotten if I hadn't reeled her in," Sheila says frantically, her eyes darting left and right over the edge of her desk as she looks for something.

"You know how it is with the new ones," I say in my most comforting voice as I pretend to care. "And it's ten times as hard nowadays with everything you say being scrutinized. Better to say nothing at all, but then you're not social enough. It's a Catch-22. She'll find her way."

"A hundred times harder than when you got into this business a decade ago. Thankfully, I don't have those issues with you. You're smart enough to delegate your social media presence to those two girls, who I must say do a wonderful job. Maybe I should find a couple like them for Eva."

I'm not listening closely, but just to be polite I mumble, "Sounds good."

What I'm thinking about is how long this is going to take and when I'm going to see Kristina again. Just five more hours.

"So, we need to talk about your next book. The publisher isn't going to wait forever, Ian. They're dying to know what's next. Nero's Nightmare was a huge success, so capitalizing on that is key. What do you think you might want to do?"

I have a brand new three book deal that I have to honor, based on the early sales of Nero's Nightmare. Within the past three months, I've thought of exactly zero ideas for the next book. I know Sheila understands, but the reality is that writing isn't something like factory work. You don't just churn out ideas every day. At least not good ones. Good ideas take time. Great ideas take even longer.

But the publisher doesn't give a fuck about good or great

ideas. They want books that will make money. Not that I'm against money, mind you. I'm a capitalist, so money is fine with me. But their wanting more money doesn't coincide with my ideas coming any faster.

However, if I don't tell Sheila something and make her think I'm working on the third book, she'll worry and then I won't have a moment's peace until I give her an idea.

So I lie.

"I'm thinking something with Marc Antony."

There. That should make her happy.

But it doesn't. Not really. I watch her unattractive face twist into an unsatisfied grimace. "Marc Antony? Are you sure?"

"Is there something wrong with Marc Antony? I'm not tied to the emperor idea as I was with the last two books. This is an entirely new series. When you pitched them the idea for this one, you told them it would be ancient Rome as the setting. So what's wrong with Antony?"

"He's just been done a lot in the past. What about that Pontius Pilate book you once mentioned to me? Now that would be a bestseller for sure."

Her enthusiasm for my jumping into some ugly religious fray makes me smile. "I did have some ideas for that, but that was years ago."

Sheila leans forward, a clear sign she wants to encourage this whole Pontius Pilate thing. "Why not explore it? An historical fiction book involving Pontius Pilate would be a hit!"

"I wrote the last two from a crime and political scandal perspective, Sheila. That wouldn't work for this, although I have to admit I'm no Pontius Pilate scholar."

I'm not trying to be self-effacing or humble. I truly only know marginally more than the average human being does about this historical figure. When I first mentioned it to her, I think I had just gotten out of rehab for the first time and was ingesting a healthy dose of religion to keep myself from going back to my old ways. Normally, I'm not really a religious person at all. Spiritual at times, but not religious.

"Well, think about it. I'll mention it and feel them out about it to see if it works for them."

That statement right there bothers me. Crossing my arms, I say, "How about an author writing what works for them? Does it always have to be what the publishers want?"

She sits back in her chair and sighs. No doubt, I'm becoming more difficult, like her young author who can't keep her mouth shut on Twitter. I don't care. Something about being a pawn who's supposed to write whatever the powers that be deem interesting has gnawed at me for a long time, and now that I'm secretly writing something on the side, their demands chafe at me more.

"You know I'm a champion of artistic integrity, Ian. You know that. You also know that money is what makes this industry go 'round. If your books don't sell, I won't be able to get you those advances you like. I would never let them tell you what to write, but understand my job here. I need to make you as marketable as possible."

I wonder aloud in frustration, "What happens to all those people who have great ideas that the publishers don't like?"

"They self-publish. It's all the rage. I'm not sure anyone writing historical fiction is terribly successful yet, but some are doing fantastic numbers. I know agents who are representing these authors and their numbers are impressive."

"Are we talking paying to print a book and getting stuck with boxes and boxes of them in someone's garage?"

Sheila smiles and her awkward appearance softens. "No. I'm talking about ebooks. You know, the Kindle and Nook. Millions of people around the world read books like that these days."

"Not until they come with the ability to produce that book smell I love."

"Well, you're old fashioned, Ian, but many people love them."

Suddenly, an idea comes to me. "You say there are people selling their own books without publishers? What genres?"

"Romance and science fiction, mostly, I think. The Kindle basically exploded because of erotica and romance, and they've led the way. Those readers buy ebooks by a much greater margin."

"Hmmm...interesting." Now the wheels in my head are really turning.

"Oh, my God! Ian, you aren't thinking about that for your books, are you?" Sheila asks in that panicked voice she used just a few minutes ago when she was talking about that other author. "Please tell me you're not."

Shaking my head, I work to put her mind at ease before that vein in her forehead explodes out from under the skin. "No. Don't worry. I was just thinking that's going to be something that will make publishers have to change and maybe authors will be able to write more of the books they want."

Sheila exhales and hangs her head for a moment before she looks up at me with a look of pure relief on her face. "Thank

God. You gave me a scare for a minute there. Can we get back to the reality of your next book with a publisher? Can I tell them about Pontius Pilate?"

"Tell them I'm mulling over ideas and deciding between Marc Antony and Pontius Pilate."

"Okay, okay. I just don't want to see you become complacent, Ian. You have real talent. After all you've been through, I'd hate to see you let it all go because you lost your passion."

I stand and give her a wink. "Not to worry, Sheila. I haven't lost my passion. Trust me."

"Good. And I hope you don't mind me saying that you look great. I was worried after our last phone call, but I'm glad to see you're looking healthy and happy."

"Thanks, Sheila. Nobody worries about me like you."

As I head toward the door, she yells after me, "I'll call you when I hear something. And don't forget about the film deal. It's almost done."

I wave goodbye and head out the door with my mind already moving on from what she wants me to think about to what I want to focus on.

Kristina.

I HOP IN a cab to head back home and as we get stuck in midday traffic, I think about Sheila's comments about self-publishing. Could it work for Silk? A bigger concern is using my name on the book. As an author of historical fiction, I likely don't have many fans who also read erotic books. Talk about an interesting Venn diagram for that group.

No, I'm going to need a pseudonym. I have no idea what I might want to call myself. Should it be something clever or sexy like names in porn? Maybe something like Ian Cox? Or Ian Cumming? I chuckle as I say the names to myself. No, they won't work. Maybe something with an initial and some generic name.

The cab passes a bank truck with the name Anderson written on the driver's side door. Nice common name. Now for an initial. My mind quickly moves to memories of watching Wheel of Fortune in my freshman dorm room at college with my roommate who was so obsessed with Vanna White he could barely get through a whole show without heading to the bathroom to jerk off. The most common letters are given in that final round—R, S, T, L, N, and E. I go through each letter, disliking the sound of most of them, but T doesn't sound bad.

T. Anderson. I like the double entendre of T and A in the name of an erotica author. Chuckling to myself, I decide that name will work. Silk by T. Anderson.

I finally reach my building and jump out of the cab, happy I've got a name and a possible means of publishing the book. The sun has finally found a way to peek out from behind the clouds that have obscured it all day, so I choose to go for a walk instead of shutting myself up inside. It doesn't take long for me to know where I'm headed.

Ten minutes later, I'm standing across the street from Kristina's building staring up at her second floor windows into her living room. I think about that first night together in that room and how she'd been so afraid I didn't like her because of what happened with some asshole. I still have no idea who he is. It hasn't occurred to me to bother to find out.

He was the past, and in this case for me, I don't give a fuck about the past.

As I stare up at that room that holds such sweet memories for me, I wonder if she's home. My mind weaves a scene of her sitting on her leather sofa, her beautiful legs curled up under her as she reads a script.

Or a book. One of mine.

Her soft brown hair falls over her shoulders, teasing the tops of her full breasts so sensitive to my touch. Those cornflower blue eyes I fell in love with as I watched her films intently read the book in her lap, her perfectly shaped pink lips occasionally moving to mouth a word as the story comes alive for her.

I crave that mouth. I crave every part of her. In just a few short weeks, I've become a slave to my need for her. Addicted. Obsessed.

Lost.

# CHAPTER NINE

## Kristina

I ARRIVE AT Ian's apartment to find him deep in work on our book, his dark eyes flashing with inspiration as his fingers fly across the keyboard. I love watching him create like this.

After a few minutes, he sits back and smiles at me. "Just finished another chapter. I love how it's coming. Take a look."

He opens his arms for me, and I sit on his lap to read what he's written, sure it's as wonderful as everything else he's written. Before I can read a word, Ian pulls my face to his and kisses me long and deep. My body yearns for his touch, yearns for him to make love to me right now.

"I missed you," he whispers in a hoarse voice that hits me deep inside. "I've missed feeling of you next to me."

"I missed you too," I say as I slide my fingers through his dark hair. "I thought about you today. I was reading the inscription you wrote in my copy of Caligula's Dream. Your best fan. I love that."

His hand slowly caresses the tops of my thighs, teasing me every so often when he sneaks a finger over the front of my panties already damp from my desire for him. I watch his tongue slowly glide over his lower lip as his gaze travels to where his hand comes to rest, and I'm desperate for him to ease the ache inside me.

"I love how wet you get just from my touch," he says and presses his fingertip to my clit, sending a jolt of need through my body.

"I want you, Ian. Please don't tease."

He removes his hand from under my skirt and kisses me softly on the lips. "After we read the scene I just wrote."

I can't help but pout at his insistence in reading instead of getting me off, but I try to be understanding, even as he quickly shifts from lover mode to author mode. He turns the laptop to face me and begins to read and it doesn't take long for a sense of uneasiness to creep in between us.

His eyes fix on the words that tell how Kate Silk stands on the street across from her lover's house thinking about how much she cares for him, but all I hear is the story of a woman stalking a man. After too many brushes with the media and paparazzi, I feel nothing but dread at the idea of someone watching me from the street below.

I thought Ian felt the same way, but as he continues to read I realize Kate is him. Has he stood across the street from my building and watched my apartment windows for any sign of me like his character does? I want to ask him, but I'm too afraid of the answer.

Ian's fingers stroke the insides of my thighs as he speaks, but all I want to do is run. With every word, I'm more convinced than ever that the scene he's written is one he's lived out before with me.

I need to get away from this place.

I need to get away from him.

"Ian, I'm not feeling well," I say suddenly, tearing him out of his work.

He looks confused, but his expression changes to concern and he asks, "Are you okay? Is something wrong?"

Those dark eyes look at me like I'm more important than anything else in his world, but I can't forget how I felt as he read to me just moments before. I need to get out there now before he realizes I don't like what he's done.

"My stomach is upset. I need to go home."

He says nothing but studies my face for a long moment. "Is something wrong, Kristina?"

The edge in his voice tells me he knows something's wrong. I need to leave. Standing, I look for where I dropped my purse on the way in. "Just don't feel well. I'll call you after I lie down for a bit."

I scramble toward the door, forgetting to even kiss him as I leave like I always do. He follows me and catches my arm as I reach for the door. "I don't even get a kiss goodbye?"

I don't want to face him now. He scares me. But slowly, I turn to see him standing behind me, a look of hurt in his eyes. For a moment, I regret my fear. He's been nothing but sweet and accepting of me. The problem is even as that regret makes me feel bad, the fear of being stalked makes me feel much worse.

"Of course. I'm sorry," I say before I lean in and kiss him as I have every time I left his apartment.

This time is different, though. I can't come back here.

He tenderly cradles my face and looks into my eyes as if he's searching for the answer to why I seem so different. His gaze unnerves me, and I say in a shaky voice, "I'm sure it's just a touch of the bug or something. I'll call you."

"You don't want me to call you a cab? I know you only live a few blocks away, but if you're sick, you don't want to walk all that way."

He knows I'm lying. I see it in his eyes. He knows and he can't figure out what's wrong.

"I think a little fresh air will be good for me."

"Do you want me to walk you home?"

"No. I'll call you later."

His hands slip from my face, and I turn toward the door. A quick twist of the doorknob and I pull the door open and leave as he calls after me to be careful. I don't look back, afraid of feeling bad if I see hurt in his eyes or terrified if I see he knows I don't plan to come back here ever again.

I frantically press the down arrow to get the elevator to come, hoping he doesn't decide to ignore what I said and walk me home. It feels like it takes forever for it to finally arrive, and I step in and sag against the metal walls as I press the button for the ground floor. I let out a deep sigh as if I've been holding my breath for too long and look down to see my hands shaking.

The elevator doors open and I bolt out into the lobby, nearly running over the doorman as he stands talking to a woman about the weather or something. I hear him wish me a good night just as I hit the doors to the outside, but I don't reply.

The October wind hits me as I step onto the sidewalk, making me all the more conscious of how much I want to be safe and sound in my home. I run down the block toward my building, turning around once or twice to see if Ian's behind me, but I don't see him. Maybe he believed my lie.

When I finally reach my apartment, I truly do feel sick to

my stomach. The vision of him standing on the street watching my every move as I walk around my apartment blissfully ignorant of being stalked terrifies me.

But deep inside a tiny voice whispers that he would never hurt me. Ian cares for me. I'm his muse. He would never mean to frighten me intentionally.

I want to think all this is true, but then I remember him reading that scene so full of details of his character watching the one she loves and all I feel is afraid.

Afraid of him.

Closing my apartment door, I fasten every lock and deadbolt, something I never do when I'm home. I see his book sitting where I left it on my coffee table when I walk to my windows to draw the shades and a pang of loss bites at my heart. Curling up on the couch, I hold the book to my chest and sob. Had I been wrong to leave him? Was that voice that told me Ian would never hurt me right, or was my fear of him stalking me like a crazed fan right?

I pick up my phone to text him, but I don't know the words to say. Finally, my fingers type the only words that make sense.

I can't see you anymore.

Seconds later, his text comes in.

Why?

I just can't. I'm sorry.

He answers immediately with a text that breaks my heart. *I love you. Please don't leave me.*

As the tears roll down my face, I type I'm sorry. We can't be together anymore.

He doesn't answer, and my sadness grows until I want to call him and know why he won't speak to me anymore. I know it's crazy. I love him too, but I know my fear is real. How will I go on without him after everything we've been to one another?

My therapist is right. I am addicted to people. No, not people. Him. I'm addicted to him.

How will I be able to let him go?

As the reality of life without Ian settles into my brain, my phone vibrates against my leg one more time. Looking down, I see his reply to me.

There is no running from what we are, Kristina. I crave your touch as much you crave mine. There's no point in denying it. We will see each other again.

Terror courses through me as I read his words again and again. *We will see each other again.* I walk to the window to see if he's standing down on the sidewalk across the street watching me, waiting for me to open the blinds and see him. People walk past my building, but he's not there. I stand there for a long time peeking out to see if he ever shows up.

He doesn't.

In some small way, I wish he would. I know that's crazier than even I want to admit, but I'm disappointed when I finally step away from the window an hour later. I sit back down on the couch where he and I first kissed and made love and read over his message one more time.

There is no running from what we are, Kristina.

# Adore

## K.M. SCOTT

Addiction and obsession brought Ian and Kristina together, and real life tore them apart.

For Ian, Kristina is everything. What began as an obsession has morphed into that something more he so wanted. Kristina is his muse and so much more, but now both of them must make choices that may change everything.

For Kristina, Ian offers all that she's ever wanted. Love. Passion. Adoration. But these come with a price, and the cost of loving him may be more than she's willing to pay.

# CHAPTER ONE

## *Ian*

THE SMOOTH TASTE of vodka washes over my tongue on its way down to where it can do the most damage. Its strength isn't diluted by orange juice or anything else like that. That's for people wanting to enjoy what they're drinking. Enjoying isn't on the menu tonight. Getting fucking blasted so I can't think anymore?

Yeah. That's what I want.

I bothered to get dressed today. That's a change from the past six days. I think somewhere in my mind I mark this day as some kind of ugly anniversary. Seven days since Kristina told me she didn't want to see me anymore.

One week alone without her.

It's been a long week of endless drinking all alone in my apartment. I think I might have eaten a few times in that span. Not that eating is high on my list of priorities. Either is showering, writing, or doing anything that doesn't involve my efforts to forget.

There is no goal other than forgetting, but I know that's futile. I can't forget her. I may say I want to, but that's the last thing I truly want to do. I want to remember every beautiful inch of her body as my hands caressed her silky skin. I want to remember the gentle sound of her voice as she asked me about my work. I want to remember her smile as she lay next to me in bed after we lost ourselves in each other.

I want to remember her. All of her.

I spent the first few days trying to figure out why she doesn't want to see me. What did I do to make her run away? Every time I asked myself that question, my mind came up with the long list of my faults, any one of which could have made her not want me.

*You shouldn't have told her about your addictions* my brain whispers.

No, she understood. I know she did.

*You shouldn't have told her about wanting her before you even met her* it murmurs.

No, she's an actress. They understand being desired by fans.

*You shouldn't have asked her to be your muse* my brain wonders.

No, she loved that. It couldn't be that. She loved it as much as I did.

Lifting the vodka bottle to my lips, I take another gulp and let it slowly trickle down my throat before I set today's companion on the table in front of me. I lean my head back and close my eyes as the alcohol hits my stomach, and for a second the pain eases.

But it doesn't last.

The problem is that I can't turn my brain off. Even with all this vodka in me, my mind can still remember. Like it's on some mission to make sure I don't forget her, it forces me to watch as it replays our time together.

Eyes closed, I can almost feel her on my lap, her thighs spread as she settles onto me. My hands find their place on her hips directing her movement. She looks down at me and gives me one of those sweet smiles that belie how sensual a being she truly is as she rides my cock like no other woman ever has.

"Fuck me, Ian," she whispers lightly against my lips, ratcheting my desire up even higher. I obey. How could I not? Fucking her gives me more than physical release. It lifts my spirit from the darkness that surrounds me to that light and gentle place she provides.

I open my eyes and look around my apartment, disappointed to admit it was just a memory. I grab my phone from the table and scroll through her messages to me. Reading each one, I still can't understand why she left. My fingers hover over the empty space under the last message I sent her. I want to tell her I miss her. That I'm sorry for whatever I did. That I can fix it. Everything can be fixed so it all goes back to the way it was. I can do that.

But they remain frozen hovering over my phone because like every time before when I told myself I should text her, a tiny voice in the back of my mind whispers those dark words and stops me.

*Fuck her. She doesn't want to see me? Well, I don't want to fucking see her. She's a Hollywood bitch whose life is a fucking mess. Even her therapist thinks so. For fuck's sake, she thinks she has an addiction to people.*

But if she's addicted to people, which in far less stupid terms means she's addicted to their approval and love, how could she leave me?

It always comes back to that question. Every time my mind

spins out of control, that voice asks that one question that hurts to even think about because I know addiction. I know the feeling of needing something or someone so fucking bad that your body aches without relief. I know there's no talking yourself out of it if you're addicted.

It's a need, not a want.

So if she has that addiction to people, why didn't she become addicted to me like I did to her?

I clutch my legs as a wave of pain washes over me. My fingernails dig into my thighs just above my knees as the need for her takes me over, and my forearms hurt like someone is twisting them. My muscles ache like someone has placed a heavy object on them, pressing down on me and threatening to crush me with its weight.

I know this feeling. We're old friends. Or enemies, depending on how you view things.

My body craves her. Like the drugs, she got into my system and became part of me. Now that she's gone, every other part of me desperately longs for the missing part.

Maybe if I just text her and ask why she left. Maybe she'll see I care and need her back.

*Fuck her. I don't need her. I can live without her.*

No, I can't.

I should try to write. Our book waits for me to return to it like some lost orphan who can't understand why its parent abandoned them. Our book. That's the problem. It's not my book. It's ours. Hers and mine. That's why I can't write. She's not here.

Without my muse, I'm lost. Without my Kristina, I can't do it.

Silk will have to wait. Maybe I can find another muse. In whatever stupor I'm in, this sounds like a wonderful idea. Muses can't be that hard to find. Desperate women who want to be adored must be a dime a dozen. Sure. Modern life has made it easy to find them.

Hello, Netflix, my old friend. Show me what you got.

I scroll through the lines of offerings but see little of interest. A blonde would be nice. Kate Silk should have been a blonde the whole time. What was I thinking? Like the world wants another common brown-haired heroine.

Some flick about an outbreak of something catches my eye, and I begin watching it looking for my new muse. I know she's here. My blurry vision isn't helping the search, though. I see a woman, but she's not right. Too trashy. Another enters the scene and she's wrong too. Too sterile.

After about fifteen minutes of what turns out to be a goddamned zombie movie, I go back to the main screen. There's a story in itself—me searching for a muse in a fucking zombie film. Maybe I'll include that in the acknowledgements. *To the hot, half-rotted piece of ass I watched for a quarter of a fucking hour. Literally.* More scrolling through more films I can't imagine anyone thought would be successful brings me to my favorites.

No, I don't need my favorites. I need something new. Someone new.

But the photos from Kristina's films sit there lined up in a row for me to watch. I can't help but chuckle as I think, "Well, I guess we know where Netflix stands on the issue of me and Kristina."

I click on the film that started it all. That remake of The

Misfits. I've watched this so many times I could act out the parts myself, but as I sit here in my living room fucked up from too much vodka, I watch it feeling like I'm seeing her for the first time in ages. I wait with eager anticipation for the moment when I know she'll be in the picture. The first time her face appears on the screen, my heart leaps in my chest.

Missing her for the past week has been nothing compared to how I feel as I watch her. I can't go on like this. Every second she's in front of me and I can see her but not touch her or speak to her is killing me.

I need to talk to her. No. Talking is never good, at least not for me. Like most writers, I'm my worst when my mouth is open. No, words come much better from me when they're written. When I have the time to choose the perfect ones to express my thoughts. When I can construct my sentences exactly so she'll understand my true feelings.

Then I'll be able to say the right things.

She always thought I said the perfect words. I remember her saying that.

I reach for my phone and go to her messages again. My thumbs hover over the letters as I think about what I want to say. Jesus, now isn't the time for writer's block. I want to tell her so much. Need to tell her so much. I'm sorry. I don't know what I did, but I'm sorry. Tell me what I did so I can make up for it. Come to me and let me fix this.

None of those words show up on my phone because my fingers never move. After convincing myself I shouldn't do anything, I throw the phone away from me, disgusted. I hate myself for doing nothing.

I can't go on like this.

✧   ✧   ✧

TEN O'CLOCK ON Wednesday night turns out to be a busy time on the streets of the Upper West Side. Maybe there's some street festival or some event being held, but as the October wind bites at my cheeks, I can't imagine that's the case. Maybe I'm just one of legions of people smashed and needing to see someone, like love zombies who can't do anything but drag their empty selves to where their heart lives. More people out actually works for me tonight, though, since I'm hoping to be invisible.

Not that I'm some huge star or anything like that. I'm no Stephen King or James Patterson, for Christ's sake. It's true I'm a New York Times bestseller, but that doesn't translate into instant notoriety, especially for someone who writes historical fiction. Well, maybe Dan Brown can't walk the streets where he lives without a mob attacking him to take a picture or sign something. My handful of literary successes have allowed me to still be somewhat invisible to most people, however.

I walk the blocks toward her brownstone building slowly and deliberately, mainly because I'm loaded. Every time I take a deep breath and let it out, the smoke from the cold nearly knocks me over from the vodka smell.

The sidewalk is surprisingly uneven now that I'm walking it without her. She always wrapped her arm in mine as we walked. Or maybe it's the effect of the vodka. I don't know. I just know where I'm going.

Her building faces a small patch of grass with a few trees on it. Not really a park, it's more like a front yard of some planned building that never came to fruition. It sits there as a testament to someone's hopes and dreams that never came true. I position myself under one of the trees in the shadows and look up toward the second floor to see her windows darkened.

She isn't there.

Where is she? Why is she out on a Wednesday at just after ten at night?

Before I can stop myself, my mind begins to spiral out of control with scenarios of her out having a good time with someone else. I've spent the entire week since losing her a total fucking mess, and she's out enjoying life. She's probably with someone. Another man. A man who wants her like I do.

No. He can't want her like I do. No one wants her like I do. They merely want to fuck her or watch her act out their stupid parts. I want to watch her sleep next to me. I want to see her smile when I read her the story of us. I want to feel her come apart from my touch. I want her to know I love her more than I can say.

A surge of rage and hate pushes through my body making me want to hit something. My fists ball up at my side as my mind spins with ideas, but then the sinking feeling in my stomach from the reality that she's gone makes me weak. Stumbling back against the hard trunk of one of the trees, I try to get my emotions under control.

And then I see her. But not just her. I see her step out of a cab with someone. A man. He escorts her up the stairs to the front door while I stand there and watch, my heart in my throat as I wait to see if she kisses him. She's wearing the pink shirt she wore the night we first met at Jax's and a pair of jeans she never wore the entire time we were together. Her long brown hair falls over her shoulders making her even sexier than she could ever know because she has no idea how incredible she looks.

She's smiling at something he must have said. Hate rushes through me again. Not for her, though. If only I could hate her, then this would all be so much simpler.

I don't hate her. I wish it were that easy.

He leans down to kiss her, and it takes every ounce of my willpower to stop me from running across the street to tackle him to the ground and never let him touch her again. Pressing my lips together, I want to close my eyes so I don't see her kiss him, but I can't. It's as if some sadistic force is forcing them open so I must watch.

I know what he's feeling as her lips touch his. He wants more. That's the effect she has. One taste won't be enough. He's thinking he wants her to invite him up to her apartment so he can have more of her. More of those lips on his lips. On his cock.

She pulls away and smiles, but I watch in shock as she enters her building and he walks back down the stairs to the cab I hadn't even noticed was still there. She didn't invite him in.

What does it matter? She's moved on.

BY THE TIME I arrive home, my mind's a mixture of loathing and jealousy that threatens to eat me up. I hate her. I love her. I want to wrap my arms around her and never let her go. I miss her. I crave her touch on my skin so bad I ache.

I fall onto the couch and close my eyes, trying to remember anything other than the sight of her kissing that man. My mind begins to race through every moment with her. I struggle to focus on any one time, desperate for one memory that doesn't seem tainted by what I just saw.

My heart slams against my chest and cold sweat pours down over my face. I miss her so much. But then slowly, the images in my mind begin to fade away until one memory comes into focus.

*Kristina smiles at me as she takes my finger in her mouth to taste the sugar left on my fingertip. She looks adorable sucking the sweetness from my skin.*

*"Taste good?" I ask as I slide my finger from her mouth.*

*Her answer is to kiss me gently on the lips before she runs her tongue over her bottom lip and whispers, "I'd rather have something else to suck on."*

*I know that might not be entirely true. She's only sucked me off twice before, and while each time she seemed enthusiastic, I know she's never finished anyone else off but me.*

*"First we taste this martini I made you. Then we can figure out what you should do with that pretty mouth of yours."*

*Handing her the sugar-rimmed glass, I watch her take a sip of the caramel appletini we've spent the last half hour concocting. The drink only took about ten minutes. The rest of the time would be considered more foreplay than drink making.*

*That's how it is with her. I know she might be considered needy by some men, but I adore that neediness that would turn others off. I understand it. When I look into her blue eyes and see what can only be described as a craving to be touched or kissed, I know how she feels.*

*I feel it too.*

*"It's very sweet, Ian," she says, smacking her lips.*

*"Then it's perfect for you."*

*Kristina places her drink on the counter and nuzzles my neck,* sending strings of excitement racing through my body. "Maybe I want something less sweet."

"I can do less sweet too," I say and tug hard on her hair, pulling her head back so she has to look at me. I look down into those cornflower blue eyes staring up at me with such need. "I can definitely do less sweet."

Biting her lip, she moans softly. "Yes. Please."

What she wants is to be dominated. Not with whips, chains, or any of that other bullshit that's more props than anything else. No, what she wants is me to make her body surrender like no other man has.

I pull her hair harder into my grip, and she doesn't wince in pain so much as in pleasure. A tiny moan escapes from her lips, making my cock swell. I want to conquer her, to make her mine and only mine.

My hand roughly slides down to between her legs and I thrust two fingers into her already dripping pussy. Her eyes grow wide at the invasion, and I ask, "Whose is this?"

"Yours," she says in the sweetest voice I've ever heard.

"Say my name," I order. "Whose is this?"

"Ian's."

I slowly slide my fingers out of her only to ram them back into her warm and willing body. She wants it rougher, but not yet. Eventually.

"Fucking right." I unzip my pants and take out my rock hard cock. She glances down toward it and bites her lip again. "And whose cock is the only one you want?"

Tentatively, she reaches out to touch me, stroking me from base to head. "Yours. I mean, Ian's."

I tighten my hold in her hair. "If you can't remember my

name, I think it's time for you to learn it."

Her eyes widen because she knows what's coming next. I tear off her skirt and blouse, sending buttons flying everywhere around my kitchen, before I push her up against the wall. Her face wild with excitement, she whimpers as I lift her and command her to wrap her legs around my waist, and then I slam into that wet cunt that's only mine and fuck her harder than I ever imagined she could handle.

She takes every pound, every slam into her body and begs for more. I sink my teeth into her shoulder, and she cries out but doesn't plead for me to stop. I know her legs ache from clutching me. I know she must want to stop, but she doesn't. Not until she gives me what I want. Not until I give her what she wants.

I feel her body begin to contract around my cock, surrendering to all the pain and pleasure I've given her. She whimpers, "Ian, don't stop…harder…harder…"

I thrust my hips forward once more and bury myself in her as deep as I can as she clings to me more with every moment. Her release rushes through her and sends me over the edge, and I flood her body with all I have. I have no idea how long we stay there like that, our bodies trembling against one another and our breathing heavy and sated.

She's small and broken afterward, but she's mine to cradle and whisper tender words to. I carry her to the bed and hold her until all the pain eases away and all that's left are the most exquisite moments between two people who need each other. My hands, which had inflicted so much on her as we fucked, now gently stroke her skin in love. She entwines her fingers in mine and curls our hands together under her chin as I tell her how much I adore her and mean every word as if my life depended on their truth. I listen to her breathing as she drifts off to sleep, and just before I close my eyes, I hear her sigh contentedly.

I've never been happier with another soul in my life.

I open my eyes as the reality of my lonely rooms bears down on me. I don't know how to go on feeling like this. I don't want to go on feeling like this. I need something to help me not feel at all.

# CHAPTER TWO

## *Kristina*

I SIT IN front of my makeup mirror hating what stares back at me. Lines and wrinkles already and I'm only in my twenties. I use the finest creams and lotions. Why don't they work on me? My skin looks ruddy and uncared for.

My eyes, all red-rimmed and watery looking, tell the story of who I've become in the past week. I cry all the time when I'm alone, which is far too often. I cry when I read those texts I sent him. I cry when I see the texts he's sent me. I cry that he hasn't sent me any more.

I'm a mess. A stereotypical Hollywood mess, complete with bad skin and red eyes.

I think back to my lunch with Cilla that day when all she could talk about was how I glowed. Now that's gone and all I am is the miserable wretch that stares back at me as I try to cover her up with makeup.

Magazines I've appeared in sit stacked on a table next to me, but no matter how many times I thumb through their glossy pages, the compliments don't feel real. Gorgeous eyes. Beautiful smile. Healthy skin. They all rave about my look, but it's all lies.

I'm all lies.

I ran away from Ian because he scared me, but I've been miserable without him since. I thought I saw him last night, but the more I think about it, the more I know that was all in my mind. It seemed so real, though. I was on my front stairs with Gavin, a fellow actor I hope to work with in that film I screen tested for, and as he leaned in to kiss me goodnight, I thought I caught a glimpse of Ian standing in the trees across the street.

*Stop doing this! You're a Hollywood star, Kristina Richards! You can meet another man—hundreds of them, if you want, anytime you want.*

I say this every time I feel down and want to go back to Ian, and it works. For a few minutes anyway. Sometimes if I'm busy during the day or I go out and see lots of men looking at me, it works for a few hours. But eventually, the truth comes back and I'm alone in my apartment missing him so much it hurts.

There's not enough concealer to hide my dark circles and bags now. I put more on, but that only makes it worse. Frustrated, I throw it aside and move on to creating the face the world expects. Foundation for even, glowing skin that's having a hard time finding its glow lately. Grey eyeliner and jet black mascara for smoky eyes that cry more than seduce these days. Grey eye shadow to complete that look.

I throw the shadow brush down onto my makeup table and bury my face in my hands. No matter how much I apply, it can't change the truth. My miserable inside shows all over my outside. Tears flow down my cheeks, and I don't stop them. I can't. It's like I have an inexhaustible supply of them.

All I can think of is him. What's he doing now? Is he

finished with our book? Is it even our book to him anymore? I can't help but cry harder at the thought that it's not our book anymore. I was his muse. He adored me and wanted to write because of me.

And what did I do? I ran away.

*But he scared me. I know that scene he wrote with his character was actually about him. He was watching me.*

As soon as the words form in my head, my brain discounts them as nonsense.

*He adored you, and you ran away like a child who couldn't handle being watched. Millions of people watch you every day. Do you run away from being an actress to become a sheep herder hidden away on some farm? No! So why did you run away from him?*

Shaking my head, I answer my own question as I try to push those thoughts away. I don't know why. I was scared. Now all I feel is lonely without him.

But if he loved me so much, why hasn't he come back? Why hasn't he tried to contact me since that night? There have been no flowers, no calls, no texts. No anything.

I lower my hands to see the mess my face has become from my tears and makeup mixing together. *This is why you're alone. You're not beautiful, no matter how many magazines say so. They lie. Everyone lies when they say you're beautiful and gorgeous because if you were, Ian would have come by now.*

No! I can't let those demons in me do this every time I look in the mirror. I grab a tissue and clean the mascara from under my eyes, but it's no use. I can't do this. No matter how much makeup I put on my face, it will never hide how unhappy I am.

✧ ✧ ✧

A HAND WAVES from the back of the very dark bar, and I squint my eyes to see whose it is. My friend Sienna stands from her seat and calls my name, so I begin to make my way through the crowds of smiling and laughing people who all look happier than I feel. I reach her and see she's found us a table far enough away from the front of the bar that we'll have at least a little privacy.

She's in a black dress that makes her long blond hair stand out more than usual, and I see by the number of men around her that it will be the usual when we're out. A line of potential second husbands stretching out the door to meet her. Not that I blame them. Between a knockout body and a gorgeous face, she physically has it all going for her. Add to those intelligence and a wickedly sharp sense of humor, and Sienna's the whole package.

"Kristina, I thought we said nine. It's quarter to ten. I'm already half in the bag from waiting here, not to mention the half dozen or so men I've had to brush off because it's a girls' night out."

"I'm sorry," I say as I sit down with my back to the crowd. "It took me longer than usual to get my makeup right."

She narrows her eyes to a judgmental squint and studies my face. "Have you been drinking already?"

I shake my head. "No. Why?"

"Your eyes are all glassy looking. What are you doing?"

Instantly more self-conscious than when I walked in the door, I lower my head. "Nothing. Nothing at all."

"Did your makeup artist friend give you something again? I

told you not to trust her. That woman is bad news."

"No. Nothing."

Sadie, the woman who's been the makeup artist on my last two films, isn't the type of person Sienna would ever spend any real time with. She's not the right class, in her mind. It also doesn't help that she gave me some pills one time to help me with insomnia that was crippling me and making it impossible to work. They made me a little crazy for a few days, but in Sienna's eyes, it was intentional.

"Then what's up with you? Cilla gave me chapter and verse about whatever regimen you've begun using and how you were glowing like a goddamned nuclear reactor. No offense, but either she's blind or the effects have worn off."

I rub my fingertips over my cheek as if to feel if the evidence of my misery is written all over my face. "You know how she is. It's always something to rave about with her."

The waiter arrives just in time to save me from more of this interrogation, and I order a merlot. Tonight's definitely a merlot night. No sweet and fruity red wines for me. If I'm going to look like shit, I might as well get shitfaced.

Sienna gives my wrist a squeeze and launches back into her questioning. "So who is this mystery man you've begun to see lately? Cilla couldn't talk about much of anything else, except your glowing, of course. I want details."

"Wouldn't you rather tell me all about your new movie? I mean, this is looking like it's going to be the one," I say, hoping to use her inherent actor's ego to my advantage, but she isn't having any of it. Unlike Cilla, Sienna knows when bullshit is being thrown her way. It's one of the reasons I consider her such a dear friend.

"Kristina, what's going on here? You look like shit, show up nearly an hour late, and now you don't want to tell me about this guy. You can tell me. This is Sienna you're talking to, not some stranger. We've talked each other through all the ups and downs. Well, talked and drank, which is perfect since we're in a bar. I promise to keep the alcohol flowing if you promise to talk. You look like you need it."

I want so much to tell someone about Ian and how much I miss him. I'm not even afraid of turning into a sobbing mess in public. At least I'd be able to unburden myself of my misery. But I can't because I promised him I wouldn't tell anyone about us and I keep my promises.

Even if there isn't an us anymore.

"We aren't seeing each other now. It's over."

Sienna's expression tells me how awful I must look. Her deep brown eyes fill with pity, and she gives my wrist another squeeze, this time one of those empathetic "I'm here for you" squeezes. "What happened?"

"I really don't want to talk about it, Sienna. It's just over. I feel terrible about it, though, so if this girls' night can help me forget, I'd really appreciate it."

"Got it!" she says with loads of enthusiasm as she raises her hand to get the attention of the waiter. "We're going to need something more than wine then."

The man returns to our table and she instructs him to bring over a bottle of his finest cognac. Never a huge fan of brandy, I grimace at the thought of a cognac hangover. As he walks away, I lean toward her and say, "I'm not really a big cognac drinker, Sienna."

"Honey, the cognac isn't to drink so much as to advertise

for a certain kind of man. Look around this bar. You've got beer drinkers, who you can do better than; wine drinkers, who aren't really what I think would help you forget anyone; and liquor drinkers. Within that last group are men who understand that if a woman can afford to drink the finest cognac in the house, then she's expecting a certain level of man. That's the man I'm trying to find for you tonight."

The thought of going with anyone other than Ian fills me with dread. I try to pretend that I'm all for her plan, but inside I wish I was back in my apartment on my couch reading his book instead of sitting in a bar full of men Sienna plans on having audition for the role of my next boyfriend.

"I'm not ready to meet anyone new yet," I say as the bottle of cognac arrives at our table.

Sienna pours each of us a drink and lifts her glass to make a toast. "I'm not talking about starting some long term relationship, Kristina. Tonight's about finding someone to give you a good lay and make you forget the mystery man. To great sex and its healing powers!"

I clink my glass and lift it to my lips to take a drink. I have to admit it does taste nice. Maybe I've only had cheaper cognac before.

Her plan works almost instantly, and within a few minutes men begin to surround our table, each one dying to join us at what's obviously a celebration. If they only knew how depressed I truly am, they'd be running away instead of doing their best to win us. I smile and laugh at their jokes, but I can't help but notice that most of them are far more interested in Sienna than in me.

Not that this is a bad thing. The idea to drink and then

fuck Ian out of my mind was never going to work, no matter how I tried. Sienna may not believe it, but I know the truth. I love him and nothing and no one else could change that. Love isn't something that can just be replaced.

"My name is Brian. What's yours?" a voice says, tearing me out of my fog of thinking about where I really want to be at that moment.

I look at the man seated next to me and smile. Attractive with wavy brown hair and brown eyes, he looks like a banker or businessman in his expensive grey pinstriped suit. "I'm Kristina. It's nice to meet you, Brian."

"You look out of place here, Kristina. By that I mean, you don't look like you want to be here."

So perfect strangers can see it too.

"No, I'm having a good time. My friend and I are out for a girls' night out." Looking across the table, I see Sienna has a man on each side of her, both working hard for her attention.

"It just seems your heart isn't in this," he says with a gentle smile that shows his very white teeth.

"I'm not as good at it as Sienna, I think. Some people shine in crowds. Others are less comfortable and prefer one-on-one."

I take a drink of my wine and feel a rush of heat cross my cheeks as I realize I've just intimated I want to be alone with him. I don't, but at that moment as the merlot settles into me, I don't want to be alone. He might not be the man I want, but at least he's someone who likes me.

"Would you like another drink?"

My wine glass is almost empty, so I nod. "That would be nice. Thank you."

Brian raises his arm to get the server's attention and then

turns his attention back to me. "Kristina, what do you do for a living?"

"I'm an actress." I don't say it, but I can't help thinking I'm not a very successful one since I'm able to sit in a bar with hundreds of people around and not be noticed, however.

He nods and pretends to be interested, but I see in his eyes a look of disappointment as he explains his job as a day trader. I listen intently for any sign that he has the passion I love to find in people, but Brian is a businessman through and through. There's nothing really wrong with that, but I like my men to be more intense and creative.

Like Ian.

We continue to talk, each of us pretending there's anything interesting about the other person beyond looks, but Sienna's plan has failed. Looking across the table, I see that's only partially true. I might not have met anyone I have any interest in, but by the look on her face, she's definitely interested in the blond man sitting close to her.

At least one of us will be happy tonight.

I look at Brian and say, "I think I'm going to head home. It was very nice to meet you." Stretching my hand across the table, I tap on Sienna's arm to get her attention. "I'm going home. I'm just going to catch a cab, so don't worry about me. Talk to you later."

"Are you sure? There's more cognac. We can move to the other side of the bar, if you like." Sienna's not-so-subtle way of asking if I'm leaving because I dislike Brian makes me laugh, and after rolling my eyes toward him to hopefully show him I'm not leaving because of him, I shake my head.

"I think it's just an early night for me. Enjoy yourself."

I turn to say goodbye to Brian, but he's standing now and I sense he's looking to take our conversation outside. Why I can't imagine since neither one of us set anything on fire with our discussion of how exciting we think our jobs are.

Sienna gives me a look as if to say, "Is it okay he's going?" but I just nod and smile. Some company as I wait for a cab won't be a horrible thing, even if it's just someone silently standing next to me.

Of course, the minute I get outside it seems that every cab in the city has disappeared suddenly. I look up and down the street over and over, but nothing. It's like fate is forcing me to move on, even though I don't want to.

"I can give you a ride, if you like. My company has a car service we use, so I can have it drop you off anywhere you like."

I stop my head swiveling left and right and say, "That's really nice of you. I'm just going to take a cab, I think. But thank you."

"There's not a cab in sight. Let me get you a car and I can take you right to your apartment."

I look once more up and down the block and sigh. I know I shouldn't do it, but I have no other way home and my apartment is miles away from this bar in Brooklyn. With a sigh, I relent and say, "Okay. Thanks."

Brian calls the car service and then says, "If you're nervous, I can stay here and not join you. I don't want you to think I'm some kind of creepy stalker guy. I'm just a nice guy trying to help someone get home."

Hanging my head, I say quietly, "Thank you. I'm not really a miserable person. Really. I've just been through something recently and my friend wanted to show me a good time. The odds were pretty much stacked against her with that, though."

"I don't think you're miserable. You seem nice. Nothing like what I imagined an actress would be like. You're down-to-earth. I like that."

I thank him for the compliment and we talk for a while about the weather, our careers again, and other noncommittal, superficial topics until a black town car pulls up. As I climb into the backseat, he stands at the door waiting for me to say whether he can join me or not. I can't be a total bitch, so waving him in, I say, "Please join me. It's the least I can do since you got me a ride home."

Brian and I talk the whole way to the Upper West Side, and in some way, I realize I do like him. Not in any romantic way, but as a person, he seems nice. That doesn't mean I trust him, though, so instead of telling the driver my address, I tell him Ian's. I'll just get out there and after the car drives away, I'll make my way home.

The car pulls up to the entrance of Ian's building and I turn toward Brian. "Thank you. This was very nice of you."

Smiling, he leans in and kisses me. I don't know if it should make me feel something for him, but all I feel is how much I miss Ian. I kiss him back and quickly get out of the car. He's probably disappointed I didn't ask for his number or give him mine, but I don't care.

The car speeds down the street away from Ian's building, and I know I should just turn away and walk home, but I can't. I know he's up there right now. This was a mistake. I shouldn't have gotten out here. Now all I want to do is see him.

The doorman recognizes me and gives me a big smile. "Good evening, Miss Richards! It's nice to see you again."

I smile meekly, knowing what I'm about to do is a mistake. Walking toward the door, I wish him a good evening as he lets me into the building, thrilled to know Ian never told him not to, and my heart begins to beat wildly. I should just turn around and go home, but he's just a few floors up. I can't stop myself.

Pressing the button for the elevator, I tell myself this is a mistake. He's never texted or called back after telling me we'd see each other again. What if he's changed his mind? What if he's found someone else to be his muse?

My heart sinks at the thought of him writing because of another woman. Being his muse had made me special. If he replaced me...

The elevator dings to let me know I'm at his floor and as I step out into the hallway leading to his apartment, fear grips me making it nearly impossible to walk toward his door. I can see it, that familiar entrance to his home I've walked through so many times before, but now it just looks like a black void.

Like what lies behind it isn't somewhere I'm welcome anymore.

With every step, my fear grows until I reach the end of the hallway and hear noises from inside his apartment. Is he watching television? I lift my hand to knock, but a sound stops me dead. Placing my ear next to the door, I listen and hear a moan.

A woman's moan.

I can't move from that spot, yet that's all I want to do. I desperately want to run away and never come back here again. Unable to leave, I can't help but cry. He's in there with another woman. Another muse. I've been replaced.

Like some pitiful, unwanted animal, I stay there on his doorstep as the sounds of him with someone else fill my ears. Finally, they become too much and I can't stand it anymore. Running away, I stumble to the elevator as my tears blind me and I press the buttons to get me out of there before he sees me and knows how pathetic I truly am.

# CHAPTER THREE

## *Ian*

I OPEN THE door just as the last sight of Kristina disappears into the elevator. For a moment, I consider running after her, but I stop myself. I'm half-naked standing in my doorway after fucking a woman I picked up in a bar. This isn't exactly the way I want the woman I love to see me.

Jessica, or whatever her name is, wants to cuddle like we're some romantic couple, but I quickly send her on her way with a smile and an empty promise that we have to do this again sometime. I needed her to help me forget Kristina. She didn't do the job, but that's not her fault.

Grabbing my phone, I type out a text and even though I know she heard me fucking someone else, I hope she'll read it.

Kristina, I miss you. Why did you run away when I opened the door?

Not exactly my best prose, but texting isn't my medium.

I sit and wait for her to answer as I fantasize about when we finally will see each other again. I want to look into those beautiful cornflower blue eyes and see that she missed me like I missed her. I can't wait to feel her lips touch mine in a kiss that makes us both forget whatever it was that broke us up. My body hurts I want her so badly, and only she can ease this ache inside.

My phone vibrates across the top of the table, and my heart slams against my chest as I anticipate her answer. Hands shaking, I pick it up and begin to read, knowing immediately that she's just as moving in text as she is in person.

How could you forget me so quickly? Wasn't I your muse? You've already replaced me. How could you do that?

The palpable hurt in her words makes me feel like someone's stabbing me in the chest. I don't know why she left, but this isn't the message of a woman who doesn't want to see a man.

Her texts continue to come as she pours her heart out to me.

Didn't what we were to each other mean anything to you?

I thought when you told me you couldn't think of anyone else that you meant it. I heard you with her when I came to your door.

My fingers twitch as I think about what to type back to her. This isn't my best way of communicating, so whatever I say will probably come out all fucked up. Better for me to just listen.

A few minutes later, a much longer message comes in and she breaks my heart with just a few words.

I can't bear the silence from your end. Are you getting

these messages? Don't you care that I miss you? Please say something. I can't go on like this. Do you miss me like I miss you? I lie in bed at night thinking about you and wishing you'd call, but you never do. Why?

As much as I know I should message her back and tell her how I feel—how I miss her more than I can even describe and how I feel like part of my body's been ripped away without her in my life—I don't. Maybe I want the chance to say what's in my heart in person. Maybe I don't know what to say.

Or maybe I'm punishing her in some tiny way for leaving me.

Whatever the reason, I don't answer her. Instead, for the first time in over a week, I want to write. Turning my laptop on, I wait for it to warm up as a hundred ideas for Silk race through my mind. The creative floodgates open, and I can barely keep up with all that I want to write. By the time my fingers hit the keyboard for the first time since she left, it's like they're on fire.

I type like a madman, words flowing through my hands like never before. I'm inspired by Kristina again. My muse has returned. A week ago, my creativity had dried up, gone with the woman I adored, but now I can see the end of the book. All those nights of missing her and being awash in alcohol are past now.

My writing comes out in ways that are entirely new to me. Always a very deliberate author, I'm now a man on a mission. Our book must be completed.

Nearly two hours later, I sit back and look at what Kristina's return to my life has brought to me. The first draft of

Silk is finished. I've never been prouder of any creative effort in my life, and I know it's all due to her.

I take a shower, shave for the first time in eight days, and dress in clothes I know she'll love. Now to convince her to see me after what I did earlier. Seated back on my couch, I type the best words I have and hope they'll be enough.

Come to me. I miss you and need you. I was lost without you.

She doesn't answer. I wait ten minutes. Then twenty minutes. Finally, at thirty minutes I begin to think I might never see her again.

No. I told her we'd see each other again, and we will. I don't know how and I don't know when, but we will.

I'll make sure of that.

A knock on my front door stirs me from my thoughts, and I walk toward it knowing it's her even before I look through the peephole. I feel her close to me again. It's like a fire inside my chest that burns only for her.

I open it slowly, barely containing my impatience to have her by my side again. She's standing there, her eyes wide and filled with insecurity. I don't blame her. How could I? The last time she stood in that very spot she heard me fucking another woman.

"Please don't send me away again," she says quietly in a plaintive voice that makes me want her even more.

"I never sent you away."

She steps into my arms and in one long moment everything I've ever wanted is mine again. Her body melds to mine like a missing part finally returned. Standing there in my doorway, I hold her and I'm happy.

I feel her sob against my chest and squeeze my arms around her to bring her closer. I want to crawl inside her so she can never leave me again. She sweetly fingers the buttons on my shirt and asks, "Is she still here?"

"No. She was nothing, Kristina."

She looks up at me with hurt-filled eyes. "Then why did you go with her?"

"I tried to forget you, so I went to a bar and picked someone up. I thought maybe being with someone else would work, but all it did was make me miss you more. Then when you came to the door before, I had sense you were there so I went to the door looking for you."

"I heard you with her."

I don't know what to say to this, so I pull her into the apartment and close the door. Wrapping my arms around her, I whisper against the top of her head, "I'm sorry. Forgive me."

"I wanted to die when I heard those sounds coming from in here."

Tilting her head up so she has to look at me, I kiss her gently on the lips. "You have to forgive me, Kristina. Tell me you can."

She hangs her head. "I want to say no, to tell you I can never forgive you, Ian." She stops and stays silent for so long that I wonder if she truly can't forgive me. Then she speaks, and my world is right again. "I can't, though. I just can't."

I lift her chin with my finger and look down into that beautiful face looking up at me. "Forgive me and know I'll never touch another woman."

"Never?" she asks, not believing me.

"Never. How could I want anyone but my muse?"

She smiles and I know she'll forgive me.

I kiss her forehead and pull back to ask her a much harder question. Looking into her eyes, I look for the truth as I ask, "Why did you run away from me?"

Her smile fades into a deep frown. "You frightened me."

"How?" A surge of anger, not at her but at myself, rushes through me at the thought that anything I did made her frightened.

"When you wrote that scene about Kate standing outside the house of the man she loves. She was stalking him, and I thought you wrote that because you did that to me. I know you would never hurt me, but it scared me. So I ran away."

Backing up, I release her, now angry with her too. "I did do that. Just like the character, I stood outside your apartment one night and watched just to see you. But that you think me doing that would harm you makes me wonder if you know me at all, Kristina."

She reaches out to touch me, but I won't let her. The frustration and fear of losing me again registers in her expression. When she speaks, it's even clearer. "Ian, don't say that. I know you. Don't say I don't."

"You say you know me, but you think I'd hurt you? You think missing you so much that I stand out on the sidewalk across the street from your building praying for just a glimpse of you is me wanting to hurt you?"

I back up even further from her and watch the tears well in her eyes. This reunion isn't turning out how I'd hoped it would, but I can't change who I am and she deserves to know that.

Kristina grabs my hand and holds it tight. "I'm sorry. I've spent so much time worrying about stalkers. I didn't mean that I was afraid you'd hurt me, though. Tell me you know that. Please tell me you know that."

I try to pull my hand away, but she refuses to let go and I pull her into me. For a long moment, we stare at each other afraid of what the next words may be from the other's mouth. I can't do anything but admit who I am again and remind her of the kind of man she's with.

"I'm addicted to you. I have been since the first time I saw you, days before meeting you that first night. It's who I am. I became addicted to how you make me feel, and that night I stood outside looking up at your windows, I wanted to feel that. I can't change this, Kristina."

"You're addicted to me like a drug?" she asks in a confused voice.

I nod. "Just like a drug. When I'm with you, I feel like the man I want to be but most times can't be. But with you, I can. When I'm not with you, I crave your touch, the taste of your lips, the sound of your voice, your smile when I read what I've written to you. Most of the time, I'm okay just knowing I'll see you again, but other times…"

My voice trails off as I remember how I felt standing outside her apartment staring up at her windows. "Other times, like that night, I want so much to see you that I'd willingly hide in the shadows just for a glimpse of you from the street below."

My confession doesn't frighten her, but I see in her eyes her confusion. Her therapist was wrong. She doesn't get addicted to people. If she did, she'd know exactly what this feels like.

"I missed you so much. I couldn't eat. I couldn't sleep. I

couldn't do anything. I'm sorry I got scared. I was being stupid."

I kiss her lips and cradle her face. "You weren't stupid. I never thought that would frighten you, but you weren't stupid."

She's quiet for a moment, and then the question she asks me makes me more jealous than I ever thought possible. "What if I slept with someone else too?"

All at once, I want to push her away and hold her to me. I bite out, "Did you?"

"No, but I can tell it bothers you. Now you know how I feel."

I drop my hands from her face and walk away from her. "Feelings aren't like that. I can't know what you feel any more than you can know what I feel, other than if we tell each other."

"Then let me tell you how I feel. Like my heart was being ripped from my chest. I heard you in here with her. Heard her making the same sounds I make when you make love to me. I wanted to run away but all I could do was stand there and listen to you with her. That's how I feel, Ian!"

I turn around to face her. "You said you forgave me."

"I did, but that doesn't mean it doesn't still hurt to think about it. Maybe I should go out and fuck another man. I could have tonight. I met someone at a bar and he gave me a ride here. I could call him and then maybe you'd know how I feel."

"Don't."

"Don't what? Make you understand what it feels like when you know the person you care about is with someone else? Imagine yourself outside my apartment door hearing me moan another man's name as he fucks me. I'm on his lap straddling his hips riding his cock and I make that noise you love—the one like a whimper right before I come. Imagine hearing that, Ian. And then I want you to just forgive me."

Her anger isn't just at me. I know that. But it doesn't change how much her words fucking hurt. I hate the man she met tonight. I don't care that she didn't do anything with him. I hate him.

And I love her.

I walk to her and can't hold back. I want her. I need her. "Not another fucking word, Kristina. You're mine. No one else. Do you understand?"

"No, I don't," she sobs. "I don't understand how to forget you with her, Ian. Make me understand."

Stuffing my hands into her hair, I pull her head back and kiss her hard. Her mouth surrenders to mine and as I snake my tongue past her lips to tease hers, an ache in my hard cock spreads throughout my body.

"I need you so fucking bad," I whisper against her lips. "I never needed her like you. I never wanted her like you."

Kristina's hands slide down my chest to unbutton my pants, her fingers fumbling with the zipper as we kiss. Finally, she slides her hand beneath my boxer briefs and palms my cock, and it stiffens even more. "Tell me what you did with her."

"No," I groan as she slowly strokes my cock.

"Then I'll assume you did the same things with her and won't do them again. Tell me."

I tug her hair harder and close my eyes as she rubs the head of my cock. "I took her from behind. I could pretend it was you if I didn't see her face."

Kristina kisses me as she plays with my cock and then says,

"Then you can't do that with me just like you won't let me use my fingers with you."

I want her so bad at that moment, I agree. "Deal. Now get those clothes off unless you want them to end up ripped off your body."

She slides her skirt down her legs to reveal nothing underneath. Her pussy, clean shaven and bare, makes me want to bury my face in her, and as she strips off her sweater, I drop to my knees to taste her. With my thumbs, I open her folds so no part of her is hidden to me and gently flick my tongue up her gorgeous wet slit, loving her taste on my tongue. Musky and sweet, she's all I want in my mouth.

Her hands tighten in my hair when my tongue reaches her clit, and I suck it into my mouth, knowing what it will do to her. Above me, she moans my name and my cock twitches its need to be inside her.

I stand and kiss her, letting her taste her own juices. "That's what I crave when you're not here. The taste of that pretty cunt on my tongue."

Biting her lip, she leads me toward the windows. I know what she wants. She wants to show the world as much as she's mine, I'm hers. I step out of the rest of my clothes and pull her body to me. "Not feeling so shy anymore?"

She shakes her head and smiles not-so-innocently. "Not tonight. I want everyone to see us."

I wrap my arm around her waist and pull her to me. "Come here. I want you on your knees sucking my cock."

Slowly, she lowers herself to the floor and opens her mouth. I guide my cock between her lips and thrust hard so the head butts up against the back of her throat. I want to fuck her face like I want to fuck her cunt.

Hard and deep.

Her hand wraps around the base, giving her some control, but I push my hands into her hair and grip tightly to direct her as she sucks me. I love the feel of her mouth and tongue gliding over my skin while she looks up at me with those gentle eyes as I ram my cock into her.

I want to claim her. I want anyone who sees her to know that mouth is only for me. I want my cum to mark her as mine.

It doesn't take long for just the sight of her sucking me off to get me there, and I gently slide my fingertips over her jaw as a sign that I'm about to come. She knows and doesn't stop, taking all of me into her mouth as I shoot down her throat. Eyes closed, she continues to suck as I empty my balls into her.

Sitting back on her heels, she licks her lips and smiles up at me. "I'm getting better at that, don't you think?"

I tilt her chin up toward me. "What does my Kristina want?"

"You. I want you inside me."

I lower myself to the floor and pushing her hair off her face, kiss her long and deep. I love her. I want her. But even more than that, I need her. Only she can make me happy. I trace the outline of her beautiful lower lip with the pad of my thumb, and she takes it into her mouth, sucking the tip so erotically my cock strains against my body in need.

As she looks up at me with those blue eyes so sweet, I say in a low voice, "I want you from behind." I know what I said before, but I can't allow anything to come between us.

"Ian…" she says, pleading for me to do as she asked earlier.

"I want us to share everything. Nothing can stand between us."

# CHAPTER FOUR

## *Kristina*

"**B**UT YOU DID that—"

"We'll never get past that if it's always between us. Give me this, and I'll give you anything your heart desires, Kristina."

I close my eyes and think about how I felt as I stood outside his door listening to him with her. He's right. I'll never be able to forget that if it remains between us.

But my stomach turns at the idea of being with him like that now.

Slowly, I shake my head. I can't do it.

"Open your eyes and look at me, Kristina."

His words aren't a request, but I don't want to look at him. He's pushing too hard, and a tiny part inside me wants to run away again. "No."

"Don't do this. Don't shut me out. Give me what I asked and everything I am is yours."

His words sound strained, as if my refusal hurts him. Slowly, I open my eyes and see the pain in his gaze as he watches me. "I'm scared, Ian. Scared you're going to ask for this tonight and then leave me tomorrow. Scared I don't mean as much to you as you do to me."

"You're everything to me, Kristina. Every fucking thing. I spent every day here missing you so much it hurt. My body ached without you. I couldn't think about anything else. I couldn't write. I couldn't do anything without you. Baby, I need you so much I'm lost."

I hang my head to hide my tears I can't hold back anymore. "It hurts so much to know that you were with her. But like you said, you can't know how that feels because you aren't feeling it. Maybe I should go."

"And do what? Run away again?"

His words edge with sharpness, and I look up to see anger in his face. I don't deserve that anger, but if he wanted to feel it, then I'd hurt him too.

"No. If I leave, I'm going to find someone else to fuck tonight. Then you'll know how much it hurts, Ian."

"I told you don't say that," he whispers, his voice bristling with rage.

"Don't say I want you to understand how much you hurt me?"

He slides his hands into my hair and tugs roughly before he whispers against my lips, "Don't talk about you with someone else."

"Not just with someone else, Ian. Imagine knowing I was going down on another man, sucking his cock dry like I do with you. Imagine knowing what you thought was so special is nothing but something so common I could find it with someone I meet in a bar."

His fingers tremble with anger against my head, but I know I'm getting through to him. I want him to feel what I felt, so I say the words I know will seal the pain into him. "Imagine another man getting me off and feeling like I'm his, Ian."

The hurt radiates off him. His eyes narrow and he winces as the meaning of my words sink into his mind. I don't know if I should be afraid, but I'm governed by pain so much that I can't stop.

"Does that hurt?"

When he finally speaks, his words are carefully measured but I know I've succeeded. "Kristina, I want to put this behind us. You left me. What I did with that woman meant nothing to me, but you with someone else would mean a great deal to me."

"How much?"

"How much what?" he asks as he presses his body tightly to mine.

"How much would me fucking another man mean to you, Ian?" When he doesn't answer, I ask the question again, louder this time. "How much would it mean to you if I fucked another man, Ian?"

I see something flash in his eyes, and he stands me up and spins me around to face the window and the outside world I so wanted to see me claim him just a few minutes ago. With his palm pressed against my throat, he whispers low and deep in my ear, "You want to hear me say I hate the idea of you with someone else, Kristina? That I'd want to kill him if I knew you'd been with him? That just the thought of it makes my fucking chest hurt like someone's carving into me? Is that what you want?"

Staring at the reflection of him standing behind me, I see the agony in his eyes as he speaks those words, and I answer truthfully. "Yes."

He slides his hand between my legs and thrusts two fingers inside me, making my legs go weak when he adds the pad of his thumb to press on my clit. "Then hear me now. You're mine. Only I get to be inside you. Only I get to taste your body. And yes, I would kill him if I found out you'd been with another man."

I can't help but moan as he speaks and his fingers fuck me. But can I let him be with me like he was with her?

"I don't want to hear another thing about anyone else, Kristina. Do you understand? There is no one else for me, and there is no one else for you. Now put your hands against the window and brace yourself."

The thought of protesting—of saying no—passes through my mind, but before I have the chance to say anything, he's so deep inside me I feel like I can't breathe. I push my damp palms against the glass, feeling its smooth surface slide under my touch, but his hands on my hips hold me fast to him, making sure I don't fall.

Each thrust into me pushes my body forward, and each time he leaves me I fall back, my body searching for what only he can give me. His fingers press hard into the flesh covering my hipbones, but whatever pain I feel is masked by the pleasure his cock sliding in and out of me provides.

His lips skim my neck and he says low in my ear, "I missed you so fucking much, Kristina. I couldn't do anything but think of you and hope the pain of being without you went away someday soon. But without you, it would never have left me."

Balancing with one hand against the glass, I cradle his cheek with my free hand as he begins to slow his movement into my body. "I missed you so much, Ian."

"Promise me you'll never leave again," he says in a hoarse voice as he buries himself in me and I feel his release flood my insides.

The sensation of him filling me sends me tumbling over the edge. Clinging to him as his cock pulses inside me, I swear to never leave him again. "I promise. Never."

His hips slow their thrusting, and in a whisper I barely hear, he says, "I love you, Kristina. Please don't leave me."

Ian slides out of my body and wraps his arms around me as he gently places kisses on my cheek. Leaning back, I rest my head on his chest and listen to his heartbeat as it gradually returns to normal after our lovemaking.

"I love you, Ian," I say quietly as he strokes my hair. "And I'm sorry. I should have never run away like I did."

"I told you we'd see one another again. I never doubted it."

As he continues to gently caress me, I think back to that message he sent the night I left him. Had he truly never doubted that we'd see each other again? For all my belief that I'd loved him before, it wasn't until I missed him that I realized how deeply I needed him. Had he felt that before I left?

✧    ✧    ✧

WE LIE IN his bed silently holding one another as the last remnants of the pain and sadness of the past week slip away. I think about how much I missed him—his touch, his voice, his eyes when he looks at me like he can't go on without me. I don't want to lose him again. We're both messed up. I know that. But can't messed up people be happy too?

I want that so much—to be happy just like we are at this

moment. With my head rested on his chest, I trace my fingertip down over his lean stomach to the thin, dark line of hair that leads to his cock. Touching the soft down, I feel his skin tremble beneath my fingers and look up at him to see a smile on his face.

"Were you sleeping?"

"Not exactly, but all it takes is one touch of your hand on me and I'm wide awake."

"Is it early?" I ask, unsure if I've even slept this night.

Ian leans over toward the night table to see his alarm clock and groans. "Not even six yet. Go back to sleep."

"You don't want me to...?" I leave my question incomplete, but he pulls me up to kiss me on the lips.

"Later. Now I just want to feel you in my arms."

His disinterest in sex strangely makes me happy. I'd worried more than once that everything we are revolves around our physical connection, but with his refusal of me going down on him I feel like our emotional connection is at least as meaningful to him as it is to me.

"Unless you really want to twist my arm."

I hear the teasing in his voice and smile. "Just so I'm clear on this, we aren't just sex, are we?"

My attempt at being lighthearted falls flat. His expression hardens, and he asks, "Do you think all I care about is fucking you?"

"No, no," I protest, but it's too late. I've ruined everything. "I'm sorry. I didn't mean to make it sound like that."

Taking my face in his hands, he cradles my cheeks and kisses me on the tip of my nose. "I don't want you to ever think that. Tell me you know that."

I nod. "I do. I didn't mean to ruin our nice time together. I'm sorry."

"Don't be sorry, Kristina. You didn't ruin anything. I guess it's natural to wonder if all we are is sex since it's so incredible between us."

"It's just never been like this for me before with anyone."

"I'll take that as a compliment."

Ian's lack of mention about my sexual abilities makes me want to ask if he's had a relationship like this before, but I'm afraid to know the answer. What if sex is always like this for him and I'm nothing special?

I nuzzle his neck and silently hope that our time together is important to him, inhaling the earthy, masculine scent of his skin. He smooths his hand over my hair and down my back, and as if he can read my mind, whispers in a deep voice, "No one has ever made me crave them like you do. I'm lost when you're not around, but I'm only slightly better when you're next to me and I want so fucking bad to be inside you."

The way he professes his need for me makes me want to please him. I want him to love me like no man ever has before. Like every man always said they did.

Ian stirs under me, gently pushing me off him as he slips out of bed. Still naked, he flashes me a smile. "I'll be right back. I want you to hear something."

My gaze is fixed on his very grabbable ass as he walks across the bedroom floor to head out to the living room. Lean and strong, his body looks like it's built to please a woman. A gentle ache settles in between my legs as I remember how his ass felt as I squeezed it just before my orgasm tore through me the last time we made love.

As I daydream about Ian's body, he returns with his laptop and slides back into bed next to me. "I want to read you what I wrote yesterday."

"Okay. What part is this?"

As he types something, he looks down at me next to him and smiles. "The end."

Surprised, I sit up and snuggle his arm. "You finished it?"

"Yeah. I couldn't write the whole time you were gone, but as soon as you began to text me, it was like I couldn't stop the words from coming." He kisses the top of my head and adds, "I couldn't do it without my muse."

Just hearing those words makes my heart fill with joy. I'm still his muse and he needs me. Nothing could make me happier at this moment. I look up at him and gaze into those nearly jet black eyes so intent on the words he's written as they wait for him on the screen.

"I can't wait for you to hear this. I created a male character halfway through, so I had to double back to the beginning, but as I reached what I thought was the end, something felt like it was missing, so I had his character end the book instead of Kate's."

"What's his name?"

"Sean."

"This sounds vaguely familiar to someone I know. Don't you think?"

I know what he's done. His story about me has morphed into the story of us. And I love him for it.

The sheepish look on his face charms me. Pressing my cheek to his shoulder, I lean over and curl my arm around his as he begins to read me the words he's given to Kate's hero, Sean.

"I put the two of them in a situation where they had to do without one another, and until you texted me today, I couldn't find the words I needed to bring them back together. They just sat there, lonely and alone, and then I suddenly knew what to say. So here's their reunion I wrote before I asked you to come back to me."

*She opens the door, and for the first time in what feels like months I see her. Her deep blue eyes that make me feel like I could get lost in them and be happy for the rest of my life. Her gentle smile that belies the sensual woman I know her to be. Her body, the taut and toned muscles my touch remembers that make my cock hard even before I know if she'll take me back.*

*Her delicate mouth—those lips that have taken me to places of ecstasy like no other woman has ever done—she opens her mouth to speak, but for a moment says nothing. Has she changed her mind?*

*"Sean."*

*She speaks my name like a gentle plea, and I step forward to take her into my arms, needing to feel her next to me. Resting her head on my chest, she whispers, "I missed you so much."*

*I caress her back as she quietly sobs against me. "I'm sorry, Kate. I'm sorry I fucked up."*

*"Tell me you can accept who I am," she begs, looking up at me with a look in those gorgeous blue eyes that practically breaks my heart in two. "Tell me what I am is enough."*

*Cradling her face in my hands, I struggle to choke back the emotion she creates in me. I'm supposed to be the man, the one she turns to when she needs someone strong to hold her up, but I left her when she needed me most. What kind of fucking man does that?*

*"Baby, I love every part of you. The good part that makes me believe in the sweetness life can offer when you find the person you're meant to be with. The bad part that other men can't handle but I can't do without. I love all of you."*

*Kate closes her eyes and hangs her head. "You deserve someone who's more good than bad. That's not me."*

*I can't let her torment herself like this. She deserves to know how much I need her. Tilting her head so she looks up at me, I kiss her softly, like a whisper, and begin saying what I should have said the moment I knew how much I loved her.*

*"My beautiful, broken girl, you can't see what you are to me? I need you more than the air I breathe or the food I eat to survive. The whole time you weren't by my side, I felt like a part of me was missing, like someone had taken away a part of my being and left a gaping hole nothing could fill. You're everything to me."*

*"Why if I ruin that?" she asks, the fear filling her eyes.*

*"I won't let you ruin what we have, baby. I'll be strong enough for both of us. I promise. I need you too much to lose you."*

Ian stops reading and turns to look at me. "It's a first draft, but I like how it's turning out."

Sitting up, I kiss him deeply, trying to convey how much I love what he's written. When I pull away, he smiles at me and I know he understands.

"So they live happily ever after?" I ask, hoping Kate and Sean get that at the end of their story.

He shakes his head. "Not quite yet. I thought I only had one story in me, but as I neared the end, I realized I didn't want to finish their story, so there will be a Silk Two."

"Another book? Will I be your muse for that one too?"

Placing the laptop on the nightstand next to him, Ian kisses me. "I can't do this without you, Kristina."

Hearing him say that makes what I felt just a few hours ago meaningless. People in love do stupid things. I left Ian because I was afraid, and he slept with someone to try to forget me. Both of us didn't want to admit the truth of who we are together.

I need him as much as he needs me. That's what love is with us.

# CHAPTER FIVE

## *Ian*

WHEN KRISTINA LEAVES just before nine a.m., I feel like I'm walking on air. I've written a complete book without heroin. The one soul on this earth I love is back in my life, and the words that had been trapped inside me now flow freely again.

I can't help thinking life is good.

And then at just after noon, it gets even better. Someone knocking at my door rouses me from my focus on plotting out the second Silk book, and when I answer it I see Sheila standing there in all her glory. Dressed in a yellow sweater and a gunmetal grey skirt that seems to accentuate all her rough edges, she's not exactly a sight for sore eyes, but I know if she's come all the way to my apartment she has good news about something. Plus, she's holding a bottle in her hands, which tells me it's likely very good news.

"Ian," she says with a huge smile as she marches past me into my home. "I bring good news. Where should I sit?"

Closing the door, I follow her into the living room and offer her a chair I never use. "Please, sit. What good news?"

Sheila sits and awkwardly folds her long legs to the left, but the effect is almost grotesque and I can't take my eyes off how large and bulbous her kneecaps are. For a moment, I'm unable to concentrate as I wonder if I've ever seen knees like hers. She's already talking by the time I regain my focus, so I'm forced to admit I need her to repeat what she's just said.

"Sorry, Sheila. You lost me there for a second. Can you start from the top?"

Her face twists into a look of suspicion as she narrows her eyes. "Have you been…?" Her question trails off, and I know she's afraid to finish the last part because of what my answer might be.

I shake my head. "No, I haven't been doing anything like that. I promise. I just lost my focus for a second. Nothing big. Just early in the day for me."

She's silent for a long moment, almost like she's mentally weighing the veracity of my statement against how I look, but then she smiles. "Okay. As I was saying, the publisher loves the idea of Marc Antony. Seems he's all the rage because of some biopic that's due to come out early next year. I had no idea about it when I told you to basically shelve the idea, of course. I hope you won't hold that against me."

I wave my hand in the air. "No bad feelings. Everyone's entitled to their opinions. I know you love my work and how much you've done to get it out there."

"I really have, and I think the publisher is thrilled to be having this to run with. I hope you can begin immediately. They want this for next fall's releases. That means you literally have weeks, Ian. Weeks. Can you do it?"

Real fear settles into my brain at her words. Weeks. A Marc Antony book will take weeks or months just to research, even if

I do decide to go with a similar format to my past two historical fiction novels.

"How long do I really have?" I ask knowing I likely have months instead of weeks.

"Maybe three months," she says in the most somber tone she's ever used with me about writing. I know what's coming next. "Is that going to put too much pressure on you, Ian?"

Her question is like a life size reality check dropped into the center of the room. I practically have to lean to the side to see her it's taking up so much space between us. The fact is I've never been very good under pressure after the book's been written. Adding pressure to the normal stress of writing a book sounds like a recipe for disaster, I'm sure.

But I'm different now. I have Kristina, and I don't think about snorting that shit up my nose every other minute of the day. For the first time since I wrote my first book, I know I can write without the junk coursing through my veins.

I can't tell Sheila any of this, though. Kristina must remain my secret. So I do my best to convince my agent that I won't become a doped up mess over this book. "I'll be fine. Months is very different than weeks. I'm more concerned with the research required for a Marc Antony book. Guess this means I'll be heading back to Rome."

A sheepish look crosses her face. "They won't give you the advance until you submit the manuscript, though, Ian. I'm sorry. I tried. I really did. But I couldn't fight them with much when they threw your past in my face. I really am sorry."

The truth of who I am stings, but she's not to blame. Either is my publisher. My past isn't going to disappear simply because I say it should. "I understand, Sheila."

"I was able to get you a very healthy advance of $75,000, though, when the book is submitted. I hope that helps a little."

"It does," I say, admitting while it's the smallest advance I've ever received, especially after having two bestselling books, it's not bad considering what's happened in the past.

"And they want a book tour this time. Well, actually, I convinced them that a book tour would be a great thing. They were hesitant to agree after what happened on the Caligula's Dream tour, but I told them those days are behind you."

I see the fear in her eyes as she talks about my first and last book tour. I'd fucked that up royally, for sure. Ten cities in two weeks and I'd barely made it through three signings before I fell apart and the rest of the dates had to be cancelled. Cringing as I remember her showing up in my hotel room with two of Albert's assistants to whisk me out of the building before anyone else found out how much a mess I was, I hang my head in shame. She really does take care of me, and until recently, I've been little more than a hassle.

"Thank you, Sheila. I really mean that. I know I've been a lot of trouble, and the fact that my books do well doesn't make up for what you've had to deal with in the past."

A smile brightens her face making her almost appealing. "As long as you're taking care of yourself and not doing that terrible stuff anymore, I'm happy. You're one of my favorite authors, Ian."

I think she's telling the truth, as hard as that is to believe. As she hands me the bottle of champagne to open, she adds, "And at least I don't have to worry about you sounding off on Twitter or Facebook, for God's sake. Just that alone makes you a treasure in my book."

Walking into the kitchen, I ask, "Is your newbie author doing any better?"

"No," she yells from the living room, "and I'm seriously thinking she's enjoying the notoriety she's receiving from angering people. I think she actually believes that nonsense of there being no bad publicity."

I pop the cork and return to my seat with the open bottle and two champagne glasses. Placing them on the table, I pour each of us a drink to toast her great work for me. "Not in this business. Your reputation is everything in the book business. I learned that the hard way."

Sheila takes her glass and lifts it in the air. "But you learned. I'm worried this one isn't interested in learning from her mistakes."

Raising my glass, I make an apropos toast. "To learning from one's mistakes before it's too late."

"Hear, hear!" she says with a smile before she takes a sip of champagne. "So now for the question I have to ask, Ian. Have you written anything for the Marc Antony project?"

I know I'm fortunate enough to have some good in my history with my publisher, which means I don't need much more than Sheila's first-rate agenting skills to persuade them on a project. The problem that creates is that I don't need to write anything, not even a synopsis, before they agree to run with an idea. Now that they've said yes, the writing has to begin immediately.

Deciding to answer with the truth, I shake my head. "Not yet. But I've got a lot of ideas, so there's no need to worry. You can count on me. As we've been talking, I've already been planning a trip to Rome and what I'm thinking the story will be about."

Sheila lets out a heavy sigh, as if my answer has taken the weight of the world off her shoulders. "That's good. That's what I want to hear. Well, actually, I would have loved it if you said you'd already begun work on this, but I'll take planning over nothing."

"What is it they say? Baby steps? I promise I won't let you down."

I finish my glass of champagne quickly, knowing that she's eagle-eyeing every move I make, and place my empty glass on the table even though I want another drink. I don't need to have her worrying about my alcohol consumption too.

"I believe you. I do. I just worry. You know how I am. All my authors are like my children, so I worry about all of you. I like to think that's what makes me such a good agent."

"You're a great agent. Don't ever doubt that because we're assholes who don't know how to behave."

My sudden expression of caring makes her uneasy, and she shifts in her seat. "You're not an asshole, Ian. You're one of my favorites. It's just that with your issues—" She doesn't finish her sentence, as always uncomfortable saying the word heroin.

"I'm better now. I promise. I wrote all of Nero's Nightmare without the heroin, so I'm good now, Sheila."

Leaning forward, she places her glass on the table. "Good. I'm happy to hear that, Ian. I really am." She rises from the chair and flings her purse over her shoulder. "I'll leave you so you can begin working on Marc Antony's story. You're going to go to Rome again, but call me after you get back."

I walk her to the door. "I will. As soon as I get back."

In her typical fashion, she pulls me to her in a bear hug and whispers in my ear, "I know this one will be great too. Don't forget that if the going gets tough I'm just a phone call away."

As she releases me, I smile at her kindness. "I won't. And thanks again for coming by. I'll talk to you soon."

Sheila walks away with a pleased look on her face that tells me she believed what I'd said. Not that I'd lied, but I can't deny how much I'd had to pretend for her. It was all for the best anyway. If I told her about Kristina and Silk, it would just cause her more grief, and I don't want to be that for her anymore.

Eager to put that thought out of my mind, I busy myself with preparations for the trip to Rome. I need to make air and hotel reservations, along with contacting Dr. Farelli again. Hopefully, his secretary still likes me well enough to let me past her or I'd have to sic Albert on her again.

I can't wait to tell Kristina about the trip. During the day, I'll conduct my research while she shops or visits tourist attractions, and afterward we'll have dinner in the finest restaurants and take long walks to the Trevi Fountain and the Forum where I'll tell her the history of the city and all about my previous trips there.

Everything finally has turned the corner. My work. My private life. Everything.

# CHAPTER SIX

## *Kristina*

M Y PUBLICIST CALLS me just as I'm on my way home to tell me she has to see me. Joanne sounds hyper on most days, but today her voice reminds me of an old style record put on the wrong speed or some overexcited cartoon chipmunk. I'm barely able to understand her, but I agree to see her, knowing if I don't that she'll simply call Jennie, my agent, and God knows I don't need her worry piling on top of my happiness.

During my cab ride to Joanne's office, I think about my reunion with Ian. Finally, after all my silliness, we're back together. But I can't help silently admit to myself that even thinking about him comes with a shadow of hurt from knowing he slept with that other woman.

I imagine what she looks like since all I know about her is how she sounds while Ian was inside her. I hate the fact that all I know about her is something so intimate yet I don't even know her name or what color hair she has. In my mind's eye, I see her as a blond. Yes, she must be a blond so she can be different from me. No, a fake, platinum blond so she's the opposite of what I look like. And she has beady little eyes and mascara that clumps on her skimpy eyelashes.

Is her hair long like mine? Did he bury his hands in her hair as they made love and tug, sending a mix of pain and pleasure down her spine like he does when he pulls my hair? Did she enjoy it like I do, or did she tell him to stop hurting her?

Quickly, my mind spirals out of control with images of them together. His eyes staring into hers as he enters her, their darkness seeming to fill his entire eyes as passion takes him over. His lips kissing her neck and breasts as he murmurs the sexiest, dirtiest thoughts he has. His hands sliding down her side and grabbing her hips as he pumps his cock into her.

Shaking my head, I struggle to push the images out of my mind. No! I can't think like this. I can't let my insecurities overrun me until all that's left of what I have with him is petty jealousy. I left him. Left him with no explanation. I did this to us. If I want Ian to be mine, I have to accept my responsibility for him ending up with another woman. If I want us to work out, I have to face my fears and self-doubts.

I have to stop running away.

The cab stops in front of Joanne's building, and as I hop out onto the sidewalk, I take a deep breath to clear my head. I can be the woman Ian thinks I am, the sensual woman he professed his love to and wrote that beautiful story for. All I need to do is believe in myself. He loves me, and I love him.

Now to deal with my publicist.

Joanne Jenkins has been my publicist since I began in this business, and in all the time I've known her, her office hasn't changed. It's still that tiny white box with walls cluttered from too many framed clippings in newspapers and magazines. The rest of the world may be online, but not her. For Joanne, life still revolves around getting mentioned in gossip columns people can hold in their hands and stuff into their briefcases and purses.

Her assistant sits outside her office at an old desk that reminds me of the kind the woman at the DMV in my hometown in Indiana sat at the day I went in to take my driving test. Metal and tan, it makes a hollow noise every time her knees bang into it. Charlene is a lovely person, but I can't imagine how someone so jittery can work with another so hyper person such as Joanne. It's almost as if they create too much energy for the tiny space they occupy.

A pretty woman with a round face, Charlene has the kind of blond hair I imagined a few minutes ago for the woman Ian had sex with, and I find it hard not to frown as I approach her today. She sees me and with her usual perkiness says, "Kristina, it's so wonderful to see you! Joanne will be just a few minutes, so please take a seat. How is everything going?"

I look around at the chairs near her desk and choose the one farthest away. "Fine. Everything's fine."

"That's great! Let me buzz Joanne and see what's holding her up."

I want to say it hasn't even been thirty seconds since she told me she'd be a few minutes, but I don't, instead choosing to just smile. Joanne answers her in a sharp tone unmistakable over the loudspeaker and before Charlene can begin to talk me up again, my publicist appears in her doorway waving her hand to beckon me in.

She ushers me into her tiny office and begins talking before I can even sit down in front of her desk. Excited about some gossip concerning another actress, she rambles on and I catch bits and pieces as I try to get my bearings. I've spent so much time with Ian recently that I've gotten used to the calmness he projects. Between Charlene and Joanne, I feel like I'm being assaulted on all sides. I don't know how much my psyche can take of them today.

"So I wanted to talk to you about Vancouver. Have you heard anything yet? What do you think?" she asks in Gatling gun fashion.

Shaking my head, I say, "No, not yet. I hope to hear something this week, though."

Joanne flips her hand through her brunette bob and pops a stick of gum into her mouth. "Okay, well when you hear anything, we need to promote the hell out of this. You've been entirely too quiet lately, and I don't like that. I want the press to be dying to get at you."

"I've just been taking some down time, Joanne. The public understands that."

"The public understands nothing but what we feed them, Kristina. I thought you knew that. If we tell them you've been sick, we'll get sympathy. If we tell them you just needed time off, we'll get resentment at the idea that an actress needs time off. They don't understand that becoming an entirely different person for their amusement is hard work."

"I think you might just see the glass half empty," I say, half-joking and half-serious.

"Call me Machiavellian, but I understand the public, honey. I've been doing this since you were an innocent baby out there in the Midwest. Do you remember Eliza Gibson?"

Quickly, I try to remember hearing that name somewhere,

but I can think of nothing. "No. Who's she?"

"She was an actress who decided that her career shouldn't dictate her entire existence. Foolish girl! I warned her. I told her the public has a very short attention span and even shorter memory. I told her they'd forget her if she didn't tend to her career like a careful gardener tends to his garden. She wouldn't listen. She needed some time off to get her head together or some bullshit like that. And before she knew it, she was yesterday's news and there was nothing I could do to fix that."

I can't help but roll my eyes. Some down time between projects and Joanne already thinks I'm on my way to becoming a has-been. "It's not the same, and you know it."

Her arms flail out to the sides of her head. "What I know is my job, and my job is to keep you front and center so Middle America doesn't forget you."

"What would you have me do? It's only been a few months. I can't help it that I'm not a drug addict or alcoholic in and out of rehab every other month."

Joanne leans forward and sighs. "I wish we could have gotten more mileage out of that John Stinson business."

Her mention of my public humiliation and being left brokenhearted as if it was something good makes me cringe. Looking down toward my lap, I say in a low voice, "Sorry my misery didn't last long enough for you."

"Well, whatever it was for you privately, it was a boon professionally. The public loves a tragic story, and that son of a bitch served us up one on a silver platter. You should thank him for that, dear."

"I'll make sure to do that the next time I see him with the woman he dumped me for," I mumble.

"Cheer up! Men are a dime a dozen in this world. Just look at me. I've been married three times. Divorced three times too, but the possibility of number four is always right around the corner. As long as someone like you picks men who can help her when it ends, that's all that matters."

My publicist continues to talk about the sad ending of my relationship with John, but I tune her out, preferring to think about how happy I am with Ian. As different from that bastard as night from day, he's thoughtful and sensual. John was just a good looking stud who never cared about anything but getting laid and moving up the ladder of success.

I wish I could tell her about Ian to prove to her I'm not some pathetic mess who needs to be torn apart to stay interesting to the movie-going public. My relationship with Ian makes me happy and proud, but I know the dangers of letting the world know about us. He can't afford that, even if it would help me.

"So I want you to let me know the minute you hear anything about the part. I want to get the news out there and blanket the media with it. You're on the verge of becoming a huge movie star, Kristina. We don't want to lose a minute of the spotlight."

"I will. Don't worry."

I get up to leave, exhausted and on the verge of feeling like shit after our meeting, but she stops me and almost as an afterthought says, "And if you get together with anyone, make sure he's famous, would you? It would make a world of difference. Too many stars are hooking up with nobodies these days, and I can't tell you how hard it is to spin gold out of something like that."

"Thanks, Joanne. I'll keep that in mind as I look for love," I say, my words dripping with sarcasm she seems to miss entirely.

"Good, good, good. Tell Jennie I said hi and to take my calls every so often."

"I will."

Happy to be away from the emotional chaos of Joanne and her rapid fire talking, I head over to my agent's office a few blocks away. A few years younger but in an entirely different league professionally than my publicist, Jennie's never liked her, and I think I'm beginning to see why. I can totally understand why she'd not want to take her calls.

For Jennie, her place in my professional life is less one of orders and directions and more one of support. That she's entirely worried I'm going to leave her at any moment for another agent doesn't lessen how much I like her. And compared to my friends' agents, she's a gem.

Her office is only slightly bigger than my publicist's, but the dimensions have been rendered meaningless because of the way she's arranged it. The beige walls are practically bare, with just a sparse collection of framed nature photos hanging on them. At first glance, her wooden desk and workstation seem like they're too big for such a small space, but they're the only furniture someone sees as they sit there with her because she's cleverly turned a closet at the back of the room into a walk-in bookcase. So while she works in very much the same size office as Joanne, the effect couldn't be more different.

Jennie extends her well-manicured hand out to shake mine as I'm shown in to her office. "Kristina, how are you? You look wonderful and completely rested. Whatever you're doing, it's working."

"Thank you. I feel good. I'm ready to go back to work, so I hope you have good news for me."

Her plum colored lips hitch up at the corners into a gentle smile that goes all the way to her dark green eyes, letting me know she's genuinely happy to tell me what she has to say. "I do. Your audition blew them away. I knew it would, but they made their decision this morning. They want you, Kristina. The part of Cherise is yours, if you want it."

This is what I've been waiting to hear for weeks. I'd auditioned for the part of Cherise Johnson, a down-on-her-luck prostitute trying to change her life in spite of the man she loves doing everything in his power to keep her under his control and weak, but I'd considered myself a longshot for the part, at best. Bigger names than me had expressed interest in the role, and I worried I looked too Midwest, white bread for it. I'd shown up to the audition in costume, fully ready to show them I was Cherise Johnson, and even though I'd thought it had gone well, I still didn't feel sure I'd convinced them I could do it.

I believed I could, though, and now that I'd get the chance, I'd show everyone I could do it.

"That's wonderful, Jennie! I'm so happy," I say, barely able to contain my giddiness at the news.

"Shooting begins in a few weeks in Vancouver, so get yourself packed and ready to go. They're sending everything over by courier later today, so once it all gets here, you can sign on the dotted line and the deal with be made. You're going to be incredible, Kristina. I just know it."

"I think so too," I say, not caring for once that I sound like I'm bragging.

"This could be it—the big break you've been looking for.

This role has everything. You're really going to get the chance to stretch your limits with this one. You beat out some big names."

The way she says that makes me think she's most impressed by that fact. Hilary Swank and Natalie Portman had been the frontrunners the last time I heard, and knowing I got the role instead of them thrills me more than I could say. It seems to thrill Jennie too.

"I know. I can't believe it now that it's sunken in."

"Finally, a role to show them your chops. I've been waiting for a role like this for you since you came to me, you know that?"

"Thank you, Jennie. You always believed in me. That means so much to me."

"You promise when they announce your name for the Oscar you won't drop me for a flashier agent out there in LA?" she asks, her expression suddenly far more serious than it was a minute ago.

I know this is one of her biggest fears. Since I signed with her, she's worried almost constantly about me leaving her for another agent. Not that I would. I like her in my professional life. Compared to virtually everyone else who surrounds me, she feels like the calm in the middle of a storm. That's too important to me to lose.

"I'm not going anywhere, Jen. You've stuck with me through minor roles and critics saying I wasn't living up to the hype and my looks. If this role means doors begin to open for me, I'm going to be going through them with you. I don't want another agent. They're all too much like Joanne."

Jennie makes a noise that sounds like pure disgust at the

mention of my publicist. "I know she's been with you nearly as long as I have, but her vision for you troubles me. She loved the media circus that came from your breakup with John. I can't tell you how many times she called me to discuss how we could use this to further your career."

I shrug and try to act nonchalant about the one topic I'd rather not discuss. "Joanne sees things from a different perspective, I guess."

My agent screws her face into an expression of disgust. "She's like an ambulance chaser." Quickly, she holds up her hands and shakes her head. "I'm sorry. That's not appropriate for me to say. I just didn't like the glee she seemed to feel at your heartbreak."

"It's over now, so it's all in the past. I'm onto bigger and better things," I say with a smile, genuinely feeling good.

Jennie levels her gaze on me. "Are we still talking about your career or something else here?"

I want to share how happy I am with Ian, but my promise to him to keep our relationship private echoes in my ears. So I tell a lie, more a sin of omission really. "My career, of course, but I'm feeling really good about my personal life too. I'm over that John mess and ready for a new love."

"That's what I love to hear! Just keep that positive attitude and I know things will work out. Now get yourself home and start packing. I'll give you a call when I get the papers."

"Okay." Extending my hand, I shake hers and say, "Thanks so much again, Jennie. I couldn't have gotten this without your help."

She takes me into her arms for a hug. "Nonsense. I'm just the messenger. You're the one they're dying to work with, so go show them what you got, kid."

I leave her office feeling like I'm walking on air. This film is my big chance. After years of working hard at my craft and taking roles other actresses saw as beneath them, I finally had the opportunity to break out and show the world what I could do with my talent.

But what about Ian and me? The idea of leaving him for months to go shoot a movie in Vancouver makes me break out in a cold sweat. One week we were apart and he slept with another woman. But that was because I left him, I remind myself.

But I'll be leaving him now too. He's become so much a part of my life that imagining it without him scares the hell out of me. What if he doesn't want to wait for me?

I hurry to his apartment to see him, debating all the way there whether I should tell him my good news or not. I know he'll be happy for me because he loves me, but it's so early in the relationship to be apart for so long. He answers his door and I throw my arms around him, already missing the feel of his body next to mine.

"Kristina, what's wrong? Did something happen?" he asks, not knowing how much my good news is torturing me at that moment.

"I missed you. That's all."

Closing the door, he takes me by the hand to the couch and practically beaming says, "I have wonderful news. My publisher agreed to the Marc Antony book, so I need to travel to Rome to research before I begin writing. What do you say to a month in the Eternal City?"

His eyes are wide with excitement as he tells me his good

news, and I can't bring myself to say no, even though I know there's no way I can take this trip with him and begin work on the film at the same time. As he waits for my answer, I see how much this means to him, so I nod and smile as I tell him I can't wait for our trip together.

"As soon as I knew I'd be going there again, I looked into making reservations for us. Oh, Kristina, you're going to love it there. We'll see the sights and it will be the best trip I've ever had to Rome."

He describes all the plans he's making, and all I can think is how he included me in them without any prodding from me. No man has ever put me first like this. How am I going to ever tell him I can't go because of my work?

"And I have another surprise for you. Silk is ready. I'm going to self-publish it tonight or tomorrow. Our story isn't going to be just ours anymore."

"What does that mean? Aren't you going to use a pseudonym?"

"Yes, but as a writer, I know once a story is published, it no longer really stays mine. I have no idea if anyone will want to read it or even be able to find it, but it's ready."

I kiss him and swipe a dark stray lock of hair from his forehead. "I know people are going to love it. How couldn't they? You wrote it."

"Maybe I'm not a very good writer if it's not historical fiction," he says in a voice that makes me think he truly isn't sure about readers loving our story.

I trace the outline of his lower lip and lean in to gently suck it into my mouth. Giving it a tiny nip, I see the desire in his eyes and let go. "You're a great writer all the time, Ian, and the story you've told in Silk is sensual and erotic. I just know people will love it."

Sliding his hands down to cup my ass, he pulls me to him and I feel his already hard cock. "I'd planned on telling you all about the plans I'm making for our trip, but that can wait. Right now, I'd rather be balls deep inside you than talk about anything else."

"More research for your writing?"

Ian shakes his head as he sensually drags his lips down my neck. "Not exactly."

I don't stop him, and for a few moments I'm able to push the reality of what I have to tell him out of my mind. His love for me comes through in every touch of his hand and every kiss. Gently, he pulls my skirt down my body and kneeling in front of me, Ian looks up with his dark eyes and gives me one of his sexy smiles I love so much.

"I can't tell you how happy I am that I get to spend time in one of my favorite places in the world with the woman I love."

As he slides his hands up my thigh and presses his lips to my sex, my body begins to soar. I want to be able to lose myself in him like always, but I can't forget that at some point I'm going to have to tell him the truth and ruin all his plans.

# CHAPTER SEVEN

## *Ian*

WHEN I TOLD Kristina I wasn't even sure anyone would find Silk, I wasn't kidding. Forget about the needle in the haystack. Selling a book online seems akin to the task of finding one particular tiny piece of hay in a haystack. How anyone sells any real number of books baffles me, but Sheila had said that some authors were doing it, so I figure I'll jump in with both feet and upload Silk to all the major sales outlets that sell my historical fiction books and will take my self-published one.

It's almost too easy. I know nothing about formatting a book to be published, but with a little reading about it online, I'm ready to go. I agree to read a friend's book in exchange for a simple very sexy cover and then it's time to upload.

For two days I watch our book just sit there as nobody finds it. I'm not really surprised given the nature of the major sites. Again, Silk is just one tiny piece of hay in their big haystacks. Then on the third day, there's one sale. One. As I check the sales totals each day, I have to wonder how anyone makes any kind of living this way.

It's definitely not something that grows organically, but for my first foray into erotica, I'm happy. A few more people buy it, and slowly reviews trickle in that show readers loving Kate and Sean as much as I loved writing them. It's no bestseller, but I'm pleased.

Then just about five days after it's published, I happen to be surfing through the channels as I wait for Kristina one night and see a reporter on one of the entertainment news shows say that actress Kristina Richards mentioned the book she's reading now is Silk. Stunned to hear that, I ask her about it when she arrives.

"They were asking me bunches of questions. Did you see the whole thing? What part did you see?" she asks in an excited voice as I pour her a glass of wine.

"Not much. Just the part about the book. Was there anything else they asked you that I should know about?"

Taking the glass from my hand, she shakes her head and asks in a shaky voice, "Like what? What else would they ask me?"

She's nervous. It's clear in the way she's acting, but I don't know why. "You didn't say anything about us, did you?"

Kristina sighs, visibly relieved by my question. "No, no. Is that what you were worried about? I told you I won't say anything."

"Did you say you knew the author of Silk?" I press further, still wondering why she was so nervous a minute ago.

"No. I just mentioned it in the hopes that maybe if they included that on their program that it could help it get seen. Has it?"

"Not in any appreciable way yet," I say with a smile, still incredulous about how anyone makes a living as an author this way.

Kristina gives me a tiny kiss and smiles up at me. "I'm not a huge name, so maybe nobody cares what I read in my spare time. The interviewer did ask me what it was about, so I told her. Did they include that in the show?"

"No, not that I saw. It might have helped. You know what they say. Sex sells."

My joke makes her giggle and she nuzzles my neck. "Mmmm...yes it does."

Taking her in my arms, I kiss the tender skin just below her ear and ask, "Have you been thinking about our trip? Are you excited about it?"

Her neck and shoulders tense up, and I lift my head to see her beautiful blue eyes clouded over. She forces a smile, but something's wrong. I can see it. Nodding, she answers, "I haven't thought much about it yet, but I'm very excited. I've never been to Rome."

I want to break the tension that's settled in between us, although I have no idea why it has, so I ask, "Not even for a film? I thought movie stars travelled around the world."

Scrunching up her face, she says, "Some might, but I haven't yet."

There's a pregnant pause as I watch her silently struggle to decide whether or not she wants to continue talking. She's hiding something from me, but what? Backing away from her, I lean against the counter and fold my arms across my chest.

"Is something wrong, Kristina?"

"No. Why would something be wrong?"

Every person in the world who has something they're hiding has asked that question in response to being asked if something is wrong. I don't know what it is, but if she won't tell me, my gut says it's bad. I walk past her into the living room, hoping that when she follows me she'll tell me what's wrong.

I watch her as she comes toward me on the couch. If any poker player ever had a tell like she does, they'd lose their shirt every hand. My girl is a terrible liar.

"Why did you walk away like that?" she asks as she sits down next to me, cuddling up to my side.

"Just seemed like the thing to do so we don't get into a fight tonight."

I turn to see her blue eyes wide with surprise. "What would we fight about? I don't understand."

Studying her body language, I believe her, strangely enough. The worried tone in her voice says she doesn't understand what we'd fight about because I suspect she doesn't realize how clearly guilty she looks and whatever she's not telling me is much worse than the sin of omission she's committing.

"We promised to be truthful always, Kristina. Something in the way you're acting tells me you're not being truthful."

That sweetness I love in her slips away, leaving a frown on her beautiful mouth. "I think I better go."

"Wouldn't you rather just tell me what's wrong?"

She says nothing and stands to leave. "I have to go home, Ian."

Fuck if she hasn't called my bluff. I no more want her to leave than I want her to keep secrets from me, but if I have to choose between the two, I'll deal with the secrets if only she'll stay. I jump up from the couch and stop her.

"Don't go."

She hangs her head and whispers, "I have to. You don't trust me."

I don't want to let her go, but she tugs her hand from my hold, and for a long moment, I stand there watching her leave like the jackass I am as my mind plays tug of war over begging her to stay and letting her walk out.

With every step she takes, I feel like I'm losing part of myself. Why did I do this? Do I really need to know every thought she has every minute of the day? What am I? Some insecure teenage boy?

"Kristina, stay."

I walk toward the door to catch up with her, but something about her is different now. She doesn't want to stay.

"I'm sorry. I shouldn't have pushed like that. Stay and we can talk about Rome and how much fun we're going to have together there."

Kristina turns to face me with a look that chills my heart. Part anger, part sadness, her expression tells me I've made a mistake. "I'm going to go home now. I love you, but I need to go."

She leans forward and kisses me deeply, making me hate myself all the more for the bullshit I've caused tonight. I want to feel her beneath me as I make love to her. I want to show her I know I made a mistake and can make up for it.

I hold her hand, not ready for her to leave, and quietly say, "I'm sorry."

"I know. I am too. I'll call you tomorrow."

And with that, her fingers slip from my hold and she walks slowly to the elevator as I stand there knowing I fucked up. I

K . M . SCOTT

could run after her and plead for her to come back, but my silent accusations have made her walls go up, and there's nothing I can do tonight to bring them down.

✧   ✧   ✧

I OPEN MY eyes and how much I miss Kristina floods my brain before I can even put together a coherent thought about anything else. She should be next to me, making that adorable snoring noise she makes when she sleeps and blushing when she realizes I've been watching her and loving that cute pout her mouth does.

Scrubbing the sleep from my eyes, I stretch my arms and legs, missing the ache in my muscles from making love I always have after spending the night with her. God, I'm such a fuck!

The need to call her presses down on me, so I roll over and grab my phone from the nightstand. Three rings and the worry that I've fucked up worse than I thought begins to dawn on me. My call goes to voicemail and just hearing her gentle voice tell me she'll call me back as soon as she can makes me wince in pain.

I don't leave a voicemail and instead go straight for the text. Not that it's my best way of communicating by any means, but desperate times call for desperate measures. Tapping away with my thumbs, I do my best to tell her how much I miss her without unraveling emotions all over her phone.

I'm lying here in bed missing the feel of your body against mine.

She doesn't text back immediately, and my demons begin

to take over. I'm sure she's with someone else. That guy she met at the bar she told me about. The guy who I saw kiss her on her doorstep that night. It doesn't matter who he is. He isn't me.

Five minutes later, I'm out of bed and dressed to go to her place. I screwed up and I know it, so I need to do something about it.

My phone vibrates against the top of the nightstand, and relief floods my mind. I look down to see her text back to me.

I miss you too.

Snatching my phone up, I quickly text back. Come to me. We can spend all day in bed. I need you.

I hit SEND and wait for her reply. Minute after minute ticks by, but she doesn't answer. I feel like she's punishing me, but if she is, I deserve it. I silently will my phone to vibrate like I have some control over any of it. Hell, I barely have control over myself.

After the tenth time of me telling my phone to give me her text, it vibrates and I look down to see what she's said.

I think it might be better for us to spend the day apart.

Each word feels like someone's stabbing me in the gut. Apart. I hadn't been wrong. She was hiding something from me.

Knowing me like she does, she has to expect me to do something. My legs move even before I make the decision to go to her. Grabbing my coat, I have to slow myself down so I don't run full speed directly to her apartment. As it is, I'm barely able to keep myself to a walk as my feet pound the sidewalk toward her building just blocks away.

Ten minutes later, I'm in front of the brownstone where her apartment is and look up to see her staring down at me from her living room window. She doesn't look frightened or angry that I'm there. And she doesn't look surprised.

If anything, she looks pleased to see me.

I tear up the stairs from the sidewalk and find the front door open for me. She unlocked it knowing I'd come. I take the stairs inside by twos and in less than a minute I'm at her door. I hear her. She's waiting for me to knock, to come to her.

Two sharp bangs on the door and she opens it. "Why are you here?"

"You know why. For the same reason you came to my apartment that other night."

She bites her lower lip and knits her brows like the thought causes her pain. "I don't want to think of that night."

"Let me in, Kristina. Let me show you how much I missed you."

Closing her eyes, she takes a deep breath in and lets it out, her shoulders sagging from her inability to stay angry at me. Without a word, she steps aside for me to come in.

I walk past and wrap my arms around her when she closes the door, needing to feel her against me. She doesn't move away to deny me this pleasure and leans her head back against my chest like she needs this too.

Quietly, in a small voice, she says, "Tell me how much you missed me."

Sliding my hand up the front of her neck, I feel the warmth of her skin against mine. I'm overcome with how much I missed this. Dipping my head, I press my lips to the shell of her ear and whisper, "I woke up this morning and my skin hurt because I needed you so much, but I didn't feel the ache I always feel after we make love."

She covers my hand with hers and whimpers softly as she arches her back. Her breasts graze my arm, and I feel her nipples hard from excitement. I love how responsive she is to my touch and my words.

"I feel like a part of me is missing when you aren't with me. Like someone's torn away something necessary and I can't go on without it, Kristina."

"Whatever this is we have between us makes me crazy, Ian."

Turning her to face me, I lift her chin so she has to look at me. "There's nothing wrong with being in crazy in love, Kristina."

"I don't want to be crazy. Crazy gets people hurt. I don't want to hurt you or have you hurt me."

I place a soft kiss on her lips and whisper, "Sometimes love hurts. That doesn't mean it isn't love."

She asks with a frown, "Why did you act like that toward me last night?"

I don't know why I acted like that. Because I thought she was lying. Because I worried she was holding something back. Pressing my forehead to hers, I answer her as truthfully as I can. "Because I'm fucked up and being with me means you see that. I just want to know you won't run away because of it."

"I would never hurt you intentionally, Ian." She leans her cheek against my hand and looks so sad. "I swear."

"I know. You're sweet and gentle and I'm a fucked up mess without you."

"Maybe we should take a couple weeks off."

Grabbing a fistful of her hair in my hand, I tug hard as my fears threaten to overrun me. Her eyes fill with tears, and I frantically say, "No. I don't want to take any time off from us, Kristina. Tell me you don't want to either."

"Please let go. You're hurting me!"

I loosen my hold on her hair and kiss her hard on the lips. She fights against my kiss for a moment, but then her mouth softens and meets my passion with hers.

"Tell me you don't want us to end," I say with a lump in my throat. "Don't leave me, baby."

Kristina grabs at my shirt and tears it off me. Buttons fly everywhere and she sobs against my chest, "I hate the idea of losing you. I don't know what I'd do if I didn't have you."

"Then why did you say we should take some time off?" I ask as I begin to undress her.

Shaking her head, she fumbles with my pants to get them off while I tug her jeans down her legs. "I don't know. I don't know. I just thought maybe if we weren't together that we wouldn't get hurt."

We're caught up in this cycle of madness and need, and I know it's spinning out of control. I don't want to stop it, though. I can't. The idea of my world without Kristina makes me break out in a cold sweat. I need her. I love her. And even though I know she's hiding something, I don't care.

All I care about is being inside her.

She wraps her arms around my neck, clinging to me as I push her back against the hallway wall. Open and needy for me, her body envelopes me as I thrust my cock deep into her cunt. We fuck with abandon like Kate and Sean, and as she whimpers my name over and over, I begin to feel like I'm flying.

This is the high she gives me. The high I'm desperately addicted to. The high I can't do without.

Panting as I take her toward her orgasm, she pleads in my ear, "Ian, promise you won't ever let me go. Please promise."

The fear in her eyes warns of some problem we'll have to deal with eventually, but at that moment, I don't care. I don't care what she's done. All I care about is having her in my life. I grip her hips tightly as the first sweet squeeze of her cunt on my cock tells me she's just about there and answer in a groan, "I promise. I couldn't live without you."

She throws her head back as her release tears through her, and as she bucks wildly against me, I come with one last hard plunge into her, the two of us drenched in sweat and holding on to one another.

When her body ceases to tremble, she rests her head on my shoulder and says in barely a whisper, as if the words are too frightening to speak out loud, "I thought I could be without you. I was wrong. What are we going to do, Ian?"

I gently stroke her back. "There's nothing to do. This is what we are."

I've never said more truthful words than those. There is nothing the two of us can do. Maybe her therapist was right and she becomes addicted to people. I thought that was bullshit psychobabble, but I'm as addicted to Kristina as I am to how she makes me feel. I don't know anymore. Nothing I've ever been addicted to ever felt like this.

❖   ❖   ❖

A LITTLE MORE than a week later, the story of our love exploded and hit the New York Times bestseller list. Silk by T. Anderson, some unknown erotica writer who self-published the story Kristina inspired that first night as I watched her movies and fell for her, hit #5.

I stand in my kitchen after letting her in and casually announce the news. "Silk hit the Times list."

Kristina's face is the purest example of confusion as my news sinks in. "Do you mean our book?"

My smile stretches wide at that. "Yes. Number five."

"Oh my God! Ian! That's wonderful! How, though? You used a pen name no one knows."

I take her in my arms and kiss her sweetly, loving her naiveté. "You did this. First you inspired me and agreed to be my muse, and then you mentioned the book in that interview. That's what did it. My beautiful muse, you did this."

Kristina leans back and I see she has tears in her eyes. "I did this? Me?"

"All you."

Hugging me, she says, "Oh, Ian, I can't believe it. But it wasn't just me. Your story is why people bought it and made it a bestseller. It's you, not me."

I tip her head back and look down into those beautiful blue eyes I love. "It's us. We did this. And I think I'm going to write another one."

"Do you know what the story's about?"

"I don't know yet, but as long as I have my muse, I know it will be great."

She hugs me tightly to her again as I think about Rome and how the next chapter in our story will unfold. It will be there that the next book comes to be.

# CHAPTER EIGHT

## *Kristina*

I STAY IN bed late after three nights of celebrating Silk's success with Ian. What had begun as a torrid love affair has morphed into something so consuming, so part of me that even being away from him makes me uncomfortable. But I've done exactly what my therapist said to and let things happen naturally. It's just that natural for Ian and me isn't really natural.

In less than twenty-four hours, we're scheduled to fly to Rome, and I still haven't told him I can't go with him. I've tried. I really have. But every time I think it's the right moment to dash all his plans for us, he says something cute or funny about how much he's looking forward to our trip. How can I break his heart like that?

Closing my eyes, I curse my bad luck. For the first time ever, I have everything I want in life. It's just my luck that fate says I can't have it all at the same time. I can't turn down the role I've wanted so badly. That would be career suicide, and I'd be crazy to let that opportunity slip through my hands.

But the mere thought of losing Ian makes me feel hollow inside. If only I'd told him when I found out. Now when I have to ruin the Rome trip, he'll know I've been holding out on him and essentially lying for days and days. He gave me the chance to tell the truth that night, but like a fool I didn't take it.

Now I've made things ten times worse.

Desperate for some sound advice, I call Sienna. Unlike Priscilla, she always has clever ideas. She'll know what I should do.

"Kristina, I was just thinking about you," she says as she answers the phone.

"Really? Why?"

"A bunch of reasons. First is that guy I met that night when we went out just left my place. Oh my, that man knows how to fuck. Honey, you must get yourself someone like him."

I smile at the knowledge that I already have a man who knows just how to take care of me in that respect. Ian and I may be crazy together, but when it comes to sex, he's exactly what every man should be.

"I'm happy you're having a good time, Sienna."

"A good time doesn't even begin to describe it. All we do is fuck. I love it! He hasn't said anything about dating or a relationship and I couldn't be happier. Tell me things got better for you since that night. What happened with that banker you were talking to that night? Is he pinching your pennies these days?"

I can't help but giggle at the cute way she says things. Cute and blunt. "No, nothing happened. He just gave me a ride home. He wasn't really my type, you know?"

"Yeah, he did have a sort of boring thing going on. You're too sweet and fun for that kind of life. I'm not getting a three-piece suit and tie vibe for the kind of man you need. You need a little freakier, I think."

"I'll be sure to work on that, Sienna."

"So why are you calling me at eight a.m.? Did you just send some hot guy home?"

"No, nothing like that. I just needed some advice."

I hear the rustling of her sheets and comforter as she sits up to listen to what I have to say. "Advice? Is something wrong?"

"Yes and no. I need to figure out how to break bad news to someone."

"Do it like you tear off a Band-Aid—fast. Just say what you have to say and then deal with their reaction. How bad is the news we're talking about here?"

"Bad. It's going to disappoint this person a lot. I feel terrible about it too."

"Life is full of disappointment, Kristina. Adults deal. It isn't Cilla, is it?"

"No." That would be easy. Cilla can be difficult at times, but nothing ever seems to bother her for long. She's got a thoughtless streak in her that comes in handy at times like this.

"Because if it is her, I say do it slow and torture her. She left me hanging last weekend when I went out to LA to see her, so I'm still pissed at her."

"Sorry. I can't help you there. This isn't about her. It's about someone I really care for and don't want to hurt."

"That mystery man you were trying to get over that night we went out?" she asks, her voice full of curiosity.

I know I shouldn't mention anything even vaguely about Ian, but I say, "Yes, but I can't tell you any more than that about him."

"Nothing? You're not good at keeping secrets, Kristina. I'll get it out of you."

"Please don't try. It's bad enough I might be hurting him by giving him this bad news. I don't want to betray him too."

"Why would telling me about some guy betray him?" she asks now very curious.

"Because he asked me to keep our relationship a secret," I confess, knowing she'll think the worst, which she does.

"He's married. That's it. Married. He's a married son of a bitch who's cheating on his wife with you," she pronounces.

"He's not married," I say with a chuckle. If Ian is married, his wife sure doesn't seem to be much a part of his life.

"Are you sure? He doesn't want anyone to know about you two. Sounds like a married man to me."

"No, he's not married and I can't tell you any more about him. I just need to know how to break bad news without hurting him."

"Are you breaking it off with him?"

"No. I just need to cancel a trip we planned on taking because of work."

"Oh, that's not a big deal. You can take a trip anytime. Just tell him you need to reschedule."

If only it was that easy. I could have done that if I told him when I found out about Vancouver. Now it was too late.

"It's not that easy. I've lied for a while about it, saying I'd go. He has no idea."

"Why'd you do that?"

The explanation of why I'd made such a dumb choice would take too long, so I just mumble, "I don't know. I didn't want to disappoint him."

"So now you get to disappoint and hurt him. Well, I still

say do it fast. Get it over with so you can move on to bigger and better things."

Sienna's words make my heart pound in my chest. I don't want to move on to anything. I just want to find a way to tell Ian that even though I love him I can't go to Rome like he wants. It sounds so simple when I say it in my head, but I know when I'm standing in front of him and I see the disappointment in those dark eyes of his that I'll feel terrible.

"Okay. Thanks Sienna. I guess I'll try it that way."

She squeals loudly into the phone, so I pull it away from my ear as she begins to talk about some show she's watching. Not exactly the way I wanted to begin my morning.

"Oh my God! Kristina! You're on Good Morning America!" I hear her scream.

Quickly, I pull the phone back to my ear as I search for the remote buried in the blankets. "What do you mean?"

"They're talking about your new film you begin shooting in Vancouver right now in their Hollywood news segment. Did you put it on?"

My television turns on and there as big as life is my face in a box to the right of the pretty blond woman who reports on all things pop news and Hollywood gossip, including it seems me this morning. She's got all the details about the film and how I'll be there in just a few days.

"Is this what you were talking about, Kristina? This is the reason you can't go on that trip with the mystery guy?"

"Yeah, it is," I say as the blond woman moves on to some other news story.

"Well, if he watches Good Morning America, he already knows. They might have done the dirty work for you."

Terror races through my mind at the thought that Ian has just found out the truth I've been hiding for over a week from of all places a morning news show. "I have to go," I say frantically as I leap out of bed to get dressed. "I'll talk to you later, Sienna."

I don't give her a chance to answer before I click END and throw my phone on the bed. I run into the bathroom and see my messy hair in the mirror, but I don't have time to make myself even close to presentable. I need to get to Ian before this news ruins everything.

Dashing out the door, I remember I left my phone on the bed so I race back and grab it only to see a text waiting for me. I take a deep breath and open my messages to see it's from Ian.

When were you going to tell me about Vancouver?

My heart sinks as I read the words. He saw the same thing Sienna and I saw. The sense of betrayal hangs off every word. Quickly, I text back a tepid excuse, but I know whatever I say can't change the fact that I lied.

I'm sorry. I didn't mean to lie.

My answer is pathetic. Whatever I meant to do, I kept my new film from him and now I've hurt the man I love for no reason other than my cowardice.

I want to explain to him, but I don't know what to say. I wait for him to text back, to tell me how disappointed he is in me, but he doesn't. His silence crushes me, so I finally try my best to explain why I did what I did. I have to try.

I wanted to tell you but then you were so excited about

the Rome trip and I didn't want to disappoint you. I never meant to lie. I love you, Ian. Please call me.

I click SEND and wait for him to call, but after five minutes I know he won't. His anger comes through loud and clear in the silence. Then he texts me and my worst fears are realized.

Without trust, we have nothing, Kristina.

He won't let me convince him to forgive me through texts, so I run out of my apartment and down the stairs to the sidewalk, half expecting him to be there waiting for me. But that can't happen today because I've hurt him.

As I run the blocks toward his apartment, I think about all the love he's shown me and I feel like the guilt is going to crush me. I have to see him to tell him I'm sorry and I'll do anything to make this up to him. We can go to Rome together as soon as I finish working on Original Sin. It won't be forever. I'll only be gone for a few months.

His building's doorman is a friendly face waiting to open the door to the lobby. Rushing past him, I hurry to catch the elevator, frantically pressing the button to get to his floor and wishing for once the elevator wasn't so slow. It's the longest minute of my life, and when the elevator doors open, I lurch out into his hallway on unsteady legs, weak from the feeling of sickness in my stomach.

Even before I knock on his door, I know he's not there. I feel a sense of missing him already. But I knock anyway, a futile effort that makes me feel like I have some control over getting him back.

I don't, though.

No one answers my knocking and somewhere deep inside I worry he's gone. Gone from here, gone from New York, gone from my life. I begin to unravel, desperate to tell him my side of the story. If only I could explain myself, if only he could see how devastated I am that what I've done has ruined what we had.

I don't know where to go to find him, so I walk the streets back to my place as I text him over and over, but he never replies. Hour after hour passes, but if he's getting my messages he's not responding. Finally, I cry myself to sleep after I send him one last text and pray he'll finally answer me.

I love you, Ian. Please tell me you still love me too. Tell me it's not too late for me to fix this.

After tossing and turning for hours, I wake up determined to repair the damage I've done. I know I can if he'll just give me a chance. I pack my bags for our trip to Rome, knowing that if I don't show up on the set for the beginning of shooting, my career might suffer but I don't care about that. All I care about is getting Ian back.

I have the cab take me to his apartment, sure that he'll be there because our flight doesn't leave for four hours. Standing in front of his door with my suitcase, I knock and listen to hear him inside as he comes to let me in. I rehearsed what I plan to say on my way here. Now all I need is the chance to show him how much I love him.

As I wait for him to answer the door, I see an envelope sticking out from underneath it. Bending down, I pick it up and see it's addressed to me. My heart slams against my chest as my hands begin to shake. I don't want to read it, but I open it anyway and see the words that break my heart.

*Kristina,*

*Every time I asked you if you had something to tell me, you lied. Was everything we were a lie? I've gone to Rome. Don't try to contact me.*

*Ian*

The tears roll down my cheeks as I read his words so filled with the pain I caused. I can't let him leave without me. I have to do this, even if it means ruining everything I've worked for in my career. I send him one more text to let him know I'm not giving up on us as I race downstairs to catch a cab to the airport.

I won't let you go without a fight. I'm coming to you.

# CHAPTER NINE

## *Ian*

I SIT IN the airport lounge waiting to board my plane and reading Kristina's texts after she found my letter I left her. I won't lie. Knowing this bothers her gives me at least some modicum of pleasure after feeling like I'd been kicked in the fucking stomach as I watched that morning show. Nothing like finding out the woman you love has been lying to you for days, even after you gave her more than enough chances to come clean.

Not that I can't forgive her. I can. I don't have a choice, to be honest. I love her too much to even think I can go on without her.

My phone vibrates against my glass of scotch, and I see it's Kristina. My eyes scan her text and I smile.

Don't give up on us. Please.

My instinct is to message her back and tell her I couldn't give up on what she is to me any more than I could give up breathing. Avoiding her for the last day has been pure torture. My hands yearn to touch her. I crave the feel of her skin on mine, the taste of her lips as she kisses me when I slide my cock into her and bury myself inside her body. My body aches from not having her next to me. I miss her smile, her voice, her laughter.

I miss her. And even though I'm hurt she lied, I just want her back with me so we can go to Rome and fall in love all over again.

I grab my phone and text back to her.

I can't give you up. Come to me.

Immediately, she answers my text with one of her own filled with that need so familiar in my life.

Promise you'll wait for me. Don't leave me here without you.

Texting back, I tell her what I know she wants to hear.

Meet me at Gate B 39. I left your ticket at the Delta desk.
I love you.

I sit there as people come and go on their way to wherever they're going and wonder how many of them are like Kristina and me. Most people sleepwalk through life. They pretend to love, pretend to care about those around them. They fake it, phone in love and lust and all the things in life that make it worth living. People float in and out of their lives with little more than a nod in recognition.

But not us. Since the moment I met her, every part of me has felt alive like never before. With the first touch of my hand, she's been mine. When I see her after she's been gone for mere hours, it's like my eyes can't open wide enough to take in all of her. I want to touch her, feel her breath as I take it away with a kiss on her gorgeous lips or the perfect word whispered in her ear.

I finish my scotch and look at the time. One hour until boarding. Looking down at my phone, I begin to worry she won't make it before we have to leave. For the first time since I sat there in my apartment watching that insipid morning news show discuss how the woman I love had lied to me, the thought occurs to me that Kristina might truly choose something over me.

My stomach knots from the betrayal this thought brings with it. How could she? I'd never choose anyone or anything over her. I can't. She's as necessary to me as the food I eat and the air I breathe. It's never a choice to need her.

Something in leaving to go somewhere else fills me with dread. When she left that night after I'd frightened her, I never doubted I'd see her again. Never doubted we'd be together again. Now as I sit in this lounge watching planes take off to faraway places, a niggling feeling gnaws at me that if she doesn't come to Rome with me, it's over.

We're over.

A little voice inside me asks the obvious question. How could that be? I'm no less addicted to her than I was to heroin, even more. Heroin only made me feel good and helped me forget what terrified me. Kristina gives me what no drug ever could.

Love in return. And that love makes me a better man. No drug has ever done that for me.

So how could this be the end of us? Am I not addicted to

how incredible she makes me feel anymore?

Closing my eyes, I silently pray she shows up and I don't have to answer any of these questions. I don't want to think of life without her.

I wait until I can't anymore and slowly walk to the gate. My hands sweat and my legs feel weak. Looking up, I see the sign for Gate B 39 and stop to look around. People file past me as the flight attendants begin to call for first class boarding. I should get on the plane, but I can't.

Not without Kristina. She's coming. I just need to wait a little longer.

First class finishes boarding and I'm still standing in line. The petite brunette flight attendant gives me a confused look as if to ask, "Are you coming?"

I flash her a weak smile and step back out of line as she announces that coach class can now begin boarding. More people file past me into the tube that leads to the plane as I search left and right for Kristina.

My phone vibrates and I know even before I look that I don't want to read the message. I can't avoid it, though, so I bring it up on the screen and see everything I've dreaded since yesterday.

I tried to get there but I can't.

There's more, but I can't read it. Stuffing my phone back into my pocket, I get into line and make my way to the flight attendant. She gives me a sad look like she knows I've just spent the last fifteen minutes waiting for someone who was never going to show. Giving me a tepid smile, she wishes me a good flight and sends me down the tube to board the plane alone.

A few minutes later, I'm settled into my seat and look over at the empty seat next to me, my chest tightening as the reality sinks in. Kristina chose something over us.

Over me.

I look at my phone as everyone around me tells the attendant their drink orders and feel too sick to my stomach to even try to down any more alcohol. Her message sits there on my phone staring up at me. Dismissing me.

> My publicist caught me as I tried to go to you and stopped me. I want to be there with you, but I can't give up the chance this film offers me. Please forgive me.

My fingers don't move to text back. I have nothing to say.

> Please answer me. Say something. Anything. Please! Tell me we're going to be okay. Tell me you forgive me. Please Ian.

The plane's engines roar and we begin to taxi down the runway as I finally answer her message with one last text of my own.

> Goodbye

As I turn my phone off, she texts again telling me she won't let me go and that she loves me, but I don't have anything else to say. The plane takes off into the air above Kennedy, and for me I'm not going to Rome so much as leaving her.

Leaving everything we were, including our story, behind. Whatever we had she ruined by lying to me.

Halfway over the Atlantic, I read over her messages again and see one that came in after I turned off my phone. Full of the sadness I feel, it shows the strength I love in her, and I silently pray she means what she wrote.

> You said there was no running from what we are, Ian. I can't let this be goodbye. You can't either. We will see each other again.

# Shatter

## K.M. SCOTT

For Ian Anwell, addiction is a way of life. He can't remember a time when he wasn't addicted to something—heroin, alcohol, whatever made him feel good. But his newest addiction is better than all the others combined. Kristina makes him feel like the man he's always wanted to be.

But addicts have a habit of wrecking things, even those they hold dear.

For Kristina Richards, Ian is everything. Love. Lust. Obsession. But even as she falls deeper in love with him and the madness they create together, she finds something she never expected to find in her time with him.

She finds strength she never knew she had.

# CHAPTER ONE

## *Ian*

F IVE WEEKS. I haven't seen or heard from Kristina in five weeks. Until this morning as I boarded the plane to return to New York, I would have lied if someone asked me if I still thought about her. I would have said no. Lying would have been easy four thousand miles away in that beautiful city I so looked forward to sharing with her.

Now that I'm back in New York, lying isn't as easy anymore. The minute I stepped off the plane I felt her pull on me. For all that this city has meant in my life, after Kristina it simply reminds me of her.

I look around my apartment and see her. Everything is a memory that tortures me. The couch where we sat together as I read the words that enchanted her. The kitchen where I found joy in making meals just for her. The bed where we lost ourselves in one another. My stomach tightens as I think about us. I can't be here right now.

Dropping my bags, I head out into a November storm that's nothing less than raw. The feel of the cold rain on my face matches my mood. I don't know where I'm going, but I walk fast, making the rain pelt my skin even harder. At some point I realize I'm walking toward Kristina's place and stop dead in the middle of an intersection.

A car screeches to a stop, barely missing me, and the driver screams, "Get the fuck out of the way!"

His words barely register as I try to figure out where to go. I live in a city with practically limitless opportunities to do things, but I don't know where to go or what to do to forget Kristina. For five weeks, I thought I'd gotten over her. I'd lied to myself, aided by the benefit of distance, but I couldn't do that anymore.

Stumbling toward the sidewalk, I hear the guy bark again, "Get your head out of your ass!"

He has no idea how accurate his assessment of me is. I find an awning to get out of the rain as it begins to pour down and watch as a couple madly in love kisses next to me. Their happiness brings a dull ache to my chest, and I turn away, unable to watch them. I wanted Kristina and me to be that happy, but it wasn't meant to be.

I could call her now that I'm back. I could tell her I forgive her for lying to me and letting me leave. But I can't lie that well. Not to her. I can't forgive her either.

That's not true. I could forgive her for lying to me. I've lied for so many years I don't even know the truth about some things anymore, so lying is a sin I can forgive.

Letting me go isn't.

Knowing that she very well might lose me forever if she let me get on that plane alone and still letting it happen I can't forgive. By doing that, she showed she doesn't love me like I love her.

Madly. Completely. As if every breath I take depends on

having her in my life.

I was able to lie for five long weeks as I buried myself in research and Marc Antony's life. And drugs. I pretended like I didn't love her more than life itself.

Now I can't anymore.

The couple next to me walks away as I stand there unsure of what to do now that I've admitted the truth to myself. I can't forgive her, but I can't live without her.

The rain begins to slow to a light drizzle, so I head out from underneath the store awning back toward my apartment. I need a drink. I need something else. I know I shouldn't want it, but as I make my way back to my place, that need starts to push out all thoughts of Kristina.

No. As painful as it is to think of her, I can't let my craving for heroin take over. I've just spent five weeks deep in it, but I promised myself once I got back here I'd stop.

My legs break into a run as I desperately try to get home, my breathing creating a cloud in the icy air around me. But as I round the last corner I see it. A picture of her on a magazine cover. She looks incredible. Fresh, soft, feminine. I stop in front of the newsstand, lost in the vision of her, and then I see the words above her head.

ACTRESS KRISTINA RICHARDS IN TORRID LOVE AFFAIR

Five fucking weeks is all we've been apart and she's already involved in some torrid love affair? I can't bear to pick up the rag and flip through the pages to read the details of this incredible love match she's apparently made.

Instead I just stand there staring like some idiot until the man who owns the stand asks me if I need help. Yeah, I need help. I need some way to fucking forget the most important person in my life.

I need help.

I grimace and shake my head before I race back to my apartment, feeling unhappier than I've felt since the last time I entered rehab. By the time I get home, I want some junk so bad my hands are shaking.

Closing the front door, I press my back against it and take a deep breath, just like they taught me to do in rehab. Take a deep breath in and push all those thoughts out of your mind. The desire to feel good again—to feel nothing but pure bliss and not have to endure the pain of knowing Kristina is with someone else—that's what I want. If the only way to get it is snorting shit up my nose, then I'll take it.

Thoughts of how much I want to get high again intermingle with thoughts of how much I miss her. They wrap around my brain like some horrible dream of the perfect pleasure and pain. The feeling of floating peacefully above myself without worry or sadness one minute, pushed aside by the memory of having Kristina in my arms that I know now was all a lie the next.

I slide to the floor and hang my head, silently begging for some relief from the torture of wanting something I shouldn't have and missing someone I can't have. All I want is to forget. That's all I ask.

Why can't I just forget her?

Was she with this torrid love affair guy while she was telling me she loved me? I can't help but wonder.

Jesus, I don't want to be like this. I don't want to feel all this pain.

I struggle to my feet and feel a surge of anger course through me. I hate her. I love her. I need her. I can't stand how much I miss her. I spent five weeks researching Marc Antony and she spent that time fucking another man.

My rage takes over, and I storm across the room toward my desk where all my work for the new historical fiction book sits as a sickening reminder that she let me go. With one swipe of my arm, I send the books and papers flying onto the floor, leaving only my laptop undisturbed. For a moment, I remember the nights when Kristina and I lay in bed as I read her what I'd written and then I have the laptop in my hands ready to throw it.

I don't know how to stop my mind from racing with thoughts about her.

Slowly, I lower the laptop back down to my desk and close my eyes to concentrate on pushing all these thoughts out of my mind. Relax. Breathe. Let your mind release those thoughts and let them go.

I try, but nothing they said would work in rehab seems to be working now. Instead, all this relaxing and breathing is making me wish I had just a little junk to give me peace. That's not good.

Scotch is, though, and if that's what will help me forget Kristina and heroin for at least a little while, then scotch is just what I need. I pour myself a glass and instantly feel my body relax as the scent of the alcohol wafts up toward my nostrils. Good old scotch.

Three hours later, I've welcomed enough of my old friend back into my system that my mind isn't racing anymore. It's barely doing much of anything, but that's better than the alternative. Closing my eyes, I let the scotch slide down my throat and warm my insides as I lean back against my leather couch and look forward to the moment the alcohol knocks me out.

*I watch her walk toward me, her dark hair blowing in the cold October wind as she works to push it off her face. Flustered from her attempts to look like what she thinks is beautiful, she's more charming than she even knows. I want to take her in my arms right here on the sidewalk in front of my building and kiss her like she deserves to be kissed.*

*Long and deep and full of the love I feel for her.*

*"You didn't have to wait for me in this wind. It's like a tornado out here!" she says as she fusses with my collar.*

*I touch her hands. They feel like two blocks of ice. "Let's get upstairs. Your hands are cold."*

*She gives me a gentle smile. "You're so sweet. Do you have anything planned for us tonight?"*

*Sliding my tongue across my lips, I smile. "I do. Let's get upstairs so I can show you."*

*"I wish I could kiss you right here, you know that?" she whispers next to my cheek. "But the minute I do, you just know there will be someone with a camera right behind us."*

*I look around pretending to scope out any potential paparazzi. "I think we're in the clear. You've been laying low for a few months so the media has moved on to someone who can't keep their dirty laundry private."*

*Kristina leans away from me and knits her brows unhappily. "I don't consider you dirty laundry, Ian."*

"Well, I'm going to have to do something to change that," I say with a grin as I think about all the things I want to do to her as soon as we get upstairs.

"Let's go inside then and you can show me what you have planned."

I take her by the hand and tug her into the lobby of my building as Michael, the doorman, flashes me a knowing smile and gives me a nod. I feel like a teenager sneaking a girl into my parents' house. It's silly and stupid, but this is the effect she has on me.

Somehow this gentle soul makes my dark one lighter.

We make out in the elevator, and when the old woman from the floor above me gets on with us, there's no mistaking her look of disgust at our impropriety at kissing in public. Kristina hides her face in the collar of my wool jacket, but Mrs. Jenkins' judgment doesn't affect me. She never liked me anyway.

At least that's how I took her comment that one day that the only history worth any New Yorker's time was American history. As if studying and writing about anything older than the seventeenth century made me some kind of fucking literary criminal.

Crazy old bag.

We get off at my floor, but not before my neighbor shoots us another nasty look for having fun. She's lucky my hands are still cold or she would have gotten a real show since I can't keep them off Kristina.

As we head down my hallway, I say to her, "There's our future, you know that?"

Kristina turns toward me and shakes her head in disbelief. "Like her? I can't imagine either of us so miserable about other people's happiness."

*I unlock my front door and nod. "Age does things to people, I guess. Not that I can ever imagine cranky old Mrs. Jenkins as anything other than the person she is now. She was probably born old and crotchety."*

*Kristina giggles. "That would be one ugly baby, Ian."*

*Closing the door, I walk up behind her and slide my hands under her coat as I nuzzle her warm skin. "Enough talk about her. I've got much better things in mind."*

*"Like what?" she asks with a playful lilt to her voice.*

*She slips out of her coat, and I hang it up near the door. "I think we'll eat first and then I thought we'd relax. Maybe do a little research for something I want to put into the book."*

*Kristina gives me a knowing smile, but she has no idea what I mean. As I sat writing this afternoon while the wind blew and the raindrops hit the windows, I had an idea for a scene with Kate that I'm dying to try with my muse.*

*No woman I've ever known can play the coquette like Kristina, and my announcement about what I have planned for the night brings out the a flirtatiousness only she can carry off with a combination of demure looks and excitement in her soft blue eyes that telegraphs her desire for our time together to begin.*

*"What's for dinner?"*

*I trail my fingertip over the swell of her lower lip and suck it gently into my mouth before I pull away and say, "Fuck dinner. Follow me."*

*Taking her by the hand, I lead her to my bedroom. Of all the times we've been together on all the surfaces of my apartment, there's just one that we've never tried.*

*The bathroom. More specifically, the sunken bathtub.*

*I stop in the doorway and hear Kristina's sharp intake of*

breath as she first sees the bathroom. "I thought the bathroom I always use was impressive. What is this?"

"The couple who lived here before me had a thing for bathrooms. This was a third bedroom at one point, but they turned it into their own personal spa. I don't usually bother with it, but as I was writing this afternoon, I couldn't get the idea of you and me in that tub out of my head."

She steps into the room and slowly spins around trying to take in all the stunning design. I have to admit it's impressive. Black marble mixed with white subway tiles gives the room a sexy look. I may not need a bathroom like this, but I know luxury when I see it. A pristine white marble tub in the center of the room surrounded by a platform gives it a sunken tub feel all the way up here on the fourteenth floor.

Kristina's eyes light up as she spies the shower area. "Is that a rainfall shower? I saw that in a magazine once and swore I'd have one if I had to make fifty movies to get it."

I slip my arms around her waist and kiss her neck. "Yeah, but the scene I have in my mind takes place in the tub."

Her body melts into mine, and she leans her head back on my shoulder. "Why not both? Then you could choose between them and pick the one that works best."

"I like the way you think."

She turns in my hold and wraps her arms around my neck. "So how does this scene begin?"

Sliding her sweater dress over her head, I step back to admire her matching bra and garter belt. I swipe my tongue over my lips at the sight of Kristina so incredibly sexy and smile. "Just like this."

I unhook the fire engine red silk bra and let it slide to the marble floor, and she seductively removes her tights, garter belt, and red stiletto heels. Standing there in front of me, she's naked and more gorgeous than any woman I've ever seen in my life. My mind begins to fill with ideas that contradict the scene I'd created hours earlier, but that doesn't matter now.

"So now what happens?" she asks shyly. "How does the scene go?"

"I think we should forget all that and make it up as we go along."

Kristina bites her lower lip and smiles as her hands travel to unzip my fly. "Do you think we can improve on what you envisioned this afternoon? You are the author."

She palms my cock and strokes it as I struggle to control my desire to fuck her right there before we get anywhere close to the tub or the shower. Swallowing hard, I answer, "I think it might turn out to be even better."

"Mmmm…good. Did you happen to see me on my knees and sucking your cock when you thought about this scene?"

My eyes roll back in my head at the mere mention of her mouth on me, and nearly panting, I say, "No, but you see how improvising is making it better already?"

As she lowers herself to the floor, she licks her lips and nods. "Uh huh."

When she looks up at me with those big blue eyes so full of innocence and just a touch of bad girl, I almost come before she even slides her lips down my cock. Some women have that effect on a man, and Kristina is that woman for me.

Without another word, she wraps her hand around the base of my cock and sucks the head into her mouth with a whispersoft touch that makes my knees go weak. Her hand grips me as she strokes over my skin, sending the purest pleasure racing through my *body.*

*It's even better than I'd imagined hours earlier. It's heaven.*

*I watch her move her mouth and hand up and down me and for possibly the first time in my life, it's not just about how I physically feel. I know how tentative she still feels with this particular sex act, and still she willingly dropped to her knees to please me.*

The memory of that night hurts more now that I know whatever I was feeling was one-sided. It was all an act. She's moved on and all I'm left with is memories and missing her. I can't handle either of them.

I need something to make me forget, and scotch isn't doing it.

# CHAPTER TWO

## *Kristina*

THE CABBIE LOVES to chat to his fares, and for one of the few times in my life, I'm thankful for the distraction. Being back in New York brings all the memories of my time with Ian back with a vengeance, making me want to cry at how much I still miss him. I thought all the weeks apart while he was in Rome would help, but the loss of him in my life only gets worse every day I don't see him or hear him say one of those things that always sounded so perfect coming out of his mouth.

"The weather has been nightmarish, even for this city," the cabbie says as he weaves his way through Upper West Side traffic.

Considering it's rush hour, we're making great time, but I'm in no hurry to be back in my apartment. Too many memories there. I'll only be home for four days, and something tells me that will be too long knowing he's just a few blocks away.

"It's still better than Vancouver weather," I say as the cabbie continues to chatter on about the wind and rain the city has been getting pummeled with.

I cradle my signed copy of Caligula's Dream in my lap. Flipping to the page where Ian wrote that I was his greatest fan, I trace my fingertip over his handwriting, so strong and so masculine with its sharp angles and total lack of roundness.

I can't help but remember that first night at my apartment. He didn't know about any of the gossip that I was sure would make him not like me. Nothing about what had happened with John or all the awful things the tabloids had printed about me being so pathetic after he'd left me for that hotel slut.

None of it had mattered to Ian.

My cell phone rings as the cabbie begins to explain what he read in the Farmer's Almanac about how this winter is predicted to be a bad one for the northeast, but even my talking to someone else doesn't stop him from reporting what some groundhog or caterpillar thinks will happen over the next few months.

I answer it and see it's Cilla. "Hey you! Are you back in the Big Apple yet?"

"Hi Cilla. Yeah, I'm home for a few days. Are you here or in LA?"

She clucks her tongue like she's disgusted about what she's going to say next. "LA. But I should be back there in about a week."

"I'll be gone back to Vancouver by then."

In truth, I'm not really that disappointed I won't be able to see Cilla this week. She's never been very good at empathy, and with how I'm feeling about being back in New York, she'd just give me a hard time about being down. Even worse, she'd push and push to find out what's making me sad, which is something I definitely don't want to discuss with her.

Being upset about men isn't Cilla's style. She's more a buck-up-and-move-on type of girl.

"Aren't we just jet setters? Well, next trip then. Or I could come up to Vancouver to see you. Is it a nice city? Any good action going on up there?"

I think about what I know of the city of Vancouver. Not much. When I'm not on the set, I'm in my hotel room. Other than a few dinners out with my co-star Gavin, I haven't exactly been painting the town red.

"It's very nice there. Very hip. You might like it."

"That sounds like a pretty tepid endorsement, Kristina. Haven't you checked out the scene up there yet? You've been in the damn city for weeks."

Typical Cilla. Nothing, not even work, gets in the way of a good time for her.

"I've been a little busy. You know. With work."

I don't try to mask the sarcasm in my voice. Not that it would matter. Tone of voice isn't something she pays much attention to anyway.

"Work schmerk. You're in a major North American city, Kristina, and you're single. You should be getting out and enjoying life while you're there."

Her reminder that I'm not with Ian anymore makes my chest hurt for a moment. Taking a deep breath in, I lie, "Cilla, I'm just getting to my apartment now. Let me call you back, okay?"

"Sure! Talk to you later, hon!"

As I end the call and stuff my phone back into my purse, I look up to see the cabbie looking back at me in the rearview mirror. "We're a good five blocks from your place, miss."

I can't help but laugh. My cabbie is both weatherman and paternal figure condemning my lying to Cilla. "I know. I guess I just wanted to get off the phone."

We don't say anything more as he takes me to my place, but as I'm about to pay him the fare, he spies Ian's book in the crook of my elbow. Pointing to it, he says excitedly, "I love his books! I didn't know a thing about ancient Rome, but once I began to read him, I actually went to the library for the first time in like twenty years and got myself some books on that time period. Great stuff!"

I look down and see Ian's picture on the back cover, his face so serious as he looks at the camera. He's not like that, though. Not with me. That man is flat and somber. Ian isn't that man at all.

The urge to explain just how wonderful he is—how full of passion for his writing and for me he truly is—bubbles up inside me as the cabbie explains his favorite parts of Caligula's Dream, but I stop myself.

"He writes great books," I say, once again sounding tepid in my praise for something else. When did I become so bland?

"Have a good night."

Nodding, I grab my bag and head up the stairs to my building's front door, stopping for a moment as I unlock it to look around at the little patch of grass and trees across the street. I strain my eyes to scan the area for any sign of him. I'd so hoped beyond hope that he'd be waiting for me.

Waiting to see me.

But there's nothing but rain soaked, leafless trees and soon-to-be dead grass there.

I BARELY SET my bag down inside my apartment and I can't stand being there. Everything reminds me of how much I miss him, so I quickly leave, unsure of where I should go but desperate to find somewhere in this city that doesn't make me think of him.

The newsstand a block away is closing up as I approach it, but the man knows me from back before I ever made any hit movies, so he waves to me. He's holding something in his hand, and as I walk closer to him I see it's a magazine.

I don't remember Joanne mentioning any magazine covers coming out this month.

"Kristina Richards! How is my favorite famous movie star?"

Mr. Jacobs is a man in his sixties, I guess, with perfectly silver hair. He likes to tell stories of when his hair was black and the women fell at his feet back when he was young and before he married his wife. She's been dead for as long as I've known him, but he speaks about her like she's still at home waiting for him to return every night from his stand in my neighborhood.

"I'm fine. How are you, Mr. Jacobs?"

A huge grin spreads across his face as he holds up the magazine. On the cover is a picture of me looking pretty good considering I think it may have been taken after a long day of shooting. Above my head in bold capital letters are the words ACTRESS KRISTINA RICHARDS IN TORRID LOVE AFFAIR.

Instantly, I'm sick to my stomach as the thought of Ian seeing this races through my mind. Mr. Jacobs asks me who the lucky guy is, so I try to explain The Enquirer has it all wrong. There's no torrid anything in my life and no lucky guy. He arches his brow and gives me a skeptical look, saying, "You just don't want to tell an old man. I see."

Shaking my head, I say, "No, it's not that at all. How long has this been out?"

"About two days."

Now I'm sure Ian's seen it. I know he has. And I can only imagine how much it hurt when he did.

I have to go to him. I hurry off from the newsstand to his building, and as always, his doorman is happy to let me in. Worried how he may have reacted to seeing the headline, I ask, "Have you seen Mr. Anwell this evening?"

His usual jovial look fades a bit as he says, "He went up a few hours ago, miss."

I want to ask more about how he looked and how he seemed, but the doorman won't tell me. As I ride up in the elevator alone, my heart races at the thought of what I'll say when I finally see him. He's never texted or called after telling me goodbye, so would I find him with a new woman like last time trying to forget me again?

Barely able to keep myself from crying at the thought of finding him with someone else, I walk down his hallway to his door. Taking a deep breath, I knock and pray to God he'll answer and not have someone with him.

I knock three times, but nothing. Pressing my cheek to his door, I listen for any sounds inside, my heart slamming against my chest as the fear that he isn't alone settles into my mind. I hear nothing, though, so I knock again and say, "Ian, are you in there? Please open the door. It's Kristina."

What I get in response is silence. I put my mouth right up to the door and hope if he's inside he's listening. "Ian, I'm here. Please let me in."

Again, silence, but then I hear the door being unlocked. It

doesn't open, but I turn the doorknob and see he's at least letting me in. The lights are out and the place is dark except for the light of the TV on the far wall. This doesn't feel like his apartment at all. It's like a pall hangs over the place.

Softly, I ask, "Ian, where are you?"

He says nothing, but as I scan the room for him, I see something on the floor near the couch. Making my way in the dim light, I'm finally able to see now that my eyes have adjusted to the light.

It's him.

Sprawled out with a bottle next to him, he looks so different than I've ever seen him. His shirt is half unbuttoned and the shirt sleeves are rolled up past his elbows. In the dim light, I see him staring up at me with a hollow look in his eyes.

I crouch down in front of him and look closer. I've never seen him like this. He looks lost. Reaching out, I caress his cheek with my palm and feel the softness of his skin and the roughness of his beard just coming in.

"Oh, Ian…"

He doesn't move, but I feel his head press against my hand. Then he speaks, and I know he's seen the cover. "Why are you here? Don't you have some torrid love affair to attend to?"

Shaking my head, I try to put a happy face on while my heart is breaking to see him like this. "I missed you."

His words seem to get stuck when he tries to speak, but finally he says in a low voice full of pain, "Five weeks is all it took to forget me, I guess."

I can't stop the tears from welling in my eyes. He's done this to himself because I didn't go with him. No amount of explaining about my job or how important this role is to me will make up for lying and then letting him go. Even now, I realize for as much as this role means to my career, he means more to me than anything.

"Oh, Ian, that's not true." I hang my head and whisper, "I missed you so much. Please don't think I didn't."

In a strangled tone, he asks the question I don't want to answer. "Then why didn't you come to Rome?"

I fall to the floor in a crumbled heap. Unable to hold the tears back, I give him the only answer I can. "I never meant to hurt you. I swear I didn't."

"Well, you did."

He sounds so lonely and sad. I can't stand to hear him like this. I want to make things better, but it's like I can't reach him, even though he's sitting right next to me. It's like there's an invisible barrier between us.

I wrap my arms around his shoulders and pull him into me. He doesn't resist, but he doesn't hug me back either. In his ear, I plead, "Ian, don't shut me out. I'm here. Let me in."

"It's too late."

Leaning back away from him, I shake my head in disbelief. "No, it's not! Put your arms around me. I know you still care. If you don't still love me, then say the words. I won't believe it unless you say the words."

Ian says nothing, but I see something in his expression that tells me it isn't too late for us. I lift his hands to my mouth and kiss them, hoping for any real sign the man I love is still inside him.

"Kristina, you need to leave. I don't want you to see me like this."

Leaning my cheek against his palm, I'm confused by his

words. "What do you mean like this? Like what?"

He yanks his hands away from me and shakes his head violently. "Go away. Go back to your new boyfriend and be happy."

"There is no new boyfriend, Ian," I say as I try to pull him back toward me. I need to touch him, but he won't let me now. "I swear there's no one but you. Why won't you believe me?"

"Because you fucking let me go to Rome."

"Well, I'm not going anywhere now, so you're stuck with me."

I can't stand the distance between us even as I sit next to him. Climbing onto his lap, I fight against him pushing me away until he stops and stares up at me with so much hurt in his eyes that I almost need to turn away.

"You don't want me, Kristina. Not like this."

His head droops until his forehead presses against my shoulder. With a deep sigh, he finally wraps his arms around me and I feel his overwhelming sadness as he pulls me to him.

"Why wouldn't I want you, Ian? I love you. I wanted to go to Rome. I should have. I know that now. I'm sorry I lied. Please don't tell me to leave."

Ian lifts his head, and I see the misery in his eyes. I cradle his face and kiss him, letting all the weeks of missing him come out finally. When he kisses me back, I know how much we've both suffered. His kiss is filled with desperation as much as mine is, and for the first time since that night I met him at that bar, I feel like he truly needs me like I need him.

Closing his eyes, he leans his head back against the wall. "I don't want you to see me like this. You don't want this Ian."

"I want you. It doesn't matter who you are."

"No, you don't. I couldn't stand the pain and missing you, so I went back to it. To heroin. I just wanted to be able to forget."

His words come out practically as sobs that break my heart to hear. He's doing heroin again, and everything I said to him that night he told me about his addiction rings in my ears. But now as I sit here watching him in so much pain, I can't imagine leaving him.

I press my forehead to his. "I won't leave you. I promise."

"Why would you stay when you told me if I ever went back to using again you'd leave me?" he asks quietly.

"Because I love you."

"You won't love me like this, Kristina. You won't."

# CHAPTER THREE

## *Ian*

FOR THREE DAYS, Kristina's been here with me, but even that can't make me stop needing the shit I stick up my nose. I don't know why she stays. She shouldn't. She should stick by what she said to me that night I told her what I really am.

The problem is that last night I ran out, which leads to an entirely different problem. The heroin is bad enough. Withdrawal is so much fucking worse.

I lied to her and told her I'm done with the junk. The look of pure happiness she had when I said it made me wish more than anything else in this world that I could give it up.

But I can't. Not yet. Not now.

So this morning, I had my editor send one of his lackeys over with what looks like work but is really just a bag of poison. He's happy to hear I'm off the wagon again, so to speak, since misery always loves company.

And for a little while I'm okay, but like always, it's never enough. By the time Kristina realizes what I am, it will be too late. She'll already hate me so much she won't ever want to see me again. I know all this and still here I am hiding out in the bathroom snorting heroin while she takes a shower in the bathroom down the hall.

I sit back on the tile floor to wait for that feeling to come over me. It doesn't take a half hour like it used to. Maybe that's because I've been clean for nearly a year, but this time it hits me almost immediately. Or maybe I've lost track of time.

I don't know. All I know is that when it hits me and that feeling of euphoria comes over me, I can't think of anything but how much I love feeling like this. No pain. No worries. Nothing but pure bliss.

Only being with Kristina comes close to this, but now that I've got heroin again, even she can't equal this feeling of happiness and contentment. I wish I could feel bad about that, but in this state, no way.

When I'm like this, nothing can bother me.

"Ian, I'm out of the shower. Are you in there?"

I clean up as quickly as possible and stuff the baggie into my back pocket as I open the bathroom door to see Kristina standing there looking so fresh and sweet. God, I love her.

"Have a good one?" I ask, hoping she doesn't recognize how fucked up I am at the moment.

She giggles. "A shower? I guess. You could have come in if you needed to go to the bathroom. I don't want to monopolize it."

Shaking my head, I smile. "That's what I have two for."

We stand there in silence for a moment as she seems to study me. She's not stupid. After she found me sitting on the floor high, she naturally suspects that even though I say I'm not doing it anymore, I likely am. What she probably can't figure out is how I got it.

Good people like her don't suspect how manipulative and devious people like I can be when we want it.

"What are you planning to do today?"

I pull her to me and nuzzle her neck, knowing that it's a fifty-fifty shot if I can even fuck when I'm this high. I want to, though. I want to be buried in her wet cunt or have her down on her knees sucking my cock right there in the doorway.

"Don't know, but I have some ideas about what I want to do now."

We haven't made love since she came here three days ago, so my newfound desire for her pleases her more than I imagined. Running her hands down the front of my pants, she unzips them and takes my semi-hard cock in her palm, stroking it from base to tip. I might not be able to get a hard on like this, but the touch of her hand on my skin feels fucking incredible, like every sensation is twenty times more pleasurable than ever before.

Kristina looks down at my hardening cock and licks her lips. "Follow me."

Taking my hand, she leads me to the bedroom, and as I watch mesmerized by how much I love her, she slips out of her clothes and beckons me to her. By the time I reach the bed, I'm out of my own clothes and my cock is more than willing, but I can't be sure if I have to face her while we make love that she won't realize I'm high.

So even though I know it may still upset her, I roll her over on her stomach to take her from behind. She doesn't say a thing and angles her ass high in the air so her pussy is right there for me.

I stuff my hand in her hair and tug her up off the bed as the first inches of my cock are swallowed by her willing cunt. She's hot and wet and all mine.

In her ear, I groan, "God, I fucking need you, Kristina." I mean more than just to fuck her, but at that moment, she thinks it's just sex talk and moans as the base of my cock pushes up against her body, fully nested inside her.

She's as eager to please me as ever, so once I establish a rhythm in and out of her, she begins her own, meeting my thrusts as she pushes back against me. I love this about Kristina. Whatever we are when my cock is buried inside her isn't just me fucking her but the two of us together moving toward that sweet moment of oblivion when her cunt contracts around me and I flood her with cum.

As I think about all of this, she moans, "Ian, I want it faster. And harder."

Gripping her sides, I ram my hips forward and fill her fast and hard, just as she asked. She gasps but after a moment repeats for me to go faster and harder, pushing back against me as I remain inside her.

As much as I can in my state, I fuck her exactly how she wants it. Her hands grasp at the sheets and she moans over and over as I inch her closer to her release. I feel her body begin to surrender to my invasion, the walls of her cunt gently squeezing around my cock as she orgasms harder than I've ever felt her come before.

"Ian, don't stop! Please don't stop!"

I don't and she continues to shake from coming until I finally pull out, still hard since I haven't come yet. Heroin may make the sensations of sex one hundred percent better, but coming isn't one of those parts that are improved.

Kristina collapses on the bed and rolls over to look up at me. Her expression tells me I satisfied her, but when her gaze falls on my still hard cock, she frowns. "You didn't come. Why?"

I can't tell her the truth, so a little white lie has to serve. "I wanted you to suck me off. You know I like that."

Her frown disappears, replaced by a sexy, devilish grin. "I do. You like to see me taste myself on you, don't you?"

I nod and pull her up toward me, loving the idea of her mouth around my shaft. I still might not get off, but the feeling of her soft lips and tongue riding up and down my cock will still be incredible.

She kisses me so full of love that for a fleeting moment I hate that I'm lying to her as she lowers herself to take my cock inside her mouth. Kneeling in front of me, she looks up and runs her tongue over her lower lip, like she's dying to taste something she loves. Pulling her hair off her face, I close my fist around it while I gently caress her gorgeous mouth that in the next moment I'll fill with my cock.

Any regret for what I've done vanishes the second she gently sucks the head and moans against my skin, sending the most exquisite sensations up and down my shaft. I pull her down hard on me until she's taken every inch and I'm bumping up against the back of her throat. She never closes her eyes as I fuck her mouth just like I fucked her pussy.

I want to come. I want to fill her mouth until cum oozes out the sides and drips down her chin like beautiful lines of white love she gives me. My brain wants to, but my body has other ideas because of the heroin.

Kristina sucks my cock like every stroke down my shaft

brings her happiness. Her blue eyes stare up at me waiting for the moment when I look like my release is just upon me, but no matter how long she tries, my body isn't letting it happen.

I massage her jaw, knowing she's hurting, but I don't stop her. I'm selfish and a fucked up prick for not letting her just sit back and have her orgasm without me having one, but I don't push her away. Instead I watch in wonder as her head bobs up and down into my crotch, and with each pass I know it's hopeless.

The junk has taken away another good thing.

Finally, she looks up at me with hurt in her eyes like she's done something wrong or she's deficient and that's why I haven't come. I shake my head and ease out of her mouth as that twinge of regret finds its way back into my mind.

"I thought you liked how I do that," she says in a sweet voice that makes my heart feel like someone's run it through.

"I do. I just can't now," I answer in the kindest voice I can give.

"Oh. Why?"

I look away, afraid she can see the truth written all over my face. I've never felt so bad when I was high. Was that stuff my editor sent over shit?

"Ian, look at me. What's going on? Is there someone else you haven't told me about?"

Jesus, the pain in her voice is killing me. I can't do this. "Kristina, it's nothing."

The silence that follows makes the room feel like she and I are miles apart and she's receding more and more every second. I can't look at her and see the hurt in her eyes, so I just keep my head hung and wait for her to say something.

Anything but that she needs the truth.

But she doesn't need it. She already knows. "You didn't stop, did you?"

Again, silence, but this time it's me who can't bring myself to say the words. Instead, I just shake my head.

A sound like a gasp is all I hear, and then the bed moves as she stands up. I turn to see her getting dressed.

"Kristina," I begin, but stop, knowing she doesn't deserve some watered down excuse for why I'm like this.

"I should have done what I said I would when you told me what you were. I couldn't, though, so I stayed and believed you. What a fool I am! I've seen this so many times and still I thought you'd give it up for me."

"Don't," is all I can get out. I don't want her blaming herself. She isn't the fucked up one.

"Don't what? Don't feel like an idiot that I believed you and went against everything I knew I should do?"

I sit back against the headboard and close my eyes. I don't want her to blame herself. I just don't know what to say. It's sad, really. A fucking author who can't find the words he needs to say to say to the woman he loves.

"I know you said you'd leave, but don't. Stay. Show me you love me enough to stay."

The sound of her pants rustling as she pulls them on makes me open my eyes, and suddenly, I see her lunging toward me on the bed. Before I can lift my arms, she's on top of me swinging her arms wildly. Her delicate fists hit my face as she sobs words I can't understand.

I deserve whatever she does to me, so I don't try to grab her wrists to stop her. Maybe if she hits me hard enough or I have to watch her cry for long enough I'll finally get it through my head that I shouldn't be a slave to this shit I crave even now.

"Why, Ian? Why would you do this? Am I so unimportant to you that you'd pick drugs over me?"

Her beautiful mouth—the mouth that made me want her from the moment I first laid eyes on her on my television screen—twists into a terrible frown as the tears roll down her cheeks from those cornflower blue eyes I love so much. Her face looks ravaged by sadness.

Sadness I caused her.

"I don't want to do this, Kristina. Believe me. I want to stop."

At the moment I say that, I mean every word. I do. I just can't see how I'll stop, though. It's been only a few weeks, and all the progress I made over the past nine months is all but lost.

"I can't stay here with you. I can't watch you throw your life away, Ian."

She moves to leave, but I can't let her. I can't lose her.

Grabbing her arm as she crawls off the bed, I stare up into those gorgeous eyes so full of pain and worry I can't change her mind. Like when she was sitting there on the floor with me the night she came back, it feels like we're miles apart.

I'm losing her.

"Please don't leave. I'll stop. I swear I will. Tell me what I have to do and I'll do it. Just don't leave."

She shakes her head and begins to cry again. "I can't tell you what to do. That you don't know if you do this you'll lose me tells me all I need. I have to go."

Yanking her hand from my hold, she runs out of the room as I scramble to my feet. I reach her just as she hits the front door, and knowing this might be my last chance to ever convince her I love her, I wrap my arms around her and hold her tight.

"Let me go! I can't do this, Ian! I can't!"

She writhes in my hold and I barely hang on, but finally she stops and collapses against my chest, sobbing, "I can't do this with you. I love you too much to see you ruin us like this."

"Stay with me, Kristina. I'm begging you. Stay even though I'm fucked up. Stay even though I made the biggest mistake and you think you can't forgive me. Just stay."

For the longest moment, she says nothing and all I can think is I've lost her. I laid it all on the line and still she won't stay.

She begins to push against my hold, but instead of leaving she turns around to face me. Her cheeks are tear stained, her eyes rimmed with red, but I see love in them still.

"Why can't I leave you? Why after all these weeks without you does the thought of losing you now make me feel like I'm losing part of myself?"

I cradle her beautiful, sad face and nod because I know exactly what she feels. The mere thought of my life without her in it is too much to bear. Leaning forward, I kiss her with all the desperation inside me and when I finally pull away, I wipe her tears and say, "Because you love me as much as I love you."

"We're a mess, Ian. This love is crazy and hurts so much that I don't think I can go on."

"Stay even though everything you know about me is bad."

Closing her eyes, she presses her forehead to mine. "You aren't bad, Ian. I don't know why you're like this, but you're not bad."

"I'll stop. Don't leave me. I can do this. I can quit it."

"Oh, Ian, what if we can't get through this? What if this is just who you are?"

Pulling her to me, I kiss the top of her head. "I can't believe that. I love you, Kristina. Since the moment I met you, I've been crazy about you."

She hugs me and whispers, "I don't know what to do. I love you so much, but this scares me. You won't pick me when it comes down to it."

"I will. I'm picking you right now. Stay with me no matter what I become, and I promise when this is all over we'll have a new start."

She kisses me with such sadness I'm sure the next word out of her mouth will be goodbye. But then she smiles sweetly and I believe I can give up the junk for her.

# CHAPTER FOUR

## *Kristina*

NEVER BEFORE IN my life have I been so certain I was making the wrong choice, and still I don't leave. I look into those nearly jet black eyes staring at me so desperately as Ian waits to hear he hasn't lost me and I can't.

I can't leave him. Whatever this is between us—love, lust, or obsession—I need it. I need him. For the past five weeks I've walked around feeling like part of me had been torn out and what was left when I looked down at my phone and saw him tell me goodbye was an emptiness inside that ached day and night.

But he won't choose me over the drugs. I knew that when I told him I would leave, and I know that now as he pleads for me to stay.

And still I can't say goodbye.

I push his unruly black hair off his forehead and sigh. "I've never been so sure of anything in my life as I am right now that you're going to break my heart."

"Give me the chance to prove you wrong."

Looking down, I can't help but smile. He's naked at his front door begging me to stay. But then I remember he snuck that terrible junk in and it's still somewhere in his apartment. Angrily, I say, "You need to get rid of any you have left, or I'm gone. Period."

He nods, but I can see he won't be able to throw it out. "I don't want this job, Ian, but if I'm going to stay, I'm staying on my terms. That leaves or I leave."

His hand slides down my arm, and he weaves his fingers in mine as he leads me back to the bedroom. Pointing at his pants, he says quietly, "Back pocket. And there's probably a tiny bit left on the edge of the tub in the bathroom."

A surge of anger races through me as I remember standing in the doorway to that bathroom after my shower feeling all clean and fresh and ready to spend the day with him and all the while he was high already. I reach down and find a plastic baggie with white powder in the back pocket of his pants.

"This is it?"

"Yeah," he says in a strained voice as he stares at it in my hand.

"Fine."

Turning on my heels, I walk to the bathroom that until now had held the memory of that incredibly sexy lovemaking session we'd had that one night. From this point on, now that will be joined by the memory of me scrubbing the edge of a fucking bathtub so he can't find any more of his drugs on it.

I flush the powder down the toilet and clean the tub from top to bottom like I've never cleaned before in my life. I'm like a woman on a mission as I scrub and scrub that white marble tub until my right bicep feels like it's going to blow out of my arm. With each push of the sponge, my hair swings in my eyes, and for a moment I remember the bathroom cleaning scene in the movie Mommy Dearest as Faye Dunaway scours that tile floor while her poor little daughter watches on in horror.

The sound of Ian's footsteps on the tile as he enters the bathroom takes me out of my daydreaming, and as I wash away the last of the cleanser from the edge of the tub, I can't help but say, "Some glamourous life of a movie star, huh?"

"I'm sorry, Kristina."

I think he's genuine when he says that. I do. I just don't know if it matters much. I dry my hands on a towel and see my fingertips are all pruney like they used to get when I was a little girl and spent too much time in the bath at night.

Ian looks lost, like he doesn't know what to do with himself. Is he unsure what to do because of how angry I seem or because he's craving more of the heroin I just flushed down the toilet? As if he's reading my mind, he says as he takes my hand to kiss the back of it, "I don't know what to do when you're like this."

"Like what, Ian? Hurt? Angry? Worried that the minute I turn my back on you that you're going to have some guy come to the front door pretending to deliver something from that fuck of an editor?"

Letting my emotions out should make me feel better, but the sad look in his eyes just makes me feel terrible for being so angry at him. Hanging my head, I admit, "I'm no good at this. That's why I told you I'd leave if you went back to doing drugs. I'm not kind enough or sympathetic enough to be what you need now."

"You're exactly what I need now. I don't need someone to believe my lies when I say I don't want heroin more than anything else in the world at this moment. I don't need someone who's worried about hurting my feelings. I need you to kick my ass and make this real for me because if you don't, I won't be able to do this."

I sit on the damp edge of the tub and look up at him. "Do you really want to keep doing that more than anything?"

His expression twists into a grimace, like what I said hurt him, and he nods. "Yeah. That's how it is with me and heroin. Nearly a year without it, and now all I want is more."

"More than me," I say sadly, hating the truth.

Ian takes my hands in his and squeezes them. "No, not more than you. It's not the same. I love you. I need you. That shit fucks me up and takes control of me. You make me happier than I've ever been before in my life."

"You said you were addicted to me. Why can't you want me more than you want this?"

I sound childish and naïve, but that's how I feel. The fact that he could feel more for some white powder in a plastic bag than he feels for me is tearing me up inside. No matter how I try, I can't understand how that could be.

He gently pushes my hair out of my eyes and bends down to kiss my forehead as he whispers, "I hate that my weakness makes you doubt yourself. Don't do that."

I hang my head, and he pulls me to him to hold me. With my cheek pressed against his side, I tell him the truth. "I love you, Ian, but this hurts so much. Why did you have to go back to that awful stuff?"

As he gently strokes my hair, he says, "I'm an addict, and I turned to the one thing that I knew could take the pain away. I'm sorry, baby. I'm so sorry I'm like this."

Looking up at him, I see he's hurting still. "Why didn't you just call me? I would have taken the pain away."

"You were the reason I was in pain. I missed you so much while I was in Italy and couldn't deal with it, and then when I saw that magazine that said you were in a torrid love affair, I just wanted to forget. I just wanted to close my eyes and not hurt anymore."

Tears fill my eyes as I say, "There's no one else, Ian. Not since the day we met. You're all I think about, even during those five weeks after you said goodbye."

"I'm sorry, Kristina. I was just so torn up by how easy it seemed for you to let me go…"

Before he can finish what he's saying, I stand and shake my head at how wrong he is. "It wasn't easy to let you go to Italy without me. I wanted to go, but Joanne found out what I was planning and I couldn't. I know I should have, but I wanted this part so badly." I stop and take a deep breath. "Oh, what does it matter now? If I didn't stay, if you didn't go. It doesn't matter anymore."

He cradles my face in his hands and stares down into my eyes with so much regret that my chest tightens at seeing him like this. "I did this to us. You didn't do anything wrong. I wanted to think you did because you chose something over me, but you're here with me and I don't want to think about the mistakes we've made or the time we've lost."

"But what happens now?" I ask, almost afraid to know the answer.

"I'm going to have to kick this, but it's going to be hard for you. Everything about me is going to be nothing but bad, but I swear if you stay, I'll stop."

"Hard for me? Why?"

"I'm not going to look or act like myself as this poison leaves me. I'm going to want it more than anything, and when I can't have it, I'm going to get ugly. I just want to tell you now that I love you and when I say those things that hurt you, it's not me talking. It's the addiction."

I don't know if I can handle what he's going to be like, but I don't have a choice. I love him.

✧   ✧   ✧

WITHIN TWO DAYS, I see firsthand the ugly Ian had promised. Already in withdrawal, he looks like a twisted, horrific version of himself. I roll over as I wake in the morning and see him staring not at me but at the wall. His eyes look wild, and his skin glistens with a layer of sweat, even though it's winter outside and no warmer than seventy degrees in his apartment.

Reaching out, I go to push his hair off his damp forehead and feel his skin. It's cold even as he lies there sweating on top of the blankets. My touch makes him cringe, as if anything on his skin hurts.

"Ian, tell me what I'm supposed to do. You look so lost and in so much pain."

"Just don't go. This isn't too bad yet. When it gets bad, please don't leave me here alone or I'll find some way to get more so I don't have to go through this."

"How long will this last?"

Frowning, he shakes his head. "I don't know. A few days, maybe. I only used for a short time this time, so maybe it won't be so long. I've never stopped without going to rehab, though, so I don't know."

He curls up next to me, and I want to take him in my arms and never let him go he looks so broken and hurt. Over and over, he begs me not to leave. "I'm not going anywhere, Ian. I promise."

I gently pull him to me and he whispers so quietly against my shoulder that I can barely hear him, "I can't do this alone. Please don't leave me."

There in his bed as I lie with him in my arms, I promise him something I've never been able to promise anyone else before. "No matter what, I'll be strong for you. I won't leave you."

For hours, I stay beside him as he shakes almost uncontrollably one minute and then seems so tired he can't even keep his eyes open the next. I've never seen him so vulnerable and weak, and all I want to do is keep my promise to him to be the strength he needs.

But that part of me that's never been strong makes me doubt I can do this.

As it begins to get dark outside, Ian slowly opens his eyes and I see the fear and pain he's going through in them. "Every inch of my body hurts. I can't take this pain, baby."

"It won't be for long," I whisper as he curls up next to me, shivering even as his skin is hot against mine. "I promise it won't be for much longer."

That promise is one I can't keep because I have no idea how long he'll be like this. Even worse, my phone has been vibrating every hour on the hour, and I know it's my agent wanting to know why I'm not back in Vancouver on the set. I've avoided her all day, but I can't ignore her forever.

"I'm so thirsty. Can you get me a glass of water?"

"Okay. I'll be right back," I say as I cover him with the sheet and blanket. As I leave, I grab my phone to call Jennie and try to figure out how I'm going to explain to her that I can't go back yet.

That Ian needs me more than I need any role, and I won't leave him now.

Alone in his living room, I dial her number and prepare myself for the lecture I'm bound to get. Looking out the floor to ceiling windows that show me the city below, I hear the panic in her voice as she answers.

"Kristina, where are you? I've been calling you all day. You were supposed to be back on set this afternoon, but they say you aren't there. What's going on?"

"Jennie, I can't explain everything, but I'm not going to be able to leave New York just yet. I need you to make some excuse so I can stay here and still be able to go back to the set when I can."

"What? You have to get back there, Kristina. An entire production can't shut down for just nothing."

I look around to make sure Ian is still in the bedroom and whisper, "This isn't nothing. Someone I care about a great deal needs my help, and I can't abandon them now. Please, I'm begging you. I need you to help me. Just tell them I need a little more time. Make something up."

"Kristina, is this the torrid love affair guy from the magazine article?"

I think about Ian going through withdrawal in his bedroom and try to remember when we were torrid lovers. Smiling, I say to her, "Yes. I can't leave him now. He needs me, and I can't let him down. So tell them I'll be back in a few days more."

Jennie lets out a big sigh. "I hope you know what you're doing, honey. Okay, I'll tell them you're sick. Everyone gets sick, right? I'll say it's the flu and you're laid up sick as a dog."

"Tell them whatever you have to. I promise I'll be back in Vancouver within the week, okay?"

"Okay. Take care of yourself, Kristina. I don't want to see you get hurt."

"Thank you, Jennie. Don't worry about me. I'll be okay."

I press END and let out a sigh of relief. At least I have a few more days to be there for Ian before I'll have to return to the set. I have no idea what will happen in that time, but I can't leave him in the state he's in now.

"Kristina! Where are you?" he says in a voice more like a groan as I walk back to the bedroom with his glass of water.

I stop in the doorway at the sight of him sitting on the edge of the bed. His black hair hangs in damp clumps over his face, and his shoulders hunch over as if he's holding the weight of the world on them. His breath is coming in shallow pants, and I worry that something has happened in the few minutes I was away.

Hurrying to his side, I sit down next to him and practically feel the waves of misery coming off him. "What happened? Why aren't you in bed?"

"I was thirsty, and I didn't know where you went or if you were still here at all. I wanted to get a drink, but when I stood up, my legs gave out."

He turns to look at me and spies the glass of water in my hand. Reaching out for it, he shakes so badly I'm sure he'll drop it if I let go, so I hold it to his lips and tilt it back slightly so only a tiny bit flows into his mouth. I pull the glass away, but he grabs my hand and gently squeezes it.

"I'm so thirsty. A little more."

"It's okay. Just let me hold it. You're too weak from being in bed for so long."

Ian takes another small gulp of water, and as I take the glass away, he looks over at me and gives me a gentle smile. "I'm weak because my body is craving that poison, Kristina. You don't need to sugarcoat it."

I nod to show I understand, but I truly don't. I want to help him through this, but I'm so ignorant of everything he's feeling.

"I didn't mean to..." I let my thought trail off because I don't know what to apologize for. Instead, I press a smile onto my lips and try to sound as happy as possible, hoping that helps in some small way. "Let's get you back into bed."

He doesn't fight my suggestion, although I'm not even sure being in bed is helpful in his condition. I help him back under the covers and crawl under them myself, suddenly more tired than I've been in years.

"Are you feeling better now?" I ask as he rests his head on the pillow next to me.

Knitting his brows, he frowns at my question. "No. Worse, actually."

I press the back of my hand to his forehead and feel his skin dry and cool for the first time in hours. "You don't feel hot anymore."

As I pull my hand away, he holds it and presses his dry lips to my fingertips in a kiss. Then he looks at me with those dark eyes that still seem so lost and says, "I don't have the twenty-four hour flu, baby."

"I know. I mean, I don't know what to say here. I don't know what you're going through, so I don't know how to act," I explain, barely holding back the emotional tidal wave inside me.

"You don't have to act any way other than who you naturally are. I love you for not leaving, even though you never signed on for this with me."

My conversation with Jennie weighs on my mind as I watch him struggle to relax. He tosses and turns in what looks like agony over and over, and then just when I think it can't get any worse, he stumbles from the bed to the bathroom and makes a retching noise so terrible I jump up and run to see if he's still alive.

What I see is so much worse than everything I've watched him go through already. On his knees and holding onto the bowl of the toilet, he vomits for nearly ten minutes straight, his shoulders and back violently undulating with each heave. I stand behind him rubbing his skin and ready to help, but I can't do this.

I'm not enough. He needs more than I can give him.

Ian finally sits down on the floor and leans back against the vanity. Clearly exhausted, he looks like a shell of the man I met a few months ago as he wipes his mouth clean. I can't watch him like this anymore. It's breaking my heart.

I sit on the floor next to him and take his hand, knowing what I have to say next isn't what he wants to hear. But it's what he needs to hear. So with my emotions ready to boil over, I say quietly, "I'm not what you need, Ian. You're not going to get better like this, are you?"

Hanging his head, he slowly shakes his head. "No."

"We need to get you better, baby, so tell me what you need me to do so that can happen. Wherever you need to go, I'll get you there."

His voice raspy, he says, "Meadowbrook. My agent knows all the details. Get me my phone, please?"

I get him the cell phone and watch as he calls her to let her know he's messed up again. The pain and regret in his voice is almost too much to bear, but from what I can hear of his side of the conversation, she's understanding.

Ian hands me the phone and buries his face in his hands. My eyes fill with tears as before me what's left of him falls apart. Taking him in my arms, I feel the sadness he can't keep in anymore as his body sags against mine.

"I'm sorry, Kristina. I'm so sorry."

"Don't worry. You'll get better, and by the time you get home, I'll be back and we can pick up where we left off before all that Rome stuff and this happened."

I want so much to be able to put all that behind us, even as the fear that we can't sits in the back of my mind terrifying me. He looks up at me and all I want to do is take his pain away.

"I love you. Forgive me."

Holding him to me, I know he loves me as I love him. But is that enough? After everything we've been through, is love enough?

# CHAPTER FIVE

## *Ian*

I STEP OUT into the January chill of northern Arizona and shield my eyes from the sun beaming down on the front of Meadowbrook Drug Rehabilitation Center. Six weeks of no drugs or alcohol seems to have made me as sensitive to sunlight as a vampire, and I step back into the building to wait for Sheila, happy to be finally going home.

She's been her usual wonderful self during all of this. Somehow, she's found a way to keep my current stint in rehab off the radar of my publishers and virtually every other person on earth. I don't know how she does it, but without her, I'd be lost.

And Kristina.

Some days, the only way I got through the hours without going clear out of my fucking mind was reading her letters to me. Every week, she sent me two. The first always sounded upbeat and sweet, and the second always sounded like she felt like I did.

Like she didn't know if she could go on being there while I was here.

Just knowing I wasn't alone in this kept me sane when all I

wanted to do was unravel and never come back from it. My Kristina. After watching me hit rock bottom, she was the one who'd been brave enough to see I couldn't shake my addiction without more help than she could give me. I couldn't see that, but she could.

I love her for that and everything else she's given me.

I'm ready to return to her and make up for all the bad I've done. Running my hand through my hair, I take a deep breath and love how good I feel. Healthy and good, just like she deserves.

All her letters are stored in the bag I brought with me here, and I open it up to read her last letter she sent just two days ago. Full of love and her worry for me, I cherish it like every other one she sent.

*Dear Ian,*

*As I sit here hundreds of miles away from where you are, I feel like I'm missing a part of me. I know you had to go there, but I can't tell you how lonely I feel. Every day I say my lines and deliver a performance I try to be proud of, but I don't have you to share it with. I wish you were here so every night we could lie in bed and I could tell you all about my day. I so wish I could see the proud look in your eyes.*

*And then I think of everything you're going through there and feel ashamed that I'm here at all. How could I have ever thought this role was more important than you?*

*I believe in us, Ian. I know it's been hard, and you still have a little more to go through, but I know when we're finally together again, all the bad we've had to deal with will fade away as long as we remember we love each other.*

*The next time I see you will be like the first time. Do you remember that night at Jax's? I can't wait for that moment when I get to look into your dark eyes and feel that thrill I felt that first night we met. I'll see you soon, baby. Until then, I love you and can't stop thinking about you.*

*Love,*
*Kristina*

I fold her letter and slip it back into the envelope as I think back to our first night, smiling at the memory of how much I wanted her even then. Since that first moment when she became more than just a face on the screen, I've loved her.

"Mr. Anwell?"

I look up and see one of the facility's staff members smiling down at me. "Yes?"

"Your ride is here. It's time to go."

Sheila walks through the front doors and comes toward me with her arms open. I think she might even be happier than I am that I'm finally leaving. "Ian, you look wonderful!"

For once, I think the same about her. She's wearing jeans and a grey sweater, a look that's quite casual for her but one that she wears well. When she releases me from her hug, I say, "You look great too, Sheila. Decidedly unprofessional for once, and it looks good on you."

She rolls her eyes and blushes. "On top of getting clean, they gave you even more personality. I approve."

Grabbing my bag, I chuckle. "Well, this place is the best in the country."

"I have so much to tell you. While I was busy hiding all of this from New York, I've been greasing all sorts of wheels for your career. I'll tell you all about it on the plane ride back. For now, we need to go or we're going to be stuck in the desert, and this is definitely not the place for me. Way too dry here."

"I don't want to stay another minute longer than I have to. I've got too much to go back home for," I say as we walk out to the cab.

Sheila winks at me as we climb into the back seat and drive away. "Does this have anything to do with that woman who was at your place the day I came to take you here?"

"Yeah, it does. I didn't just get clean for me but for her too."

"I've never heard you talk about anyone like that, Ian, and I've known you for years. I like hearing you say things like that."

"You never know. All this happiness might make me lose my edge," I joke, hoping to lighten things up a bit.

Sheila shakes her head and puts on a serious look. "No, it's not like that. When you're really happy in life, you can do anything, and that includes writing another fantastic book."

"I had no idea you were such a romantic. I thought you were only a literary agent shark."

"I'm not kidding, Ian. I hope you have some happiness. You deserve it. Maybe being with this woman will help you silence your demons."

Her reference to my drug use does what my kidding couldn't, and suddenly, the mood between us turns more serious than ever before. I owe Sheila everything, and it's time I told her that.

"I can't thank you enough for what you did. Every time, I mean. You've been so much more than just an agent, and I don't tell you that enough."

"You're a great talent, Ian. It's my job to make sure you have what you need to nurture that talent."

"You know that's not all you do, so don't try to be humble. I wouldn't be alive today if you hadn't been there to save me from myself all these times when I got lost in that shit. I owe you everything. I just wanted to say thank you."

She gets all choked up and looks away out her window. A few seconds later when she's composed herself, she turns back to look at me. "Do you know that's the first time you've ever said anything like that to me? Not that I need to hear it, but it's nice."

"I should have said that a long time ago. Thanks for not giving up on me."

"Me give up on my favorite author? Never. But even though I've said this before, I mean it. I hope I never have to do that again."

"Never again. I promise. This time was worse than any other time before. I can't keep being that person anymore."

"You've got a lot to be thankful for, Ian. I hope you remember that the next time those demons make you think that horrible stuff will make you happy."

"I promise. No more."

Sheila looks genuinely thrilled to hear me swear I won't go back to heroin again, but even more, I'm happy to say the words and truly mean them.

✦ ✦ ✦

I LEAVE HER in the back of the cab outside my building and see the doorman standing at the front door ready to greet me with a smile. "Mr. Anwell, it's wonderful to see you."

"Thank you, Michael. It's good to be home."

I called Kristina when we landed, but my call went directly to voicemail. The flight got in early, so I'm about an hour ahead of my scheduled time to get home. Once I get settled in, I'll call her again because I'm dying to see her.

Unlocking my apartment door, I smell her perfume as soon as I walk in. It's been weeks and still she's right there with me. I put my bag down and head toward the couch, needing to relax after the flight back. I take a deep breath, loving the scent of her and the memories it brings back, and close my eyes. Soon we'll be back together again.

A noise down the hall makes me sit up, but before I can move to check it out, I see her walk into my living room like an angel appearing just for me. As she walks toward me, I'm speechless at how happy I am to see her.

Kristina looks down toward her hands as she fidgets with them. "I thought I'd surprise you and be waiting for you when you opened the door, but then you got back early and I didn't want to frighten you."

"It's okay. Come here. I missed you so much. I just want to feel you in my arms."

She steps forward, and I envelop her in a hug that I never want to end as she sobs, "Oh, Ian, you look so wonderful! Are you...better?"

"I am," I say, unable to keep the smile from my face as I

look at her. "You're such a sight for sore eyes. I've missed you, Kristina."

Leaning back, she cradles my face and stares into my eyes, as if trying to make up for all the lost time between us. "Every night I thought about you and how much I wished you were lying there next to me. I was so lonely without you."

"No more lonely nights. I promise. I'm done with all of it. I swear."

"I was so worried that you wouldn't be able to forgive me for not being what you needed," she says sadly. "I wanted to be, Ian. I did. I just wasn't enough."

"This was never meant to be on your shoulders, Kristina. It was unfair of me to ask you to help me."

"But I wanted to! I did. I just wanted to be strong for you, but I wasn't enough."

I shake my head and pull her close. "No more about not being enough. You're always just what I need, and you did for me what I couldn't do. You saw what I wouldn't. Without you, I don't know what would have happened, so no more about not being enough."

Quietly, we stand there in each other's arms and together find again what has always been so much a part of us. With each minute that passes, the passion and need we brought out in one another returns, and as I look down into those beautiful blue eyes, I know I'm home.

"Tonight, I'm going to begin making up for all the lost time. I'm going to worship you like you deserve, showing you how much I adore you, Kristina, and when I'm done, I'm going to start all over again so I can be sure you know I love you."

"I love the way you always know the perfect words to say.

From the first moment we met, I've loved that. And I love you, Ian, with all my heart. I swear I do."

There in her eyes I see that same look I saw the night I went with that woman. Fear and insecurity stare back at me. But she doesn't have to worry. There is no one and nothing else I love more, and tonight I'll show her that.

Dipping my head, I nuzzle the tender skin under her left ear and whisper, "I could use a long shower. Let's get this reunion started off fresh and clean."

She smiles and I take her by the hand to lead her to the bathroom where I watched her scrub away the last remnants of my demons. She gently squeezes my hand as we walk into the room, a sign she hasn't forgotten that awful day, but I want her to see that man is no more and the Ian who stands before her is the man she fell in love with.

"It's okay. Trust me?"

Her cornflower blue eyes grow wide for a moment and she nods, giving me a tiny smile I know masks her uncertainty. "I do trust you, Ian. I just…this room only makes me think of that day."

As I slide her dress down her body, I kiss the soft skin of her shoulders and assure her I intend to change her mind about this place. "I promise after tonight this room will only have the sweetest, most exquisite memories for you."

Her dress pools at her feet, leaving her standing in just black stiletto leather boots and a garter belt. God, she knows how to make me want her!

"I wanted to dress like I did that first night. You like?" she asks with a sparkle in her eyes.

Pulling her into my arms, I slide my hands down her back

to cup her ass. "I definitely like. You look sexier than I even remembered."

"I think you're overdressed then." She fumbles with the button on my pants, finally getting it unbuttoned so she can reach in and wrap her hand around my rapidly hardening cock. "We better get you out of these clothes so I'm not the only one ready for a night of hot sex."

"Hot isn't the word for it. Try scorching."

The feel of her palm sliding up my cock is better than anything I can imagine at that moment. It's been so long since anyone but me has touched any part of my body that I worry I might not last long the first time. I take a sharp breath in when she reaches the head, sure a minute more of this sweet torture will be the end of me.

I rip off my shirt and pants, throwing them off to the side, before I lift Kristina so her pussy is the perfect angle for me to thrust my cock in and bury myself in her. She's warm and wet and I enter her with one hard thrust.

"I've waited so fucking long to feel this," I groan as she rolls her hips back and forth, nearly making the top of my head blow off.

Kristina wraps her arms around my neck, and in a voice sexier than I've ever heard from her, whispers in my ear, "Fuck me. Fuck me hard and make me forget everything but your cock."

There isn't anything else in the world I'd rather do than give her just that, so I walk us over to the wall and plant my hands against the cool tile. I kiss her with all the love I have and say, "Hang on and don't let go until I make you come so fucking hard you can't take it anymore."

I feel her fingers thread together behind my neck, and I pull my hips back so only the tip of my cock remains inside her. She stares at me waiting for me to begin fucking her in earnest and smiles as she says, "Fuck me. Please…"

Ramming my cock into her, I do just that and fuck her harder than ever before. I don't last long the first time, but I don't stop. My cum only makes her cunt slicker, and I love the feel of my cock gliding over her wet skin as I bury myself in her. Each thrust elicits a gentle moan from her that only spurs me on, and by the time it's time for her to come, I'm nearly there for my second release.

Kristina bucks against me, her hips and mine crashing into each other as she rides me to that orgasm I need to give her. Her mouth devours mine with kisses that nearly take my breath away and my legs feel like they're going to give out, but I can't stop until I give her what she wants.

"Ian," she pants softly in my ear, "I'm so close. Give me what I need."

Her cunt begins to gently squeeze my cock and I know she's close. Just one more pump into her and she'll come apart all over me. Rearing back, I thrust once more and bury myself balls deep into her, and that's all it takes.

Every inch of her body tenses, and she drags her nails across my back, clawing as her orgasm rips through her. She's raw and sensual and more beautiful than she's ever been to me in that moment when her body finally surrenders to me again. I continue fucking her to my own release as she whimpers in my ear, "I love you, Ian. More than you know."

I stand there holding her to me, each of us panting after our lovemaking. It's been months since we've truly been with one another, and I don't want this to end. Not the sex but the closeness I've missed between us.

"That was incredible," she says, sweetly smiling at me. "It reminded me of the first time we were together."

"Then we can think of this as our second first time together," I suggest as I place a kiss on the tip of her nose.

"I like that. And I like this room again."

Pressing my forehead to hers, I close my eyes and tell her what I've waited all those weeks to say. "I'm sorry I ever hurt you, Kristina. I was selfish. I know what losing you feels like now, and I never want to feel that pain again. No drug, no anything in this world makes me feel as wonderful as you do."

She smiles, and in that moment, I'm happier than I thought I ever could be.

# CHAPTER SIX

## Kristina

OPENING MY EYES, I feel Ian's chest beneath my cheek and feel safe. That being with him could bring out a feeling of security after all we've been through with his drug addiction seems odd, but it's as if our relationship has weathered a trial by fire of sorts and we've come out even stronger on the other side.

I look up and see him still sleeping peacefully, his long, dark lashes resting against his skin, hiding those dark eyes so full of passion all the time. When I arrived here yesterday to surprise him when he returned, I hadn't been sure what he'd be like after all those weeks in rehab. The last I'd seen of him had devastated me—those beautiful eyes of his filled with tears as he accepted his defeat to that awful drug and that he'd have to leave me to try to be the man he wanted to be again.

But it only took a moment for me to see that the man who'd returned to me was the Ian I'd fallen madly and passionately in love with, and if there had been any doubt, our lovemaking a short time later erased any fears I'd had about us.

Ian stirs and his hand lands gently on the back of my head as I think all of this, and now all I feel is remorse at the doubt I'd harbored. If only I could have been as sure as he was all those weeks he was away…

I never meant for anything to happen. All Vancouver was supposed to be was work, but when he went to rehab and I returned to the set, I couldn't get the sight of him hitting rock bottom out of my mind. It haunted me day and night, and before long, everyone around me could tell something had happened while I was back in New York and not the flu my agent had claimed.

The sadness I felt inside showed in everything I did, and in that weakness I let someone in to make it go away for even a little while. All I'd wanted was someone to talk to, a friend to listen as I talked about how devastated seeing Ian like that had been for me. But when I tried to talk about how I felt, I couldn't because of the promise I'd made him to keep our relationship a secret.

So the sadness remained without my being able to express why I felt so unhappy all the time. I could act like I was happy on set, but as soon as the cameras stopped rolling, it was too much to bear and someone recognized that.

I never meant for anything to happen. One day Gavin was making jokes between scenes, and I smiled for the first time in days. One smile but it felt so good to be happy again. Then the next day he brought me coffee with a smiley face drawn on the cup and the words "Let's make it a great day!" written down the side. I didn't think anything of it.

And then he asked me if I'd like to grab a bite to eat and one drink led to another and before I knew it, I was naked in his arms back at his hotel room having sex with my co-star. It wasn't meaningful or even very good sex. It was just one sad and vulnerable person looking for comfort where she shouldn't have.

Ian moves his arm to tighten his hold on me and mumbles, "You up?"

Forcing a smile, I look up and see him gazing down at me with that look of love that used to make me feel like the luckiest woman in the world. Now it just makes me feel guilty as hell.

"Yeah. Want me to make some coffee?" I ask as I roll off him, eager to get away and hopefully lessen how bad I feel at this moment.

He grabs my hand before I can get far and tugs me back onto the bed next to him. "What's the hurry? We have all day, don't we?"

I have nowhere I really need to be. He knows that. Shooting is over, so I don't have to return to Vancouver, thankfully, and I've cleared the next few days to be with him. The problem is that every minute I'm with him I feel guiltier than the last.

"We do, but I thought you'd like to get back to writing. If I remember correctly, you said you wanted to write a sequel to Silk, didn't you?"

Just saying that makes me feel so fucking shitty. Now I'm using something that means so much to both of us as a reason to leave him because I'm wracked with guilt.

Ian gives me a sexy grin and runs his hands down my back to playfully squeeze my ass. "I do want to write that, but I think I need more research."

When he's sweet like this, all I want to do is stay here in his arms and forget the rest of the world exists outside of his bedroom. I want all the bad things we've done to each other to disappear so we can be happy forever right here in this bed.

As we make love, he's tender but powerful, exactly what I fell in love with all those months ago. His mouth excites me like no other man's can, and still only his cock makes me come. Each time he thrusts his body into mine, I love the feelings only he can bring out in me.

Yet still I can't forget what I've done. I live in terror that he's going to find out, and I'll lose the man I love over a couple nights of mediocre sex in a few moments of weakness.

As I STAND at his kitchen counter drinking morning coffee and watching him search through his laptop for what he began writing before he left, all I can think of is getting out of this apartment. I don't want to leave him now, but I worry the guilt is written all over my face. I need to contact Gavin and make sure he doesn't say anything to anyone about what happened between us. Maybe if he doesn't, I'll be able to find a way to live with what I did.

"My agent messaged me that she wants to meet with me ASAP," I lie.

Looking up from his computer, Ian smiles. "I guess I'll have no reason now not to get back to work, huh? Will you be back for dinner? I'm thinking I should make that risotto that you loved again."

Oh, God. How could I have cheated on someone so incredible? What the hell is wrong with me? The man was in rehab after going back to drugs because I broke his heart and my way of dealing with my sadness and loneliness while he was trying to straighten out his life was to sleep with another man?

"Okay. I'll be back for around five. Sound good? You should be able to get a lot written in that time."

Again, I use our book as manipulation. I'm such an awful person. When he leaves me, I won't even have the right to want him back after being such a rotten fucking woman.

Ian turns from his laptop and wraps his arms around my waist. Kissing me sweetly, he cradles my face and says, "I'm calling it Silk and Steel, and I have great news. While I was gone, Silk has continued selling well after hitting the bestseller lists and I've had a few agents contact T. Anderson about the rights."

"You'd leave Sheila after all she's done for you?"

"She doesn't represent this genre. I guess it seems pretty rotten of me not to go with her, but really, she doesn't do romance and erotica."

I look at his gorgeous face and can't help but get lost in those dark eyes of his. "Rotten? I don't think you're rotten. Ever."

He pulls me to him, whispering, "Thank you for forgiving me, Kristina. I know it wasn't easy to be around me while I was fucked up. Thank you for not leaving me."

Oh, Jesus! I'm going to die from the guilt if he keeps talking like this. I have to leave before he sees something's wrong, so I kiss him and force another smile. "Five o'clock, right? I'm looking forward to that risotto."

As he walks me to the front door, he says in a sexy voice, "And that will only be the beginning of our night. Drink lots of coffee today because I plan on keeping you up into the early morning hours."

I roll my eyes and smile even though I feel like a completely horrible person. "You're going to spoil me."

"Good. You deserve it. Now go so I can get to writing our

story. I love you."

Even as I tell him I love him, I know it's just a matter of time before he finds out what I've done. God, what am I going to do?

✧  ✧  ✧

I CALL SIENNA as soon as I hit the sidewalk outside Ian's building and pray she can help me figure out how to fix what I've done before he finds out and I lose the best thing in my life. She'll have some idea what I can do.

"Kristina! Tell me you're in New York!" she says excitedly into the phone.

"I am. Are you?"

"Yes! We have to get together. What are you doing now?"

"I'm calling you to save my life. I need your help, Sienna. I've made a horrible mistake, and I need you to help me fix it."

"You made a horrible mistake? I think you've made like a handful in your life, so I doubt this is that bad. I think that café you and I like is open, so meet me there in twenty and we'll solve your life crisis over some lunch and I can tell you about my new man."

"A new one or the one you were spending all your time in bed with the last time I talked to you?" I ask as I hail a cab.

"A new one! You have to keep up, girl. I'll tell you all about it when I see you. Twenty minutes."

I hang up and climb into the cab to take me to our favorite café and hopefully the solution to the mess I've created. If I can just figure out how to fix this, I know Ian and I can be happy.

SIENNA WAVES TO me as I stand at the hostess desk just inside Surge, a café more known for its decadent milkshakes than anything else. A hangout for us from years ago, its name has changed a few times since then but we still love it.

I walk through the maze of teakwood tables to join her at a back table and find she's all ready for our chat with coffee and my favorite blueberry muffins. Taking a seat, I notice the chair next to hers is pushed out.

"Did you bring that new guy with you?" I ask, hoping her answer is no.

"No. He's back at my place. Cilla is sitting here, but she had to run to the ladies' room."

"Sienna! I wanted to talk to you. Alone."

"I'm sorry. She grabbed me as I was heading out the door. I guess she's got some tragedy of her own she's dealing with. But it's okay, Kristina. We're all friends, and she knows what's said here stays here."

As Sienna finishes speaking, Cilla sits down in front of me and gives my arm a gentle squeeze. "I hear you're as unhappy as I am, honey. You know what they say. Misery loves company, right?"

"I guess. What's wrong?" I ask, hoping to keep her focused on her own misery.

"My accountant. The fucker has embezzled almost all my money!" she answers with tears in her eyes.

"Oh, I'm sorry, Cilla. What are you going to do?"

"She's back to sleeping with that awful ex-husband of hers is what she's doing," Sienna says with a tone of disgust that matches her expression. Never a fan of Priscilla's second husband, Rafe, she's always referred to him as "The Creeper" for how close an eye he kept on Cilla when they were together.

"I don't have a choice," Cilla whines. "It's not like I can just meet a man and get him to pay all my bills. Maybe ten years ago, but now as I slog toward thirty? No way."

"Enough about Cilla and The Creeper. Tell us about your tale of woe, Kristina. We might even be able to do something about that. Accountants with sticky fingers will have to be handled by the cops."

Suddenly, this doesn't seem like a good idea anymore. Sienna I can trust, but I'm not sure about Cilla. She has a nasty habit of gossiping too much. But I need Sienna's advice, so if that means Cilla has to hear some things, so be it. As long as I keep Ian's name out of everything, I should be fine.

I take a deep breath and say, "I need advice about a romance problem."

Sienna elbows Cilla nearly off the chair. "See? Now this is something I can help with. Go on, Kristina. What is it?"

"I've been seeing someone and he had to go away for a little bit, and well, I was lonely and I…" I couldn't say the words.

"You cheated on him. Got it. Were you two broken up at the time?" Sienna asks.

Shaking my head, I say quietly, "No. He had to go to rehab."

"You cheated on your boyfriend while he was in rehab, Kristina? That's not like you. You're usually the incredibly supportive girlfriend," Cilla says with a tone of judgment I don't appreciate.

"It's not like you think. Whatever. But I don't want him to find out and have that send him back to using."

Sienna wrinkles her nose. "I don't think you should hold

yourself responsible for him falling off the wagon, if he does. I'm just surprised you're with someone who's into drugs at all, though. That's definitely not like you."

"He isn't. Well, he wasn't when we got together. It's just that when I didn't go to Rome with him, he got back into it. So you see, I don't want that to happen again. I don't know what to do."

"This is the Rome guy? I guess he didn't take the bad news well. Wow."

Cilla's gaze bounces back and forth between Sienna and me as she tries to keep up with the story. "Who? What are we talking about? How about some names so I know what's going on here?"

Turning toward her, Sienna explains, "Kristina's been seeing this guy who wanted her to go to Rome with him. She lied to him and said she would, but she couldn't when it came right down to it because she had to go shoot in Vancouver. When she didn't show, he unraveled and got back into drugs."

Cilla nods like she understands, and then Sienna turns back to face me. "What kinds of drugs are we talking about here? Prescription stuff? Oxy? Cause that stuff is a bitch to kick."

"No, not Oxy. Heroin," I say quietly, already hating that the conversation has become fixated on Ian's drug problem.

"You're dating a heroin addict, Kristina? What is going on with you?" Cilla asks, still confused but willing to give her unsolicited opinion on my love life.

"Sienna, I need to know what to do about the other problem. Could we get back to that?"

Unlike Cilla, Sienna can take a hint, so she smiles and says, "Okay, I'm sorry. The whole drug thing isn't really the issue we should be talking about. You had a moment of weakness while he was in rehab and you don't want him to find out, right?"

"Yes. What do I do?"

"I think you have to go to the guy you were with and tell him it's important to keep this whole thing on the down-low. Who is it? Maybe we have some dirt on him that we can use to keep his mouth shut."

See, this is why I knew Sienna could help. I'd never think of anything like that.

I look around to see if anyone is close enough to our table to hear what I have to say and then lean in toward Sienna. "Gavin Somers. He was the lead in that movie I was filming in Vancouver. It only happened twice, but I don't want this to get out."

"Our lips are sealed, Kristina," Sienna says to assure me. "Right, Cilla?"

Cilla quickly nods. "Of course. Sealed shut."

"So I should tell him I need him to keep this to himself? What if he won't?"

"Then we get something on him and ruin his fucking life. Scorched earth, baby," Sienna says nonchalantly before she takes a sip of coffee.

"I'm not really a fan of the scorched earth policy. I mean, the whole thing with him was a mistake I'd just rather put behind me and never think of again."

Cilla walks up to the counter to get a refill on her coffee, so Sienna leans forward and whispers, "Don't worry. We'll take care of it. But I have to know. Who is this boyfriend of yours?"

I can't tell her Ian's real name, so instead I give her his pen name. "T. Anderson."

Her eyes grow wide with surprise, and the look of shock on her face tells me she's heard of him and our book. "Do you mean to tell me you're sleeping with the author of Silk? I picked it up after you mentioned it in that interview. Oh my God, Kristina! It's so fucking hot!"

Blushing, I smile, knowing exactly how hot our story is. "I know. I'm his muse, and it's about us, basically."

"I have to know! Is he as hot in person as the male character is in the book? The things Sean does to Kate—oh my everloving God! I want a man who does that to me."

I hear Cilla behind us, so I say, "Shhh. I don't want anyone to know."

She sits down and I know instantly she heard something. "Don't want anyone to know what? Tell me."

Sienna quickly changes the subject and asks her, "So what exactly do you have to do with The Creeper to get out of financial ruin?"

"Don't try to get me talking about him. I want to know who Kristina's new boyfriend is."

It's only a fake name, so I say, "His name is T. Anderson. But don't tell anyone because we want to keep our privacy, okay?"

"Okay, but who is this guy? You say his name like I should know."

"He's nobody, Cilla," I say as Sienna shoots me a look across the table to tell me we're in the clear. "Just a guy who's dating an actress."

She takes a sip of her fresh coffee and shrugs. "Then he better get used to the idea that privacy is a thing of the past. I told you a while back. It's the age of TMZ, Kristina. Privacy is so last century."

Sienna thankfully distracts her from my problems with her opinion on The Creeper, and for the first time today I'm not terrified what I have with Ian is going to be ruined by two little nights with Gavin. All I have to do is convince him that neither of our careers will benefit from anyone finding out. He's got a good thing going with the women he parades around town, a different one to each party and premier, so he'll probably agree that our little tryst should stay our little secret.

At least I hope he does.

# CHAPTER SEVEN

## *Ian*

T HE SOBER AND drug-free version of me writes even better than before I find out after realizing I've written an entire chapter by the time I need to begin getting dinner ready. Sitting back in my chair, I fold my arms behind my head, pleased with how Silk and Steel is already coming. I'd never planned a sequel since I'd never planned on much happening with the first book, but now that I'm back and into the story, I can honestly say I've never been happier writing any book.

Or happier in general. That's all because of Kristina.

I know I still have a lot of making up to do to her. A few weeks in rehab and a reunion of mind-blowing sex is a good start, but certainly not the end. She deserves so much more, and now that I'm clean, I intend of doing everything in my power to give it to her.

Starting with a romantic candlelit dinner of my world famous risotto and then another night of incredible sex. After that, I'm thinking I will spend the rest of my life showing her how much I love her and how I don't want to live without her.

I may be clean and sober, but the part of me that's susceptible to addiction hasn't gone away, and now my only addiction is Kristina.

As far as addictions go, she's a pretty fantastic one.

My email alert dings to let me know I have a new message in my inbox, and I open up an email from an agent who's tried to contact me three times since Silk hit the bestseller lists. This morning when I deleted all but the most urgent emails that I'd missed while I was gone to rehab, hers and those from two other agents and even some movie producer had gone into the trash, along with scores of spam emails about how I could increase the size of my penis and offers from some Irish lottery commission that seems to want to send me some winnings I had no idea about.

But now as I read her fourth email, I wonder if I should consider at least speaking to her about the potential for Silk concerning New York and foreign rights. I certainly don't have time to be dealing with those issues, and if there's money to be made, I'd eventually need an agent to handle the contracts. I'd thought about asking Sheila, but as I told Kristina, she doesn't rep erotica or romance authors of any type, self-published or New York.

Dinner's more important, though, so business will have to wait. Shutting my laptop, I head into the kitchen to make the best goddamned risotto I've ever created and wait for the woman I love.


KRISTINA STANDS BEHIND me watching as I slowly add the chicken stock and stir until each ladle-full is absorbed. Turning around, I wink at her. "Now you know the secret to the world's best risotto. You have to make sure to use Arborio rice and add the stock slowly. And you need to stir constantly."

She leans her chin on my shoulder and kisses me on the neck. "The world's best risotto made by the world's best guy. How long until we eat? I'm starving and this smells fantastic."

I add the final ladle of stock and continue stirring it into the rice. "A few more minutes. Not too long."

Her hands slide down my sides, and she hugs me to her, purring in my ear, "I have an idea of what we could be doing instead of all this stirring."

Turning my head, I kiss her softly, but her kiss quickly turns into something far more erotic, and for a moment I completely forget about the risotto until I feel the rice begin to stick to the bottom of the pan.

I reluctantly break the kiss, wishing dinner was done already. "Great food calls. We'll pick that up right where we left off as soon as we finish dinner."

She moans sweetly in my ear, "I want you to know I'm pouting, Ian."

I look and see her mouth turned down in an adorable pout. "I promise not too long and then once we have a dinner of this delicious risotto, I'm going to fuck you slow and easy right there in front of those windows and give our friend the show of his life."

"Yes," she moans as her hands travel down to the front of my pants. Palming my hard cock through the fabric, she says, "But I might not be able to wait for slow and easy. I might need you to fuck me hard and fast. Is that okay?"

My stirring speeds up as she strokes me from balls to tip, and for a moment I can't think of anything but being buried inside her tight cunt. Only when she moves her hand away am I able to think clearly again, and I look down to see the risotto is finally done.

"Dinner is served," I announce, barely able to keep my calm as my cock demands what Kristina is offering.

I scoop the food onto our plates and sit down, prepared to eat, but Kristina has different plans. Straddling me, she lowers herself onto my lap as her skirt rides up to show the milky white skin at the tops of her thighs. In my ear, she whispers, "Dinner is lovely, but I'm hungry for something else."

Her tongue softly glides over the shell of my ear, sending jolts of excitement through my body as she unbuttons my shirt and whispers how much she wants me to fuck her while she undoes each button.

I run my hands over the tops of those gorgeous thighs, slipping my thumbs under her skirt to feel her smooth pussy. She's not wearing anything under her clothes, so once I remove them, she's there sitting on my lap, naked and mine to do with as I please.

My cock already aches from being so hard, so by the time she takes it out of my pants, I'm ready for her and not as interested anymore in taking it easy.

"I'm not sure I can do slow right now," I say looking up at her as she stares at my cock and licks her lips.

"I don't want slow, Ian. I want wild and desperate. I want anyone who sees me after this to know your cock owned me. I want it to be obvious I'm yours."

Her words and the way she says them in her soft, seductive voice make my head spin. My hand on the back of her neck, I pull her mouth down to mine and kiss her hard, my tongue snaking in over her lips to find her tongue. My fingers find her pussy drenched and needy for me, and she moans as I slide two into her slick cunt.

"Fuck me, please. Hurry. I need to feel you inside me."

I grab her by the hips and position her over my cock ready for her. Looking up at her, I watch her squeeze her nipples, her eyes closed as she waits for me to lower her down onto me.

I don't want slow anymore either.

"Open your eyes, Kristina," I order and see her eyelids fly open. "I want you to watch when my cock slams into that pretty cunt of yours."

She bites her pouty lower lip and nods. "Yes. Do it. I need it."

Reaching up, I cup one of her perfect breasts and squeeze the deep pink nipple hard like I know she loves. "Harder?"

She rolls her hips so her pussy glides over my shaft and moans softly, "Yes."

I pinch her nipple between my thumb and forefinger and see the pain register on her face, but she doesn't want me to let up, so I do the same to the other nipple and watch as her mouth gently hangs open in ecstasy.

"Ride my cock, baby. Let me see you take it all."

My hands leave those gorgeous breasts to take their places on her hips, and I slam her down onto me, loving the vision of my cock disappearing into her body. I guide her pace, pushing her off me and then back down over and over. She rides me with abandon while I watch her, falling in love more every minute.

As she moves closer to her orgasm, she leans forward and kisses me like my lips possess everything she desires. Stuffing my hands into her hair, I close my fists and tug hard, loving the feel of her fucking me.

"I'm close," she groans against my lips. "So close."

I tilt my hips slightly so my cock glides over her G-spot and see that's all it takes. Her walls close in around my cock, squeezing it, and she comes hard as her hips buck against me and her mouth plunders mine. She's raw and so entirely feminine at that moment, and I love that I could give her this.

As her body slows from her release, she says quietly, "You didn't come. Why?"

I know what she's thinking. She's worried it's like the last time I couldn't get off because of the drugs. Smiling, I shake my head. "I was so engrossed with wanting you to come that I couldn't think of anything else."

"Oh. I worried…" Her sentence hangs in the air unfinished, but I know what she was worried about.

"No. Nothing like that. Just me watching you and loving what I see."

A tiny smile forms on that mouth I love, and she asks, "Anything else you like watching?"

I know what she means, and yes, I love watching her go down on me. She lifts herself off me and lowers to her knees. Pushing her hair back, I gaze down at her beautiful face. "I love when you suck me off, Kristina."

She runs her hand up my slick cock and licks her lips. "Only you."

I try to keep my eyes open as she slides the head into her warm mouth, but the feeling of her tongue dancing over my skin takes my breath away and I lean back to enjoy my first blowjob since leaving for rehab. All sexual positions are good, but there's nothing like a woman you adore sucking your cock and swallowing everything you give her.

Kristina lavishes attention on my cock like it's an eight inch god she worships. With every time she takes me in as far as she can go, she looks up at me with a mixture of innocence and seduction that only intensifies the experience. She's madonna and whore all in one.

And all mine.

I watch as she lets my cock pop playfully out of her mouth before she lowers her mouth to the very base to plant a kiss as she cups my balls to give them a gentle squeeze. Then she runs the tip of her tongue up the underside of my shaft, nearly taking the top of my head off, and as she reaches the swollen crown she whispers sweetly, "Is my man ready to come?"

More than ready. A few minutes more of this and I might not be able to walk until morning.

Jamming my hands into her hair, I tug her head down onto my cock so all of me is in her mouth. The tip hits the back of her throat, making her gag a little, so I lift her a few inches and say, "Suck me dry."

She does just as I command and sucks my cock like only she can. That mixture of innocence and experience melds into a blowjob better than any she's ever given me, and when I flood her mouth, she takes every drop I have to give.

And when she lifts her head to let me slip out of her mouth one last time, her smile shows me I wasn't the only one who enjoyed myself.

I pull her up onto my lap but not to fuck her again. This time I just want to hold her and tell her how much I love her. She curls up against me and whispers, "I know we had our reunion yesterday, but I just wanted to say I missed you so much when you were gone."

There's a sadness in her voice from how lonely I know she was, and I hate that I'm the reason that's there. I place a kiss on the top of her head and tell her the truth. "I never meant to hurt you, Kristina. I swear I didn't."

She shakes her head against my chest and wraps her arms around me. "You don't have to apologize. You didn't mean to hurt me. I understand now. Sometimes when you're in love you do things and when you see they hurt the person you care for, it hurts you too."

"I promise no more hurting because of that. I promise."

Looking up at me, she gives me a gentle smile and nods. "We might as well get to this dinner you made. It's probably cold by now."

"We'll just heat it up. And when we're done, I want to tell you all the news about Silk."

Kristina sits up straight on me and knits her brows. "News? Something else happened?"

I kiss the tip of her nose. "I promise to tell you everything after dinner, but I'll give one hint. How would the role of Kate Silk sound?"

Her eyes get big as her mouth drops open. "Role? Is someone thinking of making a film of your book?"

"Our book and no more details until we eat, so we better get moving."

She hurriedly puts on some of her clothes as I slip my satisfied cock back inside my pants, and even as we eat dinner, she can't help but ask to hear more about my details concerning Silk. I hold off telling her, wanting to wait until we're settled in on the couch in each other's arms to tell her about all the interest in our story.

"PLEASE TELL ME now, Ian. I'm so excited to hear about all of this," Kristina says eagerly as she cuddles up next to me on my leather couch.

I run my fingers over the ends of her hair as I explain about the emails I've received from agents, publishers, and the producer all interested in Silk. As thrilled as I knew she'd be, she's all smiles at the idea that what began with just the two of us could become something so much bigger.

Resting her head on my shoulder, she looks up with curious eyes and asks, "So what are you going to do?"

"You mean what are we going to do. It's our story, Kristina. You're my muse, and Silk wouldn't exist without you."

"I didn't do anything, Ian. You wrote this story. This is your talent they love. Your story people are talking about. I'm just a character in the book you crafted."

I shake my head at how wrong she is. "Ian Anwell writes historical fiction. He writes it pretty well too. But T. Anderson only writes when you're with him. All those weeks we weren't together and every time we've been apart even for a few days, I didn't write a word. I couldn't. Silk is our story. Without you, there is no story."

"I read it, you know. The day before you came back," she says shyly.

"What did you think?"

"It's so full of passion and love. Is that how you see us?"

"Of course. I love you."

She lowers her head. "I love you too, but I didn't realize how much you felt for me early on."

I tip her head back and kiss her softly. "From practically the moment we met. And before that I was already addicted to you."

"Another addiction," she says sadly.

"A good one, though. Being addicted to you has never hurt me."

Shaking her head, she frowns. "That's not true. There's Rome and when I ran away from you that first time. And…"

"And what? None of that was you hurting me intentionally. I know that."

She buries her head in my chest and mumbles, "I'm so sorry, Ian. I've done such awful things because I'm so stupid."

I try to get her to look at me, but she won't budge. I kiss the top of her head and say in her ear, "You didn't do anything stupid or awful. It's okay. Why don't I tell you what I was thinking about for a Silk film? I bet that will make you happy."

Kristina lifts her head, and I see she's crying. Wiping her tear-stained cheek, she sobs, "I'm not unhappy, Ian. I just regret the things I've done to hurt you."

I cradle her face in my hands and try to kiss her worries away. "You didn't hurt me. What do you think about you starring in the film, if it's ever made? I can't imagine another actress ever being able to play Kate Silk as well as the woman she's based on."

"Me? Do you think that could ever happen?" she asks in amazement.

"I won't have it any other way. It's you or no one, Kristina. There are also agents looking to talk to me about taking the book to a New York publisher too."

"Do you want to do that? Won't that be a problem with your books?"

"It might be, so I have to think long and hard about what

to do. I won't do anything without your input, though."

"As long as you're happy, I'm happy. That's all that matters to me, Ian."

I pull her close and nuzzle her neck. "You know what else? I'm going to include what we just did before dinner in Silk and Steel."

For the first time since she arrived tonight, I hear her giggle. Leaning back, I see a blush cover her cheeks at the mention of me writing that scene, and I can't help but be charmed. For as uninhibited as she is when we make love, she's still that sweet, bashful woman I met in Jax's.

And I love both the madonna part and the whore part to her equally.

# CHAPTER EIGHT

## *Kristina*

FOUR DAYS OF complete and total bliss, most of them spent in Ian's arms, have made me feel like everything in my life had turned around. My role in Original Sin has made me realize it was time for me to spread my wings and try meatier parts. Gavin has been perfectly agreeable to keeping our dalliance private as the relationship he's begun with another of our co-stars is taking off and he doesn't want to ruin his chances with her.

And best of all, Ian and I are happier than I thought two people possibly could be. The bumps in the road to this point tested us, but we've come out stronger on the other side, and I couldn't be more in love.

Life is truly good and getting better every day.

Ian moans softly in his sleep as he rolls over to lay his head on my shoulder. His scruffy beard scratches my skin, but I don't care if he forgets to shave again today like he did yesterday. Spending all day in bed leads to that, even if we did move to the shower for a while before returning to right here to spend the night, him writing and me watching him.

I never thought sitting next to someone as they write could

be so interesting. He chooses every word so carefully, just like when he speaks, so that the end result is entirely magical to the ear and the eye. Under his care, the characters come to life as he gives them terrible obstacles and forces them to make heartbreaking choices, but I know in the end Kate and Sean will end up happy, just like Ian and me.

I watch him as he sleeps so contented and like to believe that I'm a big reason why he no longer tosses and turns like he used to. I fell in love with a man who will forever struggle with addiction, and I want to be the one he can't shake.

Maybe that's selfish. Maybe it's something I should be ashamed of because I want him to not be able to live without me like I can't without him.

I don't care if it is and I won't be ashamed of wanting the kind of love he gives me. Some love is worth it.

His hand rests heavily on my stomach, trapping me there next to him as he sleeps, but in truth, there's nowhere else in the world I'd rather be. I lightly trace the outline of his long fingers, noting how strong they feel even when they aren't holding me or balled into a sensual fist as he tugs at my hair in the heat of passion.

My finger glides up over his over arm, toned and lean, to his shoulder, and I stop as I reach his collarbone, afraid if I continue I'll wake him. I could lie here forever just studying him and be perfectly happy.

The only thing that would make me happier is to hear him tell me he loves me or say something sexy in his special way only he can do, his words so perfectly chosen that they can excite me without him even touching my body.

His dark hair hangs over the left side of his face, hiding his chiseled cheekbone and eye with its long lashes. I want to reach out and run my fingertip down the bridge of his nose so straight and perfect. He's so beautiful lying there peacefully beside me as if all his demons have been slayed and what's left is the man I've adored from that first night we met.

For the first time with a man, I feel like tomorrow will be okay.

I lean over to kiss the top of his head, loving the silky feel of his hair against my lips. Inhaling deeply, I smell the light coconut and vanilla scent from the shampoo I used to wash his hair yesterday afternoon. It's warm and sensual like him, and forever it will remind me of standing in the shower with the water pouring over us and me working hard to convince him to let me use my shampoo on his hair instead of his old ordinary brand and him finally giving me a crooked smile and saying, "I can't refuse you anything, so go ahead. Do your worst."

As I reminisce about the sex that followed, my phone vibrates in my purse nearby on the floor. Looking over at Ian's nightstand, I see the clock says it's just after nine. That's entirely too early for anyone to be texting me. I ignore it and return to enjoying the thought of Ian making love to me. Texting before ten in the morning is just rude.

But my phone vibrates again two minutes later. And then three minutes after that. Whoever it is doesn't understand phone etiquette, so I try to ignore the almost constant vibrating noise coming from my purse. But by the time ten texts have come in, I begin to worry that it isn't just rudeness on someone's part but a real emergency.

Easing my arm out from underneath Ian's head, I reach for my purse and grab my phone. I swipe the screen and there in front of me I see the reason my phone is blowing up.

The one thing I dreaded more than anything else in the world has happened. Somehow, the tabloids have found out what happened in Vancouver and they're announcing it like it's a goddamned gold rush.

*Kristina, the celebrity gossip site All The Dirt is running a story about you and Gavin Somers in Vancouver saying you cheated on your boyfriend! Who the fuck is your boyfriend? Is this serious? Why do they think this is a huge story? Call me ASAP!*

Joanne's text makes my stomach clench in terror. Is the story already live? I scramble to figure out when her message came in. 9:01. And it's 9:20 already!

Another text comes in, this one from my agent. Her fourth text of the morning tells me she's confused and frightened. I know exactly how she feels.

*Joanne hasn't stopped texting me about whatever you did in Vancouver and some boyfriend here. What's happening? What is this about? Are you okay?*

No. I'm definitely not okay. I look over at Ian still sleeping peacefully as everything else in my world is crashing down around my ears. All I want is to have him hold me and tell me everything will be okay, and he's the only person I can't look to for help now.

Oh, God. What am I going to do? When he finds out what happened with Gavin, he's never going to forgive me. Why would he? He was battling his demons in that rehab center and I couldn't even stay loyal and stand by him.

I'd leave me too.

No! I can't let that happen. I have to find a way to fix this before he finds out. I can't let him be hurt this way.

Another text from my agent makes my blood run cold. *Is T. Anderson really the author Ian Anwell? Why aren't you calling me? Call me now!*

Oh my God! How did they find out?

I need to see this story, so I quickly find All The Dirt's website on my phone and read through the story as my heart pounds frantically in my chest. The title of the article is awful, and it only gets worse from there. Somehow they know everything.

How could they have found out?

### Two Timing 'Tina

*All The Dirt hears that actress Kristina Richards has been very busy lately. First she was seen kanoodling with her co-star in Original Sin Gavin Somers while they were shooting in Vancouver recently, and as you can see by the picture below, they were just as cozy as two people could be. Our source reports that cuddling in a restaurant booth isn't all they were up to either.*

*But now we here at All The Dirt hear that while she was getting hot and heavy with Gavin, her boyfriend, author Ian Anwell, was off at rehab again trying to shake his drug habit for the fifth time. So he was trying to clean up and she was getting down and dirty.*

*And what might be the biggest news of all?*

*Sources confirm that Ian Anwell, bestselling author of the historical fiction books Caligula's Dream and Nero's*

*Nightmare is, in fact, T. Anderson, the author of the book that's on everyone's ereader this year, Silk!*

*Two timing 'Tina has been very busy indeed! But the question now is: How will her boyfriend handle the news of her infidelity?*

I feel like I'm going to throw up. When Ian finds out I not only cheated on him when he was in the fight of his life but also that the world knows he's really T. Anderson and the author of an erotic book, he'll never forgive me.

My mind spins with what to do. I can't tell him. I don't know how. Maybe I can get Joanne to get that website to retract the article.

But why would they? Nothing they wrote is false. Probably a first for them.

The walls of Ian's apartment begin to feel like they're closing in on me. I need to get out of here and figure out what to do. Silently, I get out of bed and dress to leave.

To run away. In truth, that's what I'm doing.

As I turn to leave, I look at his serene face as he sleeps and choke up as tears well up in my eyes. I don't want to go, but I need to see if I can fix the damage I've caused before he gets hurt.

Who am I kidding? He's already been hurt. I can only pray that when the world finds out he's really T. Anderson that what he's feared all along won't happen. If his publisher and readers turn on his historical books, I won't be able to forgive myself.

I'm sorry, Ian. I never meant for any of this to happen.

❖   ❖   ❖

"SIENNA, PLEASE TELL me you didn't sell the details of my life to that All The Dirt website."

I see by the shock in her expression that she genuinely doesn't know what I'm talking about. I didn't think it was her, but I had to ask. Sagging against the wall outside her door, I hang my head. "I'm sorry. I never thought you'd really do that to me."

"Kristina, come inside and tell me what the hell is going on."

She takes my hand and drags me in as I begin to explain everything that's happened that morning. By the time I reach the part about my dating Ian and his secret pen name being revealed, her mouth is hanging open in shock.

"Oh my God, honey! What are you going to do?"

As I practically collapse onto her loveseat, I shake my head, trying to hold back the tears. "I don't know. And I don't know which is worse—Ian finding out I cheated on him with Gavin while he was in rehab or his secret out for everyone to see?"

Sienna gives my hand a sympathetic squeeze, but I can see in her eyes how awful even she thinks this is.

"Okay, what's the worst that can happen?"

My heart skips a beat as the thought of what the worst truly is tears through my brain. "Ian never forgiving me for betraying him not just once, but twice. Me losing the man I love."

"Okay. Well, is there any way you or your people can get this story killed?"

I shake my head. "No. They didn't report anything false, so I don't have a leg to stand on. And it doesn't matter anyway if they did. It's out there already."

"How did this happen, Kristina? Who did you tell other

than me?"

"I only told you that day at the café." Then the truth hits me. Cilla. "Oh my God! Cilla sold her story to that rag site for money, didn't she?" I ask in horror as the reality of it settles into my mind.

For a moment, Sienna can't believe it, but it's the only thing that makes sense. "I can't believe that, Kristina. Cilla's a lot of things, but she's wouldn't do this to you."

"She would if she was desperate for money, which is exactly what she is if she's back with her ex-husband. She sold the details she'd heard that day to All The Dirt and now my life is ruined."

"Oh, honey. I'm so sorry. I brought her that day. I'm to blame."

"No, you're not. This is my fault. I cheated on him."

"But how did they find out Ian's really T. Anderson? You never told me that, so Cilla couldn't have overheard it."

I close my eyes and lean my head back against the cushion. "I have no idea. I never told anyone, so they must have found out on their own."

"What are you going to do? You can't just wait for him to find out on his own, Kristina. You just left him there in his apartment without even telling him you were leaving?"

Barely holding back the tears, I hide my face in my hands. "I didn't know what to do, so I ran, like I always do when I get scared. My publicist and my agent have been texting me like mad all morning, but I don't know what to say to them either. None of it's untrue, so what's the point?"

She wraps her arm around me, and I finally let it all out, unable to keep my sadness in anymore. I've lost the one person

I love more than anyone in this world and when everyone finds out his secret, he'll be ruined.

"Oh, honey. I know it seems bad now, but things have a way of working out. It sounds clichéd, but they do. If it's true love, you guys will be able to overcome this."

Looking up, I dry my eyes. "That's pretty optimistic of you, Sienna. I had no idea you were such a romantic. But what if it wasn't true love but love just the same? I don't want to lose him."

She shakes her head and frowns. "I don't know then. I guess all you can do is hope he can forgive you."

"I have to figure out how I'm going to tell him what I've done. I better get going."

"Okay, but call me if you need anything. While you're dealing with that, I'm going to find Cilla and rip her a new one for being such a two-faced bitch."

I know Sienna means well, but even the idea of her tearing into Cilla for being the worst friend in the world can't cheer me up now. I'm going to have to fight for Ian with everything I have inside me, but what if he doesn't want me anymore?

What if he can't forgive me?

As the cab turns the corner toward Ian's building, I see the crowd of photographers and media gathered in front, and I know my problems have just gotten a hundred times worse. If they're waiting for him, the news has spread about who he really is and he has no idea.

The cabbie looks back at me in the rearview mirror. "Looks like they're onto someone famous here. You still want to get out or should I take you somewhere else?"

We slowly roll by the chaotic scene outside Ian's building,

and I look up at his living room windows wishing I was up there with him hidden away from all the madness that's about to descend upon us, all because of me. Nodding toward the cabbie still staring back at me, I give him my address instead and sink into the seat to avoid the prying eyes of the media now stalking the man I love.

I take one last look back as we turn the corner and hope to God I haven't spent my last night there with Ian. I have to find some way to convince him he should forgive me. I can't let this ruin the best thing in my life.

# CHAPTER NINE

## *Ian*

I STRETCH THE sleep from my limbs and open my eyes to see I'm alone in bed. Still tired, I roll over and wait for Kristina to return and cuddle up next to me. Looking at the clock, I see it's close to ten. I've got a full day of writing planned, but another hour or so in bed won't hurt.

The sound of my cell phone ringing wakes me up, and I open my eyes to see it's nearly noon. Turning my head, I see Kristina's side of the bed empty. I wonder where she is, but she's probably in the bathroom getting ready for the day. My phone thankfully stops ringing, but starts up again almost immediately. Still groggy, I answer my phone more concerned with why I slept so late than whoever is calling me.

"Hello?" I mumble as I work to focus my still bleary eyes.

"Ian? What are you doing?"

I vaguely recognize my agent's voice, but it sounds frantic. Definitely not what a person wants to hear first thing in the morning. "Sheila, I just woke up, but don't worry. I'm not back to doing anything bad. I just overslept today."

"You overslept? So you don't know about what's happened?" she asks, her voice in full panic mode.

"No. Did something happen?" I ask, wide awake and beginning to get worried myself. Sheila isn't the kind of woman to go off the deep end, and if she's upset about something, it must be big.

"Oh, Ian. Just when I thought you got lucky, it's all a mess. I don't believe most of it. I can't, but you need to wake up and listen to me."

I sit up and swing my legs off the bed. "Sheila, calm down. Whatever it is, I'll be fine. Just tell me what's going on and we'll handle it."

"Are you alone?"

"No." I begin to walk through the apartment and I don't see Kristina anywhere. "Well, maybe. I think Kristina must have run out for something. What does it matter if I'm alone or not, though?"

"Ian, what did you do when you went to Rome, other than drugs? Did you even research for the Marc Antony book, or was that all a lie?"

I've never felt more confused than I do at that moment. I don't know where Kristina is and nothing Sheila's saying is making sense. Leaning back against the kitchen counter, I try to clear my head, but her questions sound like madness.

"I admit I went back to doing heroin on my trip to Rome, but I spent the time researching, Sheila. What's all this about?"

"Who is T. Anderson, Ian?"

My eyes fly open wide at her mention of the pen name only Kristina and I know about. My mind begins spinning out of control as she continues to ask who T. Anderson is and if I've secretly written a book without her knowing.

"How did you find out?"

"It's all over the news, Ian! So it's true? How could you do this? I'm your agent and you kept this from me?"

"What do you mean it's all over the news?" I ask as I begin to panic like she is. "What news?"

"The gossip website All The Dirt posted an article about you being this author and being in rehab this last time. It will be on Page Six by tomorrow."

"It's not that big a deal, Sheila. I wrote a book and published it on my own. It did better than I thought it ever would, but I'm not planning on throwing away my career writing historical fiction as Ian Anwell. Somebody must have made the connection, but the two have nothing to do with one another."

Sheila is silent for a long moment and then says quietly, "It's not that easy, Ian. Those two genres don't complement each other."

"Don't worry. It was just something that came about as a result of me meeting Kristina. I don't plan on writing many more as T. Anderson, so you won't lose me."

"It's much worse than you think. Right now, your publisher is telling me that the Marc Antony project is on hold, and I'm hearing the same thing for the film of Caligula's Dream."

"Why? Does it really matter what I do under a pen name?"

"If no one had found out, it wouldn't matter, but now that people know Ian Anwell wrote Silk, you're too sexy for historical fiction."

Now I'm in full panic mode like she was a few minutes ago. "What are you saying? That my career is ruined because I wrote one erotic book? That's fucking crazy."

"Ian, I'll do what I can, but for right now, you're just not a name they want to be associated with. But there's more."

More? Like what? Do they plan to put me in the stockade in the public square for having impure thoughts?

Suddenly, the room feels like it's spinning out of control. As she begins to read from the All The Dirt post, I stumble to the table and fall into a chair. I can't believe what I'm hearing.

"Honey, I'm so sorry, but they said this about Kristina. 'All The Dirt hears that actress Kristina Richards has been very busy lately. First she was seen kanoodling with her co-star in Original Sin Gavin Somers while they were shooting in Vancouver recently, and as you can see by the picture below, they were just as cozy as two people could be. Our source reports that cuddling in a restaurant booth isn't all they were up to either.

But now we here at All The Dirt hear that while she was getting hot and heavy with Gavin, her boyfriend author Ian Anwell was off at rehab again trying to shake his drug habit for the fifth time. So he was trying to clean up and she was getting down and dirty.'"

I close my eyes as the bile begins to rise in my throat. "No. No. They're a gossip site. They got this one wrong, though. She wasn't with anyone."

Even as I defend her, I can't help but replay every moment together since I returned and every word she wrote me in those letters she sent all the while I was in rehab. Is it possible? Did she go with that guy while I was spending time getting clean so we could have a life together?

"I'm sure you're right, Ian. She clearly loves you. I saw that the night I took you to Meadowbrook."

"Yeah, these sites get shit wrong all the time, Sheila. They aren't wrong about me being T. Anderson or about Silk. I did write it," I say, working to keep my voice from shaking I'm so upset. "But if you want, I'll make it up to you for keeping it secret by letting you be my agent for it. I've had a few contact me already, in addition to a film producer interested in talking about making a movie of the story."

"I don't usually work with that genre, but for you, I'll see what I can do. Don't worry. I'll handle everything else too. I think for the time being you might want to lay low, though. This is a story the media thinks has legs with the pen name, the popularity of Silk, and the whole cheating story."

"She didn't cheat, Sheila."

"Okay, but they don't know that, so this story seems like it has all the elements the media likes. I think until everything dies down, you should go away for a little while. Take Kristina and leave as soon as you can. You still have that cabin upstate. Go there. Sit in front of a roaring fire and lay low until I can clear things up here."

I hate the idea of running away and hiding, but she's right. Staying in the city won't help matters.

"Okay, I need a little time off anyway. I'll give you a call in a few days."

"Sounds good, Ian. Don't worry. I'll handle things for you like I always have. You don't have to worry about this. Go enjoy a little R and R with Kristina."

I hear the sympathy in her voice, but it's not for what's happened to my writing career. She thinks the part of the story about Kristina is true.

And with every minute that passes, I begin to think it is too.

I LOOK AROUND my apartment where just twelve hours earlier we were happier than we'd ever been before. For four days we'd enjoyed just being with one another in the way two people in love did. Completely and sublimely in love. Now all this place feels is empty. I don't know where she is or why she left. Did she leave because this story went public and it's true?

Flipping open my laptop, I make my way to the All The Dirt website and read the post, unable to stop myself from looking at the picture of her with this guy Gavin she worked with on that film in Vancouver.

Brown hair, average build, nothing to make him noteworthy. Goofy too perfect smile. And I hate him because there she is in his arms smiling like I thought she only smiled for me.

I don't want to believe she betrayed me so completely. I don't want to believe she cheated on me with this guy and then broke her promise to me and told the world about T. Anderson and our story.

I don't, but I can't help it. Every moment that goes by without a word from her tells me I need to begin believing it.

I can't handle this. It hurts too much. I need something to help me deal with this.

Rummaging through my kitchen cabinets for anything to help me take the edge off how bad I feel, I find a bottle of whisky somebody gave me for Christmas one year. The stuff's shit, but right now, I don't care if it's fucking lighter fluid.

I just need to be something other than sober.

I pour myself a glass and down it fast, hoping it hits me and dulls the pain that's already beginning to hurt too fucking much. Another one goes down just as quick and begins to do the job.

By the third glass, my rage and hurt have subsided enough for me to at least try to understand what happened, so I call Kristina but get no answer. I wait ten minutes for her to call me back, finishing my drink and pouring myself another, but my phone doesn't make a sound.

Finally, I text her and pray to God she answers with something that doesn't make me feel even worse than I already do.

> I read the All The Dirt post. All I want to know is if it's true.

Waiting for my phone to vibrate, I try to remember any happy moment between us, but they're all blocked by the sick feeling I have that she betrayed me.

Her message comes in, and for a moment a feeling of dread washes over me. I can't put off looking at it, though, so after waiting a minute, I pick up my phone and read her text, my heart slamming against my chest as the words flow by my eyes.

> I never told anyone about our story or that you wrote it, Ian. I wouldn't do that to you. I love you. I wouldn't ruin your life like that.

My hands shake as I write the text that may be the end of all the happiness I've ever wanted.

> Did you sleep with him while I was in rehab?

Her message takes too long, and I know the answer before my phone even tells me she's texted back. When it vibrates against the top of the table where we ate every meal together, I feel empty, like someone's carved out my insides and left me hollow. I look down and read the words that tear my heart out.

Yes but it was nothing. I'm coming there right now and we'll talk. I can explain everything, Ian. I love you. Please believe me. I can explain.

As the truth of what she did becomes reality in my mind, I stand from the table and grab a bag to fill with things I'll need up at the cabin. I can't stay here and listen to the woman I love tell me the reasons why she slept with another man while I was in rehab missing her more than I'd ever missed anyone in my life.

I reach the lobby and see the doorman just as I notice the mob of photographers standing outside the front door. He recognizes me immediately and steps in front of me to shield me from them.

"Mr. Anwell, I think we should find another way for you to exit the building today."

"Good idea. I'm going to be driving, so I just need to get down to the garage." He seems to study me for a long moment, and I realize I probably reek of cheap whisky, so I add, "I'm fine. No need to worry."

"Yes, sir." Extending his arm, he guides me to the door to the garage, never moving from in front of me. "Drive safely, sir."

I head past him toward my parking spot where my BMW Series 6 is parked and smile. "Thanks."

"Do you have any instructions in case Miss Richards arrives tonight while they're still here?"

Shaking my head, I try to keep the sadness I'm feeling over losing her from my voice. "Nope. She's used to that kind of thing. She'll be fine."

"Yes, sir. Drive safely."

Driving safely is likely not going to happen since I'm pretty fucking buzzed from the cheap Christmas gift booze, so I speed out of the parking garage and head up the street, blowing the horn at the photographer vultures as I pass. For a few minutes I don't feel like I've lost everything I love and I'm all alone, but that doesn't last and as the car roars up the road to my cabin upstate, all I feel is empty.

Empty and lost without her.

# Claim

## K.M. SCOTT

Ian and Kristina's love has been tested over and over, but now one final test may be too much for them to overcome.

The only part of his life other than Kristina that meant anything to Ian—his career—lays in shambles. Now he'll have to decide if he can forgive the woman he loves for betraying his most important secret.

Kristina will do whatever it takes to get Ian back, and this time it won't be easy. But their love means too much for her to give up now.

And just when they think they've finally found happiness, their love will be challenged one last time.

# CHAPTER ONE

## *Kristina*

I STAND AT Ian's door knocking until my knuckles hurt, but he's gone. I feel it as much as I feel the emptiness inside me from sending text after text and never hearing from him. I've ruined his livelihood, but even more, I've betrayed what we had together. He loved me, and I let that all slip away because I couldn't handle a few weeks of loneliness.

Looking down at my phone, I look for a text from him but see nothing. I have to try again. I can't let this be the end.

> Ian, please let me explain. He meant nothing to me. I love you. What we have can't be over. I won't let it be.

I wait for him to reply, to say something even if it's that he hates me and never wants to see me again, but he says nothing. His silence is worse than anything he could possibly say.

> Please answer me. Tell me this isn't the end. Tell me you can forgive me like I forgave you. Just say something.

He doesn't answer and by the time I reach my apartment, I know this time he won't just let me come back. I'm going to have to fight for him.

But I don't know where he is and just as I think I might be able to figure out where he's gone, the thought of him slipping back into his old addictions stops me cold. If he goes back to doing drugs because of what I've done, I'll never be able to forgive myself.

I have to find him before he does anything, but how?

His agent will be able to tell me where he's gone, but all I know about her is her name is Sheila. I flip through the back pages of Caligula's Dream, but all I find is information about Ian's other books. That doesn't help, but maybe I can find something online that will.

I search for any information about Ian Anwell, and the first site that comes up is his website. I've visited it dozens of times and never read anything about his agent, but then again, I wasn't looking either. Clicking on the About Ian page, I read about him growing up in upstate New York, attending Cornell University and majoring in history, and living in New York City. Nothing about who represents him.

Not knowing what to do next, I google Ian's name along with the name Sheila and hope for something to come up in the search. It's worth a try. Unfortunately, some woman named Sheila Josten seems to have a very unhealthy obsession with the man I love and every link on the first page of search results sends me to her blog where she spends a lot of time talking about Ian's books.

I move to the next page and find more of his scary stalker and her love of all things Ian. Scrolling to the bottom and after reading what could best be described as a love letter from her to him, I finally find a link to an article from The Post mentioning Ian's agent, Sheila Rogers.

After searching for another few minutes, I find a phone number for her, but before I can call her, my phone rings. Excited that Ian might have finally realized we could work this all out, I answer it but it's Cilla, not Ian.

"Sweetie, I'm so sorry. I never meant to hurt you. Sienna told me what happened. I really am sorry."

"How could you do that to me, Cilla? You're supposed to be my friend."

"I didn't think all of this would happen. I swear I didn't."

I try to control my anger at her, but just hearing her lame excuse makes it rush to the surface. "You didn't think that website would run an article about me cheating on my boyfriend? Are you kidding?"

Cilla's silent for a long moment, and then she quietly says, "No, that I knew. I just didn't realize you cared so much about him. I had no idea you were dating Ian Anwell and no idea that they'd bother with him at all."

"Bother with him? You told them I cheated on him, and then they dug up who he is under a pen name. Do you have any idea how much hurt you've caused?"

"Well, actually it was the other way around, but it doesn't matter now. I'm so sorry, Kristina. I didn't know they would do that. I figured they'd focus on you and then it would die down. You know, like it did with John."

"Like it did with John? I was devastated when I found out he cheated on me with that waitress. You knew that! How many days did I stay locked away in Sienna's house because I was so broken up over that? It didn't just blow over, Cilla. Just because the tabloids stopped talking about it didn't mean it ended for me."

"Oh, honey, I'm so sorry. I just needed money and I didn't know what to do."

"You could have asked me. I would've given you money. I would have given anything to make sure Ian didn't find out. Now he won't even talk to me and all because you wanted to find a way to get some quick money."

"I'm sorry. I mean that."

"You just don't get it, Cilla. You saying you're sorry doesn't fix anything. Go tell someone who actually believes you."

I can't listen to her weak apologies anymore. Wishing I could slam the phone down and let her hear how furious I am with her, I click END and throw my phone onto my couch. Her I'm sorry's mean nothing to me.

My chest hurts at the thought that Ian is feeling how I felt when I found out John cheated on me. I remember the betrayal hurting so badly that I wasn't sure I could ever trust anyone again. I was ashamed I'd ever believed he could truly love me, and for a long time I didn't think I'd ever be strong enough again to care for someone.

And then I met Ian and for as broken as I was, he showed me I could love again and believe not only in a man but in myself too. Now with my stupid mistake, everything we've been through and everything we were lays in ruins.

How can I ever convince him that I love him and would do anything to have him back?

First, I have to convince his agent to tell me where he is. Dialing her number, I get past her assistant, but I can tell by Sheila's tone that she's not a fan of mine after what's happened.

"What can I do for you, Miss Richards?"

"Sheila, I know you saw the whole mess on that website, but I need to find him. I'm worried he's going to fall back into the drugs because of this. I don't want that to happen, and I know you don't want that either."

"I can't help you, Miss Richards. I told Ian to leave the city with you, but clearly he believes that rag like I do. He'll return when all of this dies down. In the meantime, I'll be working to do my best to save whatever's left of his career your foolishness has decimated."

"I swear I didn't tell anyone anything about Ian writing under that pen name. I wouldn't do that to him."

Sheila snorts in disgust. "You'd just cheat on him while he's in the fight of his life to get that heroin monkey off his back."

"I'm not going to deny I made a mistake, but if you'll just tell me where he is, I'll show him that it meant nothing and hopefully stop him before he starts back up on the drugs. Please, I just want a chance to make things right."

I hear nothing for a long time, like she's considering what I said, but her tone remains icy when she finally says, "I can't help you. I just hope Ian isn't so devastated by what you've done that he falls back into his bad habits. He's too talented an author to be sidelined by nonsense like this."

I want to say to her that the love we share isn't nonsense, but what's the use? The only person I need to defend myself to is Ian, and she won't help me find him. She hangs up on me before I can try to convince her again, so I call Joanne. If anyone can help, it's her.

"Kristina, I know I told you more publicity would be a good idea, but I never thought you'd give me something this fantastic. I swear I've gotten more calls and emails about you today than I've gotten for the past nine months."

"Joanne, I need your help finding Ian."

"The boyfriend?"

"Yes. I need to find him. He's left the city because of this mess, and I need to find him."

"Have you tried his agent or publicist? They probably know where he's gone off to."

Sighing in frustration, I explain who his agent is and how she refuses to tell me where he is. I know Joanne well enough to know she'll see this as a challenge, so I exaggerate how Sheila refused to help me and hope my publicist will be able to drag the information out of her.

"Give me a few minutes. I'll find out where your Ian Anwell has run off to. Just promise me if this turns out all happily ever after that you'll be sure to let me coordinate the PR campaign."

"Fine. Just help me find out where he is and I'll promise you anything."

I hang up with her and collapse onto the couch where he and I sat that first night. All I can hope is that Joanne is able to get through to Sheila. Not exactly the most subtle person, I can't imagine how she'll do it.

All I know is if anyone can, Joanne can.

So much has happened since that night Ian and I met and came back here so he could sign my copy of Caligula's Dream. How infatuated I'd been when my manager contacted me to ask if I'd like to meet Ian. To have a New York Times bestseller and one of my favorite authors want to meet me seemed too incredible for words, but he'd assured me the offer was a real one. As I sat there in that booth at Jax's waiting for him to arrive, I hoped he'd see me as intelligent and accomplished like he is. Never in my wildest dreams had I imagined we'd begin a love affair that would change our lives forever.

Now I'd lost him because of my stupid mistake, and I planned to do whatever I needed to bring him back. If Joanne could find out where he went, I'd brave hell, high water, or whatever obstacle the world threw in front of me to get to him.

As I silently promise Ian I'll do everything in my power to get him back, my phone rings. Lunging for it, I grab it from the other end of the couch and see it's Joanne calling back.

"Did you find out where he is?" I blurt out without even saying hello.

"I did. That agent of his wanted to guard the secret like it was gold in Fort Knox, but I can be pretty persuasive when I want to be. You can thank me later. For now, you need to find a way upstate. That's where your boyfriend is hiding out."

"Upstate? Where?" He'd never talked about anywhere upstate, other than where he'd grown up, but none of family still lived there, so I can't imagine where he's gone.

"He's at a cabin he owns in Hunter about two and a half hours north of the city. How are you going to get up there?"

"I don't know, but I have to get there. Text me the address. I have to find a way to get upstate. And Joanne, thanks. I owe you big."

"Damn right you do. I'll send that over right now. Be careful driving up there, Kristina. It's the middle of winter and they get a lot more snow than we do down here."

"I promise I will, but don't worry about me. I'm a Midwest girl born and bred. I learned how to drive in the snow, unlike you city folk. I'll be fine."

I hang up with Joanne feeling better than I have since I woke up next to Ian this morning. Now all I need to do is find a car, and I know just the person to help me.

Quickly I press four on my speed dial. "Sienna, it's Kristina. I need you to let me use your car."

"The Benz?" she asks, not missing a beat. Only Sienna could get a call from someone asking to use her car and not ask why in return.

"No, the Range Rover. I might run into some snow, and I'd rather be safe than sorry."

"Okay, but can I ask where you're going? After the day you've had, I'm worried about you and you asking to take my car makes me wonder what you're up to."

"I found out where Ian is. He's at a cabin he owns upstate, so I'm going up there and I'm not coming back until I've convinced him to forgive me."

Sienna chuckles. "You must be in love, Kristina. I've never heard you so intent and confident."

"I am and I'm not going to let him go without a fight."

"That's my girl! Okay, the Range Rover is yours for as long as you need it. Do you need anything else?"

Packing my suitcase, I throw some clothes in and say, "Nope. I have everything I need now that you're letting me borrow your car. I won't forget this, Sienna."

"It's okay. I'm happy to help since I feel partly to blame for everything that happened. Cilla told me she called you to apologize but you weren't willing to let her off the hook. I don't blame you."

"She ruins my life and now she wants me to be satisfied with her apology because she didn't think it would be that bad.

I can't forgive her for telling that website what I did not because it hurt me but because of what Ian's going through."

"I wouldn't forgive her if she did it to me, so you won't hear me telling you to kiss and make up."

I zip my suitcase shut. "She has her money they paid her for the story. That's all she cared about."

"Well, you're going to find Ian and convince him to forgive you, so don't even think about her. When everyone finds out it was her who betrayed you, she won't have a friend in the world. That money better be enough."

I prop my suitcase up against the wall at my front door. "I'm done packing, so I'll be at your place in a little while. Thanks again, Sienna. I don't know what I'd do without you."

"It's no biggie. I'm an incurable romantic. This is just the kind of thing I like to be involved in. I love the idea of you driving up there to win the man you love back. It's like one of your movies."

"Leave it to you to think that," I say with a giggle. "I just hope it works out like that and he lets me in. I'm worried he won't even talk to me after what's happened and I'll be stuck outside in the snow and the cold talking through a closed door trying to convince him to forgive me."

"No way. This has all the hallmarks of a great love story, Kristina. Now go get your man! And I'll be expecting details when all this dies down since you know you can trust me."

"Got it! Thanks again, Sienna. See you in a few."

I PICK UP Sienna's Range Rover at her building and after she wishes me luck, I'm on my way. I have a little over two hours to think of what I want to say to Ian to convince him that I love him and he loves me enough to forgive me.

As I drive north out of the city, I feel like I'm leaving all the madness of this day behind me. The bare trees along the sides of the highway are strangely beautiful and calming in their starkness, and the lightly falling snow makes me think of a snow globe my grandmother gave me when she visited Sea World once when I was a child.

By the time I'm an hour into the drive, the snow begins to fall much harder and faster, covering the roadway. I'm not worried, though. I'd drive through a blizzard for the chance to prove to Ian that I love him and what we have deserves a second chance.

I just hope he feels the same way.

# CHAPTER TWO

## *Ian*

THE CABIN I bought years ago before I even had my first book published gives me a place to hide out while I lick my romantic wounds. I toss my bag onto the bed in the master bedroom and head out to the living room to start a fire. Thankfully, I made the decision to hire a caretaker who's been more than diligent in his job and left me enough firewood for at least a week.

Not that I want to spend much more time than that out here in this winter wonderland. As I sit back and enjoy the fire I've created, I look out the window and see the snow falling again to add to the six or seven inches already on the ground. It would be just my luck to have a blizzard roll in and leave me stranded here in the middle of nowhere.

Or maybe that would be a good thing. Stuck in this place with sketchy internet, at least I wouldn't be able to keep up with the fallout from the All The Dirt article. I know I shouldn't care about what happens to Kristina, but even now after all that's happened, I still love her and wish she was next to me here in front of this roaring fire.

I've left her all alone to deal with the problem. Not exactly the gentlemanly thing to do. As the thought of her being stalked and besieged by those fucking reporters passes through my mind, I feel bad for a moment.

Until I remember she did this to herself.

And to me. Then all I can think is, "Fuck her."

One minute I miss her more than I can bear, and the next I hate her for betraying me. I want to forgive her for sleeping with that guy on set. Maybe I can. We've both done horrible things to one another, and I haven't forgotten that I slept with another woman. I doubt this Gavin guy meant any more to her than the woman I picked up at the bar that night as I tried to do anything to get Kristina off my mind.

It's not the fucking I can't get past. It's the fact that she betrayed me by telling the world I'm T. Anderson. That I can't forgive because it proves I can't trust her with something far more important than sex.

It shows I can't trust her with who I truly am.

God, if I ever needed the feeling of junk coursing through me, it's now. There's a difference between thinking you need it and truly wanting it, though. I could fall back into that life and lose myself again, but that's not what I want anymore. I may feel worse than I thought possible without Kristina, but I don't want heroin.

I can't say the same about scotch, however. Not that drinking myself into oblivion would be frowned upon by Sheila and anyone else worried about me. Funny how being a raging alcoholic is perfectly fine, especially if you're an author. As if doing my best Hemingway impression provides me with some ridiculous writer street cred.

What anyone thinks about me drinking to forget what

Kristina did matters not one fuck to me, though. If the fine state of New York believes it all well and good to make alcohol legal, then I'm happy to be its biggest champion.

There will be no prohibition in this cabin. Teetotaling can go fuck itself. I intend on drinking as much as it takes for my mind to finally give up the memory of her betrayal so maybe I can begin living without her in my life. Scotch and I are old friends. I can count on it to do its best.

The rest will be up to me. That's the tricky part because as I sit here now staring into the fire and wishing she was in my arms, I don't want to forget her. Like some sad masochist, I want nothing more than to think about everything she means to me. I want to remember how she tasted and how her body felt next to mine.

I want to remember everything she made me feel for fear that when the memory finally leaves me for good, she'll actually be gone.

Just like everything else I've been addicted to in my life, Kristina brings pain as much as she gives pleasure. And like those other addictions, just the thought of being with her makes me crave her all the more.

I savor the taste of the scotch as it lingers on my tongue before it slides down my throat on its way to polluting my bloodstream. Another three or four glasses and I ought to be blasted enough to at least black out.

The problem is between then and this moment, all my mind is filled with is her.

The center of me feels empty, like part of me is missing, taken away when I left. I breathe and sense a hollowness inside me and wonder if I'll always feel like this. Never before has the loss of someone from my life made me feel like they'd taken part of me with them.

I need more alcohol. All this fucking introspection can't be any good for me. Closing my eyes, I take another swig and wish for that moment when I black out to come soon.

Unfortunately, my mind wants to flourish on the scotch tonight. I've been betrayed once again by something so dear to me.

Fuck.

Trying to think of something other than the shitstorm my life has turned into, I fail miserably as my mind returns to one idea over and over. Kristina. Jesus Christ, am I ever going to be able to forget her?

I think about the night she cuddled next to me as I read her what I'd written in Silk earlier that day. Her blue eyes filled with awe at the story I told of us, she squeezed my arm whenever I read a part she really liked. The woman who'd begun as just an actress on my television screen who enthralled me listened to my words as if they meant the world to her. I'd never felt more accomplished than I had that night when she smiled up at me as I read her our story.

A little voice inside my head whispers, "She's an actress, Ian. She was acting. You stroked her ego, and they like that. But you were no more special than any other man to her. How could you be? A drug addict who's gotten lucky with a few books?"

I hate that fucking voice. It's like some demented version of that cricket in that children's cartoon who exists only to ensure I'm miserable.

Shaking my head, I push that motherfucker and his bullshit

out of my head. He's wrong. What Kristina and I had was more than some superficial Hollywood actress sleeping away her insecurities in some guy's bed.

We were in love.

Are in love.

Hanging my head, I sigh. Were in love. It's time I admit to myself that whatever we were isn't anymore.

My phone rings to rouse me from this funk I'm quickly slipping into, but for a moment I dread the idea of answering it as I avoid Kristina. Thankfully, Sheila's name appears on the screen, and I answer hoping she's got something good to tell me.

"Ian, are you at the cabin yet?"

"Yeah. Got here a little while ago."

"Good. I think some time away from the hustle and bustle of the city will do you a world of good."

Sheila's all about the good today, it seems.

"Thanks." I know I'm making conversation hard, but I don't have it in me to make small talk at the moment.

"So I'm calling with some fantastic news. Are you ready for it?"

I chuckle. "I've never been more ready for fantastic news, Sheila. Hit me with it."

"I have been fielding calls and emails all day about Silk! New York wants you back as T. Anderson, Ian. I think this can turn out to be something very successful for you, after all."

"That's great. Really great," I say as I try unsuccessfully to hide my disappointment at hearing her basically say my career as Ian Anwell is over.

"What's wrong? I thought you'd be thrilled to hear this

news."

"Nothing. It's great news. I'm sure you're going to get me a fantastic deal."

The phone's silent for a long moment until she quietly says, "Is this about the Marc Antony book?"

"No. Just tired after a long drive up here," I lie. It really isn't the Marc Antony book, though. It's about not being wanted by the business that's loved me as Ian Anwell since my first book.

"Don't worry about that, Ian. I think we just need to give historical readers time to get adjusted to the news of what T. Anderson writes. Believe me, there will be another author who misbehaves sooner than you can say authors behaving badly. I've got at least two authors I'm sure will unwittingly end up helping you by the end of the month."

I know she's trying to help, but even hearing about her hapless newbie authors isn't enough to make me feel good about my historical fiction career being in the shitter.

"Thanks, Sheila. I'm sure it will all work out."

"Maybe my other piece of news will make you feel better. I got a call from someone interested in making Silk into a film."

"Oh yeah?"

"He read the book and thinks it would be a great project for him. That's good news, isn't it?"

"Sure. I'll leave it in your capable hands. You always do a great job for me."

"Oh, Ian. Cheer up. It's not going to be bad forever. You never know what will show up on your doorstep at any time. It might even be something that will turn your whole day around."

I have no idea what she's talking about, but it doesn't matter. Sheila sees herself as my personal cheerleader, and that's just what she's doing. I can't dislike her for that, even though her positive yet cryptic fortune cookie sayings are less than helpful in my current mood.

"Okay. I'll see what I can do about cheering up. Give me a few days and let me know what you hear from those publishers."

"What about the film idea? I think it could be fantastic. There's a huge market for movies like that now."

"Sure. See what he has to say, and I'll think about it."

"I promise we'll make this work, Ian. Just relax up there and let me work my magic. By the time you get back to the city, you'll see it will all be better."

"Thanks, Sheila. I'll talk to you in a few days."

"Take care, Ian, and remember, it's always darkest right before the dawn."

Her attempt at helping me with pithy sayings is only making things worse, but I don't tell her that. Just because I feel like shit doesn't mean I have to make her feel that way too.

"Goodbye, Sheila."

I press END and toss my phone onto the table in front of me as the thought of a Silk movie fills my head. There's only one person in the world who can play Kate Silk. I know that, and there's no way this movie can be made without her.

So it won't be made.

I take a swig of scotch and swallow hard, wishing its effects would settle in already so I could be too fucked up to think about Kristina and how much I want to see her play the role I've written for her.

The role she played in my life for all too brief a time.

Three drinks later and I'm still unable to escape my thoughts as my mind races with what could have beens and doubts about what was. Had it ever been love? Or was all we had physical borne from my obsession with her?

No. We were off the charts great in bed, but we were more than just that. She was more than just my muse. No matter what mistakes we made, we loved each other.

I still love her.

Closing my eyes, I pray for some relief from missing Kristina.

# CHAPTER THREE

## *Kristina*

A S I TURN on to the road the directions say Ian's cabin is on, the sky seems to open up and snow falls like someone in the heavens is dumping the stuff by the truckload. I can't see more than five feet in front of me, and everywhere is pure white. The road underneath the over half foot of snow is filled with ruts and potholes which make driving even more treacherous. One moment the Range Rover is rolling along fine, and the next moment it's all I can do to keep it on the road at all.

I creep along, hoping Sienna's SUV can handle the conditions to get to the top of the hill, and finally I see what looks like a building just as I reach the crest. Leaning forward toward the windshield, I watch as I get closer and see a car parked in front of a cabin. Smoke drifts up toward the sky from the chimney, and I see the yellow glow of a light coming through a window.

My heart leaps in my chest at the thought that I've found him. Slowly, I come to a stop next to a BMW and hope if this isn't where Ian is that the people inside might be willing to help me find him. Blizzard or not, I have to get to him.

I step out of the car into snow deep enough to cover my feet and halfway up my calves. My first thought is to run up to the front door to get out of the cold and wind, but the snow makes that impossible. It's a heavy snow and I can barely walk through it, but finally I make it to the porch. Shivering, I knock on the front door.

As I stand there waiting, I look in through the windows at my eye level and see a blazing fire but no one nearby. Knocking again, I say loudly, "Excuse me. Is anyone there? I'm here from the city and I'm stranded in the snow."

For nearly five minutes I knock, but no one answers. Finally, I hang my head in disappointment and turn to go back to my car, unsure of what to do now. I can't drive in this weather, and I have less than a quarter of a tank of gas left in Sienna's Range Rover. If I have to spend the night huddled up in the driver's seat with the engine running to have heat, I won't last until morning. But what choice do I have?

My foot hits the first snow covered step when I hear, "What are you doing here?"

Ian's voice thrills me, and relief flows through me that I won't have to spend the night freezing cold in the Range Rover. Turning around, I smile as I see him standing in the doorway, but quickly I realize he's nowhere as happy to see me.

"I came to see you, but I got caught in this blizzard. I got here just in time."

"For what?" he asks, glowering down at me like never before.

"May I come in, please? It's freezing out here and my legs are wet and ice cold just from walking from the car."

He narrows his eyes to a nasty squint, and for a few

moments, I don't think he's going to let me in. Desperate to get inside the cabin and warm myself in front of the fireplace, I add, "Ian, do you want me to freeze to death out here? I know you hate me now, but even that doesn't make it okay to let me die all alone in a blizzard."

Slowly, he steps back to let me in, and as I walk past him he says in a low voice full of anger, "Just until the snow stops."

I hadn't expected him to be overjoyed to see me, but his frosty reception surprises me. Everything I rehearsed on the drive all the way there flies out of my head as I reel from how unhappy he is to have me in his presence. I'd had all these romantic notions about what would happen, and with just a few words, he's dashed them all to pieces.

Without saying another thing, he closes the front door and walks into the living room to sit in front of the fire. Feeling particularly unwelcome, I begin to strip out of my jacket, boots, and wet clothes, realizing I left my bag in the car. Not wanting to go back out into the storm, I stand at the door in just my sweater and underwear sure I don't know what to do now since he's clearly ignoring me.

"My clothes got wet, so I'm going to just let them dry by the fire," I say in my best chipper voice as I walk in front of him to arrange my pants and socks on the hearth.

He sits silently behind me, and when I turn around, his eyes are closed and his head is back. Has he fallen asleep? Taking a seat on the opposite end of the couch, I rub my blotchy red legs to get the blood flowing so they'll heat up. Never before have I felt so unwanted in his presence.

"This is a nice place," I say feebly, desperate to find a way to get him to talk to me.

It really is a nice cabin. I wouldn't have pictured him as someone who'd own a cabin out here, but like his apartment in the city, it's all modern. No log cabin look with antlers on the walls for him, not surprisingly. Instead, the kitchen has stainless steel appliances with deep brown and cream granite countertops, and the room we're sitting in has walnut hardwood floors and contemporary style furniture.

He doesn't move in response to my statement. All this silence makes me uneasy, which makes me feel like I need to fill the empty space with more talking. I tell him about my ride there and how Sienna's SUV handles well in the snow, except on the road to his cabin, my thoughts drifting into a nervous tangent when he doesn't even open his eyes at my mention of how I worried I might slide off the road and down into the ravine on my way there.

"The fire is very toasty," I mumble, hoping to see some reaction from him before I begin to ramble incoherently again in hopes of getting some response.

But I get nothing but more silence.

Finally, he opens his eyes and stares for a long moment, practically looking through me, before saying, "You shouldn't have come here."

His words aren't exactly what I'd hoped to hear, but at least he's talking.

"I had to, Ian. I couldn't let you think I betrayed you like I know you do."

He narrows his eyes again as the rest of his face turns stony to match his voice. "You didn't sleep with that guy, Kristina?"

"Yes, but—"

Before I can get the rest of my sentence out, he interrupts

me. "So you did betray me."

"You slept with someone else too, but I had to forgive you. Why can't you forgive me?"

His look hardening even more, he says quietly as he stands up from the couch, "When the snow stops, you should leave."

I reach out to grab his arm to stop him, desperate to explain what happened and how much I love him, but at the touch of my hand he lurches his body from my reach and storms away, leaving me there sitting in front of the fire alone. I so want to tell him how sorry I am and how I need him to understand how this all happened, but I can't penetrate the walls he's constructed.

I know I deserve his anger, but I just never expected him to be able to be so cold. The Ian I know and fell in love with wouldn't be able to shut me out when I'm in the same house as him. Thousands of miles away? Yeah. But not with me just feet away from him.

Does he still love me or even care for me? My stomach drops and I feel empty inside as I think this might be the end of us. I can't let what we were—what we still can be—just slip away with him closed off in a room not one hundred feet away while I sit there unable to figure out what the right words are to show him if we can forgive each other, we can overcome this.

As I try to muster up the courage to fight for him, I see a page of notes on the coffee table in front of me. Sitting down, I pick up the sheet of paper and begin to read over what he's written about the film of Silk. His agent is close to sealing the deal for the movie, and in the margin next to where he's written potential actresses for the part of Kate, he's written one name.

*Kristina Richards*

My eyes fill with tears that after all that's happened between us he still thinks of me as the only actress to play the character he's written so beautifully. I want to believe this means he still cares for me, that we still have a chance to save us.

But when did he write this? It might have been a week ago or six weeks ago. He might have written this while he was in rehab.

While I was busy feeling sorry for myself and selfishly sleeping with another man.

Oh God! I need to find a way to fix the mess I've made. I need to convince him he can believe in me again. But how?

I walk to the room he's hiding in and knock on the door. Even if he tells me to go away, I have to try.

"Ian, please talk to me."

All I hear is silence from behind the door, but I can't give up.

"I saw what you wrote about the Silk project. You still think I'm the only actress who should play her."

His shoes make a heavy noise on the wood floor as he walks toward the door and stops. I brace myself for his anger when he opens the door, but it remains closed. I know he's standing there just on the other side of it hearing what I say.

Now's the time to make my plea.

"Ian, please listen to me. I'm sorry I slept with Gavin. I should have been thinking of you while you were going through that hell. I know that. I knew that when it happened. Please forgive me."

The door opens and I see the rage in his dark eyes.

Swallowing hard, he says, "I can forgive you for that. I don't believe you care about him at all. What I can't forgive you for is betraying me and ruining my career. I trusted you, and you didn't keep our secret."

Everything in his body language screams how he blames me for all that's gone wrong in his life, and for the first time I realize how hurt he is. I didn't betray him as a girlfriend. He thinks I betrayed him as his muse.

I touch his arm and even though he wants to jerk his arm away, he doesn't. Seeing the tiniest chance to get through to him, I plead, "I never told a soul who you were or that Silk was our story. I swear it, Ian."

"You're the only person other than me who knew I was T. Anderson and knew about Silk, Kristina."

"I know, but I never told anyone. I swear. All I told Sienna was that I was dating T. Anderson. That's it. Maybe someone saw us and figured it out."

I know that makes no sense, but how could Cilla have pieced together that Ian and T. Anderson were the same person?

"Kristina, someone would have to know you and I were together. You told your friend and she sold her story to that website."

I lower my gaze and know I have to tell him the whole truth. In a quiet voice, I say, "You're not wrong about me telling Sienna I was dating you, but I swear I only told her I was with T. Anderson. But my other friend overheard me saying that, and it was Cilla who sold the story. All The Dirt must have done some digging and found out."

"How? There was nothing to connect my Ian life with my

T. Anderson pen name."

I hate what I have to say now. "I mentioned to Sienna about how I cheated while you were in rehab. Cilla wouldn't have known that part was important, but that could be how that website made the connection. I'm so sorry, Ian. I just felt so terrible about what I'd done and needed to unburden myself. I never meant for any of this to happen."

The frown he's worn since I arrived deepens and his voice falters as he says, "So you told someone about how you fucked another man while I was in rehab and that's how this happened? First you cheat on me and then because you have to make yourself feel better, you ruin my life."

We stand there looking at one another and not saying a word because he's right. Everything that's happened to hurt him is my fault. I can say I'm sorry all I want. It doesn't make up for how much he's lost.

Hanging my head, I nod as he silently closes the door in my face. I have to find some way to fix this.

I slowly walk back to the living room and sit down on the couch again to warm myself in front of the fire. God, if only I hadn't messed everything up. Why did I have to ruin what we had?

I want to remember when we weren't so lost. Before I cheated on him and betrayed his trust. Before the drugs. Before I lied.

Closing my eyes, I think back to the night he asked me to be his muse. How special I felt that night. No one had ever thought so much of me, and now I'd smashed all that to pieces with my foolishness.

If only I hadn't felt so vulnerable and alone that night

Gavin came to cheer me up.

So much of Ian and me can be summed up in that tiny phrase. If only. If only I was stronger when he needed my strength the most. If only he hadn't turned to the one thing he loved more than me.

If only what we are wasn't so full of madness.

I know I have no right to expect his forgiveness, but deep in my soul I know I can't give up trying to find some way to convince him that even though our love is crazy and destructive, it's worth fighting for.

He's worth fighting for.

# CHAPTER FOUR

## *Ian*

I PACE BACK and forth across the wood plank floor as I listen to Kristina walk out to the living room. Her being here has changed everything I felt about her betrayal. If I'd never seen her again, maybe I could have forgotten her or at least been able to pretend I didn't still love her. Christ, even if I'd had a week alone I might have been able to convince myself I could live without her.

With her here so close, I can't do any of those things.

Like a coward, I remain hidden in this bedroom instead of marching out to where she sits cozy in front of the fireplace because I can't bring myself to send her away and I can't welcome her back with open arms. I want to do both and neither at the same time.

God, I need a fucking drink.

Of course, I can't do that either since the scotch is out there with her. Fuck. I can't win, can I?

Maybe I can just fall asleep and pretend she isn't out there, close enough that I could just take her in my arms and kiss her the way I always did if I wanted to. Good fucking luck with that, right?

I lie down and close my eyes in the hopes that I can push everything out of my mind and drift off into a dream of a time when my life wasn't this mess. How long had Kristina been so integral to my happiness? Is it possible that it's only a matter of months that I've been so utterly consumed with her?

If only she still brought that same joy to my life that she did in those early days. Now everything I feel for her is tainted with betrayal.

Covering my eyes with my arm, I wish for nothing else but to forget what she's done to ruin what we were so I can return to being madly and completely in love with her. I don't want to hold this anger inside me anymore. I miss her too much and want to go back to the way we were before I chose that poison over her and made it necessary to leave her.

Maybe if I hadn't had to abandon her to go to rehab she wouldn't have felt so lonely that she turned to another man. More mistakes and more regrets borne out of my addiction.

The scent of rosemary and basil drifts into the air around me, and I inhale deeply, enjoying the smell of whatever Kristina is cooking out in the kitchen. She should have left after how I treated her, yet still she's here making this cabin more like a home than it's ever been before.

I look over toward the window and see the blizzard blowing wild outside. Perhaps that's why she stayed. Of course it is. If we were back in the city, she'd be gone and I'd be alone again.

Taking another deep breath of that delicious smell, the truth becomes impossible to avoid. I don't want to be alone again. I want Kristina.

And the only way to make that happen is to forgive her.

I slowly make my way out to the living room and sit down

on the couch without saying a word. Busy preparing dinner for us, she doesn't see me at first and I can sneak a look at her without her noticing. In all the time I've known her, I don't think she's ever looked more beautiful than she does standing there at the counter with splotches of flour on her face as she makes some kind of gravy for the pork roast the caretaker had been good enough to leave for me.

She hums a song I don't recognize as I watch her, but she must sense me staring because she looks up and in those beautiful cornflower blue eyes I see the same look of love that's always been there. That her love remains after how terrible I've been to her is a testament to her, not me. I don't deserve it, no matter what she's done.

Before she says anything, I look away toward the fire, ashamed at how I've behaved toward her. Like always, the words I need to express how I feel seem to be ironically lost.

I listen to her as she stirs the gravy and then sets the spoon down on the counter. The sound of her bare feet padding across the wood floor toward where I sit thrills and excites me, even as I pretend not to notice her. I try to focus on the crackling of the fire as it jumps off the log in the fireplace, but the pull of knowing she stands so close distracts me.

Closing my eyes, I wait for her to say the first word so this silence between us can finally end. A minute goes by without her saying a thing, though, and I open my eyes to see her standing in front of me, still only in her sweater and underwear.

"Please speak to me, Ian. I can't stand being trapped here with someone who hates me like you do. I'd leave like you want me to, but I can't yet. I'm trying to make the best of this, even though I know you don't want me here."

Her eyes tell the story of her misery. Looking up at her, I quietly admit the truth. "I don't hate you, Kristina."

"No, you just don't care about me anymore, which is worse than you hating me. At least if you hated me I could believe you still felt something."

"I care. Even though I've tried hard not to, I can't shake you. I can't shake my addiction to you."

She hangs her head and in a voice barely above a whisper, she says, "You're not addicted to me anymore. If you were, you wouldn't have been able to leave me like you did."

"I am, but like with my other addictions, I can hold out for a little while before the need presses down on me so bad that I can't stay away."

Lifting her gaze to meet mine, she gives me a tentative smile. "Does that mean you can forgive me for ruining your life?"

I reach out and slowly drag my finger down the soft skin of her thigh. "You didn't ruin my life. You are my life. Before I met you, I was merely a drunken author who had nothing in his life but scotch and success that never filled up the emptiness inside. With you, I was finally happy."

Kristina drops to her knees and presses her cheek to my leg. Gazing up at me with tears in her eyes, she says, "Oh, Ian, we can be happy again. I know we've done terrible things to each other, but can't we try again?"

My hand glides through her brown hair, and I revel in its softness. So much like who she truly is. Gentle and kind, she never meant to hurt me. I know that now. I should have always known it.

"Yes," I whisper as I stroke her cheek. "I can't stay away

from you, even if I wanted to, Kristina. Of all my addictions, you're the one I can't overcome. The one I don't want to overcome."

For a moment, she stays silent while she stares up at me, and I see the happiness fill her eyes, but then she says, "Ian, I can't tell you how happy I am to hear you want to try again. I know everything went bad because of me, but I swear I never meant all that to happen. I made such a mess of everything because I was selfish. I promise I won't be that way anymore."

"Don't say that. It wasn't all your fault. Come here."

I pull her up to kiss her lips, wishing I could take away all the sadness I hear in her words. Her mouth melds to mine as I give in to what I've wanted more than anything else. More than just my muse, she's my Kristina, the one soul who knows all my secrets and demons and still loves me.

She cradles my face and whispers against my lips, "I've missed you so much. I was worried you'd never speak to me again. I'm so sorry, Ian. I never meant to do anything to hurt you."

Pushing her hair off her face, I look up into her eyes and nod. "I know. I should have never thought you'd hurt me like that. I should have known better. I'm sorry."

Tears roll down over her cheeks, wetting my fingertips, but I receive one of her beautiful smiles. "I worried I'd never hear you say something like that to me, do you know that? Then when you were so cold when you saw me standing there at the door, I was sure everything we were had gone away forever."

"I was a fool, Kristina. I'm sorry. I never should have doubted how much you loved me."

She buries her face in the crook of my neck and wraps her

arms around me, holding me tightly as she sobs, "Promise me we can start over and we haven't ruined all that we had. Swear to me it can be great again like it was when we met."

I gently stroke her back and whisper, "We'll be great again, baby. I promise."

Kristina leans back and wipes away her tears. "This is just like that first night after you signed my book. Do you remember?"

"Yeah. I remember when I slid my hands down to your ass and you had nothing but a garter belt on. I nearly exploded out of my pants right then and there."

As I speak, I do just as I did that night and cup her ass in my hands. This time she's got underwear on, but she still excites me as much as she did the first time she was in my arms. My cock aches to be inside her, and when I slide my finger under her silk panties, I feel how wet she already is for me.

Kristina rolls her hips forward to press her needy clit against my hard cock and moans, "You're such a tease, but maybe we should wait until after dinner?"

"No fucking way," I groan as I tear her underwear off with one quick rip. "Dinner can wait. What I want is right here."

My hands squeeze her gorgeous full ass, and I slip a single finger from behind into her slick cunt. Leaning forward, she slowly runs her tongue over the shell of my ear and moans sweetly as I slide another finger in to join the first, fucking her slow and easy with them.

"Ian, I missed you so much. I felt empty when I thought about never seeing you again," she says in a voice filled with desperation.

I know exactly how she feels. Every cell in my body felt that same desperation every minute I was away from her.

Kristina rolls her hips and I curl my fingers to stroke that spot inside her I know will bring her the ecstasy she so wants and I so want to give her. She leans back with a look of pure pleasure. I watch as she bites her lower lip in that way that never fails to make her look so fucking sexy and say, "Don't think about that. Think about how my fingers feel fucking your snug cunt and how much you want to come."

"I'm so close...right there, Ian," she coos as I increase the speed of my fingers dipping into her wet pussy.

"Come for me, baby. Let me feel your juices cover my fingers."

Pitching forward, she presses her mouth to mine in a kiss while a low, sweet groan escapes from her throat into my mouth. One more thrust of my fingers into her and she comes hard, riding my hand with abandon. I watch in rapt adoration as every inch of her gives into the exquisite sensations coming from her core, loving how expressive she is when we're like this.

Her pleasure is pure and real, and I silently scold that voice inside me for making me question that. When she's with me, there's no acting or pretending.

When she's with me, she's true to her nature and lets me be true to mine.

As her legs cease their trembling from her orgasm, I slip my fingers out of her. Glistening and drenched with her, they're evidence of the truth that exists between us.

I bring them to my lips and suck them into my mouth, loving the taste of her as it dances across my tongue. Smiling, I tease, "Almost as good as going down on you."

"Almost?" she asks sweetly, still subdued from coming.

"Yeah, almost. I like burying my face in your pussy, but this will do for now."

Pulling her mouth to mine, I snake my tongue past her lips to find her tongue. I want her to taste what I taste when I eat her cunt—the sweetly musky taste of her.

She settles onto my lap and when she leans away from my kiss, smiles as she says, "That's a thing with you, isn't it? You love it when I taste myself on you, don't you?"

I nod. "Yeah. I love how raw and real it is that you don't back away from tasting yourself on my fingers or my cock after I've been inside you. It makes you even sexier, if that's possible."

"I love how you excite all my senses, you know that? I've never been with anyone who thought of taste when it came to making love."

Shrugging at the compliment, I smile. "Maybe it's because I'm an author. We're very much about all the senses. But how could anyone leave taste out of being with someone? The mouth is all about tasting. When I kiss you, I taste your tongue and your lips. When I drag my tongue over your skin, I taste it."

"And when your face is between my legs, you taste me there too," she says in strangely shy way as she traces her finger over my lower lip, exciting me.

"You mean when my tongue is deep in your cunt licking you until you come all over my face?"

I say it that way to see her blush, and she doesn't disappoint. Her cheeks turn a soft pink and her eyes widen just a bit at my words, making my cock stiffen.

Touching her cheek, I say, "I love how you get shy when I

talk like that, Kristina."

"No one has ever talked to me like you do, Ian. Everything you say is so perfect. And so sexy. Like when you asked me to be your muse. Nobody else in the world says things like that."

"My muse..." I whisper and look up into those beautiful cornflower blue eyes so gentle and caring. "I love you, Kristina. Whatever this was when we began it and whatever it became, no matter what, I've been in love with you from the moment I laid eyes on you."

She smiles even as tears of happiness fill her eyes. "I love you, Ian."

For a long moment, I stare up at her just to enjoy the sight of her with me and telling me she loves me. Me. Ian Anwell, recovering heroin addict. Borderline drunk. The man who left her alone to deal with the fallout from that online rag's article like some kind of dick.

Me.

"Is something wrong? Did I say something to upset you?" she asks in that gentle way that's charmed me from the first night.

I shake my head and tell her the truth. "No. I was just thinking how lucky I am that someone like you would even want to meet me for drinks, much less agree to be my muse and fall in love with me. That's all."

Kristina leans forward and presses her cheek to mine as she whispers in my ear, "I'm the lucky one. How many women have their own love story written for them?"

"None more incredible than you," I whisper back to her.

She sits back and gives me a deliciously wicked grin. "Right now, though, I'd much rather live out a far more erotic story with you, Mr. Anderson. What do you say we act out some scenes of our own?"

This is one of the reasons I can't live without this woman. Sweet and gentle, she also has a sensual side to her I want to satisfy even more than I want to feel satisfaction myself. What we are is rough and jagged, and I wouldn't have it any other way.

# CHAPTER FIVE

## *Kristina*

I AN WRAPS HIS arms around me and murmurs in my ear in a voice low and sexy, "Hang on. We need somewhere better than this couch for what I want to do to you."

I weave my fingers together behind his neck and hold on as he walks us to the bedroom. Staring into my eyes, he says, "After I fuck you tonight, you won't be able to think of another man."

He slides his hands down to cup my ass, carefully teasing my pussy with his fingertip and making me want him all the more.

Leaning forward, I drag the tip of my tongue over the shell of his ear and swear the truth. "Never again will I think of another man, Ian. I promise."

Ian closes his fist in my hair and tugs my head back gently. Leveling his dark gaze on mine, he says, "I plan to make sure of that."

His tone is powerful and deep, and my body aches from the sound of his voice as he promises to make me forget every other man on earth. I yearn to feel his hands on my skin and his cock inside me, filling me up like only he can. I want this to be a new beginning for us—a night that will make all the bad that's happened go away so we can be what I know we can be together.

Happy and in love.

Slowly, he lowers me to the bed and then stands there watching me as if my every moment with me enthralls him. His dark gaze travels the length of my body, and I feel its warmth as it finally settles on the space between my legs. He licks his lips and his mouth hitches up into a something like a smile, but there's a hunger in his eyes that tells me there's nothing sweet about what he plans to do with me.

He lightly trails the tip of his forefinger over the delicate skin of my inner thigh, making it quiver with anticipation, but no other part of him touches me, even though I know he sees how much I want more of him. I watch with bated breath as his fingers draw closer to my dripping wet pussy, but he stops before he reaches the evidence of how much my body hungers for his cock.

God, I want to slide my fingers down my stomach and over my clit. Just one touch. That's all I want.

But I know better.

Ian seems to read my mind and asks, "You're thinking of touching yourself, aren't you, Kristina? You want to rub that gorgeous clit, don't you?"

"Yes," I whimper, desperate to have something touch my clit so swollen with need. His fingers. His cock. His lips and tongue. My finger.

"Open your legs so I can see that pretty cunt," he orders, and I obey, hoping some relief will come soon.

Ian lowers himself to his knees and with his thumbs opens

me up so I'm completely on display for him. If I wasn't so turned on, I'd be embarrassed, but I want him too much to care about how I look close up.

"Please put your mouth on me," I beg. "Please, Ian."

"Not yet," he whispers near my skin. "I want to see you touch yourself first."

Surprised at his words, I look down at him between my legs and see a devilish look in his eyes. "I thought you didn't want me to ever do that."

"Are you embarrassed?"

"No. I just thought you didn't like me doing that."

He slowly rubs the pads of his thumbs along the crease of my legs and places a single kiss on my thigh. Looking up at me, he whispers against my skin, "That was before. We're starting over and I want to see you play with yourself. I want to see your fingers make you come while I watch."

I hesitate for a moment, but just the thought of some relief from my need makes his desire to see me masturbate something I want too. My finger quickly finds its way to my drenched pussy, and I eagerly run it over my clit, loving the sensations I'm rewarded with. Every cell in my body feels alive.

Ian watches as I dip my finger into my body and pull it out to return to my clit, coating that incredible bundle of sensitive nerves with my juices. It makes my pussy slick, and my fingers slide through over my wet skin as I begin to play with myself in earnest.

With each pass over my clit, I feel a wave of excitement wash over me as second by second I inch closer to my release. I want to come so fucking badly. Opening my legs as wide as I can, I lift my hips off the bed and rock against my hand, loving how sexy I feel knowing Ian's watching me masturbate.

He says nothing, but I hear him moan low and deep when I arch my back in ecstasy right before I come. I open my eyes for a second to see him watching with rapt attention as my finger goes to town on my clit, and for a moment I wish he'd stop me so his mouth could finish me off, but then I feel my release begin deep inside me and before I know it, my legs go weak and I bury my fingers inside me.

My eyes stay closed through the aftershocks my orgasm gives me, but I feel him move over me. My body lax from coming, I slowly open them to see him smiling down at me with a ravenous look in his eyes.

"You're so fucking beautiful when you let yourself go, you know that?"

"Am I?" I ask shyly, suddenly realizing this is the first time I've ever played with myself in front of any man.

Sucking my finger into his mouth, he flicks his tongue over it. Slowly he pulls back and says, "So fucking sexy. And you taste incredible."

He kisses me and I taste myself on his tongue like he enjoys. Raw and sensual, he groans as he runs his finger across my collarbone and under my sweater to feel the tops of my breasts. "Your cunt is the sexiest shade of pink I've ever seen. I wanted to stop you and bury my face into that pink skin to taste you, but watching you fuck yourself might have been the hottest thing I've ever seen."

I close my eyes when his fingers reach my already tightened nipples and moan as he pinches them. "I'd rather feel you touch me than my fingers, though."

He leans down and says low in my ear, "You want to feel

my fingers fuck you, Kristina?"

"No."

"No?" he asks in surprise at my answer.

Opening my eyes, I look into his and know he wants the same thing I want. "No. I want to feel your cock inside me as you fuck me long and slow. Will you fuck me like that, Ian?"

"I'm going to fuck you long and slow, baby. And then hard and fast. I want your body to crave only me from now on. Is that what you want, Kristina?"

I reach down and stroke his long, stiff cock and watch the need fill his eyes. "I want this cock and only this cock. I want to feel it deep inside me as I ride it. I want to feel it fill me up like no man ever has before. That's what I want."

Ian rolls us over so he's beneath me and cups my ass in his hands. His eyes sparkle with desire as he says, "Your wish is my command, my muse. Let me see you ride my cock."

I roll my hips, and he slides through my wet folds to my entrance. Fisting his hand in my hair, he tugs my mouth down to meet his and lifts his hips off the bed to bury his cock keep inside me in one slow thrust. Each inch feels better than the last until he's fully nested inside my body, the two of us joined in the most intimate way a man and woman can be.

His tongue dances over mine, delivering another level of sensuality to my mouth as he pumps in and out of me and I meet his thrusts with my own, riding him as he commanded. Every inch of my body craves his touch, jealous of my mouth and pussy getting all the attention.

He's everything I've ever wanted in a lover. Powerful, sensual, and focused on my complete pleasure, Ian's my own sex god to this muse.

Gently tugging my head back, he looks into my eyes and whispers in a hoarse voice full of need, "Sit up on me, baby. I want to watch you make love to me."

I feel sexier than I've ever felt with any other man. Other boyfriends made me feel self-conscious and never good enough, but not Ian. When we're together like this, his gaze never leaves me, a sign of his attentiveness and adoration. He looks at me like I truly am worthy of being called a muse, and for that, I love him all the more.

"What are you thinking about?" he asks as I realize I've become lost in my thoughts of how much I adore him.

"You," I say with a smile before he plunges his cock into me once again and hits that spot that makes my eyes want to roll into the back of my head.

He slides his hands up to my hips to control my pace, a sign he's getting close to coming and doesn't want to yet. Staring up at me, he squeezes my flesh and moans, "Slow down. I want to make this last."

I still my movement on top of him, feeling him fill me completely, and flatten my palms against his stomach to balance myself. In his eyes, I see he's working hard to hold back, but I don't want him to stop. I want to feel him explode inside me and watch the ecstasy wash over his features as he comes.

"Let me see you come apart like you love to see in me. I want to see the effect I have on you."

"Most women like a man to go for a long time," he says with a grin that looks so good on him.

Trailing my fingertip over the line of dark hair that leads from his abs to his cock, I say, "I'm not most women. We have all night, so we'll have a long time. I want to see you when I make you come."

He loosens his hold on my hips and licks his lips. "I'm sure I look like any other man, Kristina."

I shake my head, sure he couldn't be more mistaken. "No, I don't believe that. Not someone who's as sensual as you are."

"You've seen me come before."

Leaning down, I kiss his lips softly and whisper, "That was before. Everything is different now between us, isn't it?"

His gaze softens and he nods. "Yeah."

"Then show me what I do to you for the first time again."

Stroking my cheek, he says sweetly, "If that's what you want."

He lifts his hips off the bed to once again begin fucking me, and whatever sweetness that had been present a moment ago disappears as he pulls me hard down on top of him. His kiss nearly takes my breath away, and his moans tell me our lovemaking thrills him as much as it thrills me.

With a hard slap, his hand lands on my ass, sending waves of pain and pleasure racing through me. Surprised, I look down at him, and he says so sexy, "My Kristina likes it rough, doesn't she?"

Sliding up and down his cock quicker now as I inch closer to my orgasm, I moan, "Only with you."

Another hard slap stings the other cheek, and with a grunt, he pushes me hard down onto him. "Good. Now ride me and get me off, baby."

I rock and roll back and forth on him and cup my breasts to keep them from bouncing all over as I ride him with abandon. Just before I reach my climax, he pushes my hands away and sits up to take an excited nipple into his mouth. Sucking hard, he stares up at me as I come, my orgasm intensified by the feeling of his teeth sinking into the tender skin of my breast.

My thighs quiver uncontrollably as wave after wave of ecstasy rolls over me, and the incredible sensations his mouth and cock are giving me blend into a second orgasm that makes everything go dark in front of my eyes. Collapsing on top of him, I groan, "Oh my God, Ian! I've never felt like that."

He still hasn't come, so I know I have to fight the urge to curl up next to him and enjoy the afterglow of mind-blowing sex. Pushing myself back up, I look down into his eyes and see my orgasm has brought him to the brink of release.

"I'm almost there, baby. Just a few more seconds and I'll give you what you want."

My clit, still so sensitive, rubs up against the base of his cock and I feel the beginning of another orgasm start deep inside me. Rocking against him, I slide him over my G-spot and barely hold back coming again because I want to see him come apart under me.

Suddenly, Ian rolls me over onto my back and rears back, sliding his cock out of me until just the head still remains inside my pussy. A look of pure need flashes in his eyes, and for a moment he looks like a man possessed. Then he plunges into me, filling me and touching all the right places with every inch of him.

A long groan escapes his throat, and his cock twitches inside me as I begin to come again. I feel him come just as I do, and then for a long moment it's just the two of us in the world. Those dark eyes fix on me, staring into my soul, and I watch him wince like he's in pain when the last of his release flows into me.

Ian kisses me long and deep before he buries his head in the pillow next to me and whispers, "That was incredible. You're incredible."

I run my fingers down his back and feel the light layer of perspiration covering his smooth skin. I could lay here for the rest of time with him still inside me and me stroking his back as the two of us come down from the best sex we've ever had. This is what love is.

This is what we are.


A CHILL RACES down my back as I lay there in Ian's arms, and I snuggle up to his side to get warm. Wrapping his arm around me, he says, "I think the power went out. The blizzard probably knocked it out, and I don't have a generator."

"Are you trying to find a nice way to say we're going to freeze to death up here in the hinterlands?" I say, half-teasing, half-serious. I love him, but the idea of us dying Romeo and Juliet style in each other's arms as the temperature drops and we freeze solid isn't one I find very appealing.

My attempt at humor makes him chuckle. "No. We have the fire in the living room, so why don't we head out there, but I'm afraid we're going to need clothes for a little while."

We lay there in the dark, not wanting to move from our cozy spot, as I think about what I have to wear since my suitcase is still in the car. My panties sit in a pile of ripped fabric, and my pants are likely still damp from the walk to the cabin through more than half a foot of snow.

At least my sweater is still in one piece. Maybe my top half won't freeze.

"My clothes are all in the suitcase I left in the car," I mumble against his still warm skin. "Other than that, I have a sweater and a pair of pants that are still drying out near the fire."

Ian squeezes me against him and chuckles. "I have blankets. We can make our way out to the fire and curl up in front of it. I can tell you about the news my agent gave me today."

He sounds happy about whatever the news is, so I sit up and tug on his arm. "Okay, let's go. The idea of freezing to death here is getting scarier by the minute."

We walk back out to the living room naked, and sitting on the couch, we cuddle together under a white down comforter Ian grabbed on our way past one of the other bedrooms. The blazing fire instantly warms me, and I turn to see him reaching for the notes I'd read earlier.

"So Sheila called today to let me know someone contacted her about a film of Silk."

His news thrills me. "That's terrific! I think anything you write would be so wonderful as a film."

For a moment, sadness fills his eyes. "Yeah, well, not anything. The Caligula's Dream film doesn't look like it's going to happen now."

"Why?"

"The news about me being T. Anderson and writing something considered erotica made them reconsider, I guess."

I hate that he's suffering because of my stupid mistakes. Pressing my cheek to his chest, I hold him to me. "I'm so sorry, Ian. I'm sorry they did that because of what I did. I never meant for any of that to happen."

His lips gently press against the top of my head in a kiss. "It's okay. What do they say? When one door closes, another one opens? Maybe that's what this Silk film could be."

I look up to see the sadness in his eyes is gone now. "It's so exciting, isn't it? What did your agent say about when it could happen?"

"These things take a while. By the time the actors come in on a project, it's been through so many hoops most don't even make it. But at least there's interest."

"I'm so happy for you, Ian."

"For us," he says as he pulls me into his arms. "Us. It's our story. And Sheila told me she's gotten a lot of interest from New York about publishing the story too."

"That's fantastic!" I say as he hugs me tighter. "At least there's some good coming out of all that awful mess."

Ian remains quiet for a long time, and then says, "I won't give them the rights unless you're Kate Silk. You're the only one who could play her."

Tears well in my eyes as I finally understand how much Silk is our story. Looking up at him, I smile as I begin to cry. "I'd be honored if they'd consider me for the part."

"Not consider. I plan on making that one of the non-negotiable terms of the deal. Unless it's you, I won't do it."

"Why? There are any number of actresses who could do this character justice, and this is a big chance for you. You don't have to make them choose me. It's more than enough of an honor to know that this story is about you and me."

"No. Kristina, it's always been only you. I can't even imagine anyone else playing this part."

I kiss him for being so sweet. "Who do you want for the

part of Sean?"

He looks up toward the ceiling and shakes his head. "I hadn't thought about it. I guess I should have since those are going to be some pretty hot scenes."

"I think he'd have to be handsome and sexy," I tease.

"I don't want to think about some sexy handsome guy with you right now," he says, narrowing his eyes to a faux angry squint.

Trying to keep the smile from my face, I say, "Well, I guess you could demand the actor be someone hideous."

"I might want to since Silk and Steel has become far more romantic than erotic."

"Really?"

Ian nods and kisses me. "Love does that to a man."

"I like that. Love does that to a man. So what's going to happen to Kate and Sean?"

"They live happily ever after."

His dark eyes stare into mine as I wonder if that's really possible for us. "Do you think we will?"

"I think this is a whole new beginning for us, so anything's possible. How does happily ever after sound to you?"

Tapping him on the tip of his nose, I smile. "I think it sounds wonderful."

And for the first time in my life, my future with a man looks exactly that. Wonderful. And I wouldn't have it any other way.

# CHAPTER SIX

## *Ian*

KRISTINA CURLS UP against me as I tell her everything Sheila said earlier. When I'd first heard about the film and book possibilities, I hadn't cared much, but now as I watch the woman who inspired Silk and my writing, I can't help but be excited about the future, both for my work and Kristina and me.

"Do you think it will be shot in New York? It would be so great to work in the city again," she says as she hugs me.

I stroke her hair and imagine how great it would be to hold her in my arms each night and then watch her work each day. Nothing would make me happier at this moment.

"Maybe it will since it's set in New York. I'll have to see."

"I think that would be so wonderful, Ian. We could talk about the dailies and you could be there on set to see me work. I think it could be so much fun for us."

Tilting her head back, I kiss her and press my forehead to hers. "You've convinced me. I'll tell Sheila to let them know the film can only be made if it's shot in the city."

"Oh, don't do that! What if they say no because of the cost? I'd hate to see Silk not get made because of my silly ideas."

I kiss her again and shake my head. "Then it never becomes a film. I'm fine with that too. As long as I have you, nothing else matters, Kristina."

And that's the absolute of my life now. As long as I have her by my side, I don't care about anything else. They can take everything away—the writing, the fame, the money. None of it matters as much as she does.

For so long, I've lived a comfortable but empty life. The drugs and alcohol did nothing to feed my starving soul, but I kept them as my constant companions because I needed something to fill the hollowness inside. That they never succeeded didn't matter. I could lie to myself and say everything was fine. I had money and fame. What else did I need?

But deep down I knew they weren't enough.

Then I saw Kristina that night and through a drunken haze I knew I had to have her. It wasn't love at first, but lust was better than what I'd been using to forget the emptiness. But it didn't take long for my feelings to grow far deeper until I couldn't be happy without her.

She stares up at me with a pensive look. "Ian, what's going to happen to us? Are we ever going to just be okay?"

I kiss her on the forehead and shake my head. "No. We're not the kind of people to just be okay."

Kristina knits her brows and sighs. "We can't keep going on like we have. Since the first night we met, we've been on some crazy emotional rollercoaster. Do you want to stay like that?"

"We can't help what we are. Something about the two of us together is crazy. But is that so bad?"

"I don't know. How long can crazy last? At some point,

don't you want life to be like other people's?"

Shaking my head, I can't help but smile. A Hollywood star and an author would never be like other people. "Kristina, we aren't like other people. You're famous and I'm a recovering addict. I'll always be a recovering addict. We are who we are. That doesn't mean we can't be happy."

"But we've spent so much time unhappy. Don't you worry about that?"

I see the concern in her beautiful blue eyes. "No. Love isn't about being happy all the time. Love is about getting through the bad times and appreciating the good times."

"We've been through so much bad, Ian. I just worry all of this is going to burn out one day soon. Don't you worry about that?"

"No, I don't because when all the bad is stripped away, we love each other madly with the kind of passion people only dream about. Most people never feel—I mean really feel anything. They say they love, but what they really do is stay in relationships that are boring but safe. That's not us. There's nothing safe about us."

"I want to think that we're always going to be okay, but I worry, Ian. What if someday one of us wants safe?"

"Do you want safe, Kristina?"

She remains silent for a long moment, closing her eyes as her mouth turns down into a frown. I run the pad of my thumb over the swell of her bottom lip while I wait to hear her answer knowing I can't promise her safe. That's the last thing I can offer her.

"I don't know if I want safe. I just worry about what happens down the road with us."

Leaning over, I press my lips to hers in a kiss full of how much I love her. "Nothing about us has ever been safe. What we feel is raw and rough and sometimes we break each other. I don't know what's going to happen down the road. I just know I don't want to think about my life without you in it, Kristina."

"I don't want to think of my life without you in it, Ian. I don't want safety if it means you and I aren't together. I just worry that someday one of us will break us and we won't know how to put the pieces back together."

I caress her cheek, loving the feel of her soft skin. "Maybe we're just going to have to accept the fact that we belong together, broken or not. We crash, we burn, and we break everything around us, but each time we search for one another because each of us has what the other needs."

Her eyes fill with a look of confusion. "What do I have that you need? I keep messing things up for us. How could you need that?"

"I need the sweetness that's so much a part of you. I need the strength you show when things get rough between us."

She rolls her eyes and scrunches up her nose. "What strength? I wish I was strong."

"Only a strong woman would have driven all this way in a blizzard to see someone she wasn't sure would even talk to her. You are strong, Kristina, and that strength is something I want in my life. I need it. I need you. If anyone should want to leave, it's you after what I put you through."

"No, I never wanted to leave. I know I said I would when you told me the truth about your addiction that night, but how could I leave when the man I love needed me most?"

Pulling her into my arms, I hold her to me and whisper,

"You deserve so much better than what I've given you, but if you'll have me, I promise that's all in the past. I know you have no good reason to believe someone who freely admits he's always going to be a recovering heroin addict, but I mean every word."

She hugs me tightly to her and I feel her sob against my chest. "Oh Ian, how could I not want you? For all your weaknesses, you're the one person in this world who makes me feel like I'm something special."

I tilt her head back and look down into her beautiful face and smile for the simple reason that she makes me happy. "You are special. I knew that from the moment I first saw you on my television in that film. No matter who else was in the scene, you shined like no one else I'd ever seen before. I had to meet you."

"I thought it was because you wanted to sleep with me," she says with a chuckle as a blush covers the apples of her cheeks.

"There was that," I admit. "But I saw something else that night too, something that attracted me to you in a way that I'd never felt before with anyone."

"What was it?"

I think back to that night as I sat alone in my apartment like I did every other night and mindlessly stared at my TV until I saw her face. That moment is seared into my mind as the one when everything in my life changed. From then on, even when I became lost in the drugs again, I had someone who I never stopped thinking about. That had never been the case for me.

"Something in your eyes told me you might be able to accept who I was."

Kristina smiles and I see that gentleness in her eyes I saw that night. "I love that you saw something that no one else has ever seen in me, Ian."

"I'm glad all those other men missed that in you. If they didn't, you wouldn't be here with me right now."

"Did I ever tell you how nervous I was that night we met at that bar?"

I shake my head and chuckle. "No. I can't imagine why."

"When I heard you wanted to meet me, all I could think about was that this incredibly talented author who'd written one of my favorite books would be sitting across the table from me and I'd feel like a total idiot in front of you. I was so worried you'd think I was just some stupid actress."

"There's nothing stupid about you. And you didn't have to worry. I was too busy being entirely sure you'd think I was just some boring history writer."

"I love the idea that we were both so unsure that night. Every man I've ever dated always seemed so sure of himself. So sure I would fall for him because he was good looking or famous. So sure he was too charming for me to say no to. But you were thinking of me when we met, just like I was thinking of you. That's the difference."

"Sounds pretty selfless for an addict and a movie star," I joke.

She looks down at the comforter and runs her fingers over the edge of the fabric. "I guess, but those are just labels for us, Ian. I like to think of the two of us as just people who care more than they should and finally found someone who really cares too."

"I've never been accused of caring too much. Never in my

life has anyone thought that about me," I admit, suddenly ashamed of how truly selfish I am.

"I think you're very sensitive to other people. I know you don't show it a lot, but I've seen it since the moment we met. I saw it in your eyes when you looked at me that night in that booth." She lifts her hand to caress my cheek, smiling up at me now. "No one as passionate as you could ever be insensitive without trying. I like that I'm the only one who sees that side of you, though."

Her touch thrills me, as always, and I lean my head into her palm to feel more of her. I love that she sees me like that. I don't know if it's the truth, but if it isn't, it's the best lie I've ever been told.

"Now you see what I mean when I say that being with you lets me be the man I always wanted to be."

Kristina presses her lips to mine and whispers, "I love that man, Ian. I love how smart he is and how he understands me like no one else ever has. And even if we freeze to death here in this cabin in the middle of a blizzard, I want to say thank you for making me feel adored like no one else in the world."

Pulling her closer to keep her warm, I hold her to me so she can take some of my warmth. "We're not going to freeze here. There's no way we've been through all we've been through just to find happiness in time to freeze in a snowstorm. The electricity will come on again, and then we'll eat the dinner you cooked and talk about what we want to do when we get back to the city."

Her body shivers against mine, and I silently wonder if any of that will actually happen. It's only been about an hour, but the heat from the fireplace is quickly becoming too little to keep us warm. It won't take long before a down comforter and a pile of blankets won't be enough.

As we sit there, I wonder if this will be the end of us. Not exactly the way I thought I'd go. I would have put a hefty bet on my dying alone in my apartment from an overdose of heroin. I figured they'd find me partially decomposed after weeks of lying dead on my living room floor, the stench of my rotting corpse too much for even that one gruff and seasoned EMT worker there always is on the scene. Everyone would wonder how someone like me could die alone without a soul in the world curious enough to come by for weeks as I lay sprawled out, finally dead from the drugs.

"Hey, you got quiet all of a sudden. What's wrong?"

I look down at Kristina resting her head on my shoulder and smile. "Nothing. Just trying to remember my Boy Scout days in case things get really bad with this storm."

She giggles in that way that never fails to charm me and says, "I love the idea of you being a little boy in his Boy Scout uniform out in the woods. So what did you remember that will help us if it gets colder in here?"

"Not much, except for a few knots, which I don't think will help us keep warm."

"Knots, huh?" she asks with a twinkle in her eye like she's heard something intriguing.

"Yeah, but that won't keep us warm."

"True, but when we get back to the city it might make for an interesting time."

I kiss her on the tip of her nose and grin, loving this side of her. "Does my Kristina like being tied up? And how did I not know this by now?"

A sheepish look comes over her face and she bites her bottom lip. "I don't know if I do since nobody's ever done that to me, but Sienna was telling me something a while back about this thing she and her boyfriend did that sounded interesting."

"So you have a kinky friend named Sienna? Sienna who?"

"Sienna Rollins. She's an actress like me."

I think back to the countless hours I've spent on Netflix and try to place the name, but it doesn't ring a bell. "I don't think I've ever heard of her."

Proudly, Kristina says, "You will. She's a knockout blond with everything going for her and on top of all that, she's a great actress. All she needs is the right part and she's going to be a household name."

"Like you."

"Sienna's so much better than I am. She just needs the break we all wait for and she's going to set the world on fire. I just know it."

"I think it's great you're so generous like that, Kristina. I can't imagine most actors and actresses are like you."

"Sienna's my friend. I want to see good things happen for her. That's how I am with people I care about."

The lights around us flicker on and off and then come back on, ending the threat of our freezing to death out in the wilds of upstate New York. Kristina looks around and breathes a sigh of relief.

"I was starting to worry for a while there. How about I get up and see if I can get that roast in shape so we can eat?"

As she moves to leave my side, I hold her there next to me, not for warmth but because I have something I need to say. "In a minute. I want to ask you something first."

Her eyes show her worry at what my question might be, but she presses a smile onto her lips. "Okay. Shoot."

"I don't want you to think I'm saying any of this because we almost froze here because I never believed that would happen. I'm saying this because if I don't ask now and somehow I mess things up, I'll regret it for the rest of my life."

"Okay. What do you want to ask me?"

Taking her hands in mine, I bring them to my lips and kiss them before taking a deep breath. "Kristina, will you come live with me? Be my muse forever. I want to see your face when I open my eyes each morning and feel you next to me as I go to sleep each night, and in between I want the chance to show you every day how much I love you."

Tears well in her eyes and she nods her head. "Yes, I will, Ian. I will be your muse forever."

As I take her in my arms, I feel happier than I've ever felt in my life. No drug has ever made me feel like this. Only knowing Kristina loves me like I love her could make me feel so incredible.

"I love you, Ian," she whispers in my ear while I hold her tightly to me. "For all the good and all the bad we've been through, I love you with all my heart."

"I love you too, my beautiful muse. My Kristina."

# CHAPTER SEVEN

## *Kristina*

THE ROAST SOMEHOW made it through the electricity going out and as we sit down to eat, I see Ian's eyes open wide at the sight of the meal I've prepared. Looking at me, he asks, "Is it possible you're the perfect woman? Gorgeous, talented, sexy, and a great cook?"

I sit down across from him at the kitchen table and smile at his comment. "I thought the same thing that first night you made me your world famous risotto."

"That sounded pretty sexist, didn't it? I didn't mean it like that. I think anyone with all those qualities, man or woman, is pretty damn impressive."

Waving away his worry that he offended me, I say, "Not to worry. Eat up. We never know how long the electricity is going to stay on since it's still blowing around out there, and I'd hate for this meal to go to waste."

"I have an idea. Hang on," he says as he jumps out of his chair to head for a closet in the hallway. He returns a few seconds later with two white taper candles and two silver candlesticks. Placing them between us in the middle of the table, he walks to the fireplace and brings over one long matchstick. As he lights the two candles, he says sweetly, "This wonderful meal calls for candlelight, so even if the electricity goes out, we'll still have a romantic dinner for two."

When he shows this side of him—the cute and thoughtful side—I can't help falling in love with him all over again. I know his demons will never really disappear, always hiding deep inside and looking for that perfect opportunity to come out and wreak havoc on him again, but I love him. The good, the bad, and the worst of him. I love all of it.

"I love it, Ian. It's perfect."

By the time we finish our dinner, he's convinced I am the perfect woman, and even though I know I'm nowhere close to being that, I'm happy to let him think that. He sits across from me with a completely satisfied look in his eyes, and I like that I could make that happen.

"Would you like to hear what I'm going to write for the second Silk book?" he asks as I clear the plates from the table.

"You know what the story is now?"

"I think so. Would you like to hear about it?"

I quickly run some hot water over the dirty dishes and return to my seat to hear all about his new book. "Yes! I'm dying to know what happens to Kate and Sean. You didn't give them a happily ever after in the first book, so will they get one in this book?"

Ian nods as a sexy grin spreads across his lips. "Yes. They'll get their happily ever after in this one. Not that I'm going to make it easy for them. They're going to have to get through a lot of obstacles before they find their happiness."

"Sort of like us?"

"Exactly like us. It is our story, after all."

A feeling of dread comes over me for a moment. "Does that mean you're going to have her go back to her addiction?"

The smile he wore just a few seconds earlier fades and he knits his brows. "Yeah. Kate's going to have to get through her heroin addiction to find real happiness with Sean."

I instantly begin to worry that writing about that will be too much for Ian. Will he want to go back to it himself because he's living it again through his character? Will he give in to the temptation?

He reaches across the table and clutches my hand. "Don't worry. I'll be okay. You'll be right there with me, and every day I'll read you what I wrote. I think it will be good for me."

"How?"

"This part of me is never going away, Kristina. I need to be able to live with the reality of who I can be and what it will do to my life if I let myself go back to that. Don't worry. I know what I can lose if I do."

"You mean me?"

"I know you stayed last time, but I'm not a fool. I know how bad that was for you, and there's no reason for me to believe you'll stay if it happens again, no matter how much you love me. I won't risk that again. I promise."

"I'm just worried it will bring back all those feelings and be too much for you."

Ian takes a deep breath and slowly exhales as concern settles into his expression. "I know. And it might bring back a lot of things I wish I could forget, but my desire for that poison isn't something I can just pretend never existed. It did, and it will for the rest of my life. That's how addiction is."

I hate hearing him say he'll always want that awful drug. Of all the things about his addiction, that's the worst. Knowing no matter how much he fights it and how long he stays clean, somewhere inside him is a part that will always want it.

He comes around the table and kneeling next to me, looks up at me with those dark eyes that always seem so full of passion. "I promise, Kristina. No more of that. I'll do whatever I have to do to fight those demons. I choose you—I choose us—over that shit. I don't want to lose you and all the wonderful things being with you makes me feel."

Cradling his face, I can't help but believe him. He's the man I love. I just pray to God he's telling the truth.

"I want more than anything for you to never touch that stuff again, Ian. You're such a wonderful man. You're a good person, and I think you believe what you say. I want you to be happy, and I've never seen you so miserable as when you were high. That man wasn't the Ian I know. That man was so lost, and I didn't know how to get to him."

He covers my hands with his and nods his understanding. "I know. I don't want that for us. I want us to be happy, and I know heroin has no place in any happiness we'll ever have. I just want you to know I haven't done anything this time. We ran into a problem and I came here, but I didn't go back to it."

I quietly admit what had been in the back of my mind since hearing he left the city. "I was afraid you might have. More than the snowstorm and even the chance that you might turn me away, I feared I'd find you high and lost to me again."

"I didn't do it. I swear. I'm not going to tell you I didn't try to get blasted drunk to forget how hurt I was, but nothing else. I promise. Never again."

Leaning down, I kiss him and say, "I'm so sorry for what

happened. I never meant to hurt you. I love you."

His smile tells me he's truly forgiven me. "I know I'm as much to blame. You deserved more than a junkie."

"Promise me something?"

"Anything."

"Promise me we can forget all this and be happy again. I want us to be happy like we used to be before everything got all messed up."

"I promise. This is a new chance for us. We're starting over and have the ability to be as happy as we want."

"Good. You know what I want now?"

He understands the tone in my voice and slowly runs his hands up over my thighs. "I think I know, but why don't you tell me what you want?"

A tiny moan escapes my throat as his thumbs graze the very tops of my legs. "I want my gorgeous author boyfriend to make love to me over there on that couch in front of the fire."

"Your wish is my command, my muse." Ian stands and holds his hand out for me to take it. I weave my fingers through his, and he asks, "Anything in particular you'd like?"

As he guides me to the couch, I think about his question and there isn't anything in particular I want. Other than him completely lost in me and me completely lost in him.

He turns to face me and kisses me deeply, nearly taking my breath away and making my knees go weak. "I'm going to worship every beautiful inch of your body. When I'm done with you, you won't be able to think of anything but how much I love you. Now lie back and let me get down to work."

I do as he commands and lie back on the couch. Crawling up my body, he gently pulls my sweater over my head, leaving me naked in front of him.

Beginning at my ankles, he slowly kisses up one leg and then the other until his mouth is ever so close to my excited pussy. I let my legs fall open to the sides, eager for him to press his mouth to my clit and give me what I want, but he has other plans.

He looks up at me as he nips at the tender skin of my left thigh and then says, "I know I told you this before, but your cunt is the prettiest pink I've ever seen in my life. Just seeing it makes me want to bury my face in you."

"I wish you would."

"Not yet. I want your body primed for me, so sit back and let yourself enjoy what I'm about to do."

I watch as he drags his tongue up toward my core, stopping just as his mouth reaches the crease of my leg. Over and over, he teases me like this, every so often letting his lips graze my pussy lightly and making me want him so fucking badly. No matter how much I whimper and beg, he still persists in teasing me, but I know the waiting will be worth it.

When he finally presses his mouth to me, it's like heaven. His tongue flat, he drags it up over my tender skin, moaning against my body until he reaches my clit. I watch in rapt attention as he hovers over that point of perfect pleasure and gazes up at me with a look of the devil in his eyes.

"Ready or should I wait a little more?"

I bury my hands in his hair and pull his head toward my body, dying to feel his mouth on me. He doesn't resist at all, as hungry for me as I am for him, and the first touch of his tongue on my clit sends a jolt of pleasure racing through my body like electricity coursing through me.

My fingertips tingle as he sucks my clit between his lips, and just as I'm sure I can't take another second of this sweet torture, he gently bites down and it's like fireworks exploding behind my eyes as my orgasm takes me over. I ride his mouth as waves of pleasure wash over me, and as the exquisite tremors begin to subside, he flicks his tongue and slides two fingers inside me, curling them perfectly against that sweet spot he knows will make me come again.

And then I come for the second time, this time even harder than the first, my hands holding his head so I don't miss a moment of the pleasure his mouth provides. Time ceases to exist in those moments when I feel like I'm floating above myself, and when he finally sits back away from me, I can't imagine how I'm going to continue feeling like this.

I open my eyes to see him smacking his lips like he's just enjoyed a favorite treat. He grins like a naughty schoolboy, and I can't help but smile.

"You look like the cat who just ate the canary," I tease.

"I love the taste of you on my tongue." He brings his fingers to his mouth and sucks me off them. "I want you to know that just in case I someday have some kind of difficulty getting it up that I'll be more than happy to spend all my time making you come that way."

Reaching out for him, I take him by the hand to pull him down on top of me. "I do love that, but I think I'd miss the feeling of you inside me. We'll just have to get you the little blue pill."

His hard cock nudges up against me, and Ian groans in my ear, "Thankfully, that's not a problem I have now. Now my cock gets hard every time you're anywhere nearby."

I spread my legs wide to take him inside me, and he lifts his hips off the couch. I want to feel him fill me like only he can, but in my ear I hear him say, "I want you on my lap like the first time we were together."

Sitting up, he pulls me on top of him and in a second my thighs are straddling him as his cock waits for me so sit down on him. Slowly, I lower myself down and feel him enter me, filling me until there's no space between us and we're together in the most intimate way.

I kiss him and taste myself on his lips and tongue as he begins to thrust his cock in and out of me. His hands hold my hips firmly, and in my ear he moans, "I love it when you ride me like this. Let me watch you come apart for me, Kristina."

Raising myself up, I slide down his cock again as he sucks a nipple hard into his mouth. He knows what I like and what gets me off, and he gives it to me like no one else ever has. I ride him, my hips rocking back and forth, while he bites down on my excited nipple, sending waves of delight rushing through my body.

I watch him move from one breast to the other, each one receiving his attention and ratcheting up my desire with every gentle nip of my skin. The mouth that just brought me such pleasure now gives me the pain I crave to get off.

Inside, my orgasm begins to unwind slowly like coiled snake until I'm bucking wildly on his lap needing the release I know he can give me. Leaning back, he watches me inch toward that moment of sweet abandon, all the while guiding my movement with his hands on my hips. I'm so close. Just a few more passes of his cock over that spot inside me and I'll come apart.

Ian lets go of my left hip and moves his hand between us. Sliding his finger over my swollen and needy clit, his touch finally sends me over the edge and my orgasm explodes inside me. I throw my head back as every nerve in my body comes alive and focuses on that spot where his fingertip still rests.

For a long moment, I forget everything but him inside me. I forget all the good and the bad we've been through. I forget the drugs and Cilla's betrayal. I forget everything that tore us apart and all I can think of is how incredible my body feels on his.

"I love watching you when you come. You're so erotic and sensual, just like a woman should be."

I open my eyes and look down at me staring up at me with wonder in his eyes, like what I am to him is something amazing. Leaning down, I kiss him and say, "Only with you. I've never been like this with anyone else. I think it's you who makes me feel that way."

"What way?"

"Sensual. Like I'm sexy and it's something that feels natural."

"Good because it is something natural. I see it every time we're together, and I love it. I love that you never pretend to be something other than what you are."

I look down at where his body and mine are still joined and frown. "You didn't come."

"I had to work at it, if that makes you feel better about my not coming. I almost couldn't hold back at one point."

"Why did you then?" I say, pouting because I love when I can make him come that way.

"Because as much as I enjoy coming from being inside you,

I love coming from your mouth even more. You know that."

"I think you have an unhealthy obsession with my going down on you, Ian."

"I think you love it as much as I do."

What I love is that when I suck his cock he's happy. I still wonder from time to time if I'm really any good at it or if he's just inclined to come easier that way, but it doesn't matter. No man has ever taken my body to the heights he has, so if my going down on him gives him pleasure, who am I to say it shouldn't be that way?

I lift myself off him and look down to see his cock glistening with my juices. Lowering myself to the floor, I wrap my fingers around him and look up to see him watching me as if he can't wait for me to put my mouth on his skin. For so long I thought this part of sex demeaning to women, an act that made us subservient and less than the man, but now I see with the right person, it's just another way to bring the man you adore pleasure.

And as I watch him come, I know this is something even he doesn't realize means something to me. That my touch, my mouth, can excite him and I can take all he has makes me feel like that sensual being I've always wanted to be.

# CHAPTER EIGHT

## *Ian*

W E LIE IN each other's arms after a third night straight of
lovemaking that only reinforced how much I love
Kristina. No other woman has ever made me feel so entirely
devoted to her happiness, and although it's not my usual way of
feeling, I genuinely enjoy being the reason she smiles.

Me. Ian Anwell. The reason someone so incredibly sweet
and gentle is happy. As I feel her move against me and make
that adorable snoring noise, I have a hard time believing I could
be so lucky.

The storm outside ended two days ago, so the roads should
be passable enough to let us leave and start our life together
back in my apartment. I've had enough of the sticks.

I gently smooth my hand over her soft hair, caressing her
back up and down and feeling more content than I could ever
imagine being. Today, we'll drive back to the city and move her
into my apartment, and after a few days of settling in, which I
intend on spending in bed as much as possible, I'll get working
on Silk and Steel in earnest and see what magic Sheila can work
with Silk.

For the first time in my adult life, I can't wait for what's about to happen.

Kristina stirs and gazes up at me with a questioning look in her blue eyes. "I woke you up, didn't I?"

"No, not this time. I've been awake for a while."

She blushes in her adorable way and smiles. "Good. I thought my snoring woke you up again. Are you sure you want me to move in knowing I spend my nights as a little chainsaw?"

Pulling her to me, I press a kiss to the top of her head. "I'm sure I can't wait to have you live with me. I was just thinking about it, in fact."

"I can't wait either, Ian."

I slide under her and my hands travel down her back to squeeze her ass. "Me too. I'll cook every night for you after I write all day, and we'll spend long hours making love in every room and on every surface. And in the mornings, we'll get up and fuck like crazy people in that shower you love."

Biting her lip, she smiles at my plans and asks, "What about when I have to work?"

"Then I'll text you too many times a day and tell you how much I love you, and when you come home, I'll cook for you and we'll make love over and over every night to make up for all the time you were away. And I'll tell you every morning how much I love waking up next to you."

"Your little chainsaw," she says with a giggle.

I kiss her softly and nuzzle her neck. "My little chainsaw."

This is what we can be when the madness we are subsides for even a short time. Sweetness and love. I could spend the rest of my life just like this with her cuddled up against me.

"What about when we fight?"

I take a deep breath in. "We'll never fight."

Kristina looks at me and shakes her head, her expression serious now. "You know we're going to fight, Ian. What's going to happen when we do?"

"We'll fight like we love. Completely. Madly. Wildly. And if the fight is my fault, I promise to only be an asshole for twenty-four hours. But you need to remember who I am, Kristina. I'm going to be jealous of other men I think want you. I'm going to be possessive when I shouldn't be, even though I won't want to be. You're my addiction."

She kisses me and cups my face with her hands. "And I promise to love you even when we're fighting completely, madly, and wildly because you're the only man I want to be with."

We stay there silent in each other's arms with the knowledge that no matter what happens, who we are will always be based on the love we have for one another. It's raw and ragged sometimes, and smooth as silk at other times, but it's always the most honest emotion we share between us.

I love her with utterly all I have, and she loves me with all she has. Anything less for us wouldn't be real.

Breaking the silence, I whisper in her ear, "Although I'd usually say we should stay here and enjoy ourselves, I think we should get back to the city as soon as we can. The storm's over, so I think we can leave whenever we're ready."

She rolls off me and kisses my cheek. "Okay. Give me a little bit and I'll be ready to go. I just have to grab a shower and get back into my clothes. They should be dry by now."

"You don't want me to go out to the car and get your bag?"

"No, it's okay. As long as I don't have to put on wet clothes, I'll be fine."

I love it when she's cute, and as she slips from the bed, she flashes me an adorable smile. "It's not like I've spent much time in them since I got here."

An hour later after I've dug both vehicles out of the snow drifts that nearly cover my car, we're ready to go back to reality, which includes the media mess we ran away from just a few days ago. I check the fireplace and turn off the lights, already missing our time here, but no matter what we have to deal with back in the city, we have each other.

And that's all that matters.

Kristina stands at the front door waiting for me, and wrapping my arms around her, I pull her close. "Ready?"

She looks up into my eyes with worry written all over her face. "Do you think we should stay longer to let all that business die down back there?"

"No. I am who I am, and that's not going to change. As Ian Anwell, I write historical fiction, and as T. Anderson, I wrote our story and I'm writing even more of it. It is what it is. As long as I know you're by my side, everything will be fine. So let's go back and show the world we're together and then hope they go away."

"What if they don't?"

"Then that gives us even more reasons to stay inside in bed. I wouldn't worry, though. Today we might be newsworthy, but trust me. There will be a celebrity who does something tomorrow that will make us as boring as yesterday's news. That you can depend on."

"Okay. I'll follow you and after I give Sienna her car back, I'll just go to your place. I have a suitcase full of clothes and everything I need, so I'm all set. I can go to my apartment in a few days."

"Perfect. Be careful on the hill. I've driven that road in the snow a few times and it can be treacherous."

With a big smile, she says, "Got it! I'm more worried about you, though. Sienna's SUV is made for this type of weather, but all you have is a car."

"Don't worry about me. I grew up around this type of weather, so I know how to handle it. Ready?"

She kisses me sweetly and buttons up the last button on her coat. "Ready. See you in a few."

THE ROADS LEADING back to the city aren't as bad as I'd feared they'd be, and as I drive I can't help but daydream about how life has turned out. What began as my obsession with Kristina as she acted on my television screen has become the kind of love I never believed someone like me would ever have. Addicts just don't get those happily ever afters. Not in real life, anyway. Only in books and in movies do they get that second chance because of a great woman who truly loves them. The reality is usually far harsher.

A life alone always fighting the demons that live inside and want more than anything to resurface and take over.

But that's not me anymore. Yes, I'll always be a recovering heroin addict. That's a truth that will never go away, so I have no choice. I have to face it. But I'm more than that, and for a long time I didn't think I was.

Until Kristina. She makes me see no matter what that junk offers, I can have better. I want better. I want that elusive happily ever after so popular in the fiction I write and the movies she makes and so rare in real life.

I look in the rearview mirror to see her behind me smiling like she knows I'm looking back at her. I wave and watch her wave back and blow me a kiss. Even such a small gesture makes my heart swell with the happiness only she can give me.

But then her expression morphs into one of horror, and in a flash, everything changes. Like some slow-motion replay, I take my gaze from her back to the road and see the truck rounding the turn into our lane. I swerve to avoid it, but it's no use. He's going too fast and he sideswipes the car, tearing off the mirror next to me. His front end rips down the side of my car, and the noise of metal crushing metal fills my ears.

I lose control and then there's only spinning. Frantically, I try to see Kristina, but it's all happening so fast now. At some point, I don't hear the screeching sound of metal on metal anymore, and everything becomes a blur. I press on the brake over and over, but it's no use. I crash through the guardrail and careen down the side of an embankment.

Trees fly by me as visions of my life rush through my mind. They're just pieces of my life, actually, but they make up the whole of who I am.

Me with my parents at the house I grew up in on a spring day, the sun warming my face as my father tossed a baseball toward my glove.

The day I graduated with honors from Cornell and the look of sadness on my mother's face when she congratulated me, wishing my father could have lived long enough to see that day too.

Standing in the rain at my father's grave later that day with my diploma and hoping somehow he saw what I'd achieved.

The moment I learned my first book would be published.

That first time I tried heroin and the euphoric sensation of flying it brought with it.

The feeling of complete and utter failure as I walked into rehab the last time.

Alone in my apartment and seeing the most beautiful woman in the world appear on my television screen for the first time.

My mind's a jumble of fear and confusion, but somewhere in all that fleeting memories of my time with Kristina begin to appear in my mind. They calm me so as my car finally hits the bottom of the ravine and the air bag explodes into me, I'm relaxed. As the shock of what happened settles into me, I feel my head fall forward toward the inflated air bag and then there's nothing but darkness.

*Kristina sits next to me quietly reading what I wrote that afternoon as I absentmindedly play with the ends of her hair, twirling them around my finger and then releasing them to do it again. I'm nervous to hear her thoughts and opinions on the story so far. Will she like it or will she think it's useless drivel that makes her question agreeing to be my muse?*

*I call Silk our story, but in truth it's hers. I write only because she inspires me. Without her, there is no Silk. Without her, there is no story to be told.*

*If she knew how much she means to me. I say the words I love you, but they never seem to be enough to convey what I feel for her. They're hackneyed and tired, overused by people who have no idea what love is and desperate souls who think they're some kind of magic to keep others in their lives long after they've decided they no longer want to stick around.*

*I wish I knew better words for how she makes me feel. Yes, I* love her, but it's more than just that. I love her. I adore her. She brings out the best in me, things I never knew existed inside me or were possible for me. I'm the man I've always dreamed of being with her.

Because of her.

Turning to face me, she looks at me with watery eyes. Is she sad? Does the story I've written about her make her unhappy?

"Ian, this is beautiful," she says in a quiet voice, instantly calming my fears. "I love this story. You've made Kate everything I wish I ever was. She's strong and fearless, but she loves Sean with everything she has."

"Do you like Sean? Do you think I wrote him the right way for her? I want the reader to see how much he goes through for her and still loves her more than even he can understand."

Kristina's smile lights up her face. "Oh yes! He's just what she needs. The part where she won't let him in because she's afraid that her feelings aren't what his are made me cry. She kept telling him that he didn't want her and that she was no good for him, but he knew the truth. He knew she didn't just care about the physical thing between them. He knew there was more. I love that."

I kiss her gently on the lips and take a deep breath in, happy my muse loves the story I've written because of her.

"What happens next? Do you know?" she asks as she leans her head on my shoulder. "I want to hear all about it."

I lean my head on hers and close my laptop. "Not yet. The story isn't finished. I have some more to write."

"Will they end up happy, Ian? Is that how this ends?"

"I don't know yet. I haven't written the rest of their story."

Kristina wraps her arms around my waist and sighs. "I want them to be happy."

I open my eyes, unsure of where I am. Sharp pain tears through the top of my head. I run my palm over my cheek and pull my hand away to see blood. Slowly, the accident filters through my brain and I remember being run off the road and sent down the embankment. I look around to see if anyone has come to help and see the back of Kristina's SUV nearby on fire.

PANIC RUSHES THROUGH me at the thought that she's trapped in there. I need to get out of this fucking car to help her! I try to move, but my left arm is stuck between the door and the seat. It should hurt, I think, but that doesn't matter now. I have to get to Kristina.

I pound on the window hoping someone will hear me. I can't watch her burn to death in that car and not do anything, so I scream, "Help! Help us! Get her out of there!"

My voice begins to give out I scream so loud, but a terrifying thought creeps into my mind as I see the flames engulf Kristina's car. Help won't arrive in time to save her and I can't save her trapped here. She'll die because I couldn't save her.

Why isn't she screaming for help? Tears come to my eyes as the thought of her already dead from the accident forms in my brain. No. God, no! Don't let her be dead already.

"Kristina! Can you hear me? Answer me! Kristina!" I yell as loud as I can and hope she hears my pleas. But I hear nothing in return.

I begin to feel weak and keeping my eyes open becomes difficult. Somewhere nearby the sound of sirens floats down to where we wait, but it's too late.

My eyes close as I accept the reality. It's too late.

# CHAPTER NINE

## *Ian*

I OPEN MY eyes slowly to see the stark white walls surrounding me. I don't know this place or where I am. I'm in a bed, and I hear machines beeping and buzzing around my head. Directly in front of me is a window but not to the outside.

I'm in a hospital.

"Ian, can you hear me?" a gentle voice asks.

I turn to see an older woman leaning over me with a look of happiness on her face, which I hope means whatever I'm in the hospital for isn't going to kill me. Her soft brown eyes stare down into mine as she waits for my answer, and I nod.

"Yes," I croak out, my throat instantly hurting from just that one word.

As I raise my hand to massage my throat, the woman moves over to a table and quickly returns with a cup of water. "Here, drink this. Your throat is tight because you haven't spoken for a while."

I take a sip of water and close my eyes as it slowly hydrates my parched throat. A few more sips and I feel ready to risk speaking again. Swallowing hard, I say, "Where am I?"

"Columbia Memorial. You've been here for nearly five days."

Five days? But I don't recognize the hospital name as one in the city. "Where is this hospital?"

"Hudson, New York."

My mind races through memories of that day when my car careened off the side of that mountain road. I look down in horror at my left arm and remember it mangled and bloody. Now all I see are bandages.

Confused, I ask her, "My arm?"

The look of happiness on the woman's face morphs into one of concern, and she presses a fake smile onto her worried face. "They tried…I think I better let the doctor answer your questions. Let me go find him."

As she moves away toward the door, I reach out with my right hand to grab her arm and say, "I need to find out about Kristina. Is she okay? What happened to her?"

"I'm sorry. Let me get the doctor and he can help you. Just one minute."

She hurries from the room with an expression that tells me she's as confused as I am, but why? Is it because they couldn't save her?

I lay there for over an hour waiting for someone to come in and explain what's going on, all the while my heart sinking lower and lower at the thought that Kristina's gone. She's gone because I couldn't save her.

I see Sheila stop in front of the window to my room. When our eyes meet, she begins to cry and covers her face, which makes me sure however I may feel that I don't look as good as I think I do.

She walks into the room slowly, wiping her tears from her cheeks as she approaches the side of my bed. Dressed in jeans and a short sleeve blue and white print top, she looks like she always has. Not incredibly feminine or even attractive, but like herself.

"Oh, Ian! What happened? How do you feel? Do you know who I am?" she says on a sob as she squeezes my hand.

"Of course. You're my agent, Sheila Rogers."

"Yes, yes! They didn't know if you'd have any permanent brain damage after the accident. It was awful! I got the call that you'd crashed your car down a ravine and I rushed up here. I've hoped every day that you'd finally wake up."

"Where's Kristina? I need to see her. Is she here? Did they bring her here?"

Sheila gives me the same confused look that the other woman did and says nothing for a few moments. When she finally speaks, her words make no sense.

"I don't know, Ian. Was she in the car with you?"

"No, she was following me and that truck must have run her off the road too. Her car was on fire. Did they get to her in time? Where is she?"

After a few more moments of silence, Sheila quietly says, "I don't know, Ian. I just knew you were in the accident."

"I need to speak to her. I need to know she's okay," I say as I begin to feel real fear that she's not safe.

"Okay, okay. Don't get yourself upset. You just woke up. Take your time."

"I don't want to take my time! I need to see her. I need to let her know I'm okay and see she's okay."

Sheila closes the door and returns to my bedside. Pulling up a chair, she sits down next to me and sighs. "Ian, I'll see what I can find out. What do you remember?"

I try to remember the details of the accident, but my brain seems fuzzy on the details, so I just tell her what I know. "I was in a car accident coming back from the cabin after you told me to get out of the city. Not that I'm blaming you, but you seem a little confused about what happened. The car slid off the road and down the embankment. Kristina was following me in her car and I saw it on fire."

Sheila gives my hand a sympathetic squeeze and frowns. "Honey, I'll see what I can find out. I just know I got a call saying you'd been in an accident. There was no mention of anyone else."

I shake my head, refusing to believe what she's saying. "No. She was in the car behind me, Sheila. I need to know what happened to her."

Sheila takes my hand to calm me down, but I can't stay in that bed. I need to find Kristina and know she's okay. I don't care that I've got tubes and wires all over me. Slowly, I move my legs to try to get out of bed, but she stops me.

"Ian, please. I need you to relax. I'll help you find out what happened, but I need you to stay in bed until the doctor comes in."

"Please find out. I need to know she's okay. Why won't anyone tell me what happened to her?"

"Okay, I'll help you. I promise."

My chest feels like someone's hit me with a sledgehammer. I struggle to catch my breath as the thought that Kristina is gone fills my mind and I mumble, "I think I'm feeling tired now. I'm just going to close my eyes for a little bit. Do me a favor and tell the doctors to let me sleep, okay? They can do their tests and ask their questions later."

She nods and gives me her best fake but sympathetic smile. "Okay, Ian. I'll tell them."

I roll over and close my eyes to block out everything. Who I am. What my life is now if Kristina isn't in it. How little I have to go back to.

That the woman I love may not even be alive anymore.

✦   ✦   ✦

TWO UNSUCCESSFUL SURGERIES to fix the nerve damage in my left arm and three months of physical therapy to learn how to live without the use of it and now for the first time in what seems like forever, I'm back at my apartment. Unlike everything else in my world since I woke up in that hospital bed, it's the same as I remember. At least there's that. I might have gone into shock if I opened the door and saw LL Bean décor all over the fucking place.

The evidence of Sheila's handiwork in keeping my apartment clean after my accident can be seen in every spotless nook and cranny of my home. I've spent enough nights face down on the floor to know it never looked this clean. I feel like I've walked into some kind of showroom apartment realtors use to hook prospective buyers.

In some way, I'm a stranger in my own home it's been so long since I've been here. I look around and see Kristina everywhere. Sheila hasn't been able to find out what happened to her, so I don't even know if she's still alive. Since the accident, she's never called or come to visit or even sent a message through Sheila.

All I have of her are memories. In my love for her, I literally am alone, but now that I'm home, I plan on finding out what happened. As I have every day since I woke up in that hospital bed, I try her number but all it does is ring without anyone answering.

After walking around my place studying it like some kind of tourist in a museum, I feel drawn to the living room and sit down on the couch. I have no idea if this is what I should do. Maybe I should write. Maybe I should sleep more.

All I know is I'm alone and can do anything or nothing. My life is a blank slate.

I should consider myself lucky. How many people would kill to have enough money to do whatever they desire in life and a marketable skill if they choose to use it? How many would love to begin life anew with the chance to start all over again?

Neither of these ideas give me any comfort, though. I don't think of myself as lucky. I think of myself as someone who had everything he ever wanted and through some terrible twist of fate had it all taken away from him. I had love and happiness, and now I have neither.

I close my eyes and lean my head against the back of the couch as I try to stay sane. Sheila's biggest fear is that I'll turn back to heroin again, but I don't want that now. I don't even really want a drink now. All I want is a way to find what I've lost before I completely lose my fucking mind.

Grabbing the TV remote from the coffee table in front of me, I turn it on and immediately the Netflix screen appears and tells the story of what I'd been doing the last time I sat there in front of that screen. All of Kristina's films are there, watched but ready for me to see them again.

I choose the remake of The Misfits and sit back to wait for her to appear in front of me. My palms begins to sweat and my heart slams against my chest as each minute ticks by, and then there she is in front of me again, those beautiful cornflower blue eyes looking out as if she sees me watching her.

When she smiles, my heart fills with joy at the memory of the two of us alone and her smiling like that for me. But where is she now? I need to find her. She belongs in my arms, smiling up at me as I hold her. I need to see her look at me with those soft blue eyes and tell me she loves me.

I believe she's still alive. She has to be.

I can find nothing online that says anything about what happened to her. No mention of her death. No mention of any accident at all. Did I just imagine it all in a state of shock as I sat there at the bottom of that embankment after the accident? But if that's the case, why didn't she come to see me even once while I was in the hospital all those weeks and then the three months of rehab for my arm?

I call Albert and get him moving on the only thing that matters to me. Finding Kristina. "Albert, I need you to contact Kristina Richards's agent, publicist, manager and anyone else who might know where she is. I have to find out."

"Okay, Ian. I can do that. You feeling okay?"

Albert's newfound interest in how I feel seems genuine, but I don't want to discuss my physical or mental well-being with him now. "Yeah, I'm fine. I just need you to find out where she is."

"Okay. Give me some time and I'll see what I can find

out."

I pull my laptop out sometime after the first twenty-four hour Kristina Richards film marathon and attempt to type. The nerve damage in my left hand makes it impossible. The fingers on that hand just sit on the keyboard, useless now. I have all these ideas for the Silk and Steel story ready to pour out through my fingers, but with only working hand, I can barely write a page in two hours. Desperate to get the words out of my head, I find a pen and paper and write like I've never written before in my life. My mind works at a fevered pace, so at least I can say something good came from all of this misery.

Afterward, I'm exhausted and for two days, I sit and stare at the TV as I watch every film of hers and periodically answer Sheila's phone calls meant to calm her fears and ensure I'm not doing anything terrible to myself. But it's Albert's phone call I wait for.

"Ian, how are you feeling? Are you getting back to writing yet?" Sheila asks in that angelic voice of hers that makes the three times daily calls to check up on me not so bad.

"Maybe, but don't worry. I'm not doing anything illegal or harmful to myself," I say with a chuckle, doing my best to make her feel better about her task.

"Is there anything you need?"

I hesitate for a moment, but then answer, "No, I'm fine, Sheila." I'm anything but fine, but as soon as I hear from Albert, I'll be better.

At least I hope so.

The phone is silent for a long moment, and then she says, "I'm worried about you, Ian. I've never heard you sound so sad."

CLAIM

"I'm not back to the heroin, Sheila. I swear."

Sheila stays silent again and then says, "I'm so happy to hear that, Ian. Don't worry. Everything's going to be okay for you. You have a second chance, and now that you're back home, I'm going to be working overtime to make sure I get you the deal you deserve for Silk and get that film made, if possible."

Her mention of Silk makes my breath catch in my chest. The story of my love for Kristina. Our story.

I continue watching Kristina's films and wonder if I'm slowly losing my mind. All of this seems so familiar, yet it's been months. Thank God for Netflix, my old friend. It's the only way I can keep her in my life for now until Albert finds out where she is.

My phone rings, startling me out of my thoughts of just how miserable I truly am, and I see it's Albert calling back.

"Ian, I talked to all her people. They won't tell me where she is, but I have a friend I asked about her and he says he's heard she's left the city to live upstate."

"Really? Where?" I want to ask with who, but I can't bring myself to say the words.

"I don't know yet, but I asked him to find out. I'll let you know the minute I find out."

I return to my miserable existence, a sad loop of watching her films and then writing the continuation of our story. The words come slower now as I sink into what very well might be depression. Nothing about my life feels like it's a second chance. I'm a one-armed author who's lost his muse. I don't know where she is or even if she's okay.

All I know is that this doesn't feel like anything I can

handle.

Nearly forty minutes later, Albert calls back with the information I've been waiting for. "She's at a friend's house in Dutchess County. Some woman named Sienna Rollins. Do you know the name?"

"No. Maybe. I don't know. Who is she?" I ask, feeling like I do know the name but not sure if too much Netflix has finally totally fucked up my head.

"She's an actress. All I know about her is she divorced some billionaire businessman a couple years ago and made out like a bandit. Other than that, I only have the address of her house upstate."

He gives it to me and I write it down on a scrap of paper I immediately slip into my pocket. The address is tattooed onto my brain. It's where Kristina is, so that's where I need to be.

✧   ✧   ✧

I DRIVE UP to Sienna Rollins' multi-million dollar property in Verbank, New York and can't help but be impressed. I may never have heard of her name or seen any of her films, but she's clearly done well for herself. Not that I care about any of that.

All I care about is finding Kristina.

A middle-aged woman in a grey and white maid's uniform answers the door and after I give her my name, she ushers me into an enormous two story white foyer, instructing me to wait until she gets Mrs. Rollins. As I stand there, my stomach feels like someone's twisting it into knots as question after question forms in my mind. Why didn't Kristina tell me where she was all this time? Not one phone call in months doesn't sound like her. She's alive, but did something happen to change her feelings for me? Or did she think I died?

A tall, shapely woman with long blond hair appears in front of me in jeans and a sweatshirt as I wonder what happened to Kristina and gives me a smile that I sense is forced. A beautiful woman, she seems out of place there surrounded by all this obvious wealth.

"Mr. Anwell, I'm Sienna Rollins. What can I do for you?"

"Please call me Ian. I'm here to see Kristina. I know she's here, and I need to speak to her."

Sienna's eyes open wide, like she's surprised at what I've just said, and for a moment that forced smile fades a little. It reappears just seconds later, though, as she says, "Ian, it's very nice to meet you. I'll have to see if Kristina wants any visitors."

"Why is she here? It's been nearly five months since the accident. Does she know I'm okay? Why didn't she try to see me?"

Reaching out, Sienna takes my hand and gives it a sympathetic squeeze. "I'm probably not the right person to ask. I'll find out if Kristina can see you."

She leaves me standing there in that white foyer as my stomach continues to churn over all those questions I have. All I want is to see the woman I love and who loves me. If Sienna knows Kristina at all, she knows about me. Why wouldn't she immediately take me to see her?

I hear footsteps and see Sienna walking toward me from down a long hallway. I can tell by the look on her face that the answer is no, that I can't see Kristina. But why?

"Kristina can't see you today, Ian. Maybe another day. Let me take your number and she can call you."

"No. I want answers and I want them now. Why is she here and not back at her apartment in the city? Why wouldn't she want to see me? Why in all the time I was in the hospital didn't she even try to visit me or find out if I was okay? What's going on here?"

"I don't want to upset you, Ian. I'm really not trying to do that. I just need you to understand now isn't a good time."

"Why? What's going on with her? We left my cabin that morning happily in love and ready to move in together, and now you tell me she doesn't want to see me. I want to know why."

Sienna looks away and I consider pushing past her to find Kristina on my own, but then she turns back and says, "Come with me. Let me explain."

Leading me into an opulently decorated living room at the front of the house, she extends her arm to offer me a seat on a large white sofa. We sit down next to one another, and I wait for her to begin explaining what the hell is going on. After what seems like an eternity, she takes a deep breath and begins speaking.

"I'm sorry things have turned out so badly for you two. Kristina loved you. I want you to know that. That day of the accident, she went over that embankment too, ending up at the bottom of that ravine with you. Thankfully, her injuries weren't life threatening, but that didn't mean they weren't serious. She went through the windshield, Ian, so her injuries occurred mostly on her face."

She stops talking and a frown settles into her mouth. I know what the problem is now. "Sienna, I don't care what she looks like. I love her. Her outside doesn't matter to me."

"It matters to her, Ian. She was an actress on the verge of hitting it big, and now she feels like she's lost everything in that part of her life. I know it's only been a short time and with plastic surgery she can someday be like she was before, but she doesn't believe that. She sees herself as that person who she sees in the mirror every day. The cuts have healed, but the scars remain."

"I understand, but we can get past that. All I need is some time with her."

"It's more than that. She blames herself for the accident. She knows what happened to you. I found out and told her, and she was horrified. She thinks she's ruined your life."

I look down at my left arm and the useless hand that dangles at the end of it before I look back at Sienna. "It wasn't her fault. She did nothing to cause that accident. Just let me see her and I can explain all that to her. My life isn't ruined. I'm still here, just with one less hand I can use."

"Her emotional injuries are why she doesn't want to see you, Ian. She's just not ready, I guess. I don't know when she's going to be ready either. Most days she just sits in her room and reads her books. Your books."

"I need to see her, Sienna. I'm not leaving until I get to see her."

She shakes her head and frowns. "I can't do that, Ian. She's not ready."

# CHAPTER TEN

## *Kristina*

T HE LIGHT COMING through the window seems so bright today, and I close the curtains to block some of it out. I catch a glimpse of my reflection in the window and cringe, hating the monster that looks back at me. That woman isn't Kristina Richards. She can't be.

A part of me wants to run out to stop Sienna from sending Ian away. After all these months of being without him, just knowing he's so close makes me need him as much as ever, but I can't. Not looking like this.

I was his muse, the woman he became obsessed with after seeing my movies. The woman whose looks inspired him to write. How can I face him now looking like this? Who would want a damaged muse?

My fingertips trace the scars from my right eye and down my cheek to my jawline. Raised pink lines that make me look like a hideous stranger even to myself. How could I expect him to ever look at me the same way? I don't look like the person he fell in love with anymore.

I sit down in my chair again and hold his book to my heart, the only piece of him I have left now. Opening the cover, I turn the page to where he signed his name to his biggest fan and trace my fingertip over the sharp lines of his signature.

Does he even write now after the accident? The day Sienna finally told me about his injury flashes through my mind, as does the pain of knowing how much his loss means to him. If only I hadn't distracted him as we drove down that snowy mountain road. If only that truck hadn't come around the corner so wide. If only we'd stayed at the cabin another day or another hour. If only we'd stayed in bed for just a few minutes more, none of this would have happened.

As always, everything about us revolves around if onlys.

I wanted to tell Sienna nothing would make me happier than to see Ian again, but how can face him like this? It's better this way. He'll find another muse who will inspire him to write again.

My chest aches at the idea of another woman being that for him. Like my heart wants to believe we can be like we were again, but one glance at my reflection in the window and my brain tells my heart the awful truth.

The sound of his voice hits me like a bolt of lightning, and I listen as he demands to see me, even as Sienna tells him it's not possible. Then I hear footsteps coming down the hallway, and panic tears through me. He's coming to see me, but he can't. I can't see him like this!

Just as I reach out to lock the door, it opens and there he is. I cover my face with my hands and turn away from him, unable to even look him in the eye. "Go away, Ian. You shouldn't be here. Please go."

"No. I came here to see you, and I'm not leaving until you talk to me. I don't care if your friend calls the police and they have to drag me out of here. I need to know the answers to my questions."

"Please go. I don't have the answers you want."

I hear him walk toward me, and then his hand touches my shoulder and it's like we've never been apart. All the feelings I've tried so hard to push down deep inside so he can move on rush back to the surface, making it impossible to hold back the tears.

"I'm not going anywhere. I know about what happened to you, and it doesn't matter what you look like. I'm not the same after the accident either. It doesn't matter. Nothing matters more than I love you, Kristina."

"It does matter, Ian. Please just leave me here to live my life hidden away."

He wraps his arm around me and kisses the top of my head. "You don't have to hide. Come home with me like we planned at the cabin and be my muse again."

I can't control my sobs as they wash over me at the thought of being his muse once more. As Ian holds me to him, I whisper the truth. "I can never be your muse again. The accident made sure of that. Please just leave and let me be."

"You don't want that. I can't believe you don't love me anymore, Kristina. No matter what's happened, you're still my muse just like I'm still a writer, even though I only have one working hand. Nothing's changed."

Pulling away from him, I throw myself on the bed and hide my face in the pillow so he can't see just how wrong he is. Everything's changed. My looks are gone, just like the use of his hand, because of me. How he could want to see me again I can't understand, but even if he's willing to forgive me, it doesn't matter.

What we were can never be again.

I feel his hand caressing my back, and my body reacts like it always has to his touch. I wish I could face him so he could take me in his arms and hold me until all the bad goes away. I've missed him so much.

"Kristina, please listen to me. I know what happened to you, but I don't love you because of your outside. I love the woman you are on the inside. The way you make me a better man than I've ever been before. Your strength when I didn't have any. You stuck around when I needed you. Now I'm here when you need me."

"It's not the same, Ian. I'm not the same. Everything I was is gone. That Kristina Richards died in that accident."

"Then we have a chance to start over again. We wanted to take that chance that day. Do you remember? We were going to go back to the city and start our life together. We can still do that."

I shake my head in the pillow. "No, we can't. I can't be your muse anymore."

Ian lies down next to me and presses his lips to my ear to whisper, "Then don't be. I don't need you to be my muse. I need you to be the woman I love. Please look at me. Trust me, Kristina."

"No. I can't. I'm not that person anymore."

"And I'm not the man you fell in love with either. I'm an author who has to handwrite his books now, but I still love you the same way I did before."

Ian's mention of his injured arm only makes me cry more. I did that. I caused him to lose the ability to use his arm. "I never meant for any of this to happen. I swear, Ian. I'm so sorry."

His hand brushes the hair from the good side of my face, and he gently kisses me on my cheek. "You didn't do this to me. This happened because a truck made a wide turn and caused an accident. No one meant for any of this to happen. It just happened. But we can get past this. If you can overlook my changes, I know I can see past yours. We aren't an arm or a few scars. Tell me you know we're more than that. Tell me you remember what we were and can be again if you just give us a chance."

"No. I can't. Everything I was is gone now. I can't bear the idea of seeing what I was in your eyes when you look at me."

He's silent for so long even as he stays there next to me that I know what I feared is true. I don't blame him. He fell in love with a woman who had beauty, and now that she doesn't, he shouldn't have to stay when he doesn't want to.

"I'm sorry, Kristina. I'm sorry for making you think that I fell in love with you because of how you look. I never meant to let you think that's all you were to me."

"I was your muse, Ian. Now what am I? You don't have to say you love me because you feel bad. You never signed on to be with a woman who looks like this."

Ian kisses me again and in a voice full of pain says, "Please look at me, Kristina. Show me you still love me like I love you."

"I can't," I sob, wishing more than anything I didn't look like I do. "I can't bear to see your reaction knowing you loved how I looked."

The bed moves as he rolls away from me, and I sense he's finally given up. I don't blame him. Some things are just too much to overcome. But then just as I think he's about to leave, he sits down next to me on the side my scars are on and out of the corner of my eye I see him lift his left coat sleeve to show me his arm.

"Do you know that even though I lost the use of my arm in that accident, my biggest fear as I drove up here was that you didn't want me anymore because I'm always going to be a recovering addict?"

I hear in his words the truth he always lives with, and I can't let him think that. Turning to face him with my scarred cheek still covered by my hair, I say, "I loved you knowing who you were all along. You never lied to me about that, so I had no reason to not want you. But this isn't the same, Ian."

"I don't know what to say to make you understand I don't care what your outside looks like. What kind of writer am I who can't find the words to convince the woman I love to believe me?"

"You're a wonderful writer. Don't say that."

"I can't be that wonderful if I can't even tell you what you need to hear to trust me."

He deserves better than to think he's lacking because I am, so I muster all the courage I have inside me and slowly sit up next to him. I hang my head so my hair covers my ugliness, but his fingers gently tuck it behind my ear so my scars and everything I am now is on full display. Squeezing my eyes shut, I close them tightly to avoid the look in his eyes as he sees me for the first time.

"Look at me, please. Please, Kristina."

I shake my head and whisper, "No. I can't face you like this."

"Please, Kristina."

I can't say no, even though I wish I could, and I finally face the fear that's haunted me from the first time I saw myself after the accident. Slowly, I open my eyes to see him staring at me with that same look of love in his dark eyes that's always made me feel so adored and wanted.

With his fingertip, he caresses my cheek, touching each of my scars as he looks into my eyes. "I missed you so much, my beautiful Kristina. Please don't make me live without you anymore. Come home so we can begin the life we planned."

"I can't be an actress anymore because of how I look. What am I going to do with my life now?"

Ian leans over and kisses my damaged cheek. "I know an author who desperately needs someone to help him write. How does co-author sound?"

"Co-author? On what?"

"Silk and Steel, our story. We lived it, so you might as well get the credit too. We'll write it together." He lifts his left arm and smiles. "Of course, you'll have to do the typing since I'm pretty slow these days."

"Me, a co-author? I'm not a writer, Ian."

His mouth turns down into a frown. "Come with me anyway. Please. Don't give up on us now."

I think about all we've been through and look into his eyes still so full of love for me, even though I'm not the woman he fell in love with, and I can't say no to him. Cradling his face, I say the truest words I've spoken in months. "I don't want to give up on us, Ian. I want to go home."

His smile lights up his whole face, and he takes me into his arms. "I promise you won't regret this, Kristina. I love you."

I feel his heartbeat against my cheek and for the first time

CLAIM

in months, I feel like I'm already home again.

✧　✧　✧

IAN PRACTICALLY LEVITATES off the couch with excitement next to me as the credits roll on the HBO production of Silk. I know he's dying to hear my opinion on it, but to tease him I pretend to have to consider the answer to his question how I liked the film.

"Well? What did you think?"

"I can see why you kept it from me even when they gave you a copy to preview," I say as I turn to face him.

He's unable to keep his disappointment hidden. Crestfallen, he mumbles, "You didn't like it?"

I've tortured him enough, so I smile and throw my arms around him. "I love it! I wasn't sure how I'd feel since I always wanted to play the part of Kate, but it's wonderful, Ian."

He backs away from me and smiles from ear to ear. "I knew you'd love it. The parts the screenwriter added fit so well I can't say I'd have done better if I did it myself. I'm so happy you loved it as much as I do. They really brought Kate and Sean to life."

It's been three long years since I convinced him that the film should be made even though I couldn't play the role of Kate. We've grown stronger since the accident, and although his left arm still doesn't work and my scars are still visible in certain light even after my plastic surgery, we're as much in love as we've ever been. We still love completely and madly, and when we fight, it's with the same passion as we love. I adore him as much as he adores me, but those two damaged souls we were when we met are still inside us, demons lying in wait for a time when we're weak and they can strike again.

But after what we've been through, we're both strong. Him for me and me for him. So those addictions and obsessions that are so much a part of each of us no longer rule our life together.

Cradling his face, I kiss his lips and smile. "I don't care what critics think or anyone else. I love it because it's the story of us. And I know that it's not just our story anymore, but in my heart it will always be just you and me, Ian."

As he takes me into his arms and holds me close, he corrects me about Silk as he always has. "It was you, Kristina. Always you."

**THE END**

# About the Author

K.M. Scott writes contemporary romance stories of sexy, intense, and unforgettable love. A New York Times and USA Today bestselling author, she's been in love with romance since reading her first romance novel in junior high (she was a very curious girl!). Under her Gabrielle Bisset name, she writes paranormal and historical romance. She lives in Pennsylvania with a herd of animals and when she's not writing can be found reading or feeding her TV addiction.

Be sure to visit K.M.'s Facebook page at **facebook.com/ kmscottauthor** for all the latest on her books, along with giveaways and other goodies! And to hear all the news on K.M. Scott books first, sign up for her newsletter today and be sure to visit her website at **www.kmscottbooks.com**

# Books by K.M. Scott:

Crash Into Me (Heart of Stone #1)
Fall Into Me (Heart of Stone #2)
Give In To Me (Heart of Stone #3)
Heart of Stone Volume One Box Set
Ever After (Heart of Stone #4)
A Heart of Stone Christmas (Heart of Stone #5)
Return To Me (Heart of Stone #6)
Forever With Me (Heart of Stone #7)
Heart of Stone Volume Two Box Set
Hard As Stone (Heart of Stone #8)
Set In Stone (Heart of Stone #9)
Silent As A Stone (Heart of Stone #10)
All of Me (Heart of Stone #11)

Temptation (Club X #1)
Surrender (Club X #2)
Possession (Club X #3)
Satisfaction (Club X #4)
Acceptance (Club X #5)
The Complete Club X Series Box Set

If I Dream (Corrupted Love #1)
If You Fight (Corrupted Love #2)
If We Fall (Corrupted Love #3)
The Corrupted Love Trilogy Box Set

Crave (Addicted To You #1)
Adore (Addicted To You #2)
Shatter (Addicted To You #3)
Claim (Addicted To You #4)
The Addicted To You Box Set

In The Darkness (Project Artemis #1)
After The Storm (Project Artemis #2)
Behind The Scenes (Project Artemis #3)
The Project Artemis Box Set

Hard Work (Standalone)

## K.M.'S BOOKS ARE IN AUDIOBOOK TOO!

# Books by K.M. Scott writing as Gabrielle Bisset:

Vampire Dreams Revamped (A Sons of Navarus Prequel)
Blood Avenged (Sons of Navarus #1)
Blood Betrayed (Sons of Navarus #2)
Longing (A Sons of Navarus Short Story)
Blood Spirit (Sons of Navarus #3)
The Deepest Cut (A Sons of Navarus Short Story)
Blood Prophecy (Sons of Navarus #4)
Blood Craving (Sons of Navarus #5)
Blood Eclipse (Sons of Navarus #6)
Blood Ascendant (Sons of Navarus #7)
The Sons of Navarus Box Set #1
The Sons of Navarus Box Set #2

Stolen Destiny (Destined Ones Duet #1)
Destiny Redeemed (Destined Ones Duet #2)

Love's Master
Masquerade
The Victorian Erotic Romance Trilogy

www.ingramcontent.com/pod-product-compliance
Lightning Source LLC
Chambersburg PA
CBHW030822110726
47900CB00006B/1712